JUL - - 2013

The Linnet Bird

The Linnet Bird

a novel

LINDA HOLEMAN

CROWN PUBLISHERS
NEW YORK

Reader's Guide copyright © 2005 by Crown Publishers, an imprint of the Crown Publishing Group, a division of Random House, Inc.

This is a work of fiction. Names, characters, places, and incidents either are the product of the author's imagination or are used fictitiously.

Published in the United States by Crown Publishers, an imprint of the Crown Publishing Group, a division of Random House, Inc., New York.
www.crownpublishing.com

Originally published in Great Britain by Headline, London, in 2004.

CROWN is a trademark and the Crown colophon is a registered trademark of Random House, Inc.

Library of Congress Cataloging-in-Publication Data
Holeman, Linda, 1949–
The linnet bird : a novel / Linda Holeman.—1st ed.
    1. India—History—British occupation, 1765–1947—Fiction.   2. British—
    India—Fiction.   3. Women—India—Fiction.   4. Ex-prostitutes—Fiction.
    5. Married women—Fiction.   I. Title.
PR9199.3.H5485L56 2005
813'.54—dc22   2004025392

ISBN 1-4000-9739-8

Printed in the United States of America

Design by Lauren Dong

10 9 8 7 6 5 4 3 2 1

First American Edition

For Holly Kennedy,
who had faith in this story

A LINNET IN A GILDED CAGE

A linnet in a gilded cage,—
A linnet on a bough,—
In frosty winter one might doubt
Which bird is luckier now.

But let the trees burst out in leaf,
And nest be on the bough,
Which linnet is the luckier bird,
Oh who could doubt it now?

—CHRISTINA ROSSETTI,
Sing-Song: A Nursery Rhyme Book

Slightly smaller than a sparrow, the linnet bird was
highly sought after as a cage bird in the nineteenth century
for its melodious song.

Prologue

Calcutta, 1839

SMOKING OPIUM IS AN ART.

I look at my tray and its contents—the pipe covered in finely worked silver, the small spirit lamp, the long blunt needle, the container of *chandu,* and my row of pea-size balls of the dark brown paste. My lips are dry. I close my eyes and see it: the opium ball at the end of the needle over the flame of the lamp, the bubbling and swelling of that muddy brown until it finally turns golden. Then catching it on the edge of the pipe bowl, using the needle to stretch it into long strings until it is cooked through properly. Rolling it back into its shape and pushing it—quickly, for it must be the right consistency—into the bowl. Now holding the bowl close to the lamp, the flame licking tenderly. I see my lips close around the familiar bone mouthpiece and then a deep pull, another, and another. The sound is the steady unbroken rhythm of a heartbeat.

I open my eyes, licking my lips. It is early morning. The Indian sun will not reach its zenith for a few more hours; there is time, before the copper rays bake and shrink everything, before the servants have to splash water on the reed screens and close all the shutters. I look back to my tray.

Not yet. I will not take up my pipe yet. I have something to tell you.

Through the open windows I can hear the children's voices from the garden. I go to watch. David is playing with the *dhobi*'s son. The child's game, a seemingly senseless galloping about on long sticks, is played with careless, easy motions as only five-year-olds can play. Malti sits on the top step of the verandah. She slowly waves a horsetail whisk in front of her oval, burnished face, wreathed with the pleasure of an ayah watching her beloved charge.

The boys romp around and around the lawn of creeping *doob*. The bougainvillea and hibiscus are in scarlet display.

I never played as my son does today. At a little older than he is now I was employed for ten hours a day, six days a week, at the bookbinders on Harvey Close in Liverpool. I had never felt grass under my bare feet nor heard the song of a bird, and only rarely felt the sun's warmth upon my face. My son will never know the work I did, not the work I started with, nor the work I did later, when I was still a child but no longer young. That part of my life will forever remain closed to him, but not to you.

David has stopped, cocking his head as if listening, or puzzled. And then he stoops, reaching beneath the low hedge of plumbago.

He runs back to Malti, his face a portrait of sorrow, his hands cupping a bird. Even from here I recognize its green feathers, the brilliant red over its beak. It stirs, feebly, but is injured, one wing hanging oddly from its body. A small, common bird, the Coppersmith Barbet. *Basanta bauri*. Only yesterday I heard its familiar *pok-pok* from the mango trees. David is calling now, his voice thick with emotion. I see the sun-browned texture of his skin, the way his long slender thumbs crook tenderly in an attempt to hold on and yet not harm the helpless thing.

I think of my own hands when so young, chapped from the cold wind off the gray Mersey, stained with ink, cheap glue webbing between my fingers. And then, not many years later, tainted with that which I couldn't wash away. Lady Macbeth and her own dirty hands. And finally, just before I left my youth forever and began my voyage, I remember my hands. Nicked with cuts from paper, dry from handling books, they appeared clean, so clean, although always, at least in my mind, unable to lose the smell of too many men, of the blood. How, you are wondering, have you come from that place and arrived here?

Beside my opium tray lies the quill and paper I had Malti bring me earlier this morning.

But before I begin to write, a small time to dream. It is my last. I have made this promise before. I have thought it, whispered it, spoken it, prayed it. But this time I have sworn on my child's head, in the darkness before morning, sitting beside David's bed, listening to his shallow, sweet breaths followed by the deep answering exhalations of Malti from her pallet in the corner. I crept in, and knelt by him, and swore, his thick hair under my pale fingers.

I swore that today will be my last dream that is fed by the White Smoke. And without its aid, I fear my dreams will warp into the old and familiar nightmare, the one I have tried so long to lose.

I close the shutters tightly, darkening the room, and I light the lamp. There is a whir and crackle as a moth comes to life and flutters about the soft glow. The noise hurts. I have taken opium too many years; my senses are stretched to a thin wire, vibrating to the slightest stimuli—this beat of a moth's wings, the drop of hot rain on the back of my hand, the unexpected confusion of a patterned sari.

The opium no longer has the ability to make me happy. It simply allows me to carry on. And today, for the last time, it will still my hand, my mind, long enough to write what I must. So that my son will someday know. For him, I will write only what is important for his future. For you, I will write of it all—part truth, part memory, part nightmare—my life, the one that started so long ago, in a place so far from here.

Chapter One

Liverpool, 1823

I HAD BEEN PUT TO WORK FOR MEN BY DA IN THE WINTER OF MY eleventh year. He was dissatisfied by the small wage I earned at the bookbindery and had recently been laid off his job at the rope makers for turning up tip one too many times and spoiling the hemp in spinning.

It was a wet November night when he arrived home with Mr. Jacobs. I suppose he met him in one of the public houses; where else would he meet anyone? I heard Da say the man's name over and over, Mr. Jacobs this and Mr. Jacobs that. One or both of them were stumbling, and the knocking into the few pieces of furniture, as well as the loudness of their voices, woke me from my sleep in the blankets I laid down behind the coal box each evening. It was warmer there, close to the fireplace, and I felt I had at least a tiny degree of privacy in the one rented room on the second floor of a sagging dwelling off Vauxhall Road, in a court on Back Phoebe Anne Street.

"She's here somewhere," I heard Da say, "like a wee mouse, she is, scurrying about," and then, before I had a chance to try to make sense of why he would be looking for me, I was dragged out of my blankets and into the middle of the low-ceilinged, candlelit room.

"I thought you said she were eleven." Mr. Jacob's voice was hoarse, the words clipped with impatience.

"I told you right, Mr. Jacobs. Past eleven, now. Had her birthday well before Michaelmas."

"She's awfully small. Not even much of a shape to her yet."

"But she has a quim, sir, that you'll find soon enough. It's just delicate she is, a delicate slip of a girl. And she's a right pretty lass, you can see that for yourself," Da said, pushing back my long hair with calloused hands and pulling me closer to the candle in the middle of the table. "Where have you last seen hair like this? Golden and rich as summer's sweetest pear. And like I told you, she's pure. You'll be the first, Mr. Jacobs, and a lucky man indeed."

I pulled away from him, my mouth opening and closing in shock and horror. "Da! Da, what is it you're saying? No, Da."

Mr. Jacob's thick bottom lip extended in a pout. "She's nothing special. And how do I know you haven't duped a hundred men before me, you and her?"

"You'll know you're the first, Mr. Jacobs. Of course you'll know. Tight as a dead man's fist, you'll find her."

I yanked my arm away from Da's grasp. "You can't make me," I said, backing toward the door. "You'll never—"

Mr. Jacobs stepped in front of me now. He had only a ring of graying hair and the top of his head shone greasily in the flickering light. There was a cut, crusted over with dried blood, on the bridge of his nose. "Quite the little actress, aren't you?" he asked. "You can stop all your bluster now. You'll not get a penny, you nor your father, if I find you're not what's been promised."

In one stride, Da took my arm again, pulling me into a shadowy corner of the room. "Now, girl," he wheedled, "it's bound to happen sometime. And better here, in your own home, than somewheres out in the rain in a doorway. Many a lass does help out her family when they've fallen on hard times. And why should you be any different?"

Of course I knew a number of the older girls from the bookbinders—as well as those from the sugar refineries and the glassmakers and the potteries—who worked a few hours now and then on the twisting narrow streets down by the docks to bring in extra shillings when money was short at home. But I had always known I was different. I wasn't like them, I told myself. It was in my blood, this difference.

"Come on now. He'll pay handsomely." Da put his mouth to my ear. I smelled the sourness of his breath. "You know we've no other way, what with me put out of the job. I've always looked after you; now it's your turn to bring something in, something more than the few pennies you earn. And it's no terrible thing. Weren't I buggered meself, over and over on the ships, when I were not much older than you? And it did me no harm, did it?"

I backed away again, arms wrapped over my chest. "No, Da. Mum would never—"

Da grabbed my upper arms, giving me a rough shake. "There'll be no talk of your mother."

At an impatient snick from Mr. Jacobs, Da called over his shoulder, "Now, sir, sit yourself there, on the settle, and I'll talk some sense into my lass here."

But of course there was no talk that made sense, only—when I screamed *"You can't make me"* and tried to run for the door—a knock across my jaw that sent me flying. I felt my cheek hit the damp cold of the floor and then I knew nothing more until I was jarred back to consciousness by hot, urgent breath on my face. My shift was pushed up around my waist, and Mr. Jacobs's body was heavy on mine. His rhythmic rutting scrubbed my bottom painfully against the splintered wood of the settle and the top of my head banged against the wall with each thrust. The searing inside of me was a fresh explosion that matched his grunts, and I saw the corresponding throb of the blue vein that ran down his forehead, thick and raised as a great worm. Sweat gleamed on his upper lip, even though the fire was out and the room cold as a tomb.

But almost worse than the pain and horror of what was happening at the mercy of Mr. Jacobs was that Da—when I turned my head to look for him, hoping he might somehow be moved to come to my rescue—watched from his stool, his face fixed in a look I'd never seen before, one hand busy under the table.

I turned away, squeezing my eyes tightly, and lay limp under Mr. Jacobs. I knew I should fight but was strangely detached. My body burned raw at its center and yet my mind tripped and ran, stumbling away from Mr. Jacobs's pulsing vein and the image of Da staring with that strange attentiveness. And then I heard my mother's voice, faint but clear. She recited the second stanza of *The Green Linnet*, the Wordsworth poem that had been her favorite, and from which she drew my name:

One have I marked, the happiest guest
In all this covert of the blest:
Hail to Thee, far above the rest
In joy of voice and pinion!
Thou Linnet! in thy green array,
Presiding Spirit here today,
Dost lead the revels of the May;
And this is thy dominion.

I heard it in its entirety three times, and just before the start of its fourth repetition Mr. Jacobs gave a great shuddering groan and lay still until I feared I would be smothered. I wanted my mother's voice back, wanted to hear her again, for while I listened my body had become numb, but now she was gone, and with the absence of her voice I grew aware of everything with a terrible clarity. I felt the position of my legs, splayed impossibly wide, torn wetness, pain I had never known or imagined, Mr. Jacobs's unbearable weight. I heard the fretful wail of the baby in the room next door and the rattly breathing of Mr. Jacobs. I smelled the rankness of his flesh. I kept my eyes closed so that I saw dark starbursts on my inner lids. It seemed that time had stopped.

Finally he moved off and away but I stayed as I was, eyes shut, unmoving through the rustle of clothing being fastened and the exchange of a few words and then the rasp of the door scraping along the floor as it opened and closed.

More minutes passed, and I carefully pulled my knees together, my fingers trembling as I pulled down my shift, and still, without opening my eyes, lowered myself to the floor and crawled on hands and knees back to my little nest behind the coal box. The only sounds in the room then were my father's muttered counting and the clink of the coins and the sputter of a dying candle. I lay on my side and twisted my blanket around me, knees brought up to my chest and hands tucking my shift into the bleeding, sticky mess between my legs, weeping for my mother even though she'd been dead for a whole year, and for what was forever lost.

LATER THAT NIGHT, when I lit a candle and washed away the dried blood and spunk from my thighs, I swore that I would never again cry over what a man might do to me, for I knew it would do no good. No good at all.

Chapter Two

I WAS BORN LINNET GOW, ALTHOUGH KNOWN AS LINNY MUNT. My Christian name was given to me by my soft and dreamy mother, Frances Gow, thinking of the songbird with its twenty-four variations of a note. Munt was the surname of the man who took her in four months before my birth.

Ram Munt, the man who sold me that first time—and through the next two years—wasn't my real da, and not even my stepfather, for he and my mother had never married. He was, however, the only father I'd known, although I knew he never looked on me as his daughter. I was simply Frances's child, a burden, someone who needed to be fed.

Ram Munt had two favorite stories. The first was about his years aboard ship. He'd been little more than a boy, come alone to Liverpool from a small village in the north. Looking for a better life, he was caught by a press-gang and hauled aboard ship for an eight-month voyage. There he was introduced to sea life in the cruelest way. When the ship eventually returned to Liverpool and dropped anchor, he tried to run but was caught by another press-gang before he'd even left the docks. He sailed again but by this time he was older and stronger and wouldn't be bullied. By the time his second voyage was over the sea was in his blood and he worked on board until he had been injured one too many times by rolling barrels and the cruel, swinging hooks and the sudden mishaps on rising and falling slippery decks, and there were younger and stronger and more agile men than he to be taken on. He was hired as a spinner at the ropewalk near Williamson Square after that, his thick, damaged fingers still able to deftly wind the hemp fibers together and walk them down to the end of the room to wrap them around the reel, repeating the process all day. He retained his coarse shipboard language and his back bore the scars of many lashings, and his hands smelled of pine tar from dipping the ropes to make them stronger.

His other story was about how he'd come to take in my mother and he told it more often than his sailing tales, usually late on a Saturday night after he'd spent all evening at the Flyhouse or Ma Fenny's.

He'd pull my mother and me out of our bed—she preferred to share a pallet with me, although Ram still called her to him a few times a week—and make us sit at the table and listen while he recounted his tale of heroism, of how he'd found my mother one wet spring night. With a bully's thrust of his chest he'd go on about how he'd discovered her, drenched to the skin and wandering in the rain without a penny to her name.

Mother kept her head lowered as he told his story. She was always tired, exhausted after her fourteen-hour days at the sewing press in the Pinnock Room at the bookbinders, surrounded by piles of schoolbooks waiting to be covered: Goldsmith's *England,* Mangnall's *Questions,* Carpenter's *Spelling,* and, of course, the towering stacks of Pinnock's *Catechisms.*

"I was never one to turn away a maid in distress," Ram would go on. "I took her in, didn't I, took her in and gave her a meal and a strong fire to warm herself. She might have been proud at one point, aye, but it didn't take long to persuade her that my roof and my bed were a damn sight better than what waited for her out in the streets."

Sometimes he changed the details; in one version he stopped her as she was about to throw herself off the miasmal banks of the River Mersey into the cold gray water. In another he fought off a band of longshoremen who were trying to force themselves on her in the shadow of the old grave dock where the ships of the slave trade had once been repaired.

"In due time I even let her use my name, so she didn't have to carry the shame of a bastard child," he'd go on, looking into my face. "This is where you come from," he'd usually add at this point, glaring at me now as if I were about to argue. "And don't you forget it. No matter what fancy tales your mother puts into your head, you were born and raised on Back Phoebe Anne Street. You've the smell of the Mersey in your nostrils and you've been marked by the fish; there can be no mistake about the origins of one what bears the mark of the fish. You're the daughter of a sailor. Any fool could figure that out."

He was referring to the birthmark on the soft skin on the underside of my forearm, just above my wrist: a small, slightly raised port-wine stain in an elongated oval with two small projections at one end. It did have the shape of a tailed fish, I had to admit, but I didn't believe it had anything to do with the blood that coursed through me.

While the man I then called Da ranted this old and tedious story about his saving of my mother, I sat, like her, impassive, but only because she kept her cool thin hand on my arm, her broken thumbnail, rimmed with ink, absently stroking my birthmark. It was so much harder for me to sit quietly than it was for her, and I don't believe it had anything to do with my age. I saw then, young as I was, that she had nothing left in her to stand up to him or anyone; she accepted Ram Munt and his rude manners in a way I couldn't understand. I burned with shame for her and with hatred for him for as long as my memory went back.

While I struggled with the rage that made my breath quicken, my mother's face showed nothing as she listened to Ram's familiar chants. Had she always been so accepting, so beaten? Occasionally she tried to elicit pity for him, telling me what damage had been done to him as a boy forced aboard those ships. "He was beaten daily, and used for the men's pleasure whenever they felt the need," she'd said. "It hardened him. Try to think of what he might have been like as a boy, as a child called Ramsey," she said once. But I couldn't. Nothing would make me lose my hatred of him, for how he treated her.

After he'd stumble to bed when his weekly tirade was done, I'd put my arms around my mother. "Never mind him," I'd whisper. "Tell me about Rodney Street again," I'd urge, knowing this was her one shining moment, her only story, and her mouth would turn up in a faint smile and she'd tell me the beloved tale, one more time, about her job as a lady's maid when she came to Liverpool from Edinburgh, and her liaison with a fine young man who spent one rainy December in the grand Georgian home on Rodney Street. Mother said she was sure he was of noble blood, so fine were his features, his back so straight and hands so gentle, his manners and way of speaking enough to make her weep just remembering. His name, she said, was for her only to know, and it would do me no good to have knowledge of it. When his visit was over and he'd had to leave Liverpool, he promised her he'd be back for her by Candlemas or, at the very latest, the end of March, Lady Day. He had plans to visit America in May and he was going to take my mother with him. To America, she said.

Here my mother's face would glow softly from within and she would sit quietly, remembering. But the story had no further happiness. The fine young man didn't come back to Rodney Street, and eventually it was discovered what Frances Gow had been up to. She was unceremoniously dismissed, in shame, without a character to ensure her of another job, and it was three weeks after this, destitute and desperate, that Ram Munt had offered her shelter.

"I really had no choice, Linny, none at all," was the way she always finished. "I tried to find him—your father. I went back to the house on Rodney Street so many times and stood, hidden in shadows across the street, in case he might come again. He'd have no way to locate me, after all. And then after you were born, I had a chance to talk to the girls in the kitchen, but they swore they'd never seen him again. What else could I do, Linny? He never knew about you. If he had, he'd have married me, I know," my mother said, "for he really and truly loved me. There seemed no other way for me, and so I did what I had to do." Here she'd look in Da's direction, where he lay sprawled, facedown across the bed, his snoring a steady muffled drone.

Every few months she'd get down the carved fruitwood box she kept hidden in the back of the dish dresser. The box contained a small round mirror backed with ormolu, the Wordsworth book that contained *The Green Linnet*—the poem about my name—and a heart-shaped pendant of warm gold. Upon its surface, designed with the tiniest seed pearls, was a bird—my mother told me she thought of it as a linnet. In its beak was a branch of miniature green stones that Mother said were emeralds. Ram Munt said they were cheap glass.

"He gave me these things, your father did. The mirror, he said, because he loved to look at my face. The book, because he loved to hear my voice as I read aloud. And the pendant, he told me, was his heart to mine," she'd say, rubbing her fingers over the softly glowing surface. "It will be yours one day, Linny. To remember that you may have the smell of the Mersey in your nostrils but it doesn't run through your blood."

I always nodded and smiled; I listened to that story, over and over, right until the day my mother died, quickly and soundlessly, taken by a rapid fever that sucked her already thin body of every ounce of life. I was well past ten and had worked alongside her at the bookbinders since I'd turned six. I had started as a gatherer, collecting the massive piles of sheets sent from the printer and running them to where the folders sat at wide tables. Once they had flattened the foldings of each sheet with a small ivory or bone folding knife, the sheets were collated and then taken to the sewers. My mother had worked the sewing press, joining the groups of sheets with a curious kettle stitch. She could sew two or three thousand sheets a day. Just before my mother died I had moved up to a folder and owned my own small bone knife. If all went as planned I would eventually become a sewer when I reached fourteen.

Every Sunday, for the first year after her death, I visited her simple grave in the low-lying area of the cemetery of what was known as the Sailor's Church—for the Mersey flowed right past it at the bottom of Chapel Street. Of course it was really Our Lady and St. Nicholas Parish Church. I would stay there for some time, hidden amid the damp, nettle-fringed headstones and poorer crosses, my fingers tracing the letters of her name—Frances Gow—carved with shallow strokes into the unpainted wooden cross. I always thought of how Da wouldn't even pay to have the bells rung as she was buried, so there was only a sad pauper's funeral for her, with some of the other sewers from the bookbindery and a few of our neighbors come to stand at the end of the cemetery, and not even a cup of tea for them afterward.

My mother had deserved more than that, and I hated Da anew, each Sunday, with the memories of how he hadn't treated her properly, even in death.

On one of these visits, on an afternoon dark with rain, a great black bird watched me from a foot away, its cruel beak jabbing the thin, beaten grass. I saw its orange, unblinking eye and shivered, and as it rose into the air with a snapping of wings like wet sheets being shaken, I decided I would try to find my father. A child's dream, surely, but often it is the dream that becomes reality and necessary for hope. And so I set off further north than I had ever been in the city, up to Mount Pleasant, and by asking numerous times eventually found Rodney Street.

It was a long way from Back Phoebe Anne Street, but if the weather was clear I would often go there on a Sunday after that, walking up and down the quiet and most prestigious street in Liverpool, looking at the Georgian homes with their upper balconies of fine wrought iron. I saw girls that I knew to be my age, but how different they looked. Back on Vauxhall Road I looked like every other girl with my too-short, patched, and stained work dress, my miserable scuffed boots, my ragged shawl. The girls here wore beautiful dresses and capes of velvet. Their stockings were clean and undarned and their shoes gleamed, sometimes with silver buckles. Their hair was tied up in satin ribbons, their skin unmarked, their eyes clear as they gazed right through me. I was nothing, a poor girl from down near the docks. No one spoke to me except for one stout matron who pushed past me on the street as I stood looking at one of the fine houses. "Be on your way, girl," she huffed. "This is a respectable street. We don't need your kind here."

I ignored her. I didn't care what she or any of the other people in Mount Pleasant thought of me. I carefully studied each man I saw, whether walking along the street or riding by on horse or, if he was visible, through the windows of the polished broughams and high-wheeled phaetons, looking for the face I saw in my head, one that had gold-flecked eyes shaped like mine, that had my own fair hair.

I knew what he would look like, for I'd made him as real as my mother's story.

And at the end of each of those fruitless Sunday afternoons I'd make my way back toward the lower end of the city. As the houses grew smaller and closer together, turning to miserable and squalid dwellings, I felt the pinch of my own life. The feeling was true and alive as my heels, rubbed raw with boots from the pawnshop, grown too small.

SURELY MY MOTHER had been a lady's maid, for didn't she know how to read and write, and wasn't her voice gentle, her speech patterns— although carrying a soft Scottish brogue—cultured? And she knew the proper way to do things; she insisted that I sit up straight at our simple meals, a clean rag spread on my lap, and instructed me how to hold my knife and fork and cut small bites and chew slowly and discuss pleasant subjects at table. She helped me with my reading and even spent a few pennies from each of her pay packets buying spoiled Pinnock's *Catechisms* from the office of the bookbinders. She could purchase one of the little sixpenny schoolbooks for a ha'penny if it were flawed and unsalable—the pages put in upside down or the cover marred. This was our secret; Da would never have allowed her to spend money on anything as unimportant as a book. I kept them hidden under my own pallet and most evenings, when my mother was asleep and Da out at a tavern or public house, I'd read until I fell asleep.

My favorites of these readers were the dozens of volumes in the *Friend to Youth* series. There were questions and answers on subjects ranging from history to business to geography to poetry. Of course I couldn't be choosy; once, the only new one I had to study for a whole two weeks was *A Catechism of Mechanics: An Easy Introduction to the Knowledge of Machinery.*

My mother also taught me to look people in the face when I spoke to them and she always, always corrected my speech, telling me that if I spoke like the people on the street and in the factories I would never rise above them. "And you must get yourself away from here, Linny," she'd often say. "There's more than this, more than the street and the work. I can't bear to think of you never knowing anything else."

Da laughed at her, asking her what she meant about rising above anyone. What did she think she was getting me ready to be—did she imagine I'd become a lady's maid, as she claimed she had been? "She'll stay at the bookbinders with you, a well-respected trade, and then find someone to marry her, get her away from my table. Let someone else worry about feeding her."

But my mother never stopped planning. It was as if she were desperate, determined to never let me forget that she hadn't come from this place, and that I must leave it by any means. Dreaming of a better life for me seemed to bring her the only moments of happiness she knew.

"She could be a governess, if given a chance. She has a fine way with reading. She would be perfect as a governess," she'd said one night at supper. "If only she had the proper clothing, she might, through the church, be put in touch with the right people. It need never be mentioned she's from off Vauxhall Road. She's perfected my voice. It could be said she's come down from Scotland. Her background need never . . ." Her voice trailed off. She had a dull sheen on her brow and more than once during the meal of bacon crumbled into boiled potatoes, which she didn't touch, she put her hand to her forehead, then pulled away her fingers and looked at them, as if in surprise. "If she were but given a chance," she repeated, the unusual flush on her cheeks growing even deeper, "my girl would do me proud." There was a dangerous spark in her eyes, and interpreting it as boldness, I matched it with my own, speaking out as I never had around Ram Munt.

"I know what I'd like to do," I said, and my mother turned to me, her mouth in a strained smile, expecting, I'm sure, my agreement with her on her vague plan, even though we both knew that a girl from the low end of Liverpool could never pass as a governess. "I'd like to decorate the books at the printers."

The odd smile faded. "What do you mean?"

"I'd like to be a finisher, like Mr. Broughton in the Extra Finishing shop."

Her face darkened. "When have you been up there, to the third floor?"

"The overlooker sometimes sends me up with messages for Mr. Broughton. There are beautiful things there." I smiled, remembering. "I've seen him laying a book with gold and then stamping it with heated tools. There were ever so many tools—rounds, scrolls, diamonds, and all the letters. And Mr. Broughton can create whatever design comes out of his own head, pressing those hot shapes and letters. Oh, think of it! To create such a wondrous—" I stopped, seeing disappointment on my mother's face, hearing Ram's snicker.

"But that's not a job for a lady," my mother said. "No woman could ever do that. You know it's only boys brought in as apprentices to the finishers. And that of course only men are clever enough for the Extra Finishing. Whatever would put that idea into your head?"

Now I couldn't admit that Mr. Broughton had let me experiment more than once in those few moments of stolen time. I had washed vellum and colored initials and even stamped gold tooling into a ruined piece of calfskin. He seemed to enjoy the clandestine activities—quickly showing me this and that, glancing over his shoulder all the while—as much as I did.

Da's snicker had turned to laughter and he enjoyed himself for a full minute before telling me, as he wiped at his eyes, to do what I did best—fill his bowl with more potatoes—and to never again mention such ridiculous plans as governesses or finishers.

Later that evening the fever that had been toying with my mother for the last twenty-four hours took a firm grip.

And less than a year after she died, Da brought home Mr. Jacobs.

Chapter Three

AFTER THE VISIT FROM MR. JACOBS, RAM KEPT ME BUSY. I never again called him Da; I rarely addressed him at all, but if I did, it was by his name. Ram couldn't bring customers to our second-floor room on a regular basis, afraid that if the landlord got wind of what was going on we'd be thrown out or, worse for my father, the landlord would demand a percentage. Instead, after I came home from my ten hours at the bookbinders, he'd make me change out of my ragged and stained work dress into a clean, childish frock and pinafore he'd bought from the pawnshop. I'd plait my hair, put on the straw bonnet with blue ribbons he'd brought home along with the dress and pinafore, and then he'd take me to the customers.

I never knew how he found the men. They were always old, or so they seemed. And they were men who liked what I was then, a small, delicate child who appeared at the doors of their hotels or lodging or boarding houses, my hand held by the short, broad, loutish fellow.

There were all manner of men. Most came to Liverpool on business from London or Manchester or from Scotland or as far away as Ireland. Some were rough, and some were kind. Some took ages to finish and others were off almost as soon as I lifted my skirt and sat on the edge of the bed or leaned over a table.

While I might visit two unknown men some nights, an hour each— Ram was always waiting to knock on the door to collect the money when their time was up—there were also regulars who paid for the whole evening. I had a Monday, a Wednesday, and a Thursday. These three became quite dear to me, really, because they were the kind ones; they would rather see a child smile than cry. With them I knew what to expect and from them I learned about myself.

Monday insisted on calling me Ophelia and always wept after his rather lackluster, predictable performance, giving me bags of sweets and stroking my hair. He told me about Shakespeare, quoting from his plays and sonnets. Monday said he was a playwright as well, like Mr. Shakespeare, but could get no recognition. He said when he'd grown obsessed with his need to have his work taken seriously, ignoring all else, his wife left him, taking their young daughter. At this his tears turned to deep sobs and he would shake his head, gazing at me in the rumpled bedding as if it grieved him terribly to have me near him, and yet he couldn't keep away. "My innocent," he'd say, wringing his hands. "So innocent, so pure, but one born of a need to understand life's mysteries. I see it there in your face, your desire to make sense of all that's around you."

Wednesday simply wanted to watch me bathe and always had a copper hip bath filled with warm water waiting for me in front of a cheery fire. After I'd washed all over, soaping my hair with sweet-smelling lavender soap (he brought a new bar each week and let me take home the used one), he'd dry me with thick soft towels and carry me to the bed. He found his pleasure in looking at me and cautiously touching my skin; whether he was unable to perform or simply ashamed of something beneath the clothing he kept tightly buttoned at all times I never knew, but he didn't mind if I fell asleep. And I usually did; it was difficult to stay awake after a full day of work, followed by the warm bath and soft bed and the harmless caresses by hands smooth as kid leather. Wednesday was difficult to leave when Ram's knock was eventually heard.

But Thursday was my favorite. He loved to feed me and after our time in his room in the beautifully appointed hotel off Lord Street he always took me downstairs to the dining room, shimmering with candelabras and silver salvers and platters polished bright as mirrors. The walls, with their elegant muted wallpaper of blue and silver, were lined with oil paintings. There were tall windows steamed from the warmth of the generous fires and the bodies heated by rich food and plentiful drink and, in many cases, I suspect, thoughts of the upstairs rooms. During our time in the hotel I was instructed to call Thursday Uncle Horace. Did the people at the elaborate front desk, or those carrying clean linens and trays of food through the wide halls, or those serving us in the dining room really believe me to be his niece? Or did they simply turn a blind eye to the truth of the situation, accepting the lie with polite smiles and subservient bows or curtsies, willingly taking the coins Horace pressed into every hand?

Uncle Horace was huge of girth. Although he was quickly and easily fulfilled upstairs, he seemed unable to satisfy his insatiable appetite at the table. He ordered mounds of food, with special delicacies for me—capons with sizzling golden skin, turbot with lobster sauce, potatoes mashed and swirled into little golden-brown domes. He also bought me sweet port. I didn't care for its taste but loved its beautiful deep ruby, which reflected off the fire. Uncle Horace always insisted on a table by the fireplace.

It was there, in the gracious high-ceilinged dining room smelling of roasted meat and caramelized sugar, of hair pomade and delicate eau de toilette, of wealth and confidence, that I watched and learned all I could of how men and women of his class moved about with surety. I studied the ladies at other tables, saw how they dressed, how carefully they dabbed at their lips with their heavy damask napkins, how their laughter chimed like pleasing music. I memorized their language and their articulation, which, I now knew, was far finer than my mother's had been. It was easy, a game to play as I pretended to listen to Uncle Horace talk about his business and wealth and opulent home in the city of Dublin. I heard about his childhood in rural Ireland, and how he would sneak out with the stable boys on Sunday afternoon for road games of hurling. He told me how he'd learned to eat to take away the emptiness he had while his parents left him with the house staff, sometimes for a year at a time, as they traveled the world. He often brought me a soft spicy cake filled with currants—barmbrack, he called it—his own childhood favorite. It was baked by the ancient cook of his boyhood, still alive and living with him in his house in Dublin. The cake would be wrapped in one of his fine linen handkerchiefs and he'd urge me to take it home.

"Are you really as hungry as you appear," he'd asked me once, as I quickly but neatly sucked an oyster from its shell, "or do you eat because you know it pleases me?"

I'd touched my mouth with my napkin and then put my hands in my lap, choosing my words carefully before I spoke. Had he never known hunger? Did he have any idea that before I was brought to him I'd spent a full day with my folding knife and stack after stack of pages, my hands cramping so badly that by the end of the ten hours it felt as if pebbles had lodged under the skin of my palms, and my shoulders and wrists burned with fatigue? That I had fifteen minutes midday to visit the privy and bolt down the piece of bread and cheese I'd brought with me? "I am as I appear, I assure you, Uncle Horace," I said, "for how else could I be anything but hungry with such food put before me, and in the presence of such company?"

He'd studied me then. "You are undernourished, that I see. But there's another kind of hunger, Linny, a wary hunger for learning, for understanding, that I also see there on your face."

I raised my glass to my lips, just letting the crimson liquid touch them before I returned the glass to the snowy tablecloth. "That may well be," I answered. "Perhaps I have a hunger of the soul itself." I was repeating, word for word, what the anemic young man at the table behind me had said only moments earlier. I had no idea what it meant, although of course I knew what a soul was. I still faithfully attended Sunday services at Our Lady and St. Nicholas.

He laughed then, his hair damp with sweat, pomade melting down his neck, his round face reddened by the many glasses of port and brandy he'd drunk, first in the hotel room and then with dinner. "You're a clever little minx, I'll give you that. Come now, give me your best Irish voice, for I'm feeling a little homesick tonight."

I recited a poem and then told him some silly social snippet I'd over-heard, mimicking his own Irish cadence, for it came easily to me, creating the exact intonations of other voices.

He nodded, smiling broadly and fondly, shaking his head as if amazed. "Aren't you a wonder, then. How do you achieve that exacting pattern? Pure Dublin, it is. It's as if you've spent all your young days taking tea on Grafton Street." And then he summoned the server for a dish of pears and cream for me and brandy pudding with hard sauce for himself, and there was no more tedious talk.

❦

I MISSED SPENDING TIME with my old friends. At the bookbinders I had two friends I'd worked alongside—Minnie and Jane. Minnie was a year older than me, Jane a year younger. We had sometimes left the bookbindery together, four hours before our mothers were allowed to leave, and had lingered along the streets on the way home, talking—or perhaps only pretending—about the fancy hats and beaded reticules we would someday own, or what we would imagine to be the finest meal in the world, or other fanciful dreams of young girls. Sometimes we held hands, as true friends do.

But there was no time for friendship now; I had to rush straight off from work to prepare our plain dinner and eat and change before I was taken out by Ram each evening. Minnie and Jane accepted my story of having to hurry home to serve my stepfather his dinner or face the back of his hand and they still smiled at me often at work, but I keenly felt the loss of their companionship in my life.

Adding to my loneliness was missing the visits with the neighbors. Some evenings when the weather was mild, Mother and I had stood out in the court with other women and girls who lived in Back Phoebe Anne. I would stand beside Mother, who usually worked on a bit of darning or sewing. Other women held or nursed their babies or caught up on their mending, like Mother, and we all absently watched the younger children play their skipping and hopping and stone-tossing games. I listened to the local gossip—who had been seen with whom, what arguments had been heard through the thin walls, whose baby was sickening, and whose old gran was dying in bed. Although the other women were coarser than Mother, most with missing teeth and loud guffaws of laughter and cheeks or bottom lips stuffed with chewing tobacco, it had still been a pleasure to lean against the walls and spend a companionable half hour before bed.

Now I'd pass those women with my head down, following Ram, sure they knew what I was off to do in my clean dress and carefully plaited hair. I often heard whispers and mutterings and knew I was now one of the regular sources of gossip, but no one ever stepped forward to speak to me or to ask how I was doing. They knew their place, these women.

But I believe it was Mae Scat, from the cellar across the lane, who might have told the Ladies of Righteous Conduct about me. Mae always had a soft spot for my mother and had, more than once, put an arm around my mother's shoulders and given her a warm shake when Ram had been particularly unkind and my mother was sporting a thick lip or swollen eye. Mae Scat had, six months before my mother died, buried her third husband, had six living children, and swore she'd never let another man touch her in any way. She always said she was blessed with a fortune in having only sons, and the three oldest, strapping lads all of them, brought home the bread and coffee on which they all seemed to exist.

From the corner of my eye I had seen Mae Scat watching me as I hurried down the lane after Ram. Her thick bare arms—she never wore a shawl, no matter how cold the weather, and her face was always flushed and perspiring—were crossed over her low bosom as her head turned in my direction, and once I heard her exclaim, to no one in particular, "It ain't right. It just ain't right."

So I assumed, when the well-dressed woman knocked on our door one warm fall evening, that it was Mae Scat who had put her on to us.

"Are you Linny Munt?"

I nodded, feeling my heart begin a staccato beat. No one had ever come to our door asking for me before. I was still dressed in my stained clothes from the bookbindery; we'd just finished eating and I hadn't yet changed for my evening work.

"I'm Mrs. Poll, from the Society of Ladies of Righteous Conduct. Could I please come in and have a word?" she said, her nostrils tight and her narrow shoulders held stiffly in the dim, smelly passage outside our door.

I hadn't opened the door any wider and now looked over my shoulder at Ram to take my cue from him. Sitting on the settle, he stared into the fire as if he hadn't heard the knock or the low, rhythmic voice.

When he made no move to object, I swung the door open, stepping back, and the woman entered. She was dressed almost severely, with a navy bonnet and matching poplin spencer over a lighter blue cambric dress, but it was easy for me to see that although the short jacket and dress were plainly cut, they were of superior material. Instead of a reticule, she carried a large gray cloth bag.

"How are you this fine evening, Linny?" she asked.

I nodded, twisting my hands in my skirt. I was suddenly afraid, even though her voice was kind. She wore cotton navy gloves, and I thought, for no apparent reason, that she was wise not to wear white ones when she came down to Vauxhall.

"How old are you? I would venture a guess at ten?"

"I've just passed twelve," I said. My voice came out as little more than a whisper. I don't know what I was afraid of, although perhaps I imagined she would carry me off to the children's section of the workhouse. I had heard terrible stories of the workhouse.

She looked surprised. "Twelve. Well. I've just come to meet you and to bring you some information. Is this your father, then?" She looked behind me at Ram, who still hadn't moved or spoken.

I nodded again.

"Mr. Munt, is it not?" she called.

Ram answered with a grunt, then rose from the settle. "What's your business with us, then, since you already appear to know our names? What nosy cow has put you on to us?"

"I assure you, Mr. Munt, that I am not here to cause trouble. I'm simply checking on the well-being of the children in the area."

I let my breath out slowly. It didn't appear she was here to take me away, then.

"Well-being? What do you mean by that?" Ram demanded.

Mrs. Poll licked her lips. I saw that her temples were damp. "Making sure they are keeping well. Inviting them to partake in our Children's Hour on Sunday afternoons at the church. I have a tract you might enjoy looking at," she said then, reaching into the cloth bag and pulling out a folded paper. "There are some lovely little drawings I'll explain."

As I reached for the pamphlet she looked at my badly bruised wrist, caused by the rough handling from one of my customers a few days earlier. "How have you hurt yourself, dear?" she inquired, glancing at Ram.

I put my other hand over my wrist. "I—I don't remember," I said. But I looked up at her, wanting her to know that I couldn't tell her, that I dare not. That Ram would punish me if I spoke the truth.

"Is someone mistreating you?" she asked, although now she spoke to Ram and not to me.

Yes, yes, I wanted to cry. *Look at me, Mrs. Poll. Look at me and understand what Ram makes me do every night.*

Ram's voice went up a notch. "She only gets wot she deserves if she don't get on to her chores quick enough. It's a father's duty to see his daughter brought up right, last time I looked."

Mrs. Poll nodded. Although a slight color had started in her throat and now stained her cheeks, her voice remained firm and pleasant. "Yes. It is a father's duty to bring his children up, to feed them and make sure they are clothed. And that no harm comes to them. I can assume, then, that you are carrying out your fatherly duties?"

"You're right," Ram answered. "I am. Not that it's your place to check on me. There's no such part of the law wot tells a parent how to treat his child. And the church has no business interfering."

I bent my head over the tract, skimming the words as Ram blustered. The little tract held a verse of Scripture and announced Sunday afternoon classes for the children of the parish. *All those who attend will be served a slice of bread with jam at the end of the lesson,* I read.

"And isn't that a pity, Mr. Munt. That prevention of cruelty to children is mooted."

"Have you finished with your call, then? Because my girl here doesn't have any time to dawdle. Give that back, now, Linny," Ram told me.

As I handed it to her, I asked, "There's bread and jam for all?"

Mrs. Poll stepped closer. "I see you're able to read then, dear?"

"Oh, yes," I told her, looking up and handing her the tract. "I've been reading for a long time." *And do you hear how well I speak? Can't you see I shouldn't be here, Mrs. Poll? Can you take me home with you?* I knew the ridiculousness of my thoughts, thoughts of a silly and very young child who didn't understand life.

"Well, then." Her voice held a note of surprise. "Would you be interested in assisting in some of our Bible classes for younger children on the Sunday afternoons? It's very simple, really. We read a passage to them and sing a verse or two of a hymn and talk about God's plan for good works and good, clean living." She reached out with an unconscious gesture to tuck a stray lock of hair behind my ear and I felt myself lean into her gloved hand. She kept her hand against the side of my head for another moment and I shut my eyes, remembering my mother's touch.

Yes, yes, I would like that, I thought, *I would like that so much* and opened my mouth to say the words, but Ram spoke before I had the chance. "She ain't got no time for that business," he said. "I allow her to get on to church of a Sunday morning and say her prayers over her muvver's grave, but then she's to come on home."

"It's only an hour, Mr. Munt, and I'm sure Linny would enj—"

"As her father, I think I'm a better judge of how Linny should be spending her Sunday," he said, standing. "Come to think of it, I'm the only judge of how my daughter spends her time. That'll be all, now. And don't be expecting to see my girl at none of yer afternoons."

Mrs. Poll moved toward the door at the obvious signal that the visit—if it could be called such—was officially over. "Well, then, I will bid you a pleasant afternoon, Linny. I'll look forward to seeing you at least in church next Sunday."

I nodded, sinking my teeth into my bottom lip, wanting to run to her, to put my ink-stained hands on her gloved ones and hold on tight. I knew my life was here but I wanted to teach Bible stories to little children, and spend an afternoon with ladies who wore gloves, and have a piece of bread and jam at the end of it all. I wanted . . . I wanted so much.

But I was silent, rooted to the spot.

"And good day to you as well, Mr. Munt," Mrs. Poll said then, her pointed chin rising. She opened the door and went out, and I heard the swish of her hem on each step as she walked downstairs, and wished with all my heart that I could follow her.

I knew I would never go to the Bible classes. I knew that neither the church, nor Mrs. Poll, nor any of the other well-meaning Ladies of Righteous Conduct could help me. Even if I'd had the courage to tell her the truth about my life, what Ram had stated was true. Nobody had any business telling a parent how to treat his child, or interfering. Nobody.

❧

I TURNED THIRTEEN and knew I had grown hard. And I knew my mother would not be pleased—not because I was a whore, for that was not my fault—but because of my evil ways and my even more evil thoughts.

My daily reflections revolved, as I worked at my folding table, on planning all the ways I could kill Ram Munt. These plans were varied and usually torturous and invariably involved imagining the use of my bone-handled knife. I also planned the ways I could kill each of the men my father brought me to (except for the weeping, grieving Monday and Thursday's kindly Uncle Horace. By that time fastidious Wednesday no longer came to Liverpool on business; I greatly missed my weekly bath and had to return to washing myself with tepid water in our dented washbasin).

But the others! To me they were all the same: no matter what bearing they affected, each had the identical fascination of ensuring that the ridiculous worm nestled at the center of their bodies would grow to a snake and then find a home in which it thrashed and jerked about until its death, with a final twitch and dribble. Immediately upon entering a strange room where one of these man awaited with their cherished worm or, in many cases, with the snake ready and waiting, I would cast my eye over the furnishings. I looked for the heavy decorated flower urn that would bash in a skull with a resounding and satisfying thud, or the sharp silver fish knife on the dinner tray that could slice the jugular with one quick, smooth stroke. Of course, these were only fancy pictures that gave me pleasure, although I had indeed had to defend myself from my customers.

More than a few times I'd had to resort to kicking and biting to escape overzealous customers who attempted to use force to contort my body into ways it simply was not made to go. On another occasion, I grabbed a heavy silver paperweight and knocked it into the temple of a crippled gentleman bent on cutting the palm of my hand so he could taste my blood while receiving pleasure from me. The most frightening incident involved a customer who wore a hooded cloak and smelled overpoweringly of horse liniment. When he showed me the tools he carried in a leather satchel and I understood the depravity he expected of me, I tried to leave in spite of the grip he had on my arm. As his grip tightened, so did my resolve not to be subjected to the humiliation he had in store for me. I was able to grab the poker from the fireplace and stab him in the belly. Although I had been forced to use my left hand and knew I wasn't able to stab hard enough to puncture his skin through the thick cloak, it was enough for him to momentarily lose his hold on my arm, and I escaped.

The beatings I took from Ram when I came away empty-handed were, to me, slight in comparison to what I'd saved myself from.

But in spite of an unnerving evening here and there, the majority of the men were simple and unimaginative, wanting the most basic of releases from what they saw as their tortured state, and, like their desires, my actions were uncomplicated and often so repetitive they became mindless.

What I actually did to relieve the boredom and unpleasantness of most of these evening visits was to steal any small thing I could find that wouldn't be immediately missed—a silver buttonhook, a tiny brass compass, or a teacup or small jug or miniature trinket tray in Liverpool's favorite Fazackerley colors of gaudy red, together with blue, yellow, and green in designs of Chinese lattice fences and overdone flowers. It seemed an easy thing to slip the bit into a fold of my shawl or boot top, or even under my bonnet when the customer was busy with his clothing or any ablutions he might undertake before or after my performance. I always sold the objects at the crowded market on Great Charlotte Street on my way home from the bookbindery the next day. With a few of the coins I bought boiled sweets and cakes, which I ate before I got home so Ram wouldn't find me out. I didn't want him to know I was stealing from customers for two reasons—the immediate one being that I knew he would take the money from the sale of the items, with a wink and pat on the head. The second was less obvious but more meaningful: for him to have known of it would have robbed me of that small potency. Stealing from the men who took from me made me feel powerful in an adult way; not only was I deceiving the customers, but also Ram Munt. The objects themselves were of no importance to me. It was this new power that was the real treasure.

After buying my sweets I went straight to Armbruster's Used Goods. The place itself seemed a graveyard—all these things that had once belonged to sailors and grandparents and mothers and fathers and their children. There was a nautical section of wood and brass compasses and quadrants and spyglasses and ships' bowls of blue-and-white china, each painted with its ship's picture. There were dusty shelves of iron coffee mills and discolored brass warming pans, bellows, stacks of printed tiles carefully prised from around fireplaces, and one chipped crude Delftware bowl, with "Success to ye Prussian Hero, 1769" in poorly executed black letters. There were stale-smelling blankets and stained Welsh flannel, wrinkled striped and corded black silk handkerchiefs, scraps of faded drugget and carpets with a worn track down the center, fringes torn and hanging askew.

And the glass! Row after row of black glass bottles, emptied of their whiskey or medicine, waited alongside rummers on their short thick stems and decanters of lead crystal with their bluish hue. There was no end of them, each piece more unusual than the next, created from the leftover glass. I pictured the boys from the glassworks with their weeping raw eyes permanently damaged by the fumes from the alkali mixing with lime and sand; here were some of their efforts, the efforts that sometimes blinded them, being sold for pennies in this low-ceilinged, damp shop with its black film partway up the walls. The place and all its belongings carried the odor of mold and despair.

I passed all these sad remains of other lives and went straight to the book section. On bowed shelves were hodgepodge stacks of books with damp-warped, foxed pages, their hinges cracked, spines leaning and darkened, and covers soiled and bubbled. But they sold for only a penny or two each, sometimes an entire collection by one author marked 5*d*. I bought book after book, hiding them in my bed, and when I had done reading them either resold or traded them for others. Unlike the sweets, which were simply a treat, the books were a necessity.

Before my mother died I read from my Pinnock's at night for the pleasure of learning. But since Mr. Jacobs and the beginning of that life, no matter how exhausted my body was when I fell into my own bed afterward, my mind felt as if it were racing too quickly. Ugliness crammed my brain to the point, some nights, that I thought the top of my head might burst open in a painful, muffled explosion. I could envision all those images and sounds, all the evil smells and tastes I'd had to endure, flooding from my opened head over my pillow in a rush of foul liquid. Reading was like a quiet balm spread by a soft hand on the inside of my skull, and I depended on it to help me come back to myself long enough to fall asleep. I had to wait until the huffing snoring from across the room assured me I wouldn't be found out and then I would light a tiny rushlight and read until I could feel my mind ready to drift. I read all manner of books—from Defoe and Swift to Ann Radcliffe and Elizabeth Hamilton, from adventures to polite romance to memoir.

So all of it—the thefts and the extras they allowed me, the delicious plans of torture and murder, and my charades at putting on a patrician voice and at playing a young lady in the luxurious bedrooms and lavish dining rooms—were devised, and served, to make life bearable.

I thought, every day, of my mother and her dreams for me. I thought of what she would think of me if she could see me now—whore, liar, thief. And I swore to her every Sunday, my hand on her listing cross at Our Lady and St. Nicholas, that I would be more than this. That I would be more than the Linny Munt I was now. That I would be even more than the simpering young women I saw emerging from carriages outside the theaters, wrapped in their furs and feathers or fussing under their parasols. I would be Linny Gow and make her proud. I swore.

Chapter Four

THE LAST JOB I DID FOR RAM MUNT WAS SIX MONTHS AFTER MY thirteenth birthday. It was a cold, wet February evening when he came home grinning, a package wrapped in brown paper and tied with string tucked under his arm.

"It's a top-paying job I've found for you, my girl," he said, tossing the package onto an empty chair and motioning with his head toward the cauldron hanging over the fire. I silently filled his bowl with the turnip and carrot soup I'd made after coming home from work. I had carefully stirred in a palmful of mouse droppings I'd gathered from behind the settle. It pleased me to add a special ingredient into Ram's food each night, after I'd eaten my own share. Some nights it was a tip from the chamber pot before I emptied it into the trickling gutter that ran down the middle of our court, sometimes it was a smear of pigeon mess I'd scraped off the window ledge, sometimes it was crushed cockroaches or other scurrying beetles that ran along the hallway of our house. In a pinch I spit into the cauldron.

I was more weary than usual this night. One of the little gatherers had fainted and I had had to do her job for the hour before she recovered, running up and down the stairs with armloads of stacks, still expected to have finished all my folding by shutting time. All I wanted to do was lie on my pallet, read for ten minutes, and then close my eyes, not thinking about the next day and what it would bring.

The idea of the evening's work was overwhelming. I knew there was no point in telling Ram I was too tired. He would never hit me in the face, as a purple eye and swollen lip were not what my customers wanted to see. Instead, he would hurt me in other ways, small, sly ways—his knuckles grinding a deep bruise into the small of my back or holding a match against the underside of my arm long enough to cause a blister—nothing that would cost me a customer, just enough to make me miserable.

"We're moving up in the world, yes, moving up," he said, ignoring the spoon I set on the table and picking up the full bowl. "You'll be working with some of Liverpool's finest ladies." His damp greatcoat steamed by the fire, sending off the smell of wet dog.

I stood across from him. "Ladies?" My voice held the faintest note of contempt.

Ram slurped noisily, then hooked a chunk of carrot out of the bowl with his fingers. "It's a party, put on for some gentlemen visiting from away. I heard, down at the Flyhouse, that they was looking for a number of the best Liverpool had to offer, none of the sailor's slags from down at the docks or even them from over at Paradise. So I had my say. Oh, I says, I have exactly what you're looking for, I tells 'em. Just a girl and clean as a whistle, hair like silk. She has to be yellow-haired, the fellow says, only one with the palest of hair will do for the special job I have in mind. Well, you can't get much fairer than my girl, I tells him. And she'll do anything you please. She's a good girl, is my own Linny, I tell the young gentlemen what appears to be in charge. I told him that, Linny, that you'd do anything, and that's what he's expecting. So don't disappoint me, now. With what you'll make tonight we might start thinking about moving out of here into better lodgings." He glanced around the spotless room, then shook the piece of carrot at me. "If you do well, you'll be asked for again. This could be the beginning of a new life for us." He winked then, popping the carrot into his mouth. "Only the beginning," he repeated, chewing, a piece of brilliant orange caught up between his two browning front teeth.

THE PACKAGE CONTAINED a green dress of Spitalfields silk with an ecru-colored frill. It was used, bought at the clothes market on Fox Street, and smelled faintly of cold sweat. Before I put it on I inspected the seams for fleas. It was last year's style; I had seen that none of the fashionable ladies on Lord Street wore this design any longer. But it clung softly, the fabric smooth against my skin. After I'd changed into it and stood before Ram, he nodded appreciatively. I had never before worn a dress with a low-cut bodice and when I looked down and saw the slight new swell of my breasts, I had to fight to stop from putting up my hands to cover myself.

"Brush out your hair. No plaits tonight. You have to look your best. Yes, tonight will be very special."

I did as I was told, then, studying myself in the ormolu mirror from the fruitwood box. I took out the pendant and fastened the clasp around my neck. I admired how the gold shone against my skin, how the green stones complemented the green silk of the dress. But when I reached for my gray shawl, telling Ram I was ready, he took another look, then shook his head.

"Take off that cheap trinket," he said, his eyes skittering from the pendant to my face and back to the pendant. "It spoils the look." He licked his lips and turned away.

I closed my hand around the pendant. I knew it looked quite fine, but I also realized that seeing it would have brought the memory of my mother to Ram. *Could he actually feel guilty about what he's forced me to become?* I returned the pendant to the fruitwood box, realizing, with a sudden sharp stab of what I knew to be my own guilt, that I should never have considered wearing it. What a disgrace, after all, to my mother's memory, considering what I'd be doing within the hour.

I'll only wear it when I can feel proud of who I am, I told myself, and closed the lid of the fruitwood box with a firm click.

※※※

RAM HAD HIRED A CART and we jerked along the streets, rising higher above Liverpool's maze of lanes and alleys and courts that led up from the waterfront. Eventually I saw St. Andrew's, the Scotch kirk, and knew we were in Mount Pleasant. And then there we were, on the grand street where I had spent so many Sunday afternoons. Rodney Street. We stopped in front of one of the brightly lit Georgian houses with a door wide enough to admit our whole cart and Ram walked me to it, tucking my hand into his arm as if he were a proud father walking his daughter down the aisle. I knew the exteriors of these houses well from my Sunday visits but had never expected to step inside one.

The door was opened by a butler, a middle-age man in velvet breeches whose closed face didn't ask any questions. With no flicker of emotion he simply stepped aside, and as I pulled my arm from Ram's and hesitantly crossed the threshold, the butler abruptly closed the door in Ram's face. But Ram pushed it open before the latch could catch.

"I'm to be paid before I leave," he said. "Payment upon delivery. That was the deal struck between me and the gentleman."

I lowered my head and studied the tips of my shoes. Brown and scuffed, they were incongruous with the airiness of the green dress. I looked up to see the butler also staring at the embarrassing fact of my boots, a giveaway that no fine dress could disguise.

"One moment," he said, his voice not bothering to disguise his distaste, although his face remained impassive. He attempted to close the door again, but this time Ram pushed it harder, stepping into the foyer beside me.

"I'll be waiting right here," he said.

The butler turned, his back stiff, and went up the stairs, disappearing around a bend in the hall. We stood silently under a chandelier dancing with the light of at least thirty candles. A parlormaid walked past the entrance hall, carrying a large urn of dying flowers—they were tall and red, spiky, with similar sharp-looking greenery. I knew they must be something exotic, brought up from London, as I'd never seen the likes of them before.

The parlormaid glanced at us; her face, like the butler's, showed no interest or curiosity. From somewhere in the house there was a steady rhythmic beat.

Within moments the butler reappeared. He descended the stairs at a studied pace.

Ram couldn't wait for the feel of the coins in his hand. He hurried over to the butler, meeting him at the bottom step. The butler handed him something; from my position behind him I couldn't see what it was. Ram momentarily studied what had been handed to him and then he was brushing past me, his eyes bright and a tight smile turning up his lips. Without even a good-bye he left, leaving the door open in his excitement.

I closed it and turned to face the butler.

He looked at me—from my unpinned hair to my hated boots—and as he held out his hand for my wrap I saw something shift, almost imperceptibly, some softening that disturbed me more than his imperious manner had. He took my shawl, holding it gingerly between his thumb and first finger as if it were lousy. The parlormaid appeared and took it from him, her nose tilted in a way that indicated just how far beneath her I was.

The butler started up the stairs, and I followed. I'd never been in so magnificent a house. I put my hand on the smooth polished wood of the banister, enjoying the feel of it.

By the time we reached the top of the curved stairway, the muffled, rhythmic sound I had heard from the foyer was louder and more distinct. I could also hear an underlying sound, like someone singing. The beat stopped and the voice called out, then laughed. The laughter verged on hysteria. The butler stopped in front of a set of double doors painted a gleaming vermilion. A brass handle in the shape of intertwined snakes graced each door. He nodded once at the doors and then left.

Unsure of what was expected, I knocked. I knocked again and then, realizing it was pointless, put my hand on one of the snake handles. It was warm to the touch, as if responding to the pulse on the other side of the door. Before I had a chance to turn it, the door was opened from the other side. Hot air, scented with perfume and smoke—smoke that was dark and sweet—rushed out at me. I stepped back.

"Oh, look," cried the boy who had opened the door. "Look, Pompey. It's a baby girl. And I believe she's the one." I took him to be a few years older than me, although it was difficult to be sure.

He had brightly painted lips and spots of rouge on his cheeks, and on his head was a tiara of glass beads with a drooping ostrich feather, discolored and ratty. A gown of flowered, diaphanous material floated around him. He put his hands on my shoulders and drew me into the room. "Do you see, Pompey?"

The gaslights on the walls were set low, creating flickering shadows. Large pieces of furniture filled every corner of the room; dressers and wardrobes and sofas and chairs sat like hulking dark animals. Out of one corner came a very large man. As my eyes adjusted I saw that his skin was very black and he wore only the smallest of loincloths and a white lamé turban. He held a small drum under one arm; as he walked in my direction, he beat it with his palm, a dull, solemn beat.

I looked at the boy.

"Don't be frightened, baby girl," he said, recognizing what must have been on my face. His pupils were huge. He waved one hand at the black man, who immediately lowered the drum in front of him so that it covered his groin.

The boy laughed, and I recognized the note of hysteria I had heard moments earlier, assuming it, at the time, to be the voice of a woman.

The unfamiliar, slightly nutty odor filled my nostrils, so strong now that, combined with the wavering shadows in the room, I was suddenly giddy. There was something wrong here, something unknown that frightened me.

"I'm Clancy," the boy said. "Now, come with me. We've been waiting." He picked up my hand.

"I don't think—" I started, trying to pull my hand from his grasp, but Clancy, so willowy and slight, tightened his grip with surprising strength, squeezing my fingers until they ached.

"But of *course* you mustn't think. Thinking is such a bore," he said then. "You must only feel." And then he gave a fierce tug, and I was jerked along. Following, I saw that he had nothing on under the gown. He led me along the periphery of the room; as we walked, stepping around ottomans and low tables, I was thinking of how I could escape. It would seem that I could turn and run but for Clancy's iron grip on my hand. And for the fact that the black man—who must be Pompey—had started his sonorous drumming once more and was now close on my heels.

"Now," Clancy said, "we're here." He pulled aside a heavy brocade curtain. Behind it was another door, plain wood, incongruous with the rest of the ornate room. There was a brass key in the lock. "Go on. It's unlocked. He's waiting for you."

"Who is he?" I asked, an unknown panic making me pull back again.

But Clancy only gave me a look that was suddenly intent, and the silly smile that had been on his lips from the moment I'd first seen him now fell away, replaced by something uncertain. His expression was eerily like the one I'd seen on the butler's face less than five minutes earlier.

I also realized Clancy was much younger than I had first thought; maybe he and I were the same age after all.

He turned the knob and pushed me through the open doorway.

HERE THE PECULIAR sugary smell of smoke was stronger still and there was something else, another smell just under the sweetness. It was as if something was slowly, delicately rotting, taking its time, enjoying the journey. As the door behind me closed, the room fell into complete darkness.

"Hello?" I called. It was wrong, so wrong. I wanted nothing more than to flee.

"Come in, come in," a voice answered. It was a soft, tremulous voice, marred by some affliction.

"Is there no light, sir?" I asked, suddenly even more fearful. The voice had not been reassuring. "For I can't see a thing." I had entered so many rooms, had heard so many men's voices. Always I had been able to see what was in front of me; although there had been too many unpleasant surprises to count, never had I had to stand in the dark, afraid of who or what might make itself known to me.

There was the long slow sound of sucking and I saw a tiny red glow of light from the bowl of a pipe. Then there was the sighing release of air and a rustle of movement. The sharp rasp of a flint was followed by a sudden flare of light, and I saw a figure crouched in front of the marble fireplace. As the kindling caught and the fire grew, the figure moved away with a shuffling, uncoordinated gait, sinking, with a shallow sigh, into a deep winged chair positioned to one side of the fireplace. The shadows of the wings hid his features.

"Now you must step into the light," the man said. "And we'll see if you're what I've been hoping for. It's so difficult to get what one asks for these days. I've been quite disappointed in the selection here in Liverpool. Quite disappointed," he repeated.

I walked to the fireplace and stood in front of it.

"Turn your head; I want to see your hair."

I looked to the left, then to the right, feeling the heat of the fire behind me.

"All right, all right." The man's voice had risen a tone, as if excited. *What's wrong with the way he speaks?* I wondered again. "Come here now. We'll have a lovely drink together, shall we?"

I went toward the outline of the chair. "I'd rather not, sir. What is it you wish me to do?" I asked, feeling my nose wrinkling slightly at the sour odor that grew stronger as I neared the chair. I'd heard all the usual requests; none surprised me now, but apart from the hooded customer, I'd never known this particular threatened sensation.

"What is your name, dear?"

"Linny."

"Would you spell that, please?"

"As it sounds, sir. L-i-n-n-y."

"Is that your true Christian name?"

"No. It's Linnet, like the bird."

"Ah. The little linnet bird. Do you sing sweetly as well, child?" He didn't wait for an answer. "And yet I think I prefer Linny. Linny from Liverpool. I will remember that. Now. I want to touch it," he went on. "Your hair."

I knelt in front of him, and from my lowered position I could see him in the light from the fire as it danced across his features. It was hard to tell how old he was, for his face was dissipated, the eyelids heavy over the slightly protruding, crusty eyes. They were unfocused, as if he had just awoken; his nose was veined and his lips too wet, too red. His tongue, surprisingly small and pink, darted in and out of his mouth in an uncontrollable flicker.

"I shall pour you a drink, shall I?" His fingers strayed to a large brown bottle on a table beside his chair. "Have you ever been to France, my dear?"

I shook my head, trying not to watch his tongue; there was something obscene in its frenzied dance, which tripped each word. I put my hand under my hair and held it toward him. "It's free of nits, you'll find, sir, as I—" I began, but without warning the man's feet, in their dark blue prunella slippers, flew into the air, wheeling furiously. ·A heel caught me in the face, sending me flying onto my side. Holding my cheek, I sat up and stared in shock. The man was slipping down in the chair, on his back now and groaning, his legs working as fast as the knife sharpener who pedaled his wheel over on Seel Street. His hands gripped the armrests to keep from propelling off the chair and he cried out in short, jerky bursts of sound.

The door opened and the black man stepped into the room, bowing his head so that his high turban didn't touch the lintel. He looked down at me, then walked to the chair. As he passed, the tiny loincloth swaying, I saw that his bare foot was more than three times the length of my hand.

"It's . . . he's . . . I don't know what's wrong with him," I said. "I didn't do anything."

Pompey picked up the man, whose legs were slowing now, and held him against his bare chest as easily as if he were a child.

"Pompey. Pompey," the man cried. "Make it leave; make the pain leave me. Give me my chloral. Hurry. It's crushing my ribs."

Gently lowering him back onto the seat, Pompey picked up the brown bottle. He poured liquid into a small glass, then held the man's quivering mouth, tucking the tongue in with his long-nailed index finger as he poured the liquid down his throat. "Soon, soon, master. It is almost over," he murmured. His voice was deep and heavily accented.

The old man's mouth opened and closed like the beak of a baby bird.

I watched the strange scene, fingering the lump rising on my cheek. The thought of performing an act on this horrid man made my gorge rise.

Slowly, the man's body slowed. His spine relaxed, and all that was left in his legs was a slight trembling.

As I got to my knees, Pompey poured from the brown bottle until the glass was half full, then came toward me, holding it out. "I see you have not drunk yet, little mistress. Come. Take this. It is time." His voice was even softer now, little more than a whisper.

I shook my head, staring at his face. He had marks, I saw, wide, raised marks that were even darker than the rest of his skin, running straight down both cheeks. He had no eyelashes.

"It will not happen again—his attack—this night," he said. "He will have no more pain and you have nothing to fear." I wanted to believe the soothing voice but I couldn't.

I glanced around Pompey, seeing the man's now still form in the chair. "What am I expected to . . . what does he want?" I whispered, bending my neck back to look up into Pompey's face.

His gaze rested on my swelling cheek as he held out the glass. "Just stay quiet. Do not upset him. Drink this now, please."

"What is it?" I asked, eyeing the colorless liquid. "I don't take spirits."

"It will go better for you. Drink, little mistress," he said.

I put my hand against the glass, saying, "No, I said I—" but in one swift move Pompey had seized my jaw and tilted my throat back, forcing my lips open in the same way he had with the old man. The liquid went down in a flaming rush and I choked and coughed as Pompey let go of me. I swallowed, licking my lips, but there was only the faint whisper of sweetness.

"It is better this way," Pompey repeated, setting the glass back on the table and moving toward the door.

"But what's wrong with him?"

Pompey opened the door and stepped through. "It is called the French Welcome by some," he said, and then stopped, looking at me. I leaned forward to hear what he would say next. "Although most are more familiar with it as syphilis."

And then he closed the door firmly, and I heard the turn of the brass key.

Chapter Five

I SAT IN FRONT OF THE FIRE ON THE CARPET SWIRLING WITH RICH
jewel tones. I knew the sailors often carried diseases. I tried to think if
I'd heard of the French Welcome, or the other word that sounded like
the sly hissing of a snake. I was suddenly sleepy, my eyelids so heavy that
I had to struggle to keep them open. Finally I lowered myself so that I
was lying on my side, my back to the fire, head comfortably resting on
my curled arm. The throbbing in my cheek had completely disappeared;
there was no pain, just a lovely, sleepy, floating sensation. The man
appeared to sleep as well, breathing heavily and noisily. His tongue was
also at rest, finally, a thick line of dried saliva crusted on his bottom lip.
In the outer room Clancy was again singing to Pompey's drumming,
but the sound blended into one continuous murmur that was something
I couldn't quite recognize but inexplicably loved.

I let my eyes close, the song and the rhythm of the man's breathing
and the comforting beat of the flames at my back lulling me. And then I
was dreaming, strange and somehow dark and uneasy dreams. Soon the
dark was banished; the sun came out, shining with an unfamiliar brittle
light that hurt my closed eyes. In the dream my eyes stayed shut, and yet
I could see perfectly. I was on Salthouse Dock, walking toward the
water. Gulls flew overhead with mewling cries as their wings snapped in
the sunlight. They swung and dipped, swung and dipped, finally flying
so low that I felt the warm flutter of their wings against my eyelids, my
cheeks. One came right next to the side of my head; its beak, pointed
and sharp, snapped loudly in my ear. I was afraid; I wanted to get away
from the mechanical clacking of the beak. I ran, but the gull chased me

to the end of the pier, its cries louder now, still trying to peck me with that awful horny projection. When I could run no further I looked down at the murky water. The beak came closer; there was no choice. I jumped, and as I fell toward the water, stomach lurching upward, I saw, just under the surface, my mother's face, white and still, eyeless, her hair floating around her head like gently waving arms of seaweed.

I gasped, opening my eyes.

The man knelt over me, large shears in his hand. The shears were gleaming silver with gold handles. Strands of my hair were in the blades. His eyes glittered strangely and his breathing was raspy. Excited, vibrating trills rose from his throat and his tongue was even more frenetic than it had been earlier. "Ah!" he exclaimed in a pleased way, studying my face as I blinked, trying to clear my vision and understand what I was seeing.

I struggled to rise but he pressed me down. "Stay still, my girl, stay still. I'm not done," he said, around the slippery tongue. "I had thought you to be dead, but it's much more pleasant with one so warm and pliant." He laughed delightedly, as if surprised by this suddenly realized fact.

Striking at him with my arm, pushing him away, for he was little more than a ghost of a man, I managed to get to my feet. The room was brightly lit by the gaslights on the walls and the lamps on tables turned high. I reached upward, dully fingering short, soft tufts, all that was left on my shorn scalp. "What have you done?" I cried, my voice strange in my own ears, muffled as if I were speaking through a pillow. "Why have you cut off my hair?" It took me a long time to get out each of the two sentences.

I looked at the long strands gleaming on the vibrant hue of the carpet. Still kneeling, the man lifted one of them, running it across his face, pieces of it catching on the gummy surface of his tongue. He laughed again, pointing behind me, and now I recognized the familiar cackle of the gull.

I turned in the direction of his finger, unable to move quickly, every movement exaggerated, although my instincts screamed at me, again, to run, escape. I saw a tall standing trunk, opened vertically. Shelves lined one side, and on the shelves were large jars.

"Take a look, dear heart, do go and look," the man said.

As if pulled by invisible sticky threads I walked toward the jars, not understanding why I would do this, why I would follow this lunatic's instructions. The image of my mother's face, floating under water, seemed more real than what was happening in this room at this moment.

I looked at the rows of jars but couldn't understand what I was seeing. The jars were filled with floating shadows. Each jar had a label, written in spidery, shaky script. *Emma, Newcastle*, said one. *Loulou, Calais. Mollie, Manchester*. I kept reading the labels. *Yvette, Toulouse. Bette, Glasgow.*

"Have you ever been to France, my little Linny?" the man asked for the second time this evening. I turned, seeing him struggle to his feet. He came closer, limping heavily, one shoulder twisted forward. My eyes swiveled slowly in their sockets, seeing that his hands were behind his back.

"It's a beautiful, terrible place, is France. I spent too long there. Too long, with all the lovely girls. Sluts, my dear. All lovely sluts with their ripe quims, they were, like your young self," he said. "You shouldn't be allowed to keep on spreading your filthy diseases. Surely you've heard of Fracastoro's shepherd—do you know the poem, my lovely? *Syphilis sive morbus Gallicus.*"

He was within touching distance now. "'A shepherd once—distrust not ancient fame,'" he quoted, "'Possessed these downs, and Syphilis his name.'"

I was mesmerized by his eyes. There was no color, only round black globes, hard as marble, as coal.

"And so of course you must be stopped. You and all your kind, for nothing can end the agony you've inflicted upon me. Not the mercury salts, not the bromide nor the chloral. Temporary, all temporary relief. So I'm keeping a collection, you see, of those I've prevented from spreading the foulness. So many colors. And I've been looking for quite some time now for an addition to my collection. It had to be the perfect color," I heard him say. "And now I've found it. Linny from Liverpool."

I looked back at the jars, staring into the one closest to my face. And then I let out an involuntary noise, a strangled gasp, and tried to move away from what I realized I was seeing. But it was as if I had joined my mother now, except my hair couldn't float like hers, not anymore. I moved my arms in torpid arcs, attempting to swim through the thick air, swim away from the jars with their horrible contents of disembodied hair.

Gleaming black, rich brown, deep red and bright orange, dark blond. All floating.

The man put his hand on my shoulder and I turned with the pressure, and then something glinted above me and I thought of the gull, saw the shears in the air, silver and gold, moving toward me. Instinctively I put up my arm, not quick enough to stop the blades, but they were deflected by my forearm, and instead of stabbing into their intended target, my neck, they slid further and slashed the soft flesh over my heart in a long, crooked line, slicing through the green dress as if it were butter. I saw blood pouring from the gash, but there was no pain, no shock.

I was deeper in the water now. There was no sound but the turgid beat of my own blood in my ears. When the shears were raised over me again, I struck clumsily at the old man, and the shears flew from his hand.

I stooped and picked them up. I looked into the maddened eyes, and then my own arm rose and lowered in what I saw as slow, graceful movements that felt like a dance, and the old man fell, the shears finally and firmly planted in one of those terrible eyes, his mouth a round and trembling wet circle.

I looked at him lying at my feet and my own legs gave way, and I knew I was falling, falling, back into the Mersey where my mother waited.

<hr />

THE VOICES GREW LOUDER. I recognized the faint hysteria of the boy in the flowered dress. Clancy.

"I don't know, do I? How were we to guess he wouldn't kill her first, as he's always done? Oh. Oh, Pompey, I feel terribly lightheaded. Please. Let me lean against you."

"Christ. What a mess. Why the hell wouldn't he have given her enough chloroform to kill her before he started in on her? But she's dead now, isn't she?" asked another voice. A man, older than the boy, his voice self-assured.

"I believe so, young master." Pompey's voice. I thought of the drink he had given me. Him, not the old man.

"Well, we'll never know how this happened, will we?" the voice of the man called Young Master said, anger just under the surface. "But I knew we shouldn't have let him keep on with his sordid game. I knew we shouldn't set up another. And now look at this. I should have listened to my intuition."

I still felt nothing, although I became aware of something new, a dull, thumping surge, a minor crescendo of pain through the top half of my body. There was the fresh iron smell of blood. I felt my head being lifted and moved, my hair pushed back from my face. I was pulled up by my wrists, and cool air blew across them as my sleeves slid back.

"Look at that mark," Clancy squealed. "Like a fish."

Then I was let go, falling limply to the floor again.

"Who brought her? Was it a pimp? Will anyone come looking for her tonight?" It was the same well-bred voice, with a touch of superiority about it. A voice no one would argue with. How odd, I thought, that I could hear and understand, but felt powerless to move so much as an eyelid.

"I believe she was bought for the night, young master. No one will be looking for her until morning," Pompey said.

"What should we do, then?" asked Clancy. "Whatever shall we do about all of this? The blood. There's so much blood." His voice dissolved into tears.

"Shut up, Clancy. Dump her in the Mersey, Pompey," the man said. "Get it done right away."

"And what of your father, young master?"

There was silence except for Clancy's muffled sobbing.

"Clean him up as best you can," the superior voice ordered. "We'll leave for London as soon as humanly possible and while it's still dark. If someone should come to fetch the girl tomorrow, there'll be no sign of her, or any of us. Anyway, one less doxy is of little importance to anyone but an irate pimp.

"When we arrive in London we'll say my father died while visiting Liverpool, and have a proper burial there. Nobody has to know about any of this. Only the people in this room know what's happened here. And none of us will talk. Isn't that right, Clancy?"

"Oh my goodness, oh, of course not. But—but I'll be *haunted*, positively *haunted*, by what I've seen here tonight." Again, Clancy's voice rose to a breathless squeak. "I can't look, no, I can't look any longer."

"Pull yourself together, Clancy." Young Master's voice was thick with annoyance.

"But those dreadful scissors, his face, oh dear, I—yes, I'm going to be sick."

I felt the floor thud with running footsteps. There was a silence, longer than the first.

And then the confident voice spoke again. "I can trust you to do what must be done, Pompey," it said calmly. "I don't want anything left, especially not that cursed hair or the damn trunk. Or anyone who might speak of tonight. Anyone. You understand, don't you, Pompey?"

"Yes, young master."

I heard no more voices, but the floor vibrated with a set of heavy steps again, and there was the soft click of a door.

I moved my left arm then, and the movement brought out an unexpected and shocking pain, as if the shears had just now plunged into skin and tendon and muscle. *Help me. Somebody, please,* I tried to whisper. But my lips wouldn't move, and besides, there was nobody to help me, my mother gone, a man called Ram caring only about what coins I could bring to his hand. The pungent odor of burning hair filled the air.

"Pompey?" I finally found my voice and whispered into the thick stink that enveloped me but there was no answer and then the dark Mersey moved in, sweetly, and I let myself go to it.

"WHAT WAS THAT?"

Something had brought me back to consciousness. Was it the shout of the voice, muffled, as if by distance or barrier? Or was it a sudden jarring?

I couldn't see anything, but I also couldn't tell whether my eyes were open or not. The numbness was still there, holding me in its quietness. I realized I was rocking, gently, as if in a cradle.

The voice came again, closer now. "Gib? Gib, you hear that? Gib!"

There was a grunt, as if someone had been rudely awakened. Next a moan. "I didn't hear nuthin'. Give us a drink, then, Willy."

I was cold. Wet. I knew I was on my side. There was a sound, familiar. I strained to recognize it. Oars, small slaps as wood hit water.

"We bin out all night? Near morning, is it then, Willy?"

"No. It's just gone three by the bells." The voices came closer, the sound of rowing louder. I grew aware that I was growing wetter. Water was inching into my ear. "I heared a carriage, Gib, and then something hit the water, just over yon. Something heavy."

A burp echoed. "My missus will skin me alive, so she will. Take me to shore, Willy. I best be off home. If I can get in without waking her, she might not—"

I felt a bump near the top of my head. "By Jesus, you was right, you old bugger. What is it? What is it, Willy?"

Water closed over the side of my face. I felt it on my mouth, felt it snaking through my lips. I could taste it, foul and cold. I tried to swallow, or to spit it out, but could do neither. Nothing—not my mouth or my throat—worked.

"She's sinking, Gib. Quick, help me pull it up. It's a box of some kind. Help me haul 'er in, man. Put your elbow into it."

"It's too heavy. Here, hook this rope through the handle. We'll drag it in to shore."

The water swirled over my face momentarily and then I felt myself lifted. My mouth was now full of water. At the next lurching movement, I grew aware of a heaviness against my back, pressure, something pushing at me.

I was in a box—was it a coffin? *Am I dead?* The water threatened to choke me, a comfort, for I knew I must be alive. But where was I and what was I doing, moving along the river with something heavy shoving into my back? I heard the bottom of a skiff scraping the rough stones on the water's edge. Then the box was dragged up on the stones. I felt the vibration of them rolling under me, but still couldn't move, couldn't make a sound.

"It's a trunk. One of them big traveling ones. Let's get her open, Willy. Could be somethin' right valuable."

"I'm trying."

"Is there a lock?"

"No. But the latches are right tight. That's a good sign. Maybe there wasn't a chance for too much water to get in. Here, I got the last one, and—Jesus have mercy!"

There was a rush of freezing air and silence. I knew now that my eyes were closed; I could see nothing.

"It's two girls," the softer voice, the one I knew was Willy, finally said.

"I can see that, can't I? Lookit how they's layin'. Like spoons. And what's all them jars? They're empty. Not even lids."

"I don't know, do I? Jesus, Gib. What are we to do?"

"They're dead for sure, ain't they, Willy?"

"Must be. Lying so still like that." I heard the rustle of clothing and the softer voice came almost in my face. "Although they ain't dead by drowning; only half their heads is underwater." I smelled the beery stench of his breath.

"You're right. That front one looks about the age of your youngest, Willy." There was a tug on my shoulder. "Stabbed. Right in the heart, from what I can see."

"Same with the other?"

More rustling, more movement, this time the weight behind me shifting.

"Nope. This one has her throat cut. Maybe there's something of value on the bodies."

"Not likely. Nobody'd go to the bother of killing 'em and throwing 'em in the river without first taking any valuables."

"Hey, Willy, maybe we could sell 'em to them sawbones up at the infirmary."

The second voice grew loud. "I ain't about to get messed up with no body snatching."

"Keep yer voice down, Willy. We ain't takin' 'em from the grave-yard. They come floatin' to us, fair and square."

"No, I won't do it. I ain't selling these girls to them with bloodied hands so they can do their dirty work. Bad business, that is, cuttin' up the dead for their own learnin'. And we've got nothin' to wrap 'em in, and nothing to haul 'em in. No. I won't do it, Gib," he repeated.

I heard a soft rasp that might have been a hand scrubbing over a stubbled face. "Could be you're right. If we was to get caught with two dead girls . . ." A sigh. Now I heard the skiff rubbing on the stones in the kissing lift and fall of the shallow water on the bank. "But them dresses might fetch us somethin', Willy." The voice rose hopefully.

"There's a lot of blood. And it looks like the green one is cut down the front."

"But the blood is fresh. It would wash out easy. And my good woman is right handy with a needle and thread. We could sell 'em down at the market. That flowery one looks pricy. It might bring in a shilling or two. And the trunk itself, well, surely it would fetch a good price. Go ahead, Willy. Start on the green one. I'll get this one off. And throw out the goddamn jars."

There were rough, jerking movements behind me, the sound of glass breaking.

"I'm a Christian man, Gib, and a father. It don't feel right, stripping these girls and throwing them back into the river. Don't set right with me at all."

"Don't think about yer own girls now, Willy. I bet this dress alone—" There was a low whistle. "This ain't no girl after all. Look here."

Silence. Then, "You're right, by Jesus. What's he doin' all trumped up like that?"

I was pulled up again. "Who knows? And who cares? But this front one here is. I can tell, even with her hair all chopped off."

"She's so small."

"Stop thinkin' about it, Willy. They's dead and in no need of their clothes, whether they's boys or girls, young or old. A dress is a dress."

I'm not dead. Can't you see? I'm not dead.

The movements behind me continued. "Quit starin' like you seen a spook," the rougher voice said, and there was a rush of cold air as the body behind me was pulled away. I knew now that it was Clancy. "Lookit this throat, would you? Ear to ear. Like a big red smile, it is."

There was a small splash and then the thud as Clancy's body was dropped back behind me. "Here. Give the dress a good shake, then take it to the edge and wash that blood out."

My arm was grabbed, and two jars that must have been caught in the folds of my skirt clanged together. "Why you just standin' there, Willy?

Do wot I says. If you haven't the stomach for it, I'll look after it all. But the dresses is mine, then." I was pulled up, but in the next second dropped back. "She don't feel like the other one," the man called Gib said. "Not as cold. Willy? I'm not sure this one's dead."

My waist was kicked with the toe of a boot, and at the sudden rough movement I involuntarily emitted a watery gasp as the stinking Mersey trickled out of my mouth.

"Damn. She's alive, all right," Gib said. "But from the looks of her she'll be gone soon. She'll never miss her dress." He pulled it off my shoulder.

"Gib. No," Willy said.

"Wot?"

"You heard me, Gib. Leave her be."

"Wot you talking about? Willy?"

I felt hands under my arms, pulling me out of the trunk. The jars that were still on my dress crashed onto the slimy stones. Something warm and soft pressed against my breast. "Cold water likely slowed the bleeding," the softer voice said. "Could be the water that was to kill her saved her instead. Who'd a done this?"

I gagged suddenly and with the wretching movement brought up more watery saliva. It was as if it cleared my throat. "Pompey," I murmured. *It must have been Pompey, following orders to throw me into the Mersey. And he thought I was already dead, so there was no reason to slit my throat, as he had Clancy's.*

"Calling for her father," Willy said. "She's wanting her pappy." And then I was roughly dragged over the stones, and the pain in my breast returned, as did the blessed darkness.

Chapter Six

I WAS ROUGHLY SHAKEN.

"Wake up, girl. It's time you were awake. Come on now."

The shaking brought on such an exquisite pain that I cried out, opening my eyes and looking into the drawn face of a middle-age woman.

The pain was everywhere. I couldn't move, pinned in place by the pounding in my temples and the terrible pain in my chest.

"Rise yerself, now. You bin lyin' here the full clock round."

"Please," I whispered, trying to lick my lips. "Drink. A drink, please."

The woman appeared not to hear me. She wore a gray shift that made her look like one long, thin slice of gray—her hair, skin, and covering. "The surgeon's been in and stitched you up." She had to shout over the screams and curses and prayers that filled the air. "Get dressed; there are others wot need the bed. You'll go through that door, there," she said, pointing to one side of the long room. She dropped my boots onto the floor, then threw the green dress, stiff with blood and stinking of foul dampness, onto the edge of the bed. There was a moth-eaten brown woolen scarf stuck on the blood of the bodice. "You had nowt else with you, although the boots are a damn sight more than many we see of a night. Now move yerself."

"Surgeon?" I whispered, for the first time looking around here. "Where am I?"

"Wot?" the woman said, leaning closer.

"What is this place?" I asked again, a slow dread coming to me.

"It's the Fever Hospital of the Brownlow Hill Workhouse."

I raised my head at this, even though that movement brought a fresh wave of pain. "No one comes out of hospital alive. Am I going to die?"

The woman shook her head. "Idjit. The only reason your sort believe you die if you come to a hospital is because none come but those a breath away from dead. It's not our fault if they're too far gone to be helped. You was lucky. Some kind soul took it upon himself to drop you in front of the door with your wound bound up in that scarf. Otherwise you'd have bled to death. Hurry up now, girl. If you've no home go on up to the workhouse. You'll be assigned a job there when you're able." And then she turned and left.

I lay still, trying to breathe around the pain, trying to stop the swirling in my head, trying to remember.

The horror of what had passed came back to me as if I'd been struck. "No," I said, closing my eyes again. "No." The room, with its sweet stink. I could remember lying on the rug in the house on Rodney Street, surrounded by the smell of burning hair. The hair, and the shears. And the man . . . the man I'd killed. That I'd murdered. Was I to be found out, hauled off to jail, and eventually hanged, my body thrown into a pit of quicklime with other murderers?

What had happened after that? Another memory. It was dark, and I was wet. Was it just the dream again, the dream of my mother floating under the surface of the Mersey? But I had been cold, so cold, and now I remember thinking *Mother? Is that you, Mother?* I had felt the watery push and sway of someone floating behind me. Not Mother. Clancy. The voices of the men called Gib and Willy. It was Willy who had saved my life, who had brought me here.

Moaning involuntarily, I managed to sit up on the mattress, stained deep brown from an ancient combination of blood and vomit and urine and feces. Drawing deep breaths, I tried to quell the nausea that the pain brought on. I awkwardly pulled off the gray, threadbare shift someone had put on me, pursing my lips with the effort, not caring that the old woman in the bed less than a foot from mine was studying me with clouded eyes. There was a thick strip of blood-soaked flannel wrapped around my chest. Getting into the dress seemed an impossibility but there was no one to help. I knew the woman who had spoken to me would have been one from the workhouse herself, her face showing no flicker of compassion.

I eventually managed to get myself dressed, partly due to the torn bodice. The old woman reached out and, with a thickened yellow fingernail, touched my green silk skirt, smiling toothlessly and muttering something incomprehensible. I dropped the brown scarf onto her bed and she snatched it up, sniffing at it and patting it as if it were a small animal. I shoved my feet into my sodden boots, leaving them undone, and stumbled through the long room of groaning, piteous men and women, stumbled as if still in the nightmare. I had to pass through a number of sections of the building, unconsciously reading the names of the wards: *Insane,* with its padlocked splintered doors that didn't block the desperate shrieks and garbled voices; *Scald and Itch,* with low moans and muffled weeping; *Smallpox,* which was eerily silent, and finally, somehow worse than the screams and heavy silence, was the cacophony of lonely sounds that poured through the doors of the ward simply marked *Children.*

Stepping out into the misty gray of morning, I avoided the workhouse to the left of the hospital, taking the path that led down to the main road. I walked and walked, knowing that if I fell I would be hauled back to the workhouse. I walked as the mist blew away and a watery sun threw pale shafts. As I neared Vauxhall Road and the locks of the Leeds-Liverpool Canal, I dully noticed the early morning crowd of spectators in Lock Fields. They were watching two young men who would likely be fighting over some all-night argument in one of the many public houses that lined the area.

I walked in my heavy boots and spoiled dress, at times bent over nearly double as I struggled around the pain. People parted in front of me. I felt as old as the crone waiting to die in the next bed in the Fever Hospital, the crone who loved green.

RAM'S MOUTH OPENED when I finally fell through the door.

"Wot—" he started, but I pushed myself to my feet and wove across the floor and lowered myself onto my pallet. The pain made it impossible to lie in any position but on my back. I plucked at my blanket but couldn't get it over me. I lay with my eyes open, and Ram came to look down at me. "Wot's happened to you?" he asked, his eyes taking in the torn dress and the dirty flannel wrapped around me, my shorn hair. I saw the familiar look of growing anger around his jaw. "I thought you'd run off on me when I went round yesterday and nobody answered my knocking. Look at the state o' you. Would you not do as you were told for the gentlemen? Did they have to punish you?"

I closed my eyes.

"I should punish you as well. That dress cost me a right pretty penny," he said. "You'll have to stitch it up as best you can and sponge out the blood." His voice rose, but there was a wavering to it, a tone I hadn't heard before, as if it was an effort for him to sound angry. "They'll never take you back at the bookbindery if you lose more than a few days. And I'm out of pocket for any night work I could get you, as well, at least for a while. If you didn't look such a God-awful mess— what the hell happened to your hair?—I'd clout you one for all the trouble you've brought. Useless cunt," he growled. And then, a minute later, his voice dropped and the blanket fell over me. "Best lay still for a while," he said, and then it was his hard palm at the back of my head, lifting it, and the rim of a cup touched my lips, and when I opened my mouth cool water flowed down my throat.

I swallowed and swallowed, but made no sound. If I had been a crying sort of girl, I surely would have wept then.

EVENTUALLY THE FESTERING and oozing around the dirty sutures on my breast abated and the delirium stopped. I knew it had been some time that I'd tossed in my bed, perhaps a week or even two; all had faded into periods of pain and thirst and light and Ram with spoonfuls of watery gruel and lifting me onto the chamber pot, all mixed in with deep blackness. But that morning, an unidentifiable length of time after what I would forever call the nightmare, I sat on the edge of my pallet and looked around. I was alone, lightheaded yet strangely more alert than I could ever remember. My mind was clear, tight and sure, focused. I was coming fourteen, and I knew now I was old enough to make a choice. There were two of them: I could stay or I could leave.

If I stayed, I would go back to the desperate, exhausting tedium of the bookbindery—if they'd still have me—or if not, another factory, for pauper's wages taken by Ram Munt. And I'd also continue to be pimped out by him, receiving for those efforts nothing but the spurt of slime deposited in or on me.

If I left, my future was uncertain, but at least I would have a say in it. The choice was simple and obvious.

I went to the fruitwood box and took out the mirror. I stared at myself and saw that what I had felt happening, as I tossed on my damp sheet, was true. My face was even thinner than usual, which was a temporary thing, but it was my eyes that showed the change. They had an intenseness, grown darker and larger, and they glittered with something that I had no name for. My pale hair stood up around my head with the look of a pullet, but the lack of curls and new angular cheekbones had taken me from child to young woman.

I unwrapped the strip of muslin I had exchanged for the dirty flannel. The stitching on my breast was dark. I touched it. The skin was raised and sealed in a twisted, ropy seam. It was beginning to harden, and I knew that with the hardening of that skin something deeper had also grown dense and rigid. Resistant and unyielding.

I cleaned up the green dress and stitched the rent. I hunted out and found coins Ram had hidden away about the room—my money, what I'd earned. The only thing I was sorry about was that Ram seemed to have drunk most of it away, and it was a pitiable sum for the years of work both on my feet and on my back.

And then I ate the heel of bread I found on the table, holding my hand over my mouth as I swallowed, willing myself to keep down the first solid food I'd had for so long, took a drink of tinny water, and walked out. I left the miserable room on Back Phoebe Anne Street, left the miserable court with its trickle of human waste running down the shallow gutter in the middle, left the blocks of leaning, back-to-back, vermin-infested buildings.

I wore the sophisticated green gown and a clean shawl and a straw bonnet, and under my arm I clutched the fruitwood box with its mirror, book, pendant, and my folding knife. The bit of money was twisted in an old handkerchief, which I'd sewn onto my underskirt.

⁂

"THIS IS MY TERRITORY," the tall, raw-boned woman said, eyeing the golden fringe poking out from my bonnet as, a few hours later, I stood along Paradise Street, filled with its sailors' lodgings and doss-houses.

"It's a free street, isn't it?" I said, my tone matching hers.

"How long you bin workin'?"

"Close to three years," I told her.

"Not around 'ere, you ain't. I knows every girl in a square mile. But you do look as if you knows your way around." She studied my face. "You're young. Younger'n most. From what I can see most likely the curse ain't even on you yet."

I didn't answer.

"How old are you?"

"Fourteen." *Close enough to fourteen.*

"You want to work around here, you work for me. What do you say to that?"

"Depends," I answered, with a boldness I didn't know I was capable of. I liked it. "How much do you take?"

"'Alf of what ya makes each night. Rules are I don't abide my girls drinkin' on the job. And I've me ways to find out if youse bin cheatin' me, and if you 'as, you're out of 'ere before you can tie your bonnet strings, and I'll see to it you never gits no more customers in this area again. Understand?"

I nodded.

"You clean? My girls don't work with clap or open pox. I got a name to up'old. Only clean girls, anyone wot comes to Blue's girls knows. Were the same when I run my business down in Seven Dials in London afore I come up 'ere; my girls was all clean."

"I'm clean," I said, then purposely let my shawl drop open. I was rewarded by the slight look of disgust that filmed the woman's expression.

"Bleedin 'ell. That's fresh. You wanna work with it in that state?"

"I don't care."

She pulled a grimy yellow scarf from around her own neck. "Cover it with this for the next little while," she said. "Don't want to be scarin' 'em off first fing."

I took the scarf and arranged it over my scar.

"What's yer name?"

"Linnet," I told her. "Linnet Gow." I pulled myself taller. "Although I go by Linny."

The woman shook her head. "You wanna change your name? You got anyone from before lookin' for ya"—here she raised her chin at my chest "—that you don't want findin' ya? Well?" She tapped her foot, waiting for an answer.

"I'll stay with Linny," I said. "Linny Gow. And if anyone comes looking for me," I added, as the unshaven face of Ram Munt filled my head, "I'll look after myself."

"Fine. I got rooms ya can use, and ya can work for me as long as ya prove yourself. 'Ave trouble with a customer or any of the other girls or the ol' Bill, ya come to me. You'll find me fair, if you follow the rules." When I nodded, she smiled, revealing a missing eyetooth. Otherwise her teeth were long and square, strong-looking. "Seems like you've got pluck," she said. "Men who come down to the streets lookin' for it, they like a bit of pluck, don't they? If they want coyness and reluctance, well, I tells 'em, stay 'ome with yer good missus."

She laughed at her own joke, and I opened my mouth and made a sound that may have been interpreted by some as laughter.

MY HAIR GREW OUT and eventually I could lift my chin and straighten my shoulders without my chest pulling and aching. In exchange for a share in a cramped room to sleep in and another room, curtained into three spaces with a thin flock mattress in each, to bring customers to, I handed over half of my nightly earnings to Blue, as was our deal.

"Where'd you say you come from?" asked Lambie one night, as we sat around a greasy table in the Goat's Head.

"Back Phoebe Anne Street, off Vauxhall Road," I told her.

"Vauxhall Road? Then how is it you got that smart talk? Them wots from Vauxhall don't talk like yer does. I'm from Scottie Road meself, and I sure never learned no fancy talk."

I smiled, a true smile. "Noble blood," I said. "Noble blood, my dears." I raised my glass of sugar water, and Lambie and Sweet Girl and I toasted to noble blood, to earning more in an hour than a day in the glassworks or the pottery or the candlemakers or the sugar refinery or bookbinders, and to the freedom that comes from not giving a monkey's of what anyone thought.

"No shortage of customers for you, is there? How does she do it then, eh?" Lambie looked at Sweet Girl. "How does she pull in the most customers? And her with that." Lambie pointed a finger. I looked down. My right breast swelled gently above the graying lace of my bodice, the skin smooth and glowing with the dull sheen of pearl under the stinking sputter of the gaslight. But on the left side the wide, jagged crimson ridge ran from the top of my breast to the top of my first rib. When no one was watching I rubbed that deep puckered scar on the flatness of my left breast. It still ached sometimes, as if the blades that had sunk deep into the tender flesh there had left invisible poisoned barbs that nipped and stung even after the surgeon had cut away the destroyed flesh and clumsily stitched the ragged edges together. The nipple was spared, but the muscle and fat that caused the slight fullness of my right breast was lost on the left.

Sweet Girl shrugged. "Sure as hell I don't know, but I wish she'd send some of whatever she's got my way. Some nights are damn useless, with little but piss-dribbling poxy cocks."

"I think it's because she let's 'em pretend she's a fine lady, just stepping down for a quick fuck with her pretty little cunt all powdered and fresh. Ain't that right?"

They laughed loudly, and I raised one eyebrow at them. I knew it was my blood that made me different. And there was something else. I knew I wouldn't be staying in this life, knew there was something different, something bigger for me. Linny Gow would become a name people would remember.

Chapter Seven

I T WAS TRUE; I HAD NO SHORTAGE OF MEN. MOST I TOOK TO ONE of the tiny cubicles containing the mattress covered with layers of cheap, coarse sheets—the top soiled one taken off after each customer—on the third floor of the house on Jack Street, one of the narrow lanes that led away from Paradise. Some couldn't wait; they only wanted a quick fumble in a doorway or alley.

And of course Ram Munt had found me not long after I'd left Back Phoebe Anne Street. I wasn't hiding, and even with Ram's muddled thinking it wasn't difficult for him to figure out where I might be.

I saw him coming as I stood under a gaslight. I knew his rolling walk and the way his ears stood out from his head, and recognized that he was squiffed to the gills even in the darkness between the light poles. He was staring boldly into the faces of all the girls he passed, and I stepped even closer to the light, reaching under the back of my bonnet.

Ram's steps quickened to a bowlegged lopsided run when he realized it was me. I came toward him, arms wide as if to embrace him. When he reached me I put my left hand on his shoulder. Then I slid the glinting blade of my folding knife, honed to a deadly point, to the pulse in his neck.

"Hello, Ram," I breathed into his face. "I wondered how long it would be before I saw you here." I pressed harder and the point broke the surface of his skin; a bright crimson bead welled up.

Ram whimpered like a babe. "Linny, my girl, that's no way to say hello to your old Da," he said, his eyes shifting.

I looked at the broken veins on his cheeks, the reddened, pocked surface of his nose, grown bulbous from drinking. Of course he was stronger than I, and even in his ale-addled state could surely manage to knock both me and the knife down before I could use it to cause any real harm—he knew it and I knew it. But I felt strangely powerful, standing in the circle of light. I had imagined this scene—the scene where I held a knife to Ram Munt—so many times over the last few years that I knew my face showed him that even after this short time, I wasn't little Linny Munt anymore.

"Go away, Ram. This is my home now. You don't own me any longer." I liked the sound of my voice as I spoke up to him.

"Linny. Now Linny. Think it over."

One half of my mouth smiled. "Oh, I have, Ram. I have."

"Trouble, Linny?" It was Blue, come up behind me. Ram frowned at her.

I smiled more fully, never taking my eyes off Ram. "No, Blue, no trouble. Just someone who thought he knew me. But he's mistaken. He doesn't know me after all." I lowered the knife but kept it visible, the light glancing off it.

Ram's mouth opened, then closed. He glowered at me, looked at the knife one more time, then his gaze swung back to Blue. "She'll rob you blind," he growled. "And put on airs. A right sly little bitch, is this one. You'll be sorry you took her on."

"I'll be the judge, my man," Blue said.

Ram Munt turned and left. I watched him go and knew he wouldn't bother me again. I was almost sorry I hadn't sunk the knife deep into that pulsing vein when I'd had the chance. I realized it would have been easy to kill again. That the first killing is like losing the maidenhead—difficult, filled with pain and confusion. But once it's been done, there can be no going back. There is little to prevent the next fuck. Or murder.

❦

SUMMER CAME, and customers were more plentiful. Standing outside with the warm night air on my face and arms, my feet neither cold nor wet, could be quite pleasant at times. I liked the camaraderie of the other girls; we would stand, arm in arm, watching for carriages slowing, sometimes cracking peanuts as we laughed and gossiped. It reminded me, in a small way, of my old friendship with Minnie and Jane, of standing in the court with my mother after dinner. I realized how lonely I'd been for the last years, and how tightly Ram had controlled me. I liked my independence; although I rarely turned down a customer, I knew I could, if he was too repulsive or suspicious. I liked the freedom of knowing that whatever I earned, I could keep half. I remembered the simple girlish dreams I'd shared with Minnie and Jane as we skipped home together from the bookbinders, and now acquired paste necklaces and beaded reticules and feather bonnets from pawnshops. I popped into a chophouse for a hot pie, sometimes twice a night, and I started a collection of small, used, but fairly dear, leather books.

I felt quite grown-up with my purchases and at times, as I slipped a garish bauble over my wrist and admired it, reveled in a feeling that was close to happiness, I realize now. And where were Minnie and Jane? They would still be at the bookbinders, giving their earnings to their fathers or, possibly, by now, their husbands. They'd have left behind their girlish dreams of finery from shop windows, their wages going only to keep bread on the table and them out of the rain.

I was honest with Blue, thankful for her protection, and I knew she liked me. As I handed over half of my take one night, she gave me a wink. "Yer doing just fine for yerself, my girl," she said. "I fink you've got yer future sewn up tight, long as ya stay clean. A girl like you can make a living fer a good number o' years."

I nodded, but of course I had no intention of staying and working the streets forever. Although I had a freedom Minnie and Jane would never know, I didn't like the price I had to pay. I knew I would be leaving Paradise, leaving Liverpool, leaving all of England. I had begun to think about America—the America my mother once dreamed of. Even if she hadn't been able to leave the hard life, I planned to.

✻✻✻✻✻

I READ ABOUT THE SHIP to America on a blustery March night. It was down at an agent's office in Goree Piazza, where the slave trade once had its offices. It was now home to various shipping companies and a few public houses. Business had been slow that night and I'd hardly earned enough to make it worthwhile to stand in the blowing rain. I wasn't as comfortable down near the water; I preferred staying closer to Paradise, where the gaslights afforded a shred of safety, but every once in a while I took my chances.

Luck was with me and I'd quickly found two customers, one after another, which was enough to finish up my night. I was on my way back to Jack Street when I stopped outside an agent's office to stuff a scrap of paper down the side of my boot, where it chafed my ankle bone. As I straightened up and glanced at myself in the darkened glass of the office, I saw a newly placed advertisement with a heading in large black letters:

THE UNION LINE OF PACKETS
LIVERPOOL TO NEW YORK
FITZHUGH AND CALEB GRIMSHAW

Underneath, in smaller letters, were details: "The *Bowditch* will sail on the 5th of April. Room for one hundred fifty to two hundred passengers steerage, as well as several first- and second-class cabins. No salt will be taken; the trip is guaranteed to be dry and comfortable." The price for a first-class cabin was twenty-five pounds—*twenty-five pounds!* I thought. I couldn't imagine anyone ever managing to save that amount of money. The steerage price was five pounds ten shillings.

Even five pounds was an amount I'd never seen. I shrugged and walked on, not thinking much about it.

But as the weeks passed, I thought more and more about the advertisement. I thought about what it could mean—going to America. And one dark night when I was closer to sixteen than fifteen, my lip throbbing from a punch by a punter who'd refused to pay and then given me the quick fist for my trouble, my feet aching in their cheap boots, I started to think about the advertisement and the picture of the tall-masted sailing ship, its sails full and wide in an apparent sea breeze.

I thought about a new life—a different life, where nobody knew me and where I could start over. I knew it might be my only chance to avoid ending up like other girls I had worked with—Lambie beaten so badly she'd gone blind and ended up in the workhouse, and, just last month, Skinny Mo dead of the bloody cough after too many years on the cold, wet streets.

So I started to hoard my earnings, pawning my cheap trinkets and extra bonnets and not allowing myself to purchase any more books, much as I loved to run my hands over the softness of their covers, my fingers tracing the stamped letters. I ate less and didn't visit the drinking houses with the other girls as often. And I waited.

I knew that when the time was right for me to go, there'd be some kind of a sign. I didn't know what it would be, but it would be unmistakable.

A FEW MONTHS AFTER I made my vow to go to America I met Chinese Sally.

"Well, look who's come down in the world," Blue had said when a young woman, tall and slender, walked up to us as we stood on the street one summer evening. She carried a large and obviously heavy brocade carpetbag and wore a dainty lace frock far too fine for the street. She wore high pattens on her shoes so that her hems didn't drag through the muck. Her hair was so black it shone navy where it showed beneath her stylish bonnet. She had beautiful skin, pale and unmarked, and the color of her almond-shaped eyes shifted and reflected the light so I couldn't quite tell whether they were green or brown.

"Yer old man back in the clink again, is he?" Blue asked.

"Just for a bit, Blue. He's only got a tailpiece this time, just the three months," she said. "And he was stitched up by someone he thought was a mate. Thanks to that rotter, Louis was caught in the act." She shook her head, setting her carpetbag on the street with a tiny sigh of regret, carefully avoiding a glob of spittle. She flexed her fingers. She wore knitted gloves. "Just goes to show you can't trust anyone."

"Linny," Blue said, "this is one of my old girls, Sal. Can you make room for 'er wif you for a few months?"

"I prefer to be called Chinese Sally," she said.

She looked different than any of the rest of us on Paradise. It wasn't only her face, but her obvious style. The lace dress was new, pressed, and had been tailored to fit, not bought from a pawnshop or a market stall. And her voice was soft, cultured.

"Certainly," I said. "There's only Helen in the room with me right now." Did she notice that my voice matched hers?

Chinese Sally smiled, a small, wry smile.

"She 'as a fancy man, doesn't she," Blue told me. "A real swell. Our Sal lives with the best of 'em as long as 'er feller don't get lagged. But she's lucky she's got 'er old friends fer when times gets rough. This is the second time you've been back now, ain't it?"

The girl nodded, studying the building behind my head. "I didn't imagine I'd ever be back. We had planned to be off to London next month."

"What does your man do, then?" I asked.

"He's a mobsman," Chinese Sally told me. "Best of the best. There isn't a pickpocket in Liverpool better than my Louis." She picked up her carpetbag, stifling a dainty yawn behind her glove. "I'm all done in," she said. "I heard this morning, early, from one of Louis's men that he'd been lagged. I was nervous to go out all day in case they were watching for me, too. I thought it best to come back here and lie low until he's out." She yawned again. "I'll have a good sleep, then be out for full night's work tomorrow."

Blue nodded. "Linny, take 'er up to the room." She gave the other girl a clap on the shoulder. "Good to have ya back, Sal."

I saw Chinese Sally stiffen and her lips tighten but she didn't say anything.

"This way," I told her. "The room is over on Jack Street."

She walked beside me. "I'm Chinese Sally down on the street. But I'm Miss Sing in my true life," she said. And then she said nothing more, all the way to Jack. I left her sitting on the rumpled bed, looking around the tiny room with distaste, the carpetbag on her lap.

This wasn't her true life, then. Like me. I thought of her words the rest of the night. "In my true life," I whispered to myself, in that same superior tone Chinese Sally had used. "My true life."

❋

I GOT TO KNOW Chinese Sally well over the next few months. You do, don't you, when you sleep beside someone, when you hear them cry out in their nightmares, when you know what kind of customer they've last had by the smell they carry on them. I knew that her eyes were brown when she was feeling her best, and that they glinted green when she was angry. She was eighteen, a few years older than me, and her life with Louis sounded exciting and wonderful.

"I'm his flash girl," she told me one evening, as I sat on the bed, putting on my powder before I started work. "You know, dress up pretty and entertain the higher class of gentlemen. He buys me the fancy clothes and pays my rent on a lovely set of rooms. The gentlemen who come to visit me are of the upper caliber, none of the riffraff we have to contend with on Paradise." She smiled, a wistful smile, and fell silent.

"And it's not just the customers," she eventually went on. "The life— well, Linny, it's nothing like this." She looked at her expensive dresses, hanging on nails on the wall, then studied my face, coming to stand in front of me, holding her gloves. "You'd be a good flash girl," she said.

I set my ormolu mirror and the box of powder in my lap. "I would?"

"Of course. You've still got the freshness the gentlemen want—all your teeth, decent enough looks, your hair thick. And more than that, you've got a few manners, and a way with a phrase."

Even though she was complimenting me, I still felt slightly insulted. "A few manners? I've got more than any of the other girls here, as you well know. My mother taught me," I said, standing, letting a slightly disdainful tone creep into my voice. "Manners and proper speech."

Chinese Sally smiled, her usual careful smile, keeping her bottom lip stiff. She had two missing bottom teeth, and was loath for anyone to see the dark gap. "You may think you're quite fine, my girl," she said, "but if you were to spend some time with me, among the right people, you'd learn a thing or two about what you call 'proper'—from those actually born into the idle life. You're only a small step above the rest of the girls, and I guarantee you, a few more years here and you'll have fallen off that step and realize you really are just common baggage. And then it will be too late for any opportunities."

I stared at her. Was she right? Would I just go on, night after night, customer after customer, my dream of leaving Paradise and Liverpool just that—a dream? Would I end up diseased, dying alone?

Chinese Sally must have seen the confusion on my face. She reached out and ran one finger down my cheek. "When Louis gets out, maybe I'll bring you back with me. Would you like that?"

I shrugged, stepping back. Her finger was soft; she had a jar of lavender cream that she rubbed onto her hands before putting on her gloves each evening. "I don't know, do I?" I raised my chin and narrowed my eyes as I spoke. "I don't know what would be expected of me. It's not so bad here," I said, although she and I both knew I was bluffing.

"Well, I'll ask you again, then, shall I, when you've had a chance to think about it? You don't have to take it pushed up against a wall, you know. Not looking like you do. You could bring Louis in a tidy profit, and the sooner we can make enough to leave, the sooner Louis and I will be on our way to London. Did I tell you, Linny, that Louis is going to marry me—when the time is right, of course—once we've moved down to London? And then of course I shall stop working, for Louis will support me properly, with a fine house and a downstairs full of servants. Of course I shall have my own lady's maid."

I thought then that if I worked for Louis I could save my money even faster, and be able to book passage to America sooner than I had planned. The idea was appealing.

***

I AWOKE ONE COLD November afternoon to see Chinese Sally packing her carpetbag.

"He's out," she told me, seeing me sit up. "Louis is out. He sent word with one of his men just an hour ago." She stopped folding a chemise, her hands poised in the air. "Well? Are you coming? I sent the message back that I was bringing a new girl. You can't show up looking like a scarecrow. If you plan to join me, you'd best make yourself up smart."

I tossed aside the patched coverlet, running my hands over my hair. "Do you really think I could do it?" I said.

"First of all, when we're up there, remember to call me Miss Sing," she said, answering my question in a roundabout way. "You can call me Chinese Sally when we're on our own, but Miss Sing when we're attending the theater or at a fine eating establishment, or any other social occasion." She dug through her half-packed bag, pulling out a dress of beige watered gauze and tossing it on the bed beside me. "Here. Put this on. It'll be too big for you, but it will do for today. I can't introduce you to Louis in either of your street dresses; you look like a ragged peacock.

Louis likes a quality look. You can keep it; Louis will buy us both more clothes."

I picked up the frock, fingering the fabric. "Why, exactly, are you doing this for me?"

She stared at me. "For you? I'm not doing it for you. Do you think I have that big a heart?" She made a chuckling sound in her throat. "I told you. You'll be part of the group and that will help Louis. Louis likes when I bring in new girls. He trusts my judgment. And he rewards me very handsomely if they work out, which they usually do. If they don't . . ." She continued to look at me, although the stare now turned slightly hostile. "Well, that's not a good thing for anybody then, is it?"

I recognized her warning. The watered gauze was smooth, cool beneath my fingers. I imagined having a wardrobe full of dresses like this one.

"Just give me time for a good wash," I told her, adding, "Miss Sing," and was rewarded by her nod and that small tight smile I'd come to know so well.

<hr />

BLUE HADN'T BEEN HAPPY to lose both of us but she held no grudges. Every morning, as each of us handed over half our wages, she would assure us, "Now youse owes me nuthin', and I owes youse nuthin'." There were always girls, and if she lost one or two, it would only be for a night. "I guarantee youse'll be back," she said to me now, frowning. "Just like 'er," she continued, tossing her head in Chinese Sally's direction. Chinese Sally stood impassive, looking down the street as if she couldn't hear—and didn't care—what Blue was saying. "Youse can't count on that kind of life, up wif the nobs. It never lasts, believe me. Youse'll be crawlin' back to where youse can trust your mates and where youse knows your place. A fancy dress can only cover so much."

I gripped the now heavy fruitwood box tighter. In it was the money I'd kept hidden under a board in the room on Jack Street, as well as my folding knife and mirror and pendant and Wordsworth. I'd also packed three small books, my favorites, the ones I couldn't bear to part with.

Wearing the dress Chinese Sally had given me and the warm cape and fancy bonnet she'd lent me, I had left my old clothes behind for

Helen. And, like Chinese Sally, I didn't care what Blue said. I was leaving this place, with its stink and trouble. We walked to the corner of Chester and Roper streets and waited. Chinese Sally kept touching her hair, tying and retying her bonnet, smoothing her skirt. "When you meet Louis, Linny, extend your hand," she said. "He'll say that it's his great pleasure to make your acquaintaince, and you must reply 'No, oh no, sir, the pleasure is mine.' He may kiss your glove. Allow him to do this and then say, 'Why, thank you, sir.'" She glanced at me. "If you don't make a good impression first thing, it won't go well for me. So if you don't know what to do or say, do and say nothing. Watch me." She was speaking faster and faster. Suddenly I was nervous, frightened at what was expected of me. I hadn't known this feeling for a long time, and realized I'd fallen into a steady, easy lull on Paradise.

Within a few moments a fancy curricle pulled by two dappled horses drew up. A man emerged and stood by the open door. From all of Chinese Sally's talk, I had expected Louis to be more imposing looking. And younger. I was surprised at how short he was, and how plain. He was at least thirty; the lines around his mouth were already deep. He had a slightly sallow complexion, longish, dark hair, and yellow-brown eyes with curling lashes. There was almost something of the Eyetalian about him. Quite unremarkable, really; had I passed him on the street I might not have noticed him. I suppose that was important, him being a mobsman, working the crowds. One wouldn't want to stand out in any way.

He bowed over Chinese Sally's hand and she giggled, a sound I had never heard her make before. Then he turned to me, his eyes running over me from my bonnet to my boots.

"This is Miss Linny Gow," Chinese Sally said. "The one I sent word to you about with Dirty Joe. What do you think? Will she do?"

I straightened my shoulders.

Louis kept up his survey of me; after thirty seconds he nodded slowly and then, remembering Chinese Sally's instructions, I extended my hand. Louis looked at it and smiled, then took it in his and raised it to his lips, although he didn't actually touch them to my glove.

"How lovely to meet you, my dear," he said, his head bent over my hand and yet his eyes studying me from under those long lashes.

"It's my pleasure, sir, I'm sure," I said, with what I hoped was my prettiest smile.

He let go of my hand as if reluctant to do so. "Has Miss Sing instructed you of my expectations?"

I licked my lips. "Well, not in so many words. But I've been at the game since I was only a girl, and—"

He stepped closer and I saw the beginnings of veins on his nose. "I'll collect all your earnings directly. You'll take the customers I bring to you and never turn any away. You may be expected to entertain large numbers, with another girl, at one time. Do you understand?"

"Large numbers? You mean more than one customer at once?"

"Really, Sal. She looks like a scared rabbit," he said, turning to Chinese Sally.

"She'll be fine. I'll keep her in line," she said, as if I weren't standing in front of her.

Scared rabbit? I pushed the wool cloak Chinese Sally had lent me back from my shoulders, suddenly too warm. "Did I hear you correctly in that I won't be seeing any of the money I earn?"

"You'll have your own room and clothing—good clothing, like Sal's. You won't need money for anything. All your meals will be brought to you. You won't be going out except for the entertaining I plan."

I swallowed. There was something about him that suddenly made me think of Ram and his control over me. What was I doing? I would lose the freedom I now knew. I imagined myself a prisoner in a locked room, the door only opening to allow in a man, and then locked again. And if the man proved foul in his requests, or even caused me pain, there would be nobody to protect me, no means of escape. I took a step back. "I think not," I said.

Louis looked at Chinese Sally, and then they both looked at me. "What do you mean?" he asked, his voice turning nasty.

I took off the cloak and bonnet and handed them to Sal. "You can come back and collect the gown, if you wish," I told her. "It's not for me. I won't be any man's possession."

"Are you completely mad?" she said. "Don't you see? Nobody gives a toss about you down on Paradise. Nobody cares if you live or die. You're just another doxie on the street, with nothing to live for."

Her voice had become harder, angry, and she reached forward and shook my arm like a terrier with a rat in its jaws. The fruitwood box fell to the street, and I heard the tinkle of breaking glass. "Don't make me look a fool, Linny."

I picked up the box and held it against my chest, stepping further away from her. The November wind chilled me to the bone without the warm cloak. "At least I work for myself and make my own decisions. I choose my customers. I eat what I want, when I want. Blue looks out for me. I do as I please. You may see your life with him"—I tossed my head in Louis's direction—"as all very well, Chinese Sally, but to me it sounds little more than a bird in a cage."

"Fine, then," she said, hooking her arm through Louis's. "Stay on the street. Stay there and rot. Before you know it you'll find you're nothing but a used-up old whore who can't even give it away for a pint of ale."

Louis ignored me, helping Chinese Sally into the carriage. The door slammed and the horses moved forward, and still, I stayed where I was, thinking about what I'd just given up and what I had to go back to. Had I made the right decision? Chinese Sally had been right about no one caring whether I lived or died.

My feet and fingers grew numb with cold; my back ached from standing stiffly so long in one position. Eventually I heard the cheery whistle of the gaslight man with his ladder. The lamps were illuminated, one by one. The street glowed with a soft, deceptive light and I knew what I must do.

As I began the long walk back to Paradise I thought of the broken mirror in the box under my arm and imagined the knowing wink Blue would give me when I showed up back on the corner.

※※※

AND SO LIFE WENT ON. Winter blended to spring and spring to summer, summer to fall. I passed my sixteenth birthday, and then my seventeenth. The customers came and went like the seasons. I grew older, and my desire to leave this life grew stronger.

Chapter Eight

H E HAD HANDS THAT SMELLED OF FISH. TRYING TO PASS HIMSELF off as a gentleman with his fine black wool coat and top hat, I knew by the putrid odor ingrained in his thick fingers that he was no more than a fishmonger wearing a rented outfit for the evening. Well, we both play the game of pretending then, don't we, I thought, supporting the man's weight as he steered me into an alley, his arm draped heavily over my shoulders.

It was late October and I went about my job with weary and practiced movements. I had been with Blue for well over three years now, having had my seventeenth birthday in August. I didn't enjoy my time with the other girls as I once did, and I'd even lost the joy of reading. There seemed no time or privacy, and the energy and passion I had once felt in holding beautiful books, reading their magic and studying how they were made, had somehow trickled away.

Nor did I worry much about my appearance; I realized none of the customers cared one way or another. For the last few months thoughts of my mother came more often. As I waited for a customer to finish some nights I closed my eyes and envisioned the life she had so desperately wanted for me, away from the filth and stench of Back Phoebe Anne. I tried to picture myself at a table like the ones I remembered from the dining room with the man I called Uncle Horace, like the ones I had once read about. I saw myself among sparkling glass and china so delicate to be almost transparent; I envisioned reaching for the fish fork, the butter knife, the soup spoon, knowing when to pour the port and when the wine and when the sherry.

Now, my back pressed painfully against the rough brick of a dark building in an alley off Paradise Street—and I knew there would soon be a trail of bruises dark as inky kisses up my spine from the pressure—the thick fingers of the fishmonger's left hand searched high inside me while he shook and jiggled himself against my skirt with his right hand, trying to ready himself. I idly thought how fortunate that he was the last for the night. Surely another customer would object to the smell he was leaving on me.

It was no good. The fishmonger finally gave up, roughly pulling his fingers out of me, his elbow giving my hipbone a hard knock as he angrily buttoned his trousers.

"That'll be sixpence, sir," I said, straightening my skirt and kneading my fingers against my sore hip. "A tanner, please." I held out my hand.

"You'll get nowt. I got nothing and I'll pay for nothing," he said, walking away.

I sidestepped a puddle of streaky vomit glinting in the light from the street and caught him by the sleeve. "Now, sir," I told him, my voice never losing its sweetness. "T'wasn't my fault you weren't at your best tonight. And you did find a bit of pleasure, I'm sure, judging by your familiarity of me."

He stopped, looking down at my hand on the thick wool of his sleeve. "I'll give you tuppence and not a penny more." He dug in the pocket of his tight striped waistcoat, taking out a coin. As he handed it to me his eyes rested on the skin just above my bodice. "Could be that yer wrong. It *were* yer fault I weren't at me best. That's horrible, a right mess. Why don't you cover yerself?"

I took the coin, holding it tightly in my fist. "And why should I? For weren't it one very like yourself that caused it?"

The fishmonger mumbled something unintelligible and turned away, unbuttoning his trousers again and urinating loudly against the wall, steam rising in the cool air. I watched the puddle he created running along the veins between the cobbles.

I tucked the coin into the slit in the underside of my waistband, then carefully stepped over the filthy, uneven surface of the alley and out onto the nearly deserted street.

"Hoi! Linny!"

I peered down the dim street, trying to see through the shadows, then waved, waiting as the other girl hurried toward me.

"Did you have a good night, then, Linny?" Annabelle asked. She was chewing gingerly on a hard roll stuffed with greasy herring. Her cheekbone shone swollen.

"It hasn't been too bad, except for the last one. He couldn't bring his fine soldier to stand at attention and wouldn't pay what I asked," I told her.

Annabelle nodded. "Bugger the rotten sods and their limp cock-stands. You should carry a cutter, as I do. A sturdy blade flashing against their jewels makes 'em cough up soon enough."

I nodded, thinking of the folding knife I'd once used to threaten Ram Munt, and had call to bring out a few more times when I'd felt truly fearful. But I'd lost it last July when my untied straw bonnet had been blown off into the street in a sudden dry gust of gritty wind. I'd run to retrieve it before it was flattened by a horse's hoof. But it had danced and twirled away from me, caught up in the persistent wind, and by the time I'd caught it and brushed off the dust and put it back on, I realized my knife was gone. I retraced my steps over and over, but the bone-handled knife had disappeared, snatched up, most likely, by a street urchin with a magpie's eye. I hadn't wanted to spend the money to buy another. Now I realized Annabelle was right. More and more I had to fight—either for my money or to defend myself. The customers were getting rougher and cheaper.

"Comin' for a drink?" Annabelle asked.

"No." I yawned, blinking as the chapel bells of St. Peter's chimed five times. "I'm off to get a few hours' sleep."

Annabelle shrugged and went up the street and I made my way back to my old home, the dilapidated room on Jack Street. Now I shared it with Annabelle, Helen, and Dorie.

What I told Annabelle was true; I *was* tired. But the other reason I didn't want to go to the Goat's Head was that I didn't want to spend even one extra penny of my money. I'd saved seven pounds. The fare advertised on the posters had risen from five to seven pounds over the last two years and was always dropping or rising a few shillings, depending on the season and the ship itself, but seven pounds was a safe bet. I planned to work one more month, just one—to save a little more so that I wouldn't be penniless when I arrived in New York.

I would never be forced onto the street again.

As I silently let myself into the fetid room on Jack Street I saw two humped, motionless figures on the narrow mattress and was glad Annabelle didn't come home. Only three of us could crowd onto the narrow flock pallet; Annabelle and I, had we come home together, would have had to pull straws to see who got the bed and who would sleep on the floor. There was a definite nip in the air, and if I'd pulled the short straw, with only my shawl and extra dress to cover me, it would be unpleasant on the cold floorboards without even a strip of drugget to keep away the draft. There was a tiny fireplace so badly clogged that we hated to light it because of the clouds of black smoke we had to endure. The walls, untouched by the whitewash brush in years, were furred a delicate green by the rising damp. Rain made the rotting beams creak monotonously, and the one loose window rattled painfully in even the slightest wind. The glass was so smudged with dirt and soot inside and out that during the day the room seemed to be in a never-ending twilight.

I took off my boots and pulled off my dress so I could unhook the front stays of my corset, then, shivering, put my dress back on and wrapped my shawl around me and crowded onto the edge of the flattened stained pallet that filled the width of the closet that passed as a room. I had to shove Dorie with my hip, who in turn pressed closer to Helen, forcing her against the wall. Dorie moaned and grumbled sleepily, flinging her arm across my temple. But still, I was almost asleep by the time I turned onto my other side, facing into the dark room. With my eyes closed, I fingered the reassuring thickness of my waistband—my pendant and coins—all stuffed into the slit I made in the wide band that held my skirt to the bodice of my dress.

There was an identical opening in the waistband of my other dress, and nobody knew about my savings, not even the other girls in the room. I'd surreptitiously transfer the money and the pendant when I changed my dress each week. I'd try to wait until the other girls were gone, or, if that proved impossible, I would turn away, facing into the corner as I pulled off one dress and slipped the other over my head. I let whoever was in the room think it was because I was ashamed of my scarred torso.

The fruitwood box and the coins and books it had contained had been stolen over a year ago. The only reason my pendant had been spared was because Helen, without asking, had taken it and worn it that night. I'd been furious with her when I'd seen it around her neck when I ran into her on the street, and had demanded it back. But later, when I'd returned to Jack Street and found the room turned upside down, my box gone and even floorboards torn up, the thief finding all the money the girls and I hid under separate boards, the only thing I'd been grateful for was that Helen had decided to choose that night to borrow the pendant.

After that I'd kept it and my money with me at all times.

With sleep coming sweetly over me, I recited the rote prayer to try to keep away the nightmare, the overpowering crush of blood and hair and cold water and the plunging shears. When I was awakened by it, as was usual every third or fourth night, I'd sit up, bathed in sweat, my mouth stretched wide as I took deep, gulping gasps. The truth of that nightmare—the knowledge that I had killed a man, even though it had been to protect myself from the same fate—was like a slinking dark animal, something with sharp teeth and yellow eyes. It was always following me, sometimes close on my heels, at other times sitting some distance away, watching. Under bright gaslights or a candle's soft glow the dark animal stayed low, pushed away by the warmth and the light. But it came back with a vengeance when I was in the dark. In the growing cold of this autumn it had grown even larger. There were times, now, that I felt it so close I'd whirl around in the darkness of the street, thinking I heard it breathing. And then I knew the nightmare would come that night.

Now it had come three nights in succession, without any days of grace in between, and I'd only managed a few hours of restless sleep each night. My body ached with exhaustion and I willed myself to dream ordinary thoughts this night. I felt my eyelids easing, knew the line between my brows was erasing. Just before I let myself go, I put one hand up in the old position over my ruined breast. It comforted me to protect it, although I don't know why. And lately, I'd been moving my other hand from its usual spot, guarding my waistband. I moved it further down now, to my belly, cradling the child furled tightly there.

I KNEW IT WAS A GIRL and that I would call her Frances. I don't know exactly when or how she was conceived; I'd always been careful with my prevention—using the bit of sponge, washed out every morning and then soaked in alum and sulphate of zinc and put in place before my first customer, and then, after my last, taking out the sponge and using my syringe wrapped in a rag dripping with the same witch's brew, no matter how weary I was. It had been Blue who had taught me what to do, and I'd used the sponge and syringe faithfully as soon as my first bleeding began, only three months after I'd left Back Phoebe Anne Street for good. But of course all the girls get caught at one time or other. It had happened to me before, just at the end of my first year with Blue, only I hadn't even been aware of it until it was almost over. It was Helen, come back to Jack Street for her cloak when a cold rain had started up, who had told me what was happening. She'd found me on the bed when I should have been out working, doubled in two with pain, my face waxen and wet with sweat, and after a few questions she slipped out and brought back two pints of ale. Helen had sat beside me, forcing me to drink both pints, telling me it would be over soon, and to be glad of it. This way, she told me, I wouldn't have to pay to get rid of it.

All I'd felt, then, was relief when the cramping and clotted bleeding at last stopped. Nothing else.

But this second time had been different. For one thing, I'd realized, fairly early, that a baby had started. And I also knew it was the sign I'd been waiting for.

The trip to New York would take six weeks, longer if the weather proved poor. But that meant that if I left at the end of the month, I would arrive before the baby was due. She would be born there, in the great New World, and she would be an American. I would find a respectable job, for weren't there all sorts of jobs to be had in America, especially in the place called New York? Nobody would know me and I would create a new life for my daughter. The little girl would never know about my life—this life—in Liverpool.

For the last few months, while I waited for each customer to finish, mindlessly murmuring rote praises and moaning as if delirious with pleasure to bring them on faster, I made up the stories I would tell little Frances about the fine gentleman who had been her father and what had happened to him and how I had come to the United States of America.

And then, early one morning as I had walked back to Jack Street, the rain falling in torrents and the inky sky occasionally bleached by the sheet lightning that flashed from far out over the Mersey, illuminating the weeping rooftops, I realized, with a sudden sharp pang, that maybe my mother had done the same thing.

For the first time, I wondered if perhaps I didn't carry noble blood at all. My hand sought out the birthmark under my wet cuff, fingering the raised shape of the fish thoughtfully.

"WHEN ARE YOU getting rid of it?"

I shook my hands over the washbasin and wiped my face with a clean rag, looking down at Dorie. Helen had gone off to buy herself a hot pie, and Annabelle hadn't returned at all after the night's work, but Dorie was stretched on the bed, enjoying the space to herself before she headed out onto the street that afternoon.

I put my hands on my abdomen, wishing I'd pulled my stays tighter. "Can you tell?"

"I can. But most others wouldn't see it; you're that small. How far gone are you, then?"

"I don't know." For my own reasons I didn't want to tell Dorie that I knew it to be almost six months. "But it's been quickening a while now," I added, trying not to smile, thinking of the tiny fluttering that kept me company, cheering me when there seemed little else that could.

Dorie made a sound of disgust. "It's a right fool you are, then. Once it's quickening it's harder to get rid of. Means you must be four months along. Why didn't you do something sooner? But it's not too late, although it'll be hard on you, I grant you that. A lot more painful and messy, but it can be done if you find the right person and are willing to pay." She stuck a finger into her mouth and dug at a back molar, her face contorting, the heavy folds of her eyelids almost hiding her small eyes.

"Toothache?"

She sat up, nodding. "I'm planning to have it yanked at the barber later today. Why don't you come with me? I'll set you up, as long as you've got the money. There's someone the barber knows; I've used him."

Tying a dark blue ribbon in my hair, I shook my head and picked up my shawl.

"What do you do with all your money, Linny? You don't buy yourself any finery, or even a frock from the pawnshop. And you hardly never come to a tavern or chophouse with us no more, and Lord knows you eat next to nothing. No fancy cakes, no fruit pies. Just the slop from the stalls, jacket potatoes and oxcheeks, from what I always seen."

"I'm saving it."

"Not for a rainy day, I hope," Dorie said, laughing, her eyes disappearing again, and then she grimaced, slapping her palm to her cheek. "Ow. You'd have it all spent in one November if you was saving it for that." Her tongue probed the back of her mouth now. "You'll come with me, then?"

But I just shook my head again, leaving Dorie worrying her throbbing tooth.

❈

I KNEW SOME OF the girls who had been forced to carry a baby to birth because it couldn't be got rid of. Most left their newborns on the steps of the workhouse or a church. Only one girl that I knew, Elsie, had tried to keep hers and still stay in the game. She left it with a toothless hag during the night when she was at work, and the little thing—a well-formed boy—had appeared to be thriving for the first four or five months. But one night he wouldn't stop crying, and the old hag, trying to quiet the teething infant so the others in the packed straw-filled room wouldn't throw her out, had first cut open his gums to let the new tooth come through, and when that only intensified his screams, had, in desperation, overdosed him with Mother Bailey's Quieting Syrup. The baby fell into a deep, deadly, laudanum-laced sleep that he never awoke from. After that Elsie slipped away from Paradise and word filtered down to us she'd hanged herself in a flooded cellar off Lime Kiln Lane.

But of course no one ever knew for sure.

Chapter Nine

I WAS MORE TIRED THAN I EVER REMEMBER FEELING. IT DIDN'T matter how many hours I slept; I was still weary when I awoke late afternoon to prepare for the night. I knew it was the baby, taking what she needed to grow. My feet hurt more than ever; I saw, each dawn as I unlaced my boots, that my ankles were swollen, the skin marked with angry red creases where the leather bit into them.

This particular evening—November Fifth, Bonfire Night—I considered not going out at all. Perhaps I would celebrate Guy Fawkes by buying myself something hot to eat and then spending the night on Jack Street, listening to the fireworks. Maybe I would even treat myself to a yellow-backed penny novel and attempt to concentrate enough to read.

But even as I cleared a spot in the soot-covered window and looked down at the teeming alley below, dreaming of reading by candlelight, and of sailing away, and of playing with my pretty baby in a sunlit patch of grass in a place far from here, I knew I was only fooling myself. I would have to go out. I still had to turn over a minimum amount to Blue each night, even if I didn't pull any customers. And I wouldn't dip into my savings—I was so close that I could hear the ripple of sails in the wind.

I'd been pulling fewer and fewer tricks this last while. I worried, foremost, that little Frances would come to harm by some of my rougher customers. As well, my body was unfamiliar, heavier and unwieldy, my dresses uncomfortably tight even after letting out all the seams. I found it difficult to muster the enthusiasm necessary to elicit a favorable response, and many men, perhaps reading the unconscious unwillingness in my face and posture, would glance over me and then move on to one of the other girls.

As I laced up my boots, wincing, I realized just how badly I needed to leave it all—the damp room on Jack Street and the cold, wet streets that fanned out from Paradise in an endless maze of dark alleys filled with drunken, smelly customers. And the streets were becoming ever more dangerous. In the last three weeks three prostitutes had turned up dead, strangled and deposited down by the docks. I knew one of them; she was a pallid young thing with her two front teeth knocked out in a brawl with another whore over a customer a few months earlier. There were rumors of even more girls gone missing since the summer, but if a body never materialized, she was never declared dead.

THAT EVENING I PICKED OUT a spot on the corner of Paradise and Cable Street where I'd often had good luck. Ten bells had chimed, a cacophony from all the churches nearby—St. George's, St. Peter's, St. Thomas's—but the evening was slow so far, only three customers. I knew it often took until after eleven for business to pick up, when gentlemen on their own flooded out of the musicals and dance halls and theaters. But as it was Bonfire Night, perhaps many men, their faces ruddy with the night air and rum, would choose to go home and spend the rest of the evening watching the public fireworks with their children. It was cold; the sky, that afternoon, had been leaden and carried the smell of snow. Now a thick fog descended. On the next corner I could make out the orange glow of a burning tar barrel, lit by the drunks with nowhere to doss. The streetlamps were little more than misty orbs.

A few minutes after the echo of the last bell had died, I heard the clatter of horses' hooves behind me. I turned, momentarily blinded by the lanterns swinging on either side of a carriage. It was a fine brougham with a pair of dancing gray horses. I'd seen it before, although never its passenger. The brougham had started appearing on the streets a week ago, and one of the girls—Little Eve—had been inside.

She whispered to me, only a few evenings ago, that it was best not to get into it. "Take it from me, I was sorry. A mean sort he is," she told me. "He likes to give it down the throat or up the arse and he's brutal with his hands; he's knocked about more than me, I've heard. Look what he did." Little Eve had pulled back her bonnet to show me a red, swollen ear with an oozing scab where the lobe joined the jaw. "Pretty near tore the ear off my head. He pays well, but you'd do well to avoid him. A bit of a villain. And you never know, Linny. Who's to say he's not the very one what's killed those girls?"

I had shook my head. "You're imagining too much, Little Eve. A killer wouldn't keep coming back to the same place, would he? He'd be afraid of being caught. And besides, you're still here, aren't you?" She didn't return my smile, and carefully rearranged her bonnet over her injured ear.

Now the carriage stopped, and when the curtain was pulled aside, a very ordinary middle-age man looked out at me. An overshot jaw, sagging skin around the eyes and mouth, but nothing sinister appeared to be lurking there. Although I know well that looks mean little in this business, I usually trusted my instincts, and more than once I'd been right. Still. I thought about Little Eve's mess of an ear and stayed where I was.

"Good evening, lass," the man said. "Are ye not cold, standing in this chill?"

Scottish. Not a bad sort. Noisy, often, as they came, given to great huffing and groaning, but the cadence of their voices always reminded me of my mother and I must admit I'd a soft spot for them.

"I might be a little," I told him.

He looked me up and down, his eyes stopping on my scar. His eyes lingered there longer than necessary, his gaze seeming to caress the damaged skin. "Would ye like to come for a wee ride, then? Have a nip and warm yourself on this miserable night?" He held up a silver flask. When I still didn't come closer, he took a long drink, then put the stopper back into the flask.

"I pay well," he said. "I'll give you a sovereign."

"A sovereign?" I repeated. A whole pound was triple the amount I was hoping to save over the next month. "Did I hear you correctly, sir? You did say a sovereign?"

"I did," the man said, smiling now. His eyeteeth were very yellow. The horses stomped their heavy feet, their tails swinging through the fog, churning it, and one nodded his head testily, as if impatient at being kept waiting.

"I'm sorry, sir, but I must see it before getting in with you." I expected him to drive off then, angry at my cheek. Gentlemen in fine carriages do not like to have to prove themselves—in any way—to a girl of Paradise Street.

But the man's expression didn't change. In the next instant he held up the piece of gold, glinting in the light of the carriage lantern. "I have it here," he said.

I didn't like his smile. But a whole pound! I could stop work after tonight, and look for a ship sailing earlier. It would mean baby Frances and I could be well taken care of until I could land myself a job. Bugger Little Eve and her dire warning.

It was a lucky break, I told myself, and one I deserved.

"All right, sir," I said and stepped up to the carriage. The man opened the door from the inside and I climbed in, sitting across from him, arranging my skirt over my knees and crossing my ankles in their thick boots.

"A bit of early winter upon us, I fear," I said in my best voice.

The man held out the flask as he tucked the coin into the pocket of his fustian coat and patted it. "Later," he said. "Now. What's your name?" He pulled a tartan lap robe over his legs.

"Linny," I told him. "And I don't drink spirits, sir."

He laughed then, a deep rumble. "Well, I have found myself a rare bird, haven't I?" He put the flask to his mouth again, drinking until it was empty. Then he shook it as if its emptiness angered him, finally throwing it to the floor.

It landed at my feet, and I looked at it. Silver, with initials, but there wasn't enough light in the carriage for me to make them out.

We drove for quite a time. I couldn't see where we were going, as he'd kept the curtains drawn, but I suspected we were simply circling the streets, and once he was finished with me he would drop me back where he'd found me. Even in the darkness inside the carriage I was able to see the gleam of the man's eyes. They never left me. I tried, at first, to make conversation with him, but he appeared uninterested in talk. Eventually he motioned for me to sit beside him. I did as he bid, and immediately he ran his index finger over my scar, over and over, finally lowering his head to lick and nibble at the puckered flesh. I ground my teeth; I had been subjected to all manner of indignities, but somehow this filled me with a different revulsion. Perhaps because no one had dared touch my scar before; it was always avoided, and, in some strange turn of thought, I considered this part of me one of the only left unviolated, perhaps the only area of my body that had not been used for a man's pleasure.

When I felt I could not bear it for another second, I shifted, trying to pull away from him, and thankfully he lifted his head, but then tossed aside the lap robe, pushing me to my knees in front of him with one hand, the other working his buttons.

Still repulsed by his saliva wet and thick on my breast, I involuntarily recoiled as I was hit by his vile smell as he burst out of his trousers, more than ready. He took hold of my head on either side and pulled my face close to his groin.

I struggled, attempting to draw back, wanting to tell him that perhaps he'd prefer something else; I could suggest other manners of pleasing him, but before I could speak he grew impatient, slapping me smartly on the side of my head so that my ear rang.

I knew I would have to do as he wanted, and quickly, if I was to get away without a beating, but the first slap was immediately followed by a second, this one harder, stunning me. He tried to stand in the swaying carriage, his wool trousers slipping down to his ankles. He towered over me with his open hand raised as I struggled to right myself.

But now he was in his game, the one that all of us from the street knew too well, the gent that couldn't find his own satisfaction without bringing pain and humiliation first.

"Sir, please," I said, "give me a chance to—" but he knocked me about again, and I fell to one side, my hands flailing for something to grab. I inadvertently yanked the door handle. The door opened and I half swung out, gripping the handle for all I was worth, and then—and I'm not sure if I actually felt the man's boot under my back, shoving me out, or if he was trying to grab me and prevent me from falling—I was on my face on the hard cobbles at the side of a street.

ALL THE AIR was knocked out of me. I lay there, gasping, aware I was in the middle of a crowd. There were so many boots and horses hooves and wheels passing close to my head that I feared I would be trampled.

In the next moment there were hands under my arms and I was dragged to the relative safety in front of the buildings that lined the street. It was a woman with a small boy who had come to my aid. "Are you all right, miss?" the woman asked, and I nodded, still bent over, trying to breathe.

"We seed you," the boy said, "come flying out the carriage."

I managed to raise my head and look down the busy street. The carriage had disappeared.

I put my hand to my chest; my heart was pounding.

"Will you be all right now?" the woman asked again, and I managed to thank her for her help. She was well into middle age, her face badly lined, and a number of missing bottom teeth had shaped her chin into an inquisitive point. Under a faded burgundy bonnet with a torn brim her white hair had that particular yellow cast of one who had been blond, although her eyebrows were coarse and dark.

I looked around. Nothing was familiar. "What place is this?" I asked her.

"You're way down Richmond Row, miss," she said.

My heart sank. The carriage hadn't been circling the streets. We'd come far from the center of Liverpool.

The woman reached out and brushed at my sleeve. "Have you no reticule, my dear? No shawl?"

I cursed myself for my foolishness. As well as being shaken and losing the sovereign—if indeed the Scot had intended to give it to me—I'd even lost my shawl in the milieu inside the carriage. I saw that my skirt was dirtied with bootblacking. My hand flew to my waistband; the reassuring thickness was there, as always.

The woman was watching me.

"No. I suppose I've lost them." I didn't know how to explain the situation to the woman. Her dark eyes were kind, almost moist, it seemed, as if she were very worried over my state, even though I was a stranger to her.

"A pretty young thing like yourself," she said, as if she'd read my thoughts, "so cruelly treated." She shook her head, and her eyes filmed further. "I lost a daughter of my own; it's all too well I know how hard life can be for a young lady." We were pushed and jostled by the noisy crowd. "It's not right, one so fine as yourself, so abused," she said, having to raise her voice to be heard over the shouts and the echoing boom of distant fireworks. "You should sit and have a sup of ale, to steady your nerves." She glanced at the boy. "Why, if we had but a penny to spare, we'd surely buy you a drink."

The boy nodded, licking his lips. "I's thirsty, Ma," he said. He looked to be five or six. I was surprised at him calling the woman Ma; she appeared far too old to be his mother.

"I know, my son, but times is hard. You know your mam hasn't so much as a penny."

Even though I knew I was being taken in, for it seemed the child spoke up as if on cue, I was grateful for even the small act of being helped on the street when most would pass right by. "You must let me buy you and your son a drink," I said. "To repay your kindness."

The woman put her hand on the boy's head. His black hair was long and stiff with dirt, and his dark eyelashes crusty. He had very pale blue eyes, enormous in his small face, and his features were even. He would have been a handsome lad if he hadn't been so filthy. "That would be ever so fine. I don't care for myself, but my wee boy here has been walking for hours now and is a mite weary. We wanted to watch the fireworks and the burning of the Guy over at the park. A warm drink of barley water would pick him up ever so much. But you've lost your reticule, you said. If you've no money—" She left the sentence hanging.

"I've a bit put aside," I said.

She nodded. "There's a nice public house only a few steps up the street, if you're able."

The thought of sitting down and having a warm drink was hugely appealing at that moment. I was badly turned around; although breathing normally now, there was a sharp pain in my back. I put my hand on it, and in the next few seconds it lessened.

The woman linked her arm through mine and led me to a public house, its name—the Green Firkin—painted in fancy curled letters on the thick glass. As she pushed the door open a burst of drunken singing rushed at us, along with the smell of spilled gin and cigar smoke and sweat. We had to work our way through the customers packed shoulder to shoulder. As we approached a table in the far corner, a woman and two older men sitting there got up, and we took their places. I saw the woman nod at one of the men, and he dipped his head at her as if they knew each other.

"I've stopped here once or twice before," the woman explained. "It's a friendly place."

As soon as we seated ourselves I put my hands under the tabletop and dug into my waistband for a few coins. The woman appeared to be taking no notice of me, busy licking her fingers and rubbing at the boy's face in a pathetic attempt to clean him up.

"I'll take a hot lemon gin," she said, "and the barley water for my boy, please."

I made my way to the bar and ordered the gin, as well as barley water for myself and the child.

I managed to get the full glasses back to our table, although as soon as I set them down the pain returned, and I leaned forward, again rubbing at my lower back with my fist.

"Have you trouble, dear?" the woman asked, tossing back her gin in a deft and familiar manner. She smacked her lips with a rubbery sound, setting her empty glass back on the table.

"I must have bruised my back falling from the carriage," I told her, sitting down and taking a long draught from my glass. "I'll get myself home, and once I lay down it will be fine." I looked at her empty glass; the child's was still topped up. I realized she'd want another drink. All I wanted to do now was get away from this noisy, smoke-filled place. And I knew I was so far from Jack Street.

What a spoiled evening, I thought, as the child took the tiniest sip of his drink, watching my face. Not only did I lose my shawl and these few hours of work, but was buying gin for this woman and would have to hire a carriage to take me back to Jack Street.

As I turned to the woman to tell her I'd be on my way, the boy's full glass tipped over neatly, knocked by his arm, and the cooling, sticky liquid rushed toward me and pooled in my lap before I had a chance to move. The woman grabbed her shawl off her shoulders and mopped at my skirt, shouting at the boy for his carelessness. His face screwed up and he howled in a high, feral wail, his mouth a black square.

"Please, please," I said, shaking my head at the woman as she frantically brushed at my skirt. "It doesn't matter. It's all right," I said to the boy, for now he was grinding his grimy fists into his eyes, his howls grown even louder.

"You're going to catch it now, a good clout round the ear, that's what you'll get," the woman hollered at him, standing, her soaking shawl rolled into a bundle.

"No, Ma, no," the boy cried, jumping from his stool and running toward the door.

"Please, it's not impor—" I tried to tell the woman, but her mouth was fixed in a grim line.

"I'll catch up with him on the street, and haul him back," she told me, then hurried after him. "Wait here for me," she added over her shoulder.

I didn't intend to spend the rest of the night buying her glasses of cheap gin; I hoped that the boy was a fast runner and would have his mother—if indeed she really was his mother—chasing him far down the street so that I could slip out and into a carriage before she returned.

The pain in my back dug deeper now and I had to steady myself with my hands flat on the table as I stood to leave. When it passed, I reached down to shake out my skirt, wet and gluey from the spilled barley water, and saw, in total horror, that the waistband had been turned out. I grabbed at it, refusing to believe what I was seeing, turning it out further. It was empty. I dropped to my knees and scrabbled on the filthy floor under the table with my hands, crying, "No. No, no no." I could hear my own voice, a high, desperate shriek not unlike that of the child's moments earlier. Except that his, I realized with a sickening thud, had been a well-practiced act.

I fought my way through the packed room to the door and looked up and down the street, but it was impossible to see through the thick wall of men and women and children and horses and carts thronging the narrow street. I raced back into the bar, telling the keeper what had happened; did he know the woman and boy? Were they regulars here?

But the keeper wasn't interested. "Can't help you," he said, not even bothering to look up from the ale he was pouring.

"But—but it's everything. She stole everything I had," I wailed, although the keeper had moved down the bar and was talking to a woman sitting there.

The pain in my back was so strong now that it jolted me. My knees buckled with the sudden unexpected shock of it, and a young man who had been nursing a glass of dark ale, sitting to one side, grabbed me. "Are you ill, miss?" he asked, his hand wrapped tightly around my forearm, holding me up.

When the pain receded slightly, I felt a tremor from the man's hand pass onto my arm, and looked down at the long-fingered hand, the knobby wrist emerging from too-short sleeves. He was shaking with some kind of mild palsy. "No. I'm not ill, just sick. Sick at being robbed. Is there nothing anyone can do?" I cried again, looking into his long, plain face. His eyes—deep blue with a darker rim—were small but kind.

"Whoever robbed you will be well away. What with the Guy Fawkes celebrations and the crowds, it's easy for them to do their work."

I withdrew my arm and stood still, unable to take it in for that one moment. The enormity of what had happened was unbearable. All this time on the street, so careful with my savings, and now caught in the oldest trick. What had I been thinking? Had my brains, as well as my back, been jolted by the fall from the carriage?

"I could see you to your home, miss," the young man said. "If you're worried about walking out on your own."

I raised my head. Worried about walking out on my own? Was he blind? Did he not see me for what I was? Or perhaps he did, and thought he could slip in a free one by pretending concern. Nobody got one for free, not from me. I'd had enough taken tonight. Almost everything. I put my hands on the slight swell of my abdomen.

"I'm perfectly fine to make my way," I told him, realizing I'd have to walk. "If you'll tell me which way it is back to central Liverpool." The pain in my back had a firm grip now.

"But—but if you've been robbed, you'll have no money for a carriage. It's a long way."

He appeared genuinely concerned. But so had the woman who had just taken away my future. I had to press my lips together tightly to hold back the low moan threatening to push its way out.

"My name is Shaker," the man said. "And I can assure you that you don't look in any condition to be humping it all that distance. You've come over quite pale. Is it your back, miss?" He looked pointedly at my fist, planted into the small of my back, kneading at the pain which was now coming in a definite rhythm of gripping and then lessening waves.

"I've had a fall. It will pass soon," I said, breathing deeply as the pain ebbed.

"Could I buy you a warm drink? Would that help?" he asked, and as I opened my mouth to say no, a particularly deep pain grabbed so viciously that I did cry out this time, and without meaning to, clutched at the man's lapel.

He put his arm around my waist, holding me until the sensation lessened. "I suspect it's not your back, miss, but something else," he said, not meeting my eyes, but fixing his stare on the braided, wrapped topknot of my apollo.

I felt his fingers spread over one side of my abdomen. They pressed gently through my corset, as if probing. "Please," I said, softly now. "I just need to get home. If I can only—" But the wave crashed into me again; this time I had to bend over and the sound that came from my lips was animal-like, almost a grunt.

He picked me up, then, with one quick swoop, and the pain at that moment was too intense for me to object. He made his way through the lurching crush of bodies as I leaned against his chest, keeping my eyes shut tight. I couldn't bear to think of what was happening, what I had started to suspect, but now knew, with certainty. It was wee Frances, shaken from her warm home, shaken loose and wanting to be born. Too early, far too early. There would be no chance she would live if she came now.

Chapter Ten

I WAS ABLE TO STAND BESIDE HIM, WITH HIS SUPPORT, AS HE HAILED a carriage, and he helped me inside. "Where shall I direct the driver?" he asked, leaning in the open door. "Where is your home?"

I thought of the stifling, airless closet. The girls would be out at work for the next four or five hours. I would have to do this, alone, on the pallet on Jack Street. I felt my lips shaking as violently as the hands of the man who called himself Shaker. *No. No no no.* My head wagged with each inner *no.*

Shaker misinterpreted what he saw. "It's all right. Look." He pulled a few coins from his vest pocket. "Here. It's enough to pay the driver."

I couldn't say anything, just kept my eyes fixed on the faded wine-colored curtain over the window.

Shaker waited until the carriage jolted with the impatient shifting of the horses and there was a rough question from the driver. Finally Shaker answered and climbed in beside me.

Neither of us spoke. I concentrated on the swaying curtain, biting down through each fresh assault of pain. It was no longer only in my back, but around the front and radiating down my thighs. Within ten minutes the carriage stopped, and Shaker helped me out.

"Where are we?" I asked, looking around the dimly lit street with its row of neat two-story terraced houses sharing common walls and brick façades. I recognized traces of simple elegance in the doorways and windows, which were tall and well proportioned. I could see that the doorsteps and windowsills were well scrubbed and whitened. I cupped one hand under the rise of my abdomen in an attempt to ease the pressure.

"We're in Everton, north of the city. This is where I live—Whitefield

Lane." Shaker opened the unlocked door and led me inside. All was in darkness but for the red glow of a dying fire in a room to the left. Urged by the press of Shaker's hand on my back, I slowly made my way up a flight of narrow stairs toward a landing. A sliver of light showed under one of the two doors there. He hesitated, and in that moment the door opened and a gaunt, gray-haired woman holding a well-thumbed Bible in one hand and a candle in the other stared at us.

"What is all of this?" she demanded, her voice querulous, holding the candle in my direction. The flames cast craggy shadows on her scowling features. "Who is this person?" I saw her sharp eyes taking in the cut of my dress, my apolloed hair. I knew the odors of the alehouse— spirits and tobacco and sweat—emanated from us.

"It's a young woman in distress, Mother," Shaker said.

I didn't think my legs would hold me any longer. I clung weakly to Shaker's sleeve, and he put his arms around me to help me stand. I leaned my forehead against his chest.

"Distress? Distress?" the woman repeated. "From where I'm standing, she's just drunk. You dare to bring home a drunken whore?" I turned my face to look at her, and she stepped so close that I felt the fine spray of spittle that flew from her lips. "You disappoint me, my boy, and, much worse, you disappoint the Lord with this type of behavior."

"Mother. You don't at all understand the situat—"

"No. I don't. But I do know that I can't abide to see such a one as her under my roof." Her head swiveled on her thin, wrinkled neck as she bent to speak into my face. "Fornicator." The word came out a harsh whisper.

Shaker ignored it. "And it's our roof, Mother. Our roof, not yours."

"You give me one good reason why I should allow this, Shaker. One good reason."

"Christian charity, perhaps?" Shaker enunciated, a sarcastic impatience in the words.

This changed the woman's expression, and she stepped back.

The agony made my knees buckle, and I moaned now, feeling tremendous pressure. I held tightly to Shaker's jacket so I wouldn't fall. In the circle of his arms, I felt the tremor of his hands on my back become more violent as he spoke up to his mother.

"The young woman is about to give birth, Mother. She needs help."

Heard out loud—*give birth*—the words were horrifying.

"She doesn't look with child. Although it could be because she's skin and bone, worn down by her frenzied fornicating." The woman moved closer to me again, peering first at my belly and then at my ringless fingers and then into my face. "And why, I ask, have you brought her here? You're not . . . connected with this girl, are you?" Her rheumy eyes were boring into mine; now they grew suspicious and fearful. "Do you bear some responsibility for her state? Son? Tell me you have no responsibility toward this woman. Please." The final word was pleading.

I echoed her word as the pressure felt like iron tongs, forcing my very bones apart. "Please," I moaned to Shaker. "Please. Help me."

He dragged me into a dark room, half carrying me. His mother was relentless, following us. Wavering, monstrous shadows created by her candle danced on the walls. "Why doesn't she go home, where she belongs?"

"She's been robbed of all her money. The crowds tonight . . ." Shaker trailed off. "And she needed help," he said for the second time. "Now go, Mother. Go back to your room." His voice was low but strong. "I insist. This is not your business."

Finally, the woman said nothing more. She left, taking the candle and closing the door behind her.

My body was no longer in my control. In the darkness I heard my voice rising in a spiral, a strange, warbling call, and Shaker laid me gently on a soft surface. There was the rasp of a congreve and then the flare of light as he touched the match to the wick of an Argand lamp. In its glow I saw I was on a narrow mattress on a rope-slung frame. It seemed the pains were building on each other, the time between them shorter and shorter. Explosions of noise in the distance signaled the height of the Bonfire Night fireworks. I was being torn in two.

"It's too early. It's far too early," I whispered, drawing my knees up and apart as Shaker lit a fire in the small fireplace.

"Yes, I know," he said, almost as if to himself. "And it appears to be too far along to stop."

"I don't know what to do," I said, panting now. *And I'm afraid.*

Shaker's hands were jumping wildly as he washed them in a basin.

Water splashed over the front of his coat and he removed it. Booming and crashing rattled the glass pane of the window. "I do," he said, and then came to me.

"LET ME SEE HER."

"You don't want to do that, miss. It will only upset you."

"I said I want to see her." My words hissed as if filled with venom.

It had been over quickly; I didn't question anything Shaker had told me to do as he pushed up my dress and undid my stays and tucked my chemise up out of the way and then placed his large knuckled hands on my abdomen and began murmuring instructions. He gave me a clean pad of cotton to bite down on when the worst of the pain came. Afterward, he pulled the stained sheet from beneath me and spread a fresh one, then brought extra cloths for the bleeding and warm water and a soft flannel for washing. He left me alone and I took off my dress and corset and cleaned myself, slowly, all over. My movements were slow and heavy, and when I was done I lay back on the bed.

Morning hadn't yet come, although the light in the lamp seemed dimmer, and the darkness in the corners of the room was fading. Wind whistled at the window.

"It's my baby. You can't tell me that I have no right to see her." I tried to keep the command in my voice, but I shivered even with the blanket wrapped around me, and the last of the words fell off weakly. Shaker had opened the window a few inches, and the cool air rushed in, bringing fresh, somehow green-smelling air. The air I had breathed for so long had the heaviness of gray. The fireworks had long been over, and there were no sounds from outside. Used to the endless clatter and shouts of Jack Street, I found this room eerily quiet.

He studied me for another moment and then went to a washstand that held a porcelain basin. "Wait, then."

I closed my eyes, hearing small splashing sounds, gentle rustling. "What are you doing?" I finally asked, opening my eyes and trying to find a comfortable sitting position, pulling the blanket firmly around my shoulders.

He didn't answer but finally came to the side of the bed. He squatted beside me, lowering the decorated porcelain basin, and I looked at the tiny shape under the clean linen handkerchief that had been carefully draped over it. A miniature winding sheet.

I moved the handkerchief aside with my index finger.

She lay on her side. Shaker had washed her; her skin was clean, the soft gray-blue of a mourning dove's breast, and a fine down covered her entire body. She was perfectly formed but unbearably tiny, transparent eyelids and fingernails.

I reached out and stroked the cool velvety forehead, the arm, the back. My fingers were trembling, or perhaps not, perhaps it was the baby trembling from the vibration of the basin in Shaker's hand.

I wanted to weep. I tried, for it was as if the lining of my throat had swelled to an unbearable size, so thick and membranous that it was difficult to swallow. Saliva filled my mouth, my nose ran, but still, no tears came to my eyes.

"I'm sorry. I knew it would do no good for you to——"

I had to work at my throat and finally my voice returned, although it was only a dull croak. "Her name is Frances." I took my hand away from the baby and put it into my lap, where the other hand clenched it. "And I'm glad she didn't live. Glad, for what kind of life is it for a girl in this world? What kind of life for a girl?" I believed it at that moment.

Shaker gently set the basin back on the washstand, looking down at the baby.

"You won't dump her down a midden, will you? Give her to me and I'll take her and bury her myself."

Shaker continued to look at the dead child.

"If you want me to leave, I'll leave right now. I'll take her and go," I said, somehow angered by Shaker's stooped shoulders, his trembling hands, the sorrow that seemed to be a part of him. What right did he have to grieve for her, for my Frances? He had no right at all. He knew nothing of me, nor I of him.

I tried to swing my legs to the floor and involuntarily cried out at the sharp dark pain. The blanket fell away.

"I'll let you do whatever it is you wish with her, of course," Shaker said, turning to me now, standing so still except for the fluttering hands, which he eventually tucked under his own arms. "What is your name?"

"Linny Gow," I said, sitting there, naked but for my thin chemise. I put my palms on either side of me on the bed, preparing to push myself up. "I must go," I said.

"Why?" Shaker asked.

I didn't have an answer. My eyes went to the basin.

"Would you like to lie here, for a few hours at least, until the worst of the bleeding stops and you have enough strength to get home?" He came closer.

When I didn't answer, he continued. "You know you mustn't go right back to work. At least not for a few days. Your body needs time to heal."

Of course he knew what I was. He hadn't needed his mother to point out my occupation. He'd known right from the first moment I stepped beside him in the public house, although his manner toward me had been so respectful that I had actually believed that he might have been fooled for a short time.

At his mention of going back to work I was overcome with exhaustion. The thought of going out into the cold pre-dawn and walking all the way back to Jack Street seemed, suddenly, completely impossible. "I'll rest for an hour at the most," I told him. "Only an hour." I lay back down.

Shaker rearranged the thick wool blanket over me, and as he did so, his eyes flickered over my scar, and I heard an almost imperceptible sigh. Then he closed the window, stoked the fire, turned out the lamp, and left.

As I lay there, warm, sleepless, in the first pale rays of morning light, I looked away from the basin, toward the window. A bare wet branch touched the glass cautiously in the remains of the wind that had now died away. The sky was pearly. I thought about Shaker and for the first time wondered that he had known what to do. I thought of the sadness on his face as he held the washbasin toward me, and then later, as he stared down at my dead baby.

I AWOKE TO BRIGHT SUNLIGHT streaming through a window that was clean as any I'd ever seen. I threw back the blanket and sat up, stiff and aching everywhere, as if I'd been beaten far worse than the few blows from the Scot in the carriage. I felt skinned, both inside and out, as if even a word would produce pain. I stood slowly, my legs shaky, and dressed.

As I let down my tangled apollo and struggled with the matted tangles I looked to the washstand. In place of the basin was a small tin-plated box no longer than two of my hand lengths. Shaker must have come in while I was asleep. A box for storing jewelry was my first thought, or for special keepsakes. I went to it and ran my fingers over it, realization striking, and then opened the lid a tiny bit. I saw the crisp white of the linen handkerchief, touched it and felt the small curled contents. I closed the lid.

The rest of the room contained a broad, austere desk and a straight chair. Stacks of books were piled on the desk and one lay open. On the wall over the desk was the drawing of a man with no flesh, just muscle, sinew, and veins. There were other drawings of bones, one of a skull, split in half, with a wormy mass showing on the open side. And then I saw them, on the floor beside the desk. Jars.

For one horrible moment I was back in the brightly lit room with its terrible collection.

I went closer, afraid of what I might see. But these jars didn't contain hair. At first I thought the contents to be food storage, for shapes that I had only seen in a butcher's stall floated there. Then I realized they were organs, parts of the body, preserved, obviously, by their white, waxen appearance. Some I didn't recognize, although I did see kidneys. A heart. A liver. Looking into the last jar, I put my hand over my mouth to stifle the sound, but I wasn't fast enough. The door opened and Shaker hurried in to find me backing away from the desk.

"I'm sorry, I'm so sorry. I didn't think . . ." He was stuttering, snatching up the jar so rapidly that the large-headed fetal beginnings of a human surged and bobbed in the eddying formaldehyde.

I stared at him, stricken, feeling my own face as lifeless and bleached as the contents of the jars.

"I study the human body," Shaker said, too quickly, as if guilty.

"I . . . I wanted to be a physician. Of course it's impossible for me—a physician, or even a surgeon, even the most rudimentary of barber-surgeons—like the one who once attended to you." His eyes rested on my scar for the briefest of moments, then he shook his head. "Impossible, being the way I am—my hands," he continued, as if he needed to clarify, "but it remains a passion." He had managed to hide the jar behind his back as he spoke. "I've made some beef tea," he said, "and you should have some tartar emetic, for making the blood stronger. But you need a physician's recommendation; it's only available at the dispensary. Are you feeling terribly indisposed?" He was babbling, his tongue tripping over the words in trying to explain himself.

I had lowered myself onto the ladder-back chair at the desk. "I just became lightheaded from standing too quickly," I lied, not wanting him to think me weak. "I'll be on my way in a moment." I looked toward the pretty box on the table. "Will you be wanting your box back?"

"Oh, no. Please. You had said you wanted to bury it—her, and I thought . . ."

I studied the box, not wanting to look at Shaker as he backed out of the room. He reappeared, carrying a shawl, in less than a moment. "I'm so sorry to have upset you, Miss Gow. Please." He handed me the shawl—his mother's, of course. I put it around me. "At least have a cup of the beef tea I've prepared. It's across the hall, in my mother's room. She's just returned from church, and her room is warmer. The fire hasn't been laid downstairs yet; Nan will arrive shortly and see to things. Come and sit in the other room. Please," he added, again.

The suggestion of the meaty drink made saliva rush to my mouth. "All right. Thank you, Mr.—"

Color spread upward from Shaker's neck. "Oh, it's just Shaker, as I told you last night. Started as an unfortunate jest while I was at school but it stuck, and so it remains." He smiled briefly, revealing slightly crooked teeth, but it was a natural smile and it warmed his plain face. It crossed my mind that I hadn't seen this kind of smile on a man's face for a long, long time. Not from any of the men who looked at me. "My surname is Smallpiece. But please. I'd prefer if you'd call me Shaker. If you don't mind the informality."

"Thank you, Shaker," I said, realizing that it would indeed be ridiculous to carry on with any pretense. "For . . . last night. For helping me." I studied his trembling hands. Did they ever stop their dance? Had they shaken as he gently guided the tiny blue girl out of me?

He balled them into fists, then, and I was ashamed for staring.

"You must think me a right ninny," I said, raising my eyes. "To be robbed like that. Me, of all people. I should know the games of the street." I shrugged. "There's no way I'll ever get my money back, I know that."

Shaker jammed one hand into his pocket. "It'll be spent on cheap gin and who knows what else by now. But I went back to the Green Firkin this morning and the publican let me in, even though it's the Lord's Day. I asked him again, as you did last night, if he knew who the woman and the child were. Of course he would say he didn't; likely he would be in on it, and demand his share for letting her work his place. But I did have a look round, and found this kicked into a corner. Of course, it could be anybody's."

He pulled his hand out of his pocket and held out my pendant. At the sight of it, twirling slowly on the end of its gold chain, the grief over having all of my dreams stolen in one night came out in a dry, explosive sob. I reached for the pendant, snatching it from Shaker's fingers, and held it against my cheek.

"Her name is Frances," I said, knowing I had already told him that. "After my mother." And then, finally, it was possible to cry. After so many years. I sobbed in an embarrassing, noisy, and unfamiliar way, with a high-pitched keening, my nose running, eyes squeezed shut, rocking back and forth on the edge of the chair. I felt Shaker's hand on my shoulder, the trembling violent now, but it was a comfort nonetheless.

When I at last was able to control myself, my sobs replaced with a stuttering in my throat, wiping my eyes on the shawl, Shaker removed his hand and took a step away from me. He showed great interest in the drawing of the skinless man, then in the open book, the jars, whatever lay in view from the window. He looked everywhere but at me, as if seeing me cry had been more embarrassing to him than what he'd seen the night before as I lay on his bed and he knelt between my bent legs.

He finally rubbed his hands together nervously, clearing his throat, but he seemed unable to decide whether to go or stay, or the best way to deal with a woman in distress.

Chapter Eleven

O VER THE CUP OF STEAMING BEEF TEA IN THE ROOM ACROSS THE hall, which was, as Shaker had promised, warm, with a hearty fire blazing in a good-size fireplace, I told Shaker my plan of going to America. About how I'd been put into the business by Ram Munt, how I'd been saving every penny I could for the purpose of leaving this life in the only way open to me. How I almost had enough. How I had planned to raise my baby there in America and live a respectable life.

Why did I tell him all of this? I don't know, other than I felt that it was my duty to explain to him who I was; perhaps to thank him in the only way I could, other than offering my body—by being honest with him. And as I talked and watched his face, I realized his opinion of me mattered, something I'd never felt before.

The whole time his mother was there, in her cane rocking chair facing the long window, tatting lace. She didn't acknowledge me when Shaker accompanied me into her room, one hand resting lightly on my back. He pulled out a chair for me at the small deal table in front of the fire. Shaker acted, likewise, as if she wasn't there, and in time I also ignored her presence.

I studied the windows, clouded from the heat, framed with crisp curtains. The wide mantel boasted a round clock in an Amritsar case, crowded by a collection of china dogs. A thick fringed rug covered the floor, warm under my feet. An oak dresser beside a horsehair screen held an assortment of glass ornaments, shells, japanned trays, and gaudy biscuit boxes. The room indicated every sign of decency and prosperity.

Over the dresser hung a painting, a rendition of some foreign-looking temple in blues, greens, and whites. Although the painting itself was, even to my eye, poorly executed, the colors—the brilliant hues of the background of blues and greens surrounding the stark white of the temple—were somehow pleasing, so different from the usual watercolors seen in every hotel and dining room.

"What is that painting of?" I asked, when I'd finished my story.

Shaker looked from me to the painting and back at me, as if puzzled by my question. Or perhaps surprised. He said a strange name, something that sounded like *Tajatagra,* and changed the subject. "So you'll have to begin again, then, with saving?" Shaker asked. He continually pushed his untouched cup of tea, now grown cold, back and forth on the well-polished tabletop, just a fraction of an inch each time. He could not remain still. I suspect he didn't drink his tea as his palsied hands would cause the liquid to slop over the sides, and I also suspected that this would embarrass him.

I sighed. "I can't think of it. But of course I will. For what other option is open to me? I've lost everything, save for my mother's pendant. What choice do I have?" I repeated, and ran my fingertip around the lip of the cup.

Shaker's mother spoke then, making both of us jump. "What choice? You ask what choice you have?" She let her tatting drop into her lap and stared at me over her shoulder. "Do you not know the wonders of the Lord?" Her voice was too loud—partial deafness or simple anger?

"I used to go to church. With my mother, when she was alive, and then for a while after she died." I tried to keep my voice respectful for Shaker's sake, but already I hated this woman, with her suspicious eyes and attempt at a pious expression.

She shook her head. "And what would your mother, rest her soul, think of your sinning ways now?"

"Really, Mother," Shaker said, stealing a glance at me. The flush rose on him again.

But his mother ignored his mild admonishment. "Do you think she would approve? Do you think the Lord in His Glory approves of your wicked, filthy ways?"

I drank the last mouthful of my beef tea, then carefully set the cup onto the table.

"I'm simply a working girl, doing what I can to get by, Mrs. Smallpiece," I said, letting a slightly imperious tone creep into my voice.

The woman's eyebrows, bushy and gray, rose into her forehead. "And proud of it, by the sounds of you. You live in an underworld of prostitution and crime, making light of our concepts of respectability, of purity and prudery. Trying to pass yourself off as a lady won't work with me. I can see you trying to clamber over the fences we've had to build to protect ourselves from the inferior likes of people like you. I know you for what you are, through and through. I've known others like you. For didn't I—"

"Don't, Mother," Shaker interrupted. "Stop. It will do no one any good. You know what may happen if you upset yourse—"

"Pride has nothing to do with it, as you must know, being so well informed of my life," I interrupted, staring at the old woman. I didn't care what Shaker thought now. I wouldn't be bullied by this dried-out hag. "I started in a bookbindery beside my mother as a child of six. For my work my mother was given enough pennies a week to buy an extra bit of bacon and a loaf of cheap bread that was half chalk and a packet of tea leaves mixed with ones already used. I'm sure you know this sad story, don't you, Mrs. Smallpiece? At least in theory." I glanced around the cozy room. "You really have no idea, do you, sitting in your comfortable house in your comfortable street, knowing each day of your life that you would be cared for and watched over? If I were still working there at the bookbinders, I would now be making enough to rent a corner of a room in a lodging house, and pay half of my wage to the crimp who cheated everyone under her roof, and live on the same ration of bacon and chalky bread and weak tea. And perhaps one day I would marry and move to another corner of another stinking room, and I'd have children and still go to work at a factory, and my life would continue on until either childbearing or endless work killed me."

As I spoke, I heard my voice shift wildly, like sand under pulsing waves. I heard my drawing room voice swing into the rough northern tones of Back Phoebe Anne and Paradise. I heard the inflection of my mother's soft Scottish lilt, and then it was back to the throaty, plummy tones I had tried so hard to perfect in the candelabra-lit dining room in the hotel near Lord Street. I couldn't hold on to one voice; in my distress I was flying in all directions, the babble of a madwoman's voice as surely as my appearance was of one now.

"So I chose the only other way that I hoped might get me away from that future. Or at least I thought it would. I should have known it was only a dream. I should have listened to the person who told me I was simply a girl with the stink of the Mersey waterfront in my nostrils and I would never be any better than that," I finished, realizing my voice had, at the end, gone unpleasantly shrill. I stood, trying to ignore the cramping and rush of fresh bleeding. "I'm sorry, Shaker," I said, pointedly ignoring the old woman now. "I had no call to speak rudely to your mother but it's time I was off, back to where she believes I belong."

But Mrs. Smallpiece had also risen, and approached me, one shoulder lower than the other, her face, on that side, drawn down as well. I saw a dull fire in her faded, deep-set eyes. "I could offer you salvation. One so young as you, perhaps it hasn't set fully yet. The evil."

"Salvation?" I asked. "Salvation?" A small sly noise, a derisive snick of laughter, slipped from between my lips. I looked at Shaker, but he was studying his cup.

"If you take the Lord Jesus into your heart, offer up your soul to Him, there may be a chance for you to renounce your ways." Mrs. Smallpiece tried to lift her shoulder and her chin stuck forward. "For I also was once guilty of lustful thoughts and performed lewd acts of the flesh, yet the Lord saw fit to shine his light on me and I was pulled from the claws of the Devil. Yes, I was pulled from those claws, although not before they had sunk deep within me—" And here she flung her head in Shaker's direction. "And my punishment for my sinning was him, there, born little better than a cripple. A son useless in body, unable to provide a daughter-in-law to care for me, unable to give me grandchildren." She turned her oddly glowing eyes to Shaker. "Useless," she repeated, her voice rising to the beamed ceiling with a high, hollow echo.

I refused to look at Shaker; I kept my eyes fixed on the old woman.

Saliva bubbled on her bottom lip and her eyelids fluttered rapidly, as if the fire I had seen there threatened to burn her. "I have accepted my punishment, kept him when others would have left him to die. And for that I was saved. The Lord in His mercy is all knowing and all seeing, Hallelujah sayeth the Lord, Hallelujah oh Lord oh Lord save us." Her words came louder and faster, suddenly tripping into each other until they were merely a cacophony of grunts and garbled syllables, a speaking in tongues that sent a chill up my spine. And in the next instant her eyes rolled heavenward and her knees buckled. She fell to the floor and her body shook with rhythmic tremors, her heels beating a staccato rhythm on the floorboards.

As the acrid smell of urine filled the room I bit so hard on my bottom lip that I felt the skin split.

Shaker knelt beside his mother, his hand under her head, turning it to one side as her tongue protruded and forcing a smooth piece of wood he pulled from his pocket between her clenched gums. Eventually the tremors lessened and finally ceased. Shaker gently lowered her head to the ground, removed the spit-soaked wood, then took a handkerchief from his pocket and wiped her face. With a practiced motion he lifted her as if she were no more than a husk and laid her on the narrow bed along one wall, tucking a large flannel under her wet skirt.

He opened the window to rid the room of its smell of piss and sweat.

"I'm sorry," he said, not meeting my eyes. "She'll be fine shortly. She hasn't had one in a long while; these fits only occur when she's greatly agitated. They started after her apoplexy, a few years ago. I urge her not to excite herself," he added, finally turning to me, and there was something in his face, some quiet desperation, that made me pity him. "She'll be calm when she wakes. It's as if these occasional cataclysms allow her to return to her normal state for a long time afterward," he went on, as if assuring himself that it was all actually normal, that his life with this needy and overbearing woman was fine, that he was in some way grateful for her not abandoning him, even though it was clear it was he who had to care for her.

I looked at his mother. The sight of her yellowy sclera and the line of drool shimmering down her bristled chin made me reach for the chair behind me and I sat down heavily.

Shaker sat across from me again, his mother's still body stretched out a few feet from us. "I told you, you can rest here as long as you wish. And then I'll help you get home." He was looking at me. "How old— do you mind if I ask? How old are you?"

"Seventeen."

I saw the look of surprise flicker across his face before he could stop it. "Seventeen?"

"I've always looked younger—" I started, but in a rush of understanding realized I had misinterpreted his surprise. "How old did you think I was?" I knew, even after this brief time, that it was difficult for Shaker to hide what was in his thoughts.

"I assumed you were closer to my age—twenty-three."

I went to the small gilt-framed mirror hanging on the wall beside the window and looked at myself in bright daylight. For years I had seen myself only in the forgiving flicker of candlelight, the softening rosiness of gaslight, always in my thick layer of powder and rouge. And now I saw that I had truly become a creature of the night.

My skin, untouched by sun for so long, had the pallor and texture of a two-day mushroom. The moon-shaped scar at the side of my mouth, created by the heavy blow of a ringed hand, stood scarlet. My hair, which I had always thought of as golden, now was dry and somehow bleached of its depth of color, like winter straw. My eyelids were shadowed purple, as were the bruised-looking pouches beneath my eyes, emphasized by caked traces of powder. And my eyes themselves—the gold flecks that had once glinted in the brown irises, lighting them, were gone. The gold had disappeared, gone from my hair, and from my eyes.

I saw Shaker's face behind me. Watching me. His face held the same pinched, defeated look as mine.

I backed away, shaking my head. "What's happened to me?" I whispered, not asking Shaker but myself. I didn't know the hollow-eyed woman in the mirror. She bore a resemblance to the ruin of the woman I had called Mother. Where was Linny, little Linny Gow, the child with the clear eyes and hair like the ripest of summer's pears?

"You've had a shock," Shaker said quietly. "I expect that once you feel better—"

"No," I said, sitting again. "No. That's not it."

We sat in silence, listening to the quiet ticking of the clock. The sky was darkening and the breeze at the slightly open window lifted the strands of hair around my face. "I don't know what I mean," I finished limply.

Mrs. Smallpiece gave a small murmur and then turned her head from side to side. Shaker helped her to her feet and got her settled in her chair. Her chin slumped against her chest, but Shaker took her Bible from a shelf and put it into her loosely curled hands.

"Do you believe in signs, Miss Gow?" he asked.

He was tall; I had to tip my chin to look at him. "Signs?" I thought of the baby. She had been my sign. But how did you interpret it when the sign didn't mean what you thought it had? Was that another sign in itself?

Although the room was still quiet, sounds from outside grew louder. The urgent barking of a dog, the far-off lowing of cattle, the closer chiming of church bells. The breeze suddenly turned to wind, causing the curtain to billow in an arc, reminding me of the sail of a ship.

"I believe in signs," I finally said.

Shaker lowered the window with a thud and then, leaning against the sill, the light behind him, stared at me. "I do too, Miss Gow," he finally said.

"Linny. Please call me Linny."

A slow flush rose up his neck again. "I believe you are my sign, Linny Gow."

❊❊❊❊❊❊

IT SEEMED ODD AND YET, somehow, I did not think it strange. I simply stayed there, in the house on Whitefield Lane, with no discussion, no plan. After our conversation, Shaker had disappeared, perhaps for one hour or possibly two, as I had no notion of the time. I felt strangely detached, sitting at the polished table, as if my mind were somewhere above my body, floating loose and confused. Mrs. Smallpiece, after her brief bout of religious fervor and convulsive fit, appeared exhausted, almost as dazed as I was, as if something had fled and left her empty and either she wasn't aware or didn't care that I sat in the room with her. Eventually she slowly made her way to the horsehair screen in the corner and went behind it, emerging in a fresh dress. Then she returned to her chair and flipped the pages of her Bible endlessly but didn't read from it. The two of us sat there, separate islands, waiting, I felt, but for what I didn't know.

There were footsteps on the stairs, a heavy set and a lighter, almost scampering set, and a stout woman clattered in with an ash pail. She stopped at the sight of me and the young girl with one milky blind eye bumped into her back. Mrs. Smallpiece dully scolded her about being late. The woman dropped the empty pail. "How was I to know you were having company?" she demanded. "Does that mean extra for dinner as well? That beef might not stretch. Does Merrie have to set the table for three?"

When she didn't get an answer, she turned on her heel and stomped out of the room, her ample backside swaying indignantly. The girl ran after her. In a moment I heard thumps and knocks from the staircase, as if the woman were dusting or polishing it with a great deal more noise than was necessary.

Shaker returned, carrying a rolled-up flock mattress and crisp sheets, a new-looking pillow and blankets, which he arranged along the wall opposite his mother's bed. Mrs. Smallpiece watched but said nothing.

Then he carried in the small tin-plated box and took up the coal shovel from against the fireplace. I rose, holding the shawl tightly around me, and together we went down the stairs.

"Good day, Nan," he said, as we passed the stout woman on her knees sweeping out the sitting room fireplace. "And to you as well, Merrie." The woman stared at me openly, without replying. The girl held a figurine in one hand and a dusting rag in the other. Like the woman, her hands stopped what they were doing and she looked at us with her one dark blue eye, the milky one turned inward.

I walked beside Shaker through a number of streets. The sun had come out and it was warmer than it had been for several days. We stopped at a muddy lane that led to a small church surrounded by dark yews.

"There's a graveyard here, but we would have to seek permission. The church's rules, of course."

I nodded. "And what would the rule for an unbaptized bastard child be?" In the next sentence I answered my own question. "A shallow grave in unhallowed ground, among unclaimed drunks and paupers. No. I don't want to forever think of Frances in a place like that."

"There's somewhere else," he said, slowly. "I just didn't know what you wanted." He turned, and again I stuck to him like a shadow as we walked through the small village of Everton. I'd heard of Everton. Beyond the houses and shops was countryside. I'd never been in the country.

After a ten-minute walk we emerged onto a quiet road. Shaker stopped and parted a hedgerow and I stepped through. We stood in a small copse of hawthorne trees. The ground was soggy with fallen leaves, and twigs snapped under our feet when we moved. There was no sound but the dripping of the darkened boughs. There was the unfamiliar smell of grass after a rain. I breathed it in; the smells that were mine were the oiliness of the docks, rotting food thrown from stalls, animal and human offal in the streets, and the overpowering odors of the men—either the pungent unwashed smell of one class or too much cologne and hair pomade of another. In front of us, one brave holly bush showed the beginnings of scarlet berries in the wintry air and the long grass was soft and only beginning to lose its rich green. "I thought perhaps here," Shaker said.

"Yes," I said. "This is a good place. This is the right place for her."

Using the coal shovel, Shaker helped me bury Frances under the holly bush and then backed away. I found a small, pink-streaked rock and nestled it into the freshly turned earth at the top of the small mound, then said a prayer for her. I knelt there for a time—again, time that had no length or breadth. I was aware of Shaker somewhere behind me. Finally he put his hand under my elbow to help me up, saying, "I like to come here and think. Nobody else seems to bother with it. She won't be disturbed."

And then we walked back together in silence, slowly, because I was still weak. When we entered the dining room Nan and Merrie were just leaving and there was a pot of savory stew bubbling over a steady fire, a fresh loaf of bread on the sideboard. The three of us had our dinner in the narrow but comfortable dining room with its wallpaper an elaborate tea-rose cluster design only slightly faded, broken horizontally by a white dado freshly painted. We sat at a table smelling of beeswax polish and ate

from delicate plates. Although their pattern was unrecognizable through decades of washing, and there were a few nicks in some of the edges, the china retained an unmistakable delicacy. We sat and ate without speaking, each in our own thoughts, as if we had done this all our lives.

Chapter Twelve

I SLEPT ON THE PALLET IN MRS. SMALLPIECE'S ROOM THAT NIGHT, a deep, dreamless sleep, a sleep I hadn't had for months or maybe years, maybe since I was a child sleeping beside my mother. As I woke the next morning, through habit I put my hand to my waistband and then my belly. My eyes opened wide in the morning light as I realized both were empty, and I remembered all that had happened.

"Where is Shaker?" I asked, seeing Mrs. Smallpiece working on a piece of needlework in front of the fire. My voice surprised me; it was almost timid.

"He's at work, good, honest work, as all God-fearing people should be."

I rose and smoothed the sheets and folded the blankets, patting the pillow into shape.

"Chamber pot's behind the screen," she said, her voice pinched, as if it hurt her throat to have to offer me the opportunity to add my own night water to her smelly pot. "Best do something with that hair; you're a sight. There's a comb by the washbasin."

"Where does he work?" I asked, with that same rather cowed tone.

"At the Lyceum," she answered shortly.

"The Lyceum on Bold Street?" I knew the place well; right on the corner of Bold and Ranelagh streets, it was a Gentlemen's Club, an impressive building with a small, grassy treed semicircular area enclosed by an open iron fence. I had passed it often, admiring its columns and the broad marble steps leading to its grand recessed entrance.

She nodded once. "Hurry yourself. And when you're done take the pot down and empty it in the privy at the back, then come back up here and help me with my hair. I dismissed that useless Nan—she and her lazy bacon-faced daughter expect to be paid good money for next to no help. Now that you're here to take on their jobs," she added, and I opened my mouth to protest, but she didn't give me a chance to speak. She put down her needle and held up her hands. The joints were swollen and twisted; it must have been painful for her to sew. "More suffering for my sins," she said. "You'll be afflicted by something for your own wickedness, if you haven't been already. And the child was better born dead; it would have been an idiot, being fathered by hundreds."

I took a deep breath to stop myself from hissing something back at her, all traces of my former tentativeness disappearing with her words. A hot rage swept over me at her cruel mention of my perfect child. I stepped behind the screen, thankful to be out of her view for even the time it took me to relieve myself. And I had no intention of staying, even though I hadn't let myself think of Paradise Street since the day before. The last thing I would ever do would be servant to a miserable old woman with an eye cold as a haddock.

SHAKER ARRIVED HOME for the evening meal looking somehow different than he had when I'd first seen him in the Green Firkin. It was something more than being clean shaven, his long hair neatly combed. It went deeper than that. What had changed in his face?

We said hello to each other when he came in, both of us suddenly shy.

"I don't think she's prepared a proper meal in her life," Mrs. Smallpiece complained. "I had to talk her through every step. Although she does have strength in her hands. And you know I can barely handle the stairs, what with my legs, so at least she was of some use in the fetching and carrying."

Shaker nodded, clearing his throat as if embarrassed. "Did Nan not come in to help today, Mother? And what of little Merrie?" He looked around. "Who is serving dinner, then?"

When his mother didn't answer, I spoke up to fill the silence. "Your mother told me you work at the Lyceum. In the Gentlemen's Club. I'll serve," I said, and he stiffly lowered himself onto his chair. I took the plates of mutton and boiled potatoes from the sideboard and set one in front of Shaker, one in front of his mother, and one at my place. I passed the gravy boat, aware of the heavy pall of awkwardness that had appeared out of nowhere. Was the awkwardness because I was serving him dinner? Or was it because I was no longer in distress? Because I no longer resembled the rouged and apolloed whore who had clung to him in the public house? Or the desperate, bedraggled creature with her hair hanging around her face as she blustered over her beef tea with her pathetic story of lost dreams, or the hunched, keening mourner beside the tiny grave marked only by a pink-streaked rock?

I had combed through my hair and twisted and secured it neatly at the back of my head, my face was scrubbed clean, and I had pinned Mrs. Smallpiece's shawl primly across my chest. Did I frighten him more now, as an ordinary young woman who was waiting on him as he sat at the table?

He picked up his fork. "Please, Miss Gow. Linny. Sit down. Actually, I work in the library. As well as the News Room that's part of the club, there's a subscription library upstairs, owned by the club's members." Then he lowered his head over his food, and I was careful not to look at his attempts to get a full forkful to his mouth without losing half of it back onto the plate. Long minutes passed, broken only by the sound of the silver on china and collective chewing and swallowing.

Suddenly he looked up. "Do you read?"

"She does," Mrs. Smallpiece answered. "I had her read to me. You know these eyes of mine can barely make out the print now. And I chose Scriptures that she needed to read. 'Thou art weighed in the balance, and art found wanting' was one I thought applied to her, after her immoral life. 'Ye have plowed wickedness, ye have reaped inequity, ye have eaten the fruit of lies—'"

Shaker interrupted her. "I suspected you might," he said, as if it were I who had answered him. "And I take it you can write as well?"

"I haven't, not for a long time, but as a child I could. My mother taught me."

"I see," he said, and that was all, and I suddenly recognized that what was different about his face was his expression. He no longer had a lost look, an empty melancholy.

※

IT WAS TOO EASY to go upstairs to the soft pallet with the thick blankets after I had washed and dried the dishes.

The next morning Mrs. Smallpiece dug through her wardrobe and unceremoniously threw one of her old frocks across my pallet. The cheap, badly made, and low-cut dress I'd been wearing—my garish work-ing dress—was, I knew, completely unwearable in Everton. I put on the drab brown broadcloth, eying with chagrin the much-darned shawl and badly out-of-style bonnet she also unearthed for me. The dress was a poor fit, hanging loosely. I felt as dull as the unflattering outfit.

I once again followed Mrs. Smallpiece's instructions as she put me to work after breakfast, polishing the mismatched silver—the dinner-ware as well as a tea service and the gravy boat—peeling vegetables delivered to the back door by the costermonger, and making biscuits and the pastry for a beef pie. A gilt-edged card was delivered, and after reading it and mumbling "How pleasant," Mrs. Smallpiece deposited it on a silver tray that sat on a small mahogany table near the front door. She had me read to her again from the Bible, but after five minutes her head began to nod and finally dropped to one side, her mouth open. I wrapped her shawl around me and slipped away to the clearing with its holly bush and sat with my fingers tracing the smooth grooves of the pink-streaked stone. The pain in my body was healing but there was a deep sadness that throbbed through me ceaselessly. If I was to return to Paradise, it would have to be by tomorrow—the third day in a row I had been away—or Blue would give my spot, both on the street and in the room, to someone else.

But that night Shaker came home smiling broadly—a smile that looked out of place on his narrow face. He had secured a job for me in the library. I could start the following week.

I set the plate of biscuits on the table with a thud. "You did what?"

My tone made Shaker's smile disappear. "I said I was able to get you—"

"Did you think to ask me if I would like a job in a library? I haven't made up my mind as to what I plan to do next. You are very kind, but I've just stayed this long to get my strength back, as you suggested. I haven't made up my mind about anything."

Shaker stood there for a moment. "Haven't you?" he asked.

I fidgeted with the bread knife. "And besides, who would hire me without even meeting me? Who would hire a complete stranger?"

"I told my employer—Mr. Ebbington—that my cousin, Linny Smallpiece, the daughter of my father's brother, has come from More-cambe to live under my roof and is in sore need of a position." His voice had taken on an unfamiliar, cold quality, a quality that I recognized as indignation. Somehow it shamed me, although I refused to show it. "No, I told him when he asked, she has no letter of character, as she's spent her life caring for her invalid father, but I told him I could attest for you, and would assume full responsibility. I don't make a habit of lying, Linny," he said, "but I chose to lie today." And I felt even worse for my superior airs of a moment ago. I looked down at the crusty tops of the biscuits.

"Mr. Ebbington has put his faith in me. I have worked for him for seven years, my own position assured for me by my father before he died. He and Mr. Ebbington were good friends. The only truth in all of this is that my father did have a brother in Morecambe, although he died four years ago and had no children." His trembling had increased, moving up his arms so that his whole body now shook.

"What would I be expected to do?" I asked, after a long moment, meeting Shaker's stare.

"There wasn't even an actual position available, but Mr. Ebbington told me he had been thinking of bringing in someone with a fine hand to catch up on the recording of the books. Although I am responsible for overseeing that the ordering and receiving and placement of books is carried out properly, of course I can't write with my . . ."—he looked down at his hands with a hateful sneer—"with *these,* and although Mr. Worth, who is quite elderly, signs the books out for the members, there seems to be a problem keeping up the required recordkeeping. So that is what you would do—keep the records of the books up to date. *If,* of course, you don't find it beneath you."

I lifted my chin. His last sentence, and its tone, stung. "What is the pay?"

"A florin a week. Paid monthly, of course."

Two shillings a week. More than factory work, but not a whole sight better. And I could turn a far better profit in a few slow nights on the street. Behind me, a drop of rain fell softly on the grate, sizzling on the slow fire. The yeasty smell of the fresh biscuits filled my nostrils. The cold November rain ticked against the front windowpane, although the sound was muffled by the heavy closed curtains. The dining room was heated and fragrant with the smells of cooked food; although its furniture and fittings and floral carpets were well worn and had obviously been established in their positions for many years, somehow I found a deep comfort in this.

I imagined being out in this weather, waiting, hoping the rain wouldn't convince the customers inside the taverns and music halls to go straight to their warm beds and cold wives instead of having a quick one for less than the price of the carriage ride home. I thought of the putrid odor of the Scot in his fine brougham, of the rough, probing fingers of the fishmonger. I thought, with a queasy lurch, of raising the shears over the syphilitic lunatic's face on Rodney Street, of the press of the point of my folding knife into Ram Munt's throat under the gaslight on Paradise.

I thought of baby Frances, and the way her tiny curled fingers looked as if they were trying to hold tight. I never wanted to carry another stranger's child, knowing that should it occur again I would have to destroy it before it took a firm hold.

I thought of the tall sailing masts of the ships down at King's Dock, and knew I would never set foot on board.

I also knew I had fooled myself, as perhaps my mother had fooled me, with stories of being more than what I was, of expecting more than

I should. I knew I was giving up, but I was too weary, at that moment, to fight any longer.

"Fine. I'll take the job." The rain lashed against the window now, the accompanying wind creating a low moan around the sash. "Thank you, Shaker." And as I thanked him, I wondered when he would be coming to me for payment in exchange for what he was offering.

AFTER DINNER, Shaker asked me to come to his room, his eyes not meeting mine. I remained expressionless, nodding once. So the payment was to be immediate, then. His mother acted as if she hadn't heard his request. I wondered how Shaker would face her afterward, and also wondered why he didn't at least wait until she was asleep. I was surprised at his boldness and wondered how my healing flesh would accept him.

But I could never turn him down, no matter how often he wanted to take me. I owed him this much, at least.

When I followed him through the door he went to his desk and I straight to his bed—the same bed I had bloodied only a few days earlier—and lay on my back, turning my face to the wall as I hiked up the brown skirt. There was silence, and I looked back at Shaker to see why he hadn't begun to unbutton his trousers and come forward.

"No," he said, in a hushed, shocked voice, and I saw that he had turned scarlet, still standing by his desk. "No," he repeated, drawing his gaze from my uncovered legs. "I—I wanted to ask your help. By writing something for me. I'm unable to hold a quill, as you know."

I felt an unfamiliar heat in my cheeks, and knew that for the first time I was flushing as Shaker had, something I didn't know I was capable of. I twitched down my skirt and went to the table where a large book lay open.

"This is by Bernard Albinus," he told me, clearing his throat. His cheeks still held that high color but he spoke in a normal tone, as if he had not just seen my nakedness. "He was the most important descriptive anatomist of the last century. As well as the human skeleton, he's illustrated the muscles of the body and the complete system of the blood vessels and nerves. I've taken the book from the library an embarrassing number of times. If I could have a set of notes of the most pertinent areas of my study—those on the nervous system—I wouldn't have to keep taking the book out and trying to memorize passages. So I wondered . . . if you could write out the information I show you." He pulled out the chair for me.

"But won't your mother think . . . what will she think of me being here, in your room . . ." I left the sentence unfinished.

"Never mind about her. Much of her is no more than noise." He made the rough, clearing sound in his throat a second time. I recognized it, now, as a habit, when Shaker was uncomfortable. "She wasn't always the way you see her. I remember her laughing and enjoying herself while my father was still alive." His face softened, and his eyes took on a faraway look.

I tried to imagine Mrs. Smallpiece laughing, Shaker as a boy, and his father, the three of them sitting at the dining room table we'd just left.

"My father was a physician," Shaker volunteered, "although he did much more than simply prescribe drugs. He also chose to do the work of a surgeon, even though that was below him on the medical hierarchy. Instead of the expected—taking pulse and dealing with the hysterics and melancholy of the more affluent—he actually dealt with the body and all its frailities. He set bones, found remedies for skin diseases, performed surgeries at the infirmary. He sometimes allowed me to accompany him to the homes he visited and to listen and watch. That's where I found my love of the profession. He was a kind man, my father, knowing I could never follow his path but never speaking of it. He treated many of Liverpool's needy, usually for no payment but their gratitude. Because of that, my mother was forced to live a much more frugal life than she would have if my father had stuck to the physics for the wealthy and demanded his price. However, even though we live a fairly simple life, my father's reputation was such that my mother can still consider herself included in what she sees as the grander social scene."

"She's mentioned her friends," I told him. "I fear my presence has prevented her from inviting any of them to call."

Shaker smiled at me. "Don't worry about that. I'm pleased that she can still enjoy the small pleasures she knows as Dr. Smallpiece's widow, with her acceptance in that milieu, and the invitations she receives." He stopped, and in that moment I realized that in the short time I'd known Shaker, he had proven to be very much like the father he described.

"Shortly after my father died—seven years ago—my mother suffered that terrible apoplexy, and after that, she began seeking . . . God." He frowned, studying the illustration over his desk as if he'd forgotten I was there. "I've read of these cases more than once. It seems as if there is a connection between the two—the onset of seizures with the beginning of unnatural religious fervor."

I made a small sound, an acknowledgment, and he started, focusing on me once more. "I tried to help her. I followed all the prescribed medical treatments—restricting her fluid intake, giving emetics and purgatives. I even bled her frequently, trying to equalize her circulation. But none of it has helped. Although, as I told you, the fits are rare, at times her behavior is such that I hardly recognize her anymore." He sighed. "And you needn't worry about her demands on you. They'll stop. Nan, who has always done for us, as well as her daughter, Merrie, who looks after my mother's clothes and hair and any extra work to be done, will be back—my mother dismisses them both regularly for one infraction or another. Nan and Merrie stay away two or three days, long enough for my mother to miss them terribly, and then they simply show up again. Nan is quite used to the pattern and she and my mother understand one another."

I picked up the quill and dipped it in the ink. "What did you mean, Shaker, when you told me I was your sign?" I asked him, before I wrote the first word.

Shaker moved to the window, fussing with the curtain. "I had decided—that night in the Green Firkin—that . . ." He stopped, then continued. "I had decided to drink as much as I could, although I rarely consume much strong drink. When I felt that I had drunk enough to give me courage, I planned to go to—to the place where Frances is buried—so as not to leave my mother to deal with . . . things—and drink a potion of hemlock I had procured."

"Hemlock? Is it not a form of poison?" I knew I shouldn't have interrupted Shaker's confession, and quickly put my hand to my mouth.

From the side, I could see the corner of Shaker's lip lift slightly. "It is. I felt there was no purpose for me anymore. It seemed the cowardly way out, and yet I could think of nothing else but ending my miserable existence. I felt there was no purpose for me anymore. I had three emotions, as I stood at that dirty counter in the public house."

I waited.

"The strongest was self-pity. That because of my inabilities, I would never be the man I wanted to be. I would never be a physician or even a surgeon, the one thing I wanted to do—help people in that capacity. Although my work in the library is quietly fulfilling, it holds no . . . no passion for me. As well, my despair was also over the fact that I would never even know the simple pleasure of my own family—for what self-possessed young woman would be interested in someone like me?"

This surprised me. I had begun to see a quiet strength under Shaker's plain features, and in spite of his tremors, he carried himself with the utmost dignity. Surely he judged himself too harshly.

"The second emotion was guilt," he continued, "at leaving my mother on her own. But the self-pity won out over that. I had a letter written for her, one which I hoped would explain things, as well as instructions for her own welfare. I knew she wouldn't be destitute, as there is enough left by my father to comfortably support her until her demise. And I spoke to Nan, long ago, about the possibility—should I ever be unable to care for my mother—that she and Merrie move in and live here, caring for my mother as long as she lived, to which Nan agreed. She is a widow herself, and although my mother considers Nan much beneath her, there is nonetheless a strong and undeniable friendship between them."

He ran his fingers up and down the piping at the edge of the curtain.

"And the third?" I finally asked, when he had been silent too long.

"The third was one last tiny shred of hope. Hope that I would suddenly be shown why I shouldn't carry out my plan. I had been watching and perhaps waiting for something for over two weeks, from the time I had decided on my course of action. If there was something, some kind of indication—something that I could interpret as a sign, then I would ask for forgiveness for my bitter self-pity and go on with my life. And you, Linny, were that sign."

"In what way?"

"Because I realized I could help you."

A drip of ink fell onto the clean paper, and I watched it spread. "You mean because I'm a useless whore and you thought that you could justify your own life by changing mine into what you see as respectable?"

There was more silence and then Shaker's voice came low, in barely held back anger. "No. Because I thought—perhaps with doses of feverfew tea, mixed with a touch of rosemary, which I've read can be helpful in alleviating cramping—that the labor might stop. When I realized it was too late for that, I wanted to assist you and make sure you weren't forced to drop your baby in an alley, alone and like an animal, and then bleed to death. That's how I hoped I could help you, even if I'm not a physician or a surgeon. Just as an ordinary man who cared about the welfare of a stranger. That's how you were my sign. You enabled me to rise above the mire of my own self-absorption."

I bit at the inside of my cheek, where a small, hard lump had formed from this habit I had acquired of late. It had become something to concentrate on in order not to speak out to Mrs. Smallpiece, or when I was at a loss for words—as now.

And then Shaker came back to the desk and pointed to the passage he wanted me to start with, bringing the lamp closer. I began copying, in the best hand I could manage. We never spoke again of what he had just told me.

Chapter Thirteen

N AN AND MERRIE WERE BACK AT WORK, AS SHAKER HAD PRE-
dicted, within another day. I suspected that part of the reason Mrs.
Smallpiece greeted them so pleasantly on their return was not only so
she could be pampered in the style to which she was accustomed. I
deduced she wanted to be free to come and go on the social calls—the
luncheons and afternoon teas and church events—she so enjoyed. I
don't know whether she thought I might flee with the silver if left to my
own devices, but do know that she wasn't comfortable leaving me alone
in her home.

And when we were home together, that first week, Mrs. Smallpiece
tolerated me as long as I read to her from the Bible whenever she asked.
She had one bad day when she complained at length about her aching
joints, and on that day tried to get me to repent, to admit my wicked foulness and what she imagined to be my continued lustful thoughts. When I
stubbornly refused to bow to her demands for prayers for forgiveness,
she turned sullen and thumped my hands with her Bible, predicting my
lonely death after endless torturous suffering. She made it clear that her
Methodism had been a natural stage of her moral background, and it
obviously remained an intellectual and philosophical grounding.

I found it an easy task to accept her moods and helped her in the
same way Shaker did when she was seized with a fit upon awakening one
morning.

She was determined that I should improve my manners and decorum. She immediately began drumming the rules she felt were needed
to function as a proper young lady.

"If Shaker is allowing you to stay here—and it appears that you've accepted his completely unacceptable offer of lodging—you'll not be embarrassing me any more than you already have. I know there's no real hope for you"—here she sighed, the loud, gusty sigh of one badly inconvenienced—"but all I can do is try. Look at the way you're sitting."

I looked down at myself in Mrs. Smallpiece's cast-off dress. I was leaning into a corner of the horsehair sofa, my elbow resting on its arm, my palm supporting my cheek. My legs were stretched out and my feet comfortably crossed at the ankle.

"Sit up, girl. Straight up. Hands folded in your lap. Feet beside each other. You look like the slattern you are, lying about like that."

I straightened my spine, keeping my mouth tight. I clasped my fingers together and moved my feet so my ankles touched.

"That's better. Now stay that way for the next hour."

"What?"

"You'll say 'I'm begging your pardon, Mrs. Smallpiece?' And you'll stay that way until it feels natural. It's what every young lady should learn when she's no more than a babe."

"This can never feel natural."

"Maybe not to one born in a cellar and never brought up. But here in Everton, a lady knows how to behave at all times."

"I was not born in a cellar," I said. "And my mother did bring me up. I've also learned a thing or two about proper deportment along the way." But I also realized that no matter what I believed I knew, I recognized that Mrs. Smallpiece, for all her odd ways, had been looked after all her days, and only knew the life of a middle-class lady.

She sniffed at my argument now, went to the bookshelf, and pulled out two books which she deposited in my lap. One was called *An Appeal to the Consciences of Christians on the Subject of Dress,* and the other was simply entitled *The Proper Young Lady*. "Study the one on respectable dress on your own. But I shall expect you to read a chapter a day from the book on etiquette. Begin with chapter one; I shall question you on the items you've read each subsequent evening." She studied me and I remained immobile in the pose she'd demanded. "You must realize that your presence here has hampered my own entertaining," she said. "I cannot allow any of those ladies in my social circle to meet you until I can trust you will not humiliate me."

"I shan't humiliate you, Mrs. Smallpiece," I said, trying to keep the fierceness I felt out of my voice. "I can assure you of that."

Her expression made it clear she didn't believe me. "We'll wait and see, shall we?" she said, and turned and left the room, managing, even with her limp bombazine dress, to give the impression of a sweeping, imperious dowager.

When she was gone I shook my head in annoyance and relaxed into my former comfortable position, idly flipping through the books she'd dropped onto my skirt.

Nevertheless, I listened for her footsteps, ready to straighten my spine should she return.

AT HER SON'S REQUEST, Mrs. Smallpiece reluctantly took me to her seamstress and had three dresses made for me. They were all of the same pattern—with rounded neckline and center front-button closure. The bodice was fitted, with no boning, and the skirt wide and gathered into the waist. The only ornamentations were lace-trimmed nankeen collars with a dull sheen, a tiny strip of white lace and one crocheted button accenting each sleeve. The fabric was sturdy material, meant, I'm sure, to last for a good ten years. One dress was brown, one gray, and one navy. The dresses were disappointing in their fit and dull colors, but I thanked Mrs. Smallpiece with an enthusiasm I didn't feel.

Although she instructed Merrie to pin my hair into a severe mode, when the woman left the room I convinced the girl to adopt a more flattering and younger style. Later Mrs. Smallpiece eyed my soft ringlets but said nothing.

As I SET OFF with Shaker for my first day of work at the library, packed into a crowded carriage that ran regularly between Everton and Liverpool, my feelings swung wildly from nervousness to confusion. When we approached Liverpool's center, I knew none of the girls I had worked with would be out so early in the day. And, I told myself, even if we did pass one of them, it was unlikely she would recognize the plain brown bird in the crowd of other plain, respectable men and women on their way to work at their offices and shops.

I truly suited my name now. Never mind the linnet's voice, the beautiful variations on a tone. I had the true appearance of a female linnet, a common, small, and rather drab finch.

Had any of them—Annabelle or Helen or Dorie, or any of the other countless girls I had laughed or commiserated with over a bad customer—worried over me or missed me? Likely—at least for a day or two. And Blue might be slightly annoyed at having lost one of her hardworking girls. I imagined that by now, when I had failed to show up at the room on Jack Street or under the gaslights along Paradise, they would all simply assume the worst—that I had ended up as another murdered whore dumped someplace where no one would find her. Someone might have seen me getting into the carriage with the Scot, and that would be the last they knew of me. I had been warned, and had ignored the warning, and—just look at that, would you—she paid the price, didn't she, they would say. Would they mourn for me? Perhaps briefly, and some of them might raise a glass in my memory in the Goat's Head, but there were always girls, always someone waiting to slip into the place of one who had disappeared as easily as she had first appeared.

❋

WHEN MRS. SMALLPIECE finally felt I could be trusted not to embarrass her in public, she took me to church. Like Shaker, she introduced me as the daughter of her husband's brother—her niece—although the first time she did it, standing outside the church doors on a cold Sunday in December, I felt her arm trembling against mine through our thick woolen jackets. Whether her trembling was caused by anger at me for putting her in this position or simply because she knew she was sinning, I don't know. But to a woman like Mrs. Smallpiece, surely the sin of telling that lie—that I was a proper young woman, related through marriage—would, I'm sure, be less of a sin than having to admit that she was harboring a whore.

The minister, Mr. Lockie, who sported bushy, tangled gray eyebrows and had a nearsighted squint, also gripped my hand with an unnerving fervor as he welcomed me into his flock that morning after the service. After being introduced by Mrs. Smallpiece he studied my face intently. In all fairness, the intenseness may have been a condition of the squint. But I did indeed read something in his face, something similar to the expression Mrs. Smallpiece often wore when she looked at me—the hope of salvation through conversion that the Methodists so embraced. Did he pick up on my distasteful past and, like Mrs. Smallpiece, thrill at the possibility of saving an obviously needy soul?

The first social call she invited me on, first sternly reminding me that a blunder on my part could literally ruin her reputation, was to the home of her friend Mrs. Applegate. It was mid-December, with air so cold we could see our breath as we walked briskly to Mrs. Applegate's house a few streets over. After we were ushered into a parlor overheated by a roaring fire and the tightly packed bodies of a number of seated elderly ladies, I was introduced by Mrs. Applegate as Mrs. Smallpiece's "poor niece." Once the hostess had directed us to our seats, Mrs. Smallpiece nodded, almost imperceptibly, at my hands, reminding me I was to remove my gloves since tea was being served. She lost no time in making it abundantly clear that I had lived a sheltered life as my father's nursemaid in Morecambe, away from the company of others, and was unaccustomed to much socializing. "So please forgive her if she's slightly lacking in the convivial graces we pride ourselves on," she added, her neck rigid.

I accepted a small mince tart from the silver tray held in front of me by a young parlormaid smelling of perspiration, and deposited it on the decorated plate I held stiffly in my other hand. My mouth was too dry to eat; I knew I would choke should I attempt to take a bite of the delicacy.

The other women nodded sympathetically, having no problem eating tart after tart and drinking many cups of tea. One short woman with a nasty growth over her eyebrow shook her head sadly at Mrs. Smallpiece, as if she knew all too well the trial her friend was going through, attempting to cope with a young woman as feeble and dull-witted as Mrs. Smallpiece tried to make me appear.

Although my whole body burned with shame—for these pious, well-meaning women to think I was such a backward dolt—and also with anger toward Mrs. Smallpiece, I knew it would do me no good to take a stand and prove her wrong. So I lowered my head, studying the frilled edges of the tart. If I were to stay in Everton for at least a while, as had been my choice, instead of going back to the rough freedom of Paradise, I knew I had to fight my own instincts, to remain quiet and adopt a simpering smile. As I sat there, to calm and amuse myself I tried to imagine the expessions of shock and horror that would flood these women's faces if they could see the images that still burned so brightly in the front of my own brain, the ones of me with my customers, on my back or knees. For all their airs and graces, I knew that I surpassed these women in knowing more about life and the nature of men and women than they could ever, ever even begin to suspect.

And yet in spite of the silent games I played to survive these events, my head still pounded frequently with the effort of it, and the lump inside my cheek grew from the endless gnawing. I saw, in the gilt mirror in the room I shared with Mrs. Smallpiece, that a new line had appeared between my eyebrows.

THE COPY OF *The Proper Young Lady* grew tattered. I had most of it memorized after a few months. How tedious it all was: etiquette for the parlor, etiquette for social calls, etiquette for meeting acquaintances on the street, etiquette for introductions—there appeared to be no end to the rules and expectations. At times my head swam with trying to keep it all straight—when to remove one's bonnet and when to keep it on, likewise for gloves; never stooping to retrieve something that had dropped but waiting for a person of lesser standing to pick it up and return it; and especially—oh, especially, Mrs. Smallpiece warned me—the strict rules for dining.

"There is nothing so indicative of good breeding as manners at the table," she told me. "A lady may dress with style and carry herself on the street with dignity, and may sustain a decent conversation, but if she is not perfect at the table, dinner will betray her. While your manners—

although where you learned them I'm sure I don't know—are passable, they are definitely lacking in finesse."

Although wearisome, the lessons were simple things to learn when taken in small doses, and it pleased Mrs. Smallpiece that I responded favorably. As the months passed and I showed her that I was willing to follow her demands, she found less and less reason to berate me. Now and again I witnessed a small, tight smile cross her thin lips when I took over for her, pouring the tea and passing the sugar and cakes to callers on Saturday afternoons, or reading aloud to her in a pleasant voice from *A Family Shakespeare*—the only other book she was interested in besides her Bible. The book, the complete works of Shakespeare, had, by author Thomas Bowdler, been rewritten with all passages considered improper removed, so there was no fear of encountering any immorality.

Mrs. Smallpiece also took pleasure in watching me work on tiny, delicate stitches to decorate lawn handkerchiefs as we sat before the fire of an evening. In my hands, damp with the effort of this unfamiliar work, the fabric grew wrinkled and limp, sometimes dotted with tiny pinpricks of blood as the needle stabbed my thumb instead of the handkerchief. And although I found the work numbingly boring, it afforded me a kind of quiet, rhythmic monotony that allowed my mind to wander to places far from Everton.

Mrs. Smallpiece mistook my bent head as obedience; she thought she was converting me, and there is no one more sanctimonious than one who believes she has turned a sinner into a saint.

※※※

OVER THIS TIME Shaker viewed me as neither sinner nor saint, or perhaps as a little of both.

Not only did he never call me to his bed, he treated me with an oddly courteous respect. I knew he watched me when he thought I wasn't looking, and I could tell, from the startled embarrassment on his face and his sudden turning away, that at times he grew aroused being near me. But he never acted in any way but as a perfect gentleman, and although I suspected that his affection for me was growing, I also knew that I didn't know how to feel anything for a man. I knew men in one dimension, men like Ram Munt and Mr. Jacobs and the unspeakable man in the house on Rodney Street. It was a long and seemingly endless line of men, all alike. I knew Shaker wasn't like them in spirit, but still, I couldn't feel anything for him except a clumsy gratitude.

I had immediately loved my job at the library, surrounded by books, and felt a definite thread of connection between my life as a child, near my mother at the bookbinders, and the life here. Thoughts of my mother came to me often now, along with the comfort of clean paper, the smell of ink, the order of one page after another: it created a deeply soothing quality. I knew she would have been proud of my work. But this life, no matter how I looked at it, was a lie, a posturing and deception. I did not wear the pendant.

I sat hidden behind a high screen at a desk with my quill and ink and pile of books and recording cards all day, light streaming in from a small window on the wall behind me. I wasn't to come out into the public area while there were members about, Mr. Ebbington informed me, but as part of the position I would be allowed, like Shaker, to sign out books as if I were a member, once the library was closed for the day.

I waited for the closing of the library with anticipation every evening. The Argand lights on the polished and gleaming reading tables would be lit, sending soft shadows onto the graceful domed and pillared interior. There were scientific instruments and maps on display, as well as elegant long-case clocks and mahogany barometers. Under glass sat display books with their gold and silver clasps, their precious and valuable bindings in velvet and silk. The library collections, purchased or donated by its members, were wide ranging. I would wander through the sections—History, Voyages and Travel, Sciences, Government, Jurisprudence, Theology, and the largest section, Polite Literature—under which encyclopedias, heraldry, topography, poetry, drama, philosophical works, and novels and tales could be found. I paused among those quiet shelves and held books in my hands, inspecting their mottled or gilded edges, and ran my fingers over their covers. I inwardly rejoiced at the sensation of them, the cotton cloth with their ornamental characters, the embossed books with their patterns in relief, like cameos, and my fingers lingered especially on the costly and elaborate varieties of russian, moroccan, and calf bindings.

Every week both Shaker and I chose three books to take home with

us. While Shaker knew exactly what he wanted, searching out specifically those books dealing with medical science—although he also pro-
fessed an interest in history—my decision always took much longer.
Shaker would wait, reading one of his books, always patient, while I
roamed the aisles. At first he had recommended books for me, pointing
out volumes of poetry or drama or some of the gothic tales he had once
read and thought I might enjoy. But I had spent a long time reading
Polite Literature. Now I wanted books that would teach me ever more
about the world and its people. I found I was especially intrigued with
tales from the Voyages and Travel section.

"Do you not ever dream of taking a voyage, Shaker?" I asked one
evening, laying a book I'd chosen—Boswell's *Journal of a Tour to the
Hebrides*—on the library table. "There is such a huge world beyond
ours here."

He nodded. "I often thought of adventure when I was younger," he
admitted. "When my father was alive we would discuss all manner of
the world, its many lands and inhabitants. He did encourage me to
see more, and before his death I spent one summer in Paris at his urging. I was a little younger than you are now, and journeyed with two
other lads."

I sat down across from him, putting my elbows on the table and
leaning forward, twining my feet around the legs of my chair. I knew
Mrs. Smallpiece would go into one of her lectures if she were to see me
in such a definitely vulgar position, but she wasn't here. There was no
one in the upstairs library at this time of evening but Shaker and myself.
"What was it like? Was it as wicked as one hears?"

He smiled. "It was new and exciting. I felt quite alive. My friends
and I roamed about day after day, taking in the sights. One of my
friends is an artist; he did a series of sketches. He gave me some. I can
show you when we get home."

"Would you go back, then?"

His smile faded. "I think my days for adventure may be over." He
crossed his arms, tucking his trembling hands under them, a gesture he
did unconsciously when he spoke of himself. "And what of you, Linny?
Do you still dream of America?"

I shook my head. It seemed so far from here, farther even than it had on the streets. "I can't imagine it now, although I'm not sure why," I told him. "And yet . . ."

"And yet what?"

"There is something inside me, especially when I read these"—I put my hand atop the book that lay on the table between us—"that makes me feel unsettled. As if there is something, just beyond my grasp, waiting for me."

Shaker looked at my hand, my fingers caressing the moiré cover. Then he looked up at me. "I believe these longings are the feelings that accompany youth, Linny. But perhaps, perhaps when you . . . if you . . ."

"Perhaps what?" I prompted when he didn't continue.

He stood then. "Nothing. I sometimes speak without thinking."

"You don't," I said. "I've never heard you say anything that wasn't well thought out."

He gathered up his books, fussing with them now. "We'd better hurry or we may miss the last carriage."

I followed, wondering what he had been about to say.

⁂

ALTHOUGH I WAS NOT ALLOWED into the Club and News Room on the main floor of the Lyceum, which was for men only, I would peek in to the high-ceilinged room with its spacious windows facing Waterloo Place whenever I had the chance. Usually this was on my way to the basement to fetch more ink or paper, or to use the marvelous new apparatus in a room discreetly marked Ladies' Cloaks—a toilet with a flusher, operated mysteriously by one swift tug on a rope that hung from the wall. What a luxury! I often lingered in the lavatory longer than necessary, pulling the rope for the sheer pleasure of watching the water swirl to some distant and hidden place. I couldn't help but smile as I compared this method to my days of emptying the stained and chipped chamber pot out of our window and directly into the court on Back Phoebe Anne.

In the Club and News Room I saw men relaxing in the comfort of deep leather armchairs, enjoying a cigar and coffee or tea. Some read crisply ironed copies of the *Liverpool Mercury* or the wide range of other newspapers and periodicals available. Others quietly discussed the imminent arrivals and departures from the port. Many club members, I realized, were wealthy shipowners. A number of them had also been customers of mine at one time or another, although I had no concern of being recognized—or even noticed.

There was also a lecture hall with grand double doors on the main floor. Elaborately lettered signs, designed and produced by Mr. Worth, stood on easels outside the doors, advertising upcoming lectures on arts, literature, or sciences that were made available to members and their guests.

It was a beautiful, gracious place. Spending my days at the library and my evenings in the genteel house in Everton under Mrs. Smallpiece's strict tutelage, I knew the old Linny Gow was growing smaller and smaller, replaced by one who moved through the world with much more assurance. And how did I feel about the new person I was becoming?

I often felt a quiet sense of accomplishment, a warm glow that I might, after all, become the kind of young woman my mother had so often envisioned. And yet this was accompanied by a strange and troubling sensation of loss. I no longer shared the easy laughter and camaraderie of the girls on Paradise. I had become less spontaneous, more tightly reined. Perhaps I saw myself as less genuine. There can be no going forward, after all, without the look back over one's shoulder.

My life was becoming, I realized, both comfortable and predictable. I met Shaker's two friends, both pallid and serious but courteous young men, one of whom appeared tongue-tied in my presence. They accepted me as Shaker's cousin. Every fortnight they arrived at Whitefield Lane for dinner. The meal was always solemn and rather stuffy with Mrs. Smallpiece present, but eventually she would grow weary and retire to her room. Leaving Nan and Merrie to clear the table, the four of us would retire to the drawing room, and it was here, after Shaker and his friends had a few glasses of spirits, that the evening became informal. The more talkative of the two young men regaled me with stories of Shaker as a boy and I saw a mischievous side to Shaker those evenings that I quite enjoyed.

I kept my head about me, making sure I didn't get too caught up in the stories and laughter, aware that I had to stick to my created background. Shaker was very cognizant of this, too, I realized, often mentioning some fact about my fictitious father—his uncle—that made the story more true for me. There were odd and startling moments when I actually believed I was indeed a Smallpiece by birth.

I had, I told myself often, been given a chance at a better life, a life that anyone from a back court off Vauxhall Road would be eternally grateful for. I no longer had to spend long hours each night being cold or wet. I didn't have to squat over a chipped basin before the sun rose each morning, removing a slimy piece of sponge soaked with foul spunk. I didn't have to worry about being torn open by a man capable of growing to the size of a horse, or being bitten or slapped or pinched to help a customer grow stiff. My skirts were no longer urinated or vomited on by those reeling with drink, and my pay was given to me in a folded paper, instead of tossed onto the filthy street for me to scrabble for among dog dirt and gobs of shining spittle.

I had enough to eat. I had any book I desired at my disposal, and time to read. I had my own clean bed.

Why, then, could I not be content? Why then, did I continue to be plagued by despair, by thoughts that flew out beyond the Lyceum and the house on Whitefield Lane? My dream of America had died, and although it no longer held a fascination for me, I still imagined myself in an unknown life—completely different from one that Liverpool, with its fog, gulls, and gray shifting light over the stretching windswept emptiness of the water, had to offer. And I was restless and uneasy with my past, the old horror of what I'd done, the old troubling nightmare still haunting me from time to time.

Why could I not accept what had been offered by Shaker as a gift, be content with this life—no, this charade—as Miss Linny Smallpiece?

Chapter Fourteen

I MET FAITH VESPRY THROUGH CELINA BRUNSWICK.

Celina was dark haired and not extraordinary in any way, but her bright blue eyes fringed with heavy dark lashes had a certain attractiveness. Shaker and I were leaving the library one evening, about two months after I came to live with him, when we came upon her, walking arm in arm with her father down Bold Street.

"Miss Brunswick, Mr. Brunswick," Shaker said, stopping before the couple, tipping his hat.

"Good evening, Mr. Smallpiece," the young woman said and then she stared at me, two spots of color appearing high on her cheekbones.

"Hello, Geoffrey," the older gentleman said. *Geoffrey?*

"We haven't seen you about for quite some time," Miss Brunswick said, her eyes flickering between Shaker and me. "I am sure you've been missed at a number of functions over these last few months."

"Yes. I've been . . . busy," Shaker said. "Allow me. Mr. Brunswick, and Miss Celina Brunswick, it is my pleasure to introduce you to Miss Linny Smallpiece, late of Morecambe."

"Miss Smallpiece?" Celina asked. Her voice was cool as she took in my unfashionable outfit. She wore a long smoky blue pelisse—the color setting off her eyes—and her hands were hidden inside a fisher fur muff. Her hat had a matching fur trim. I knew by both the cut and the fabric of her clothes that they were expensive. "She's a relation, then?"

"My cousin," Shaker said, and the tightness in Celina's jaw relaxed just the tiniest bit. "She has suffered a loss—her father—and has come to live with my mother and myself. She works with me now in the library."

"She works?" Celina said, then graced me with a small smile, look-ing at the books under my arm, tilting her head and reading their titles aloud with a questioning lilt. "*Letters on the Improvement of the Mind,* by Hester Chapone? And Hannah More's *Search After Happiness?*" She raised her eyes to meet mine, a challenge in them that I didn't under-stand. "Very ambitious reading. May I take it that you are an admirer of the Bluestockings, then, Miss Smallpiece?"

I smiled uncertainly.

"My cousin enjoys a wide variety of reading," Shaker said, coming to my rescue. "I can't say that your choices apply solely to women of pedantic literary taste, do they, Linny?"

"No. Certainly not," I responded, careful to match my intonation to Celina's, although my throat was flanneled with nervousness. "Yet I must admit that yes, I do have a high regard for the Bluestockings' fearless-ness in flouting public opinion on the expected confines of the female. Oh—that appears to be our carriage," I added, as the carriage rumbled by. I wanted to get away from this woman with her superior air and crit-ical expression.

"Yes. We should hurry. It was a pleasure to see you again, Miss Brunswick. Sir." Shaker again tipped his hat.

Celina gave me a long stare from beneath half-lowered lids, and then the four of us parted company.

"She knew," I whispered to Shaker once we had taken our seats in the carriage and were heading in the direction of Everton.

"Knew what?" he asked, opening the cover of his own book.

"About me. She knew, immediately, that I didn't belong."

Shaker closed the cover. "Nonsense. You answered her admirably, if a trifle stiffly. Although she did appear less friendly than in the past. I've known her for over a year now. We were introduced at one of the lectures—on botany, I believe. Miss Brunswick is very interested in flora and fauna."

"She certainly appeared interested in me as well," I said, then added, "Geoffrey."

Shaker gave a wry smile. "It's my Christian name. But anyone who is comfortable with me calls me Shaker, as I told you."

"I think Geoffrey quite suits you. Distinguished," I said, opening my book to read for the rest of the ride home, but I noticed, before he turned back to his book, that he had colored.

THE FOLLOWING WEEK Shaker suggested that I stay after work that Friday and attend the scheduled evening lecture.

"I couldn't," I responded.

"Why not? As a member of staff you'll be allowed entrance. I'm sure Celina Brunswick will be there, so at least you'll know one person."

All the more reason not to go, I thought. "I've just . . . I've never attended anything like that." I thought of the lettered sign set up by Mr. Worth that morning. BUTTERFLIES OF INDIA, it announced, and then, in smaller, plainer letters underneath: All Members and Their Guests Welcome. "Would you come as well?"

He shook his head. "Neither India nor butterflies interest me. But it's something you might enjoy." His eyes traveled to the old bonnet of his mother's I still wore every day.

I knew I didn't look fashionable enough to attend the lecture. My clothes clearly announced my working position, and although they were passable for my job, I thought of Celina and her haughty look, her trim shape in the fitted pelisse.

"Think about it," he said.

THE FOLLOWING DAY Shaker rushed out at his lunch break, returning with a bulky paper-wrapped parcel. He carried it on his lap all the way home, his fingers spread out on it as if it gave him pleasure to touch it. Once we were at home in the drawing room, he handed it to me. I opened it; it was a gown and hooded cape. The gown was heavily figured amber silk with gigot sleeves tapering gradually to the wrist. There were scallops on the collar edge and skirt bottom. The cape was of a darker gold, and soft wool.

There was a muffled noise from Mrs. Smallpiece, who sat stiffly on the settee, her hands pressing her stomach. "Dyspepsia," she said, more loudly than necessary. "I had Merrie fetch me some caraway seeds today, but they haven't helped with the wind at all."

"I don't know if you'll like them," Shaker said, as we both turned from his mother, "but I thought perhaps for the lecture . . ."

I wished I hadn't hesitated before I spoke. "Of course. It's a perfectly lovely ensemble, Shaker."

"The woman in the shop told me you'd also need . . . the . . . others. Inside the gown." He wouldn't look at me as he said this.

I looked through the folds, a delicate powdery scent of lilac emerging from the gleaming silk, and found a set of stiffened petticoats, as well as small bustle pads to hold out the skirt from the waist.

"It's all too beautiful, Shaker," I said. "But I don't know that I should accept it."

"Just try the dress on, Linny. Please."

I did, realizing that it was indeed a wonderful dress. In my mind I compared it to Chinese Sally's dresses, and realized that in actuality those had been poorly made and had far less dignity than the figured amber silk. When I came down the stairs and into the drawing room Shaker stood, smiling, clasping his hands. "Fine," he said. "It's just fine. I knew the color would be a match for your eyes."

Mrs. Smallpiece covered her mouth to stifle a belch. "She looks perfectly respectable in her day dresses," Mrs. Smallpiece said, her voice waspish now. "You can't make a silk purse from a sow's ear," she added. "Why does she need anything new, anyway? You're only spoiling her. What she's paying for her bed and food isn't even enough."

"What do you mean, Mother? Paying?"

Mrs. Smallpiece's chin rose, but her voice held a tiny quaver. "I collected her pay packet from her for the last few months and I'll do so again at this month's end. It's only fair. There are no free rides in this world, especially for one such as her who should be eternally grateful to us."

Shaker stood in front of his mother. "You'll return that money to her," he said. "She earned it. And if I choose to buy her something to wear, so that she doesn't have to slouch around in the unflattering frocks of your choosing, it's nobody's business but mine."

I turned to study the plate rail as if inspecting it for dust, so that Mrs. Smallpiece wouldn't see my small but satisfied smile.

❈

I FELT SO PLEASED with my appearance in the new frock and cape that I did attend the butterfly lecture. Once there, however, my confidence fled, and I was horribly nervous as I made my way through the crowd. Perspiration gathered under my stays as I held my forced poise, thinking about every move I made, every murmured nicety. I spotted Celina sitting with another young woman, smaller and slighter. She had foxy red hair and dark gray eyes and was quite striking, her looks only slightly spoiled by a rather long nose.

As the crowd gathered around a table of tea and cakes after the lecture, given by Mr. Prinsep, an elderly and alarmingly florid gentleman, Celina stood across from me.

"Hello, Miss Brunswick," I said, trying to feel brave in my amber gown.

"Oh. Miss Smallpiece. I didn't recognize you," she said, not returning my smile. "Miss Smallpiece, my good friend, Miss Faith Vespry."

Faith gave me an open smile, and I noticed her gums. Her teeth were small and even. "So this is the cousin," she said. Her voice was high and breathless.

I saw Celina's elbow dig into Faith's side, but Faith appeared to ignore it. "Celina told me that Mr. Smallpiece had his cousin living with him now. How are you finding Liverpool? Where is it you're from? Was it Bristol?"

"Morecambe, Miss Vespry," I said, firmly. I was ready. As well as any of the information Shaker had passed on to me, I made sure I had read everything I could find on Morecambe and its history and had fabricated my whole past, including dates and places. I was thankful for my effortless ability to memorize.

"Do leave off the Miss. Just Faith. I know Celina thinks me so very common, insisting on being called by my Christian name. But I know we're going to be friends, don't you? Oh, I love the seaside," she hurried on, barely stopping to take a breath. "Is that charming tearoom—oh, what is it, the Archery?—still there? Mother and Father and I visited there only last year," Faith said, smiling so broadly that even more of her pink gums showed.

I was amazed, not by her openness but by how I'd managed to change myself in these last few months. Faith saw me as a contemporary, then, a young woman of a similar standing. "Yes," I fairly beamed, anxious to prove myself further. "The Archery is highly enjoyable; I've taken tea there, in the conservatory, a number of times." The lie came out so easily.

"Celina," Faith continued, her eyes not leaving me, "Miss Small-piece is not at all as you described. Not at all."

"Will you never learn to keep what you're thinking to yourself, Faith?" Celina demanded, a delicate pink staining her cheeks. She looked down into her full cup.

"Why don't you go and put some sugar in your tea," Faith responded. "It must be terribly bitter, judging by your expression."

Celina tsked in an annoyed way, then moved down the table.

"Don't mind her," Faith said. "She's not hiding it very well."

"Hiding what?"

Faith leaned closer. "Even though you're a cousin, Celina doesn't much like the idea of another woman living with Mr. Smallpiece."

I frowned, then understood by the way Faith had stressed *another woman*. "Ah. Miss Brunswick is . . . attracted to Shaker?"

Now it was Faith's turn to frown. "Shaker? That seems a cruel name."

"Oh. I must explain. It may appear cruel—an old boyhood slur that stuck—but it's what he insists on being called by those very familiar with him." I stopped. "And of course, me being family . . . it's only natural." I looked through the crowd at Celina, seeing her talking with little enthusiasm to an older woman. "Does Mr. Smallpiece know of her feelings?"

"Of course not," Faith said. "She knows there could be no hope of anything between them anyway."

"Why?"

Faith tilted her head. "But surely you must understand the situation. Celina's father would never approve of Geoffrey Smallpiece."

My lips pursed in annoyance. "Because of his affliction?"

"Poor man. He's quite hung on strings, isn't he? But that's not the most troublesome fact." She glanced around. "Of course it's all too delicate to discuss, don't you agree?"

"Yes," I said, but I didn't understand at all.

"Oh, heavens, I can't keep this mouth of mine quiet, as I'm sure you've seen by now. I do go on, don't I?"

"Well, I wouldn't—"

She pulled me into a corner. "How coarse of me to discuss financial matters. Please don't be shocked or disappointed with me. You're not, are you?"

I realized she was actually waiting for an answer. I could barely keep up with her conversation, jumping from sentence to sentence. "Disappointed? No, I'm not disappointed."

"Although I'm sure you've never met anyone quite so candid."

Now I just smiled.

"It's just that"—she looked over her shoulder and seeing Celina still involved in conversation, continued—"Mr. Brunswick is, of course, hoping to make a match for Celina that would benefit the family in all ways. There could be no hope of future advancement for either Celina or her family if she married a man like Mr. Smallpiece. Not only financially but also socially." She fanned herself with her gloves. I had not removed mine. "Heavens. If my mother were to hear me now I would be confined to my room for a week for speaking so."

Again I smiled. She really was very refreshing, but I enjoyed her company for more than that. I was still basking in the knowledge that she had assumed I was a young woman of the same standing and was speaking to me as such.

"You must be aware," she went on, leaning closer, "that your cousin appears to have little interest in taking part in any of the more important social events around Liverpool. Although he's certainly invited to a number of gatherings—his father was so well respected, after all, and the name Smallpiece is well received. And yet he doesn't care to take advantage of the standing his father left for him. Certainly you must know what I mean about him." She raised one eyebrow.

"I suppose I do," I said.

"I've heard he's very like his father before him, most charitable. Did you know your uncle well? It seemed that he was victim of unfortunate circumstances."

"Yes, he was," I agreed again, having no idea what the unfortunate circumstances she spoke of were and praying she wouldn't discuss it any further. Before I could change the subject Faith continued.

"And of course you have just suffered a loss. My condolences."

"Thank you," I murmured.

"What was your late father's profession, Miss Smallpiece?" she asked now.

A second of silence lapsed. "Please, if I'm to call you Faith, would you be comfortable calling me Linny?" I said. I was stalling for time. I couldn't believe I had forgotten to create a professional life for my supposed late father, or that Shaker had never once mentioned what his uncle did. "He . . ." I thought of the businesses and shops we passed on our way to the library, of Seel Street, which I'd walked down only the day before, and the images of Rushworth's and Draper and Seeger, both piano and organ manufacturers. "He owned his own business. Selling pianos," I said.

"Oh," Faith said, opening her reticule. "That reminds me. My mother often has musical evenings. We would love for you to come to the next one. It's a week from Thursday," she went on, handing me a calling card. "It must be difficult for you to meet people, spending all day closed up with books and then living way out in Everton, with Mr. Smallpiece obviously not trying to introduce you to society. I can't understand why he doesn't bring his mother and move closer to where everything goes on."

I tried to keep my face composed, smiling and taking the calling card.

"So. A week from Thursday," she repeated. "And of course your guardian will accompany you. It will be a surprise for Celina when she sees Mr. Smallpiece. I can't wait to see her face."

I murmured something, feeling suddenly weary. Although I was pleased at Faith's artless acceptance of me, it was hard work to try to keep up with her, needing to weigh everything I said so as not to appear a fool. Or the liar that I was.

"What did you think of Mr. Prinsep's lecture?" she asked then.

My shoulders relaxed. I had spent some time with a book on varieties of butterflies before this evening, in order to prepare myself. Now I felt on safe territory. "Some of his illustrations were beautiful, weren't they? I've never thought much about butterflies." At last. Speaking the truth. "And he made the country itself sound exotic and wonderful," I said. "I've never thought much about India, either, I realize. Quite grand, from what Mr. Prinsep recounted."

"He only told us the pretty bits. He's an artist, after all, and doesn't see the world as realists do. There are awfully wicked things in India as well as the beauty." Her voice dropped to just above a whisper. "They worship idols, and apparently there are friezes in the temples depicting . . . well, I can't speak of it. I've heard that some women swoon if they accidentally view some of the statues; they're that shocking. My brother's good friend is a lawyer in Bombay. He came home for a visit last year, and I listened in when he and my brother were speaking in private. Of course, he only told my mother and me charming stories, but I know better."

"Really," I said, pressing my lips together, trying to hold back a wide smile. Faith was perfectly delightful. In some tiny, ridiculous way she reminded me of my friends on Paradise—not that she was crude in any way at all; it was her forthright manner that was so refreshing. Or maybe I felt so pleased because Faith accepted me. She wasn't judging me or looking at me with any suspicion. She made me feel that I belonged here, that I had every right. And for this alone my gratitude was such that if I were Linny Gow, and not Linny Smallpiece, I might have hugged her.

"I sometimes think about going there!" she added breezily. "Don't you think it would be absolutely the most wonderful adventure?"

"I really wouldn't know," I said, anxious to keep listening to her, but Celina returned with the older woman and interrupted our conversation. The talk was steered into idle gossip, which held no interest for me, and I was aware of my discomfort returning now that Faith and I were no longer alone. I bade them farewell as soon as it was proper, and the doorman helped me into the hired carriage waiting to take me back to Whitefield Lane.

On the short journey my head swirled from the pretense of belonging, and from the excitement of trying to keep up with Faith's questions and comments.

That night, after I blew out the candle by my bed and stared into the darkness, I made out the shape of the crude painting over the oak dresser, and realized I'd seen a much more professional rendition among Mr. Prinsep's paintings. I smiled wryly to myself. The Taj Mahal at Agra. How much I didn't know.

SHAKER AND I went to the musical evening at the Vesprys' the next week. He took little persuading; gallantly, he invited his mother, but she declined, as I'd hoped she would. He looked very smart, wearing a well-cut suit of brown silk he obviously kept for such occasions.

The evening was pleasant. Shaker and I sat at the back of the Vesprys' drawing room, listening to the piano and harp recital. Later we were served small plates of pastries and glasses of sweet sherry. We shared the pastries, which were more delectable than any cakes I had ever tasted. I saw that in spite of Shaker's trembling he managed to eat and drink with only slight difficulty; I realized he had, in the past, been more nervous when alone with me than he was in mixed company. Later I brushed the crumbs from his lapels and his shirt front with its delicate ivory buttons, and we mingled with the crowd. I saw Celina watching Shaker, her face quite rosy, which improved her looks. Talking to Shaker so that he followed, I moved closer to her, until finally it appeared that she and I bumped into each other, although I had been fully aware that she, too, was moving toward us. The three of us spoke in a slightly stilted manner at first, but before long Celina and Shaker were involved in a conversation about the choices of the pianist. I left them and made a pretense of studying the family portraits in oil that were arranged along one wall of the drawing room, glancing back at the couple occasionally. From across the room I realized that Shaker was almost handsome, dressed so smartly, his long hair thick and shining.

Faith found me and introduced me to a man—Mr. Gerrard Beck—whom I assumed to be her suitor by the way she held his arm and smiled daintily at him, so that her gums remained hidden by her top lip. She introduced me to a number of other people whose names I promptly forgot.

Shaker spoke quite animatedly all the way home—of the music, the food, the company. He didn't mention Celina Brunswick specifically, but I felt a sense of pleasure in knowing that he had enjoyed himself.

I SAW FAITH a few days later, chancing upon her and Mr. Beck as they stood outside a shop on Bold Street, but both looked flushed and ill-tempered, as if they had been arguing, so I simply greeted them and then went on my way.

Another invitation arrived at the house on Whitefield Lane, this one for Mrs. Smallpiece and Shaker and I to attend a dinner party at the Vesprys'. This time, surprising me, Mrs. Smallpiece agreed. I sent back a reply in my best hand, stating that Mrs. Lucinda Smallpiece, Mr. Geoffrey Smallpiece, and Miss Linny Smallpiece would be pleased to attend.

There were sixteen people in attendance, including the Brunswicks. Faith seated me at her right. Shaker sat across from me with Celina on his left. Mrs. Smallpiece was farther down; beside her was a plain young woman who appeared to be a missionary, judging by her dress and her pious expression. I knew that Faith must have designed the seating.

The meal boasted a puréed soup, a saddle of mutton, and turkey in celery sauce. There were sweetbreads larded in a white sauce, as well as potatoes and kale. Dessert was an elaborate soufflé. I worried for Shaker about being faced with this meal in public but when I glanced at him, as we were being led to the table, he blinked his eye at me in what I realized was a wink. Was it an assurance that he was, after all, fine in these situations, or was it quite the opposite—him letting me know that he had complete trust in me to handle myself with the necessary decorum?

Faith and I spent much of the meal talking, although twice her mother glared at Faith, making it clear that she was to converse with others at the table. I saw that Shaker and Celina were also caught up in conversation. Shaker ate little, but it didn't appear that anyone else noticed. At one point I heard him laugh quite openly at something Mr.

Vespry said, and was shocked, realizing I had never before heard this sound. It made me smile.

AFTER THAT FAITH AND I spent more and more time together. I sensed she found it difficult to fill her days. She sometimes sent a note to the library telling me she would be coming in—her father was a member—over my lunch break, and we'd sit at my desk, behind the screen, to eat whatever she produced from her bag with the simple meal Nan had packed for me. Other times we simply walked up and down Bold Street for that half hour, arm in arm, glancing in the shop windows, neither of us particularly interested in the wares. It was more enjoyable to talk.

I grew to be comfortable with her during our time alone, mainly because with me she dropped her mindless chatter—obviously kept for the rest of company. Instead, she spoke of interesting topics—politics and her views on the Whigs, history, literature, the art movement, and so on, and asked my opinion and wanted to hear what I thought. She was clearly more well read and knowledgeable than she cared to let on in the presence of others; because I worked in a library it was obvious that she considered me of a different mind-set than her society friends, whose concerns ran to fashion and gossip. And, realizing, after that first evening of becoming acquainted, that Faith didn't seem interested in asking any more about my past—or, actually, my present—I relaxed.

Eventually I began to see that Faith, in order to conform to what was expected, was careful to keep her true self hidden most of the time. I also realized that she sensed this same careful cover in me, although the genesis of our similarity could not be compared. But for all of this I felt a begrudging admiration, as well as a growing sense of friendship.

SIX MONTHS AFTER our first meeting—it was a wet day in early June, and the rain had been coming down heavily for hours—Faith was in the sheltered portico of the Lyceum when Shaker and I stepped through the doors. She'd obviously been waiting some time; the hem of her skirt was dark, thoroughly soaked, and tendrils of deep red hair, curled by the moisture and bright with beads of rainwater, escaped from her bonnet.

"Linny, I'd like to invite you as my guest for dinner. Right now. I know we don't have a chaperone, and it's early, but could you come? I've booked us a table at the tearoom on Lord Street." Her voice was even more breathless than usual, which I attributed to waiting for me. Later I knew it to be something else.

I looked at Shaker. Obviously the unexpected invitation didn't extend to him.

"I know you don't think it proper, Mr. Smallpiece—two ladies dining on their own—but I assure you my parents have allowed me to come out. In fact, my father has just deposited me here. I'll see that she gets home safely afterward," Faith told him. "I'll hire a carriage. And we won't be late. I just . . . there's something I'd like to discuss with her."

"If she cares to join you and your parents have conceded, I will grant her permission," Shaker said, bowing slightly. When we were away from Whitefield Lane he slipped into his role as my guardian quite seamlessly.

"I'd love to, Faith," I said, meaning it. Her friendship had grown important to me. It was the only one I had, apart from my relationship with Shaker. And more and more I felt the weight of Shaker's obvious feelings for me too heavy, taking the shape of a burdensome yoke as opposed to a light cloak. I knew he was having difficulty having me so near, both at work and at home.

I now worried when I felt his breath on my cheek as he leaned too close in his room in the evenings, pointing out the work I still copied for him. I worried as I passed him a plate at dinner and his trembling fingers touched mine for longer than necessary; I worried at the pressure of his thigh against mine as we rode to and from work in the crowded carriage. I accidentally overheard him, late one night, quietly abusing himself as I silently passed his closed door and felt pity for him, and anger at myself for the suffering I caused him. Had he been another sort of man, I might have simply come into his room when his mother was asleep and allowed him to use me to relieve himself. For me the meaningless physical act would have created no more thought or sensation than a fit of sneezing. But then, had he been another sort of man, he would have claimed me months ago, whether it was at my bidding or not. And I also knew that he wanted more than a quick poke. It was clear to me, and had been from the first week of knowing him, that Shaker Smallpiece was not of the nature of most men; he would not take a whore or a woman outside of wedlock. I believe that until the time he met me he had accepted his celibacy with a studied grace. I had ruined that.

Many nights now, as I fell asleep, I tried to think of a way to not hurt him when he eventually must speak of his desire, for I knew he would not be able to withstand it much longer without some form of expression.

Chapter Fifteen

AFTER FAITH AND I BID SHAKER GOOD-BYE WE HURRIED ALONG, laughing as we attempted to stay under her bobbing umbrella. As we passed a deeply recessed doorway I saw a little girl huddled there, head covered with a thin, torn shawl. There was a bulge under the shawl at her chest that I took to be a sleeping baby. I stopped as Faith kept going.

She looked back at me. "What are you doing, Linny?" she called.

I dug in my reticule, glad I had a few pennies. I held them out to the girl and as her bare arm came from under the shawl, Faith was there, scolding over my shoulder.

"Don't give her anything, Linny," she scolded. "Don't encourage them to come up here begging." Her voice rang with contempt and yet I heard pity behind it.

The girl's arm hesitated, halfway between her own body and my hand with the coins.

"Do you have a baby there?" I asked. She looked to be eight or nine.

She nodded. "Me bruvver," she said.

"Do you have someplace to go?"

She nodded again. "But me mam's got a customer in the room; she sent me out till she were done."

Faith let out a tiny screech. "Heaven help us. Come away, Linny."

"Do you have any more spare coins?" I asked Faith, made bold by the shivering of the child, the stillness of the very small hidden baby under the shawl.

Faith opened her reticule and pulled out a coin. "That's all," she said defensively, as if I were accusing her of something. In her face I saw compassion but also fear.

I gave the coins to the girl, and as her hand closed around them, she pulled back into the recess of the doorway.

"Now hurry, we're getting soaked," Faith said and started to run. I hurried after her. The wind coming from the Mersey raced ahead of us, creating ripples on the surfaces of the puddles. Faith jumped over them as if she hadn't a care in the world, but I was suddenly heavy-hearted.

We arrived at the tearoom breathless, chests heaving from our run. Faith shook her bonnet like a wet dog, and a table of matrons near the door frowned. Faith laughed at their dour expressions, surprising both them and me. It was bad enough we had arrived unchaperoned, but to create a display was, I knew well by now, in breach of all etiquette.

As we were seated with our menus I tried to push away the image of that tiny pair in the doorway and what memories it brought back for me. "Faith? What is your opinion of that girl, the little thing with no hope for a future?" I asked.

"Opinion? Well, obviously the rich and poor—like good and evil—will always exist, won't they? It's as the Reverend Mr. Thomas Malthus expounds with his fears of overpopulation. The constant tendency of populations to grow faster than the means of subsistence is quite evident. That urchin, along with her mother—who contributes to the great social evil—must be accepted. My father, only last year, read Malthus's *Essay on the Principle of Population* and was quite fond of quoting from it often. Poverty and inequality are part of the God-given order of the universe, after all. It's a comfort to know that there is nothing to really be done."

"What if one were to try and change that order?"

"For one or for all?" she questioned, but then the well-dressed server came, and we made our choices and gave them to him. Faith leaned her elbows on the table, cupping her face in her hands. She was delightfully unladylike at times, while I stiffly attempted to retain an exacting decorum in public at all times.

"Let's talk no more of the unpleasant aspects of life," she said. "I have the most marvelous thing to tell you, Linny, and you must just listen, because you may think me mad at first. And, by the way, I do not have my parents' permission to be here and was daring enough to come to the library on my own. They believe me to be reading in my room."

I smiled as she confessed what she imagined to be a daring escapade. I thought of the roast lamb with mint sauce I had ordered. And Apple Hedgehog for dessert. I knew that the few pennies we had given to the girl would buy her a hot jacket potato, perhaps two, if the stall keeper was in good humor.

"It's this. I've decided I simply must go to India."

"India? What—"

She held up her hand. "Just listen, remember? As I told you, ages ago, it's something I've been thinking of." She fidgeted with the lace edge of her napkin. "My life feels stalled, Linny. I'm filled with . . . ennui, I suppose. I have my moods . . ." She stopped, her eyes suddenly blank, as if seeing something inside her skull.

"Moods? We all have moods, Faith," I said, but she didn't appear to hear me. In the next moment she shook her head and focused again, a big, tight smile pulling her lips back from her teeth. It was almost a grimace.

"And my father says I can go, as long as I have someone to accompany me," she continued. It was as if she wasn't aware of that lost moment. "Of course there will be a number of chaperones on board ship, married women going back to their husbands after bringing children home for schooling, or simply from a visit, but he won't hear of me going off without a companion." Her words were rushed.

"I have to interrupt," I said when she paused for a breath. "Why are you so interested in India?"

Faith looked around the slowly filling room, then waited as the server set down our bowls of leek soup floating with morsels of parsley dumplings. When he had left, she lowered her voice and leaned across the table. "To be frank, Linny, Liverpool has so little to offer in the way of interesting men."

"But what of Mr. Beck? Gerrard. He seemed very pleasant. I sensed—"

She dismissed my words with a trifling wave of her hand. "Oh, he decided to take a job down in London. We parted ways a few weeks ago. I suppose I forgot to mention it." But there was a hint of desperation about her voice that belied her flippant attitude. "And as I said, thinking about it, the choice of suitable escorts in Liverpool has become thin of late."

I thought of all the men I had known in Liverpool. She was probably right, although our opinions were based on quite different impressions.

"In fact it's becoming quite distressing. I'm sure you don't mind if I speak so openly about my . . . difficulties."

I knew, by various things Faith had said, that she was almost twenty-one. Her time for finding a husband had come and was almost gone. She had another year left, at the most. I nodded.

"And although you've still time, I don't imagine you've had the opportunity to meet too many eligible young men." She took a small spoonful of her soup. "First nursing your father, and . . . now. Your life with your aunt and cousin. It's not terribly exciting, you must admit."

I didn't reply, but she didn't appear to notice.

"So I've decided that I must go to India to meet a suitable man." I noticed her upper lip had the tiniest quiver as she attempted a gay smile. "If you were to join me, Linny, there's a very good chance you would meet somebody as well."

My mouth remained open, my spoon partway between the soup and my lips. I closed my mouth and lowered my spoon. "Join you? Did I hear you correctly, Faith? Do you mean join you in traveling to India?"

"Yes. Couldn't you just imagine—'the delightful Miss Vespry and the enigmatic Miss Smallpiece, both late of Liverpool, arrive in Calcutta in the gentle breeze of the cool season.' It sounds like a yellowback novel, doesn't it?" She had grown ever more excited, her voice quite loud now.

I put one finger to my lips to remind her that others were watching. "India, Faith? It's too much—too much for me to even imagine. I must have time to think, to—"

"Oh bother, Linny," she interrupted. "What is there to think about? Wouldn't you rather have an adventure than sit behind that screen at the library? And again, it's almost certain you would meet someone suitable."

I decided the truth—for this one moment—would be best. "Although India sounds outrageously exciting, if you must know, I'm not particularly interested in marrying right at this moment," I told her. *Or ever.*

Now it was Faith's turn to open her mouth in surprise. Then she snapped it shut. "What do you possibly mean? What else *is* there for women like us but to marry well?" she asked, confused. "What else?"

I had no answer. "What about Celina? I'm surprised you wouldn't have asked her to go with you."

"Celina isn't interested. We did discuss it, briefly, but she knows her heart already belongs to another. Even if it isn't reciprocated." She widened her eyes. "You *know* of whom I speak. But she remains hopeful and just has no interest in leaving England."

I realized at that moment that Faith must have solicited all of her unmarried friends. I was the last, her final, desperate hope.

"And your family agrees to send you?"

"Oh, yes. At least Father does. Mother is less certain, but Father thinks it's a fine idea. He has a number of friends who work for the East India Company's civil service—and understands these things better than Mother. Actually Father is intending to travel to Calcutta late next fall, but I don't want to wait that long." She hesitated, then continued. "It would be the wrong time to arrive if I waited for him. The best time of all—the season for entertainment—is the cool season. If I wait for Father it will be the end of the season and that won't do me any good at all. Dear friends of Father and Mother's—Mr. and Mrs. Waterton—have extended an invitation to host me and a companion. We could stay with them as long as . . . as necessary."

I knew she wasn't finished by the way she played with the engraved handle of her knife.

"I do believe that Mother would prefer I *didn't* marry, although of course she would never admit to that. But I know how she depends on me. She's not well, you know, and I have only two brothers." I thought back to the events at Faith's home, remembering Faith's pale, oddly bloated mother.

"So I think Mother envisions my caring for her for as long as she needs me—which I feel would be until her last breath. And well meaning as my mother can be, and not disputing that I *do* care about her—with all my heart—the idea of growing old as a spinster in that house, fussing over her, is not how I see myself. I want a chance at my own home, Linny."

In the moment of silence that followed, I almost heard the unspoken *before it's too late.*

"The British men in India outnumber women three to one," she went on. "And there are all sorts of events—luncheons and dinner parties and balls and soirees—it would be impossible not to find someone. And although India might not be the place one wants to live out one's life, there are all sorts of reasons to come home again. Oh, say you'll think about it, please, Linny." She reached across the table and I took her hand.

She lowered her voice. "I don't want to insult you," she said, "so please don't be offended. It's not difficult to understand your situation, and I know that if you were to say you'd come with me, my father would pay for a round-trip ticket as well as a suitable wardrobe and anything else needed. He would, of course, clear it with your cousin, as he is your guardian. And once we're there we would stay as guests in the home of the Watertons, who are more than happy to entertain young women from home, full of the English news they've been missing." She stopped to take a breath, then rattled on.

"I've been finding out everything about it. The journey can take anywhere from four to five months, depending on the weather. It would be terribly exciting, sailing away, around the African cape. The sights one sees! Sometimes the ships have to drop anchor at strange places, if the ship is blown off course. And the last port of call before Calcutta is Aden. Did you know that the natives at Aden have shocks of red or yellow hair? Why is that, do you think?" Her voice rose again. She appeared unable to control herself, throwing her hands about. Diners at other tables were once more surreptitiously watching, and I saw several speak behind their hands, their eyes on Faith.

"And in the warm waters of the Indian Ocean there are whales and porpoises that leap alongside the boat, as if performing for the passengers. Imagine, Linny!" In the next instant she slapped her hand to her mouth. "I'm so sorry," she said from behind her palm. "I can tell by your expression that I *have* insulted you with my overly forward offers with regards to finances. I'm too impossibly brash, I know that. Father suggests that's why no—" She stopped.

But Faith had misinterpreted my expression.

Unexpectedly, and for the first time in my life, I understood the meaning of seduction. For if Faith Vespry was attempting to seduce me with her words, she had succeeded.

Over our soup, she touched the dead dream, the one I had so carefully buried all those months ago along with my wee Frances. She had touched it, and it left me weak and trembling. It wasn't offense Faith was seeing on my face, but awakening and hunger.

THE MOST DIFFICULT ASPECT of leaving Liverpool—no, perhaps the most difficult thing I had done in my adult life—was telling Shaker I was leaving. I asked him to walk with me, a sunny Sunday a few days after my final discussion with Faith on our plans. Shaker and I wandered along a wide dusty road lined with hedgerows just outside of Everton. A large spreading elder grew near the side of the road, and I stopped there, in its shade, and told Shaker about Faith's invitation and how I wished to go. I told him that Mr. Vespry, after receiving Shaker's permission for me to accompany his daughter, would make every necessary arrangement for me to travel to India with Faith, and to be hosted while there.

He was stunned. It took a full moment for him to digest this, and then respond. "You're leaving?" he finally said. "Leaving Liverpool? Leaving England?" *Leaving me?* I thought I heard, although he didn't speak those words.

"Yes. There's a ship, the *Margery Ellen,* sailing in just over three weeks' time. It will take us around Africa, all the way to Calcutta."

"But that journey takes months. And it's dangerous. India itself is dangerous. What will you do once you're there? When do you plan to return?"

"I don't know, Shaker. I don't know what will happen when I'm there. I only know I can't let this opportunity pass. Thinking about it has given me the old feeling, the one I had about leaving here and traveling on a sailing ship, as I told you I planned since I was first on the street."

There was silence, and then something in Shaker's face shifted. "The Fishing Fleet, is it?" he asked, his jaw clenched.

"I don't understand." I found it difficult to look at him; emotions were openly playing across his face. It was as if I were seeing him naked.

"Nobody speaks of it, but it's well known, Linny. Desperate women making the long voyage in the hopes of finding someone to marry them."

I shrugged. "Well, you're right, then. That's what Faith is doing, without saying as much. I'm simply accompanying her."

"And you, Linny? You won't be putting on your best airs—the new airs, the ones you've learned while living with me—to find a husband as well?" His voice carried an undertone of cruelty I didn't know he possessed.

"Shaker. Can you really think that of me?"

He half turned so that only his profile was visible. "What else am I to think? Isn't your life here comfortable? Do you want for anything?"

I realized it wasn't cruelty at all. It was pain. "No." I was ashamed. "No, you've given me more than I ever thought I would have. A home, a position that I enjoy, security. And you ask for nothing in return. I know I'm selfish, Shaker, but I want to go. I'm sorry. You've given me everything, and yet—"

"I could give you more, Linny." He turned to face me suddenly, his voice rising, and my heart plummeted, for I knew what his next words would be. "Marry me," he said. "Please. You make me feel like I've never felt before, like I never dreamed possible." He took my hand, and his was damp. "I do love you, Linny. You must know that."

I looked down at our hands, joined and trembling.

"I don't think you love me, Shaker. I think I . . . perhaps I excite you, perhaps because of what I was. Of how you've seen me, and of what you know I've done." I was choosing my words carefully, trying to make him see that if he had taken me, as many times as he needed to, he would have burned me out of his dreams and imaginings. How could a man who had only done good love me, dirtied as I was by my past?

"What you were has nothing to do with it," he argued. "It's the way you make me feel. You brought me back from self-hatred. You showed me I could feel like a man." Then, as suddenly as he had taken my hand, he dropped it and stepped away. Now his face was ashen. "Oh. Of course. All I've spoken of is the way you've made *me* feel. I've completely ignored how I might have made you feel. But now I see. All I inspire in you is pity."

"How can you say that? I may have pitied you, for the briefest of hours at the beginning of our time together, but that was gone when I watched you and listened to you—not only your compassion toward me, but with your mother. I see you with your friends, and the members of the library, and at social events—and even with shopkeepers. I have nothing but admiration for the honest and truly caring person you are."

He shook his head in annoyance. "How could I not have seen, all this time, that the way you smiled at me, your many small kindnesses to me—they all meant nothing more than gratitude edged with pity?" He backed away.

Of course he saw it clearly, and I had no argument.

"I was so lost in my own discovery of joy, Linny, that I didn't even stop to consider yours. Forgive me." And he turned and walked stiffly toward the thick copse of trees along the side of the dusty road, and I had to admire the proud set of his shoulders.

He didn't come home until long after his mother and I had gone to bed. I couldn't sleep, worrying about him out in the dark somewhere, but eventually heard him coming up the stairs. His footsteps were slow and heavy. They stopped on the landing and I held my breath, thinking he would open our door, unsure of what he would say or do, or how I would respond. But then there was the quiet sound of his own door opening and closing, and nothing more.

✻〰〰

SHAKER DIDN'T COME TO WORK with me the next day. His mother came downstairs, telling me that Shaker had asked me to report to Mr. Ebbington that he'd caught a fever. "He's never missed a day of work. Never," she told me, her eyes and mouth softened with concern, and at that new look I caught a glimpse of the person she might have once been.

"Shall I go to see if he needs anything?" I asked, rising from my breakfast.

"No. He asked not to be disturbed," she told me, and I sat down again, pushing away the plate Nan set in front of me, suddenly unable to swallow.

I spent an anxious day at work, but when I returned Shaker was waiting for me in the street when I departed from the carriage. My heart beat harder at the sight of him—relief and anxiety. The sky was low and gray. It had rained earlier, and now the eaves of the buildings around us dripped with a steady rhythm. "Are you feeling better?" I asked, although of course I knew that his reported illness had not been physical.

"Walk with me," he said, and boldly took my hand and put it on his arm with a firmness that I had never felt before. He looked pale but resolute as we went to a nearby sweet shop with a few tables in one corner. It was a well-scrubbed place, its floors gleaming and brass polished. It was empty of customers. We ordered tea and slices of hazelnut cake.

"I've spent the last twenty-four hours sorting this out," he said, as soon as we were seated. "I'm sorry for my behavior yesterday. I'm quite ashamed."

I had to close my eyes for a second before I could trust my voice. "Please, Shaker. It's not you who should be ashamed. It's me. I'm sorry. I just . . . I don't feel anything, and don't think I ever will. Not for a man." I tried to think of a way to describe what had happened to me, inside, but I didn't know the right words.

"People rarely marry for love, Linny. They marry for companionship, for financial convenience, for security. For convention. I'm not convinced love plays that large a role for most."

I waited, in case he had more to tell me, but his mouth closed in a firm line. The only sound in the shop was the quiet *clink* of a wooden spoon beating something in a bowl behind a curtained doorway.

"I'm going to India, Shaker," I finally said, quietly. "And I believe I do love you. But not as a wife for a husband. I also believe that if I *were* able to love a man in that way, you would be that person."

His Adam's apple moved in his throat. "Then I must accept that, and be satisfied with it, mustn't I?"

We sat in silence across from each other, our tea growing cool.

"But will you promise me something? That if things don't go as you hope in India, and you have to return to England, will you come back here, to me?"

"I've told you, Shaker, I can't——"

Shaker didn't let me finish. "Not to marry me. I understand that, Linny. You made your feelings clear, and I will never ask you again. But if you ever need a place to stay, or you simply need a friend, I'll be here, always, and I'll help you in any way I can."

I reached across the table and laid my hand against his cheek. "How do I deserve you?" I asked. "Someday you'll find someone far better than I, someone who can love you in the way I can't. And you'll forget about me, as you should."

The cake lay untouched between us. We sipped at our tepid tea, but before we finished it we rose, as if by agreement, and went out onto the street. The sky had cleared, the clouds lifted, and the summer air was heavy and fragrant. The sound of children playing in the distance floated toward us. I put my arm through Shaker's and he put his hand on mine and we went slowly, surely, with no more words, toward the house on Whitefield Lane.

⟿

THAT NIGHT I WENT to his room. His eyes were open, facing the door as I came through it, almost as if he were waiting for me, although I had given no indication that I would visit him. It crossed my mind that perhaps he had waited for me other nights, even though he had acted, the first time I presented myself to him to thank him—in the only way I knew—as if he could not lower himself so.

I knelt beside his bed in my thin nightdress, stroking his brow. And this time he did not turn away. This time he sat up, pulling back the coverlet, and I thought, then, that perhaps my old whore's ways might never leave me, that I would always be willing to offer up my body. But in the next instant I felt a strange rush of confusion—for suddenly I saw that it was not just me offering him a part of myself in gratitude, but the other way round.

I pulled my nightdress over my head, allowing him to see me in the moonlight. He drew one deep breath and held it. I settled myself beside him, and he expelled his breath in a long, shaky exhalation. We lay, facing each other, eventually breathing in unison. His bedshirt smelled of carbolic soap. When I kissed his mouth it smelled faintly of parsley, a clean and refreshing smell. My own mouth had been violated in so many ways, but I had never kissed anyone before. The feel of his lips on mine was pleasing.

Slowly, gently, although trembling violently, Shaker tightened his arms around me, his lips responding to mine, and I felt him against me, ready, with only that brief, sweet contact.

I turned on my back, pulling him atop me, and used my own hand—for his quivered too terribly—to guide him inside me, and lay very still, my bent knees hugging his hips. Within a short time his body ceased its uncontrollable shaking, and then, slowly, as if with a former familiarity, we moved together. His cheek, as he lowered it to mine, was wet with tears.

Afterward he was still, completely still, in a manner I had never witnessed. It was as if his trembling had, temporarily, flowed out of him along with his physical release. And my throat constricted, aching, as I watched him sleeping on my scarred breast, his lashes damp. He was a man of honor, to be trusted. He would keep me safe.

And I knew, with a sad certainty, that safety was not the only thing I wanted.

Chapter Sixteen

I WATCHED AS WE SAILED AWAY FROM LIVERPOOL. I SAW THE GRAY smoke over the factory chimneys. Under my feet, the deck tilted. I smelled metal and steel—the anchors, chains, clamps, hasps. The scent of tar brought back the image of Ram Munt and his hands.

My own hands held the railing, wet with fog. My heart pounded; I was sailing away, sailing, as in my dreams, from the place that had brought me mainly misery. *This is not my true life,* Chinese Sally's words rang in my head. And now I was sailing toward a new place, what must be the beginning of my true life.

I watched the chimney pots of Liverpool grow small. I thought of Shaker, the light limning his body as he stood on the dock, one hand lifted in a final farewell.

August 1830

My dearest Shaker,

It is over a month since we left Liverpool on this tall-masted frigate, and today is my birthday. Today I am eighteen, and to celebrate this occasion I am writing to you. I know this letter cannot be posted for months, but I am feeling a strange sense of loneliness tonight, and the act of putting quill to paper always comforts me. I daily record this life aboard ship in my journal— the one you gave me as a parting gift—but tonight I felt inclined to address my written words to you. This is the first let- ter I have ever written.

I have taken to the life at sea as if I had been born to it. How strange; as I write this, I think of my stepfather's words. Because my arm bears the mark of a fish, he often told me I was the daughter of a sailor. Of course I didn't believe him; my mother's story of my noble father is much more compelling, and it is the one I will always believe. And yet my feeling aboard this vessel is that the sea—in all its strength and mystery—does speak to me in a language I understand.

The accommodations are cramped and less than clean; we are below deck, in a room separated from other women by strung canvas. There is little light or air; the doorway opens into the steerage. Faith and I share our tiny cubicle, with its bucket behind a suspended piece of calico, with a large, whey-faced woman of indeterminate age, Mrs. Cavendish. She has lived in Delhi for fourteen years and has made this voyage a number of times. After a visit home, she is now returning to her husband, a general in the Indian army. Because of her seniority, Mrs. Cavendish chose the bed nearest the door. Faith and I are relegated to string hammocks. Although Faith appeared crestfallen at sleeping in a sling bed for the next number of months, I secretly love the way my hammock swings with the rock of the waves, and, so cradled, feel the unraveling of the tangles of my former life as I drift to sleep each night.

I am learning card games—whist and piquet and ecarte and lanterloo. I simply decline joining in when asked until I've observed each game enough times to be confident of the rules. Occasionally there is dancing on board as well, and I take these opportunities to ensure I will be able to conduct myself without embarrassment. Do you ever dance, Shaker? I don't recall you mentioning.

To date I have perfected the minuet and the quadrille, and know my *dos-à-dos* and promenade. I sail from partner to partner—although most of us are women!—on those evenings when the sea is calm and some of the passengers can be persuaded to bring out the instruments they have brought—violins and clarinets and violas—and perform.

Do you know, Shaker, that most people are too much about

preening and being watched to observe others? This has been in my favor while acquiring these needed skills before we arrive in India. It is all Faith chatters about on her good days—the dances and salons and evenings of cards we would attend. Even she doesn't seem aware that I am a novice at these things, although I have come to see that Faith is, like many of the others, one who enjoys being watched, and doesn't always observe keenly that which is around her.

We take our meals in the dining room, and are enjoying the luxury of fresh meat because of cows and sheep brought on board, as well as root vegetables that are still plump and tasty—although I don't see how much longer they will remain fresh.

For much of the time during these first weeks on the gray Atlantic I have wrapped warmly and spent many hours on the deck, either sitting on a bench and studying the books on India Faith and I have brought—the customs, the weather, and learning what I can of Hindi—or else walking briskly, stepping over coiled rope and stacks of chain, breathing in the cool salty breeze and marveling at the endless furrowlike swells of the metallic waves.

I am sorry to report that Faith has grown wan, sighing and constantly warning me that I am looking far too ruddy-complexioned from the wind, and that I should spend more time below, resting, as she does. But I have spent enough of my life in small, foul-smelling quarters.

I am filled with strange optimism, Shaker, an odd, cheery nudging that is unfamiliar. I am pleased by it. I do hope you are keeping well, and visiting with friends and accepting social invitations. It's important that you spend time with others.

Yours,
Linny

September 1830

Dear Shaker,

I trust you will read these letters in order, as this one, written three weeks after the first, will tell a very different tale of my life aboard ship. Although the sea is still my ally, it has shown its other face.

Fooled by the even waves and steady wind giving us good speed for our first month, Shaker, I imagined the rest of the voyage would be uneventful and easy. But a storm blew up on our sixth week at sea. The sky grew dark and ominous mid-morning, the wind whipping and cruelly cold, and by afternoon the waves had transformed into huge jagged crags. Sitting in the shifting dining room, we were advised by the gruff captain to retire to our cabins and lash ourselves to our beds until it had blown over. Faith turned to Mrs. Cavendish immediately, her mouth open as if confused. Dear Mrs. Cavendish, who has taken us under her wing, tried to console her. "I've seen many a storm, my dear," she said. "They get even worse as we round the Cape. Usually it's possible to ride them through."

"Usually?" Faith replied, the color around her mouth and eyes edging into a delicate yellow-green. "You mean . . . does a ship ever—" She couldn't finish the sentence. I stared at her. Had she really not considered the possibility of dying en route to India, Shaker? Of the ship overturning in a storm just like this one? Of pirates, in the warm Indian Ocean, attacking the ship and looting it for the passengers' goods, possibly killing anyone who got in their way? I had thought of all of these eventualities—and more—although they held little concern for me. But Faith . . . for one so clever about some things, about others she is woefully naïve.

Mrs. Cavendish murmured into her ear, patting her arm. "We'll get you some Jamaica gingerroot; that will help settle your stomach for at least the next little while," she said comfortingly, and the two of them, supporting each other on the sliding floor, lurched out. But I had to stay for just a few more minutes and watch, through a porthole in the dining room, what was happening to the ocean.

It was the landscape of a monstrous dream. The waves had become sheer cliffs rearing up in front of us and we rode up, up into that face and then plunged, sickeningly, down its other side, only to be faced with yet another and another of the seemingly endless walls of water. A deckhand, seeing me being thrown violently from side to side while hanging on to the brass rail that ran around the wall of the dining room, shouted at me, cursing, and I managed to get down the gangway and to our cabin, my clothes thoroughly soaked.

The storm was terrible but—as I am here to write about it—I survived! And, as you can see, I am now quite enjoying recounting the drama of it all to you. I never believed myself one for drama. Perhaps it is the freedom I feel that is loosening it within me.

Mrs. Cavendish is bullying me off to bed, so I shall obediently retire.

Yours,
Linny

I didn't wish to describe to Shaker in too much detail what happened during that first storm. It was, if nothing else, rather indelicate, not the sort of topic one who is attempting to be a cultured young woman should think of transcribing on paper.

When I had finally stumbled downstairs during the storm, Faith was in her sling bed, a number of scarves and shawls tied around her middle and knotted into the ropes of the bed. She moaned steadily, a low, sonorous cry, and just as I was flung onto my own hammock she angled her neck over the side and vomited, a huge splashing puddle of reeking yellow. I secured myself in my bed, heart pounding as I heard muffled, weak cries all around me, my initial excitement at the wildness of the storm being replaced first by apprehension and then by growing panic.

During the next hours I questioned—for the first time—leaving

Liverpool and the safety and security of life with Shaker. Breathing in the stink of tar and vomit and bodily expulsions, unable to hear anything but the crashing of waves and howling of the wind, I lost track of night and day. I was shaken about in the complete darkness, imagining with every bang and groan of the timbers that the icy water would surely burst through, filling my nose and mouth, drowning me as I lay lashed to my hammock. I lived in my old nightmare of cold water closing over me, of drowning in the Mersey, for what felt like days. Alternately I gasped for breath in the airless room or shivered, my clothes damp from my own sweat. I was convulsively sick, my stomach and bowels emptying where I lay. My voided body continued to heave until I tasted the metallic heat of blood on my lips, knowing the lining of my stomach was being torn away.

I longed for Whitefield Lane, for Jack Street, even for Back Phoebe Anne. I kept my eyes squeezed shut and waited to die; in fact, I believe that for indescribably bereft moments I wished for it. There has only been one other time in my life when I felt this close to death.

EVENTUALLY I BECAME AWARE that I had been asleep and was now rocking gently. I opened my eyes and saw that the door was open and secured by its hook to the wall. Dim light filtered into the disastrous, foul mess of our room. I heard Faith's voice, pure and high as a child's, and realized it was this that had woken me.

"Linny? Answer me. Linny?"

I twisted to look toward her hammock. I saw that Mrs. Cavendish's bed was empty, stripped of its sheets and blankets. "Where is Mrs. Cavendish?" My voice was a hoarse croak, my throat raw from vomiting.

"She went on deck to wash her bedding. I don't think I can move."

I feebly plucked at the scarves and shawls that had stopped me from being pitched to the floor and tossed about in the slime like a pebble, then sat up, grimacing at the pulling of the soiled crust of my undergarments. I stood, shakily, my rib cage and abdomen feeling bruised from the endless contractions of my empty stomach. Helping untie Faith, I gave her a half-smile. "Aren't we the pair, though? I think the only solution is a bucket of saltwater dashed over us."

"Don't joke, Linny. I'm too weak to even cry. I don't think I'll ever recover from this."

"You will," I told her.

"You're awake, then, girls," came Mrs. Cavendish's booming voice from the doorway. "Come on, change all your clothing and get it and your bedding up on deck, and we'll get this place cleaned up in no time. Now, that storm wasn't as bad as some I've seen. Once our ship was hit astern, and the force of that water burst over the deck and right below, straight into my room. I can assure you I make a most becoming mermaid." She gave a hearty laugh. "And I can also assure you that storm won't be the last on this voyage."

Faith erupted into sobs, and it took us a good ten minutes to help her compose herself enough to rise.

❦

ON THE WEST COAST of Africa our ship was blown off course by another storm; this one sent us close to Brazil, and took us another three weeks to resume course. During this time I studied my Hindi and wrote in my journal and continued writing unposted letters to Shaker.

We had been at sea for three months. Now the food had lost any semblance of being enjoyable; the only meat left was preserved pork, tough and stringy and salty. All sense of order had left the dining room; food was thrown unceremoniously on the tables and whoever had the stomach for it that day reached out and grabbed. The water had turned the color of strong tea and tasted as bad as it looked and smelled. The heat grew intense, and we stripped off our woolen dresses and wore light muslin—until we approached the Cape of Good Hope, where the weather once again grew chilly. As we neared that imaginary line where the Atlantic Ocean meets the Indian, we saw ourselves in danger of being dashed against the shore when a sudden shift in the winds caught the billows in a dizzying rush. We stopped briefly at the Cape for new supplies and then were off into warmer waters. But we were soon caught in a seasonal hurricane. The ship lurched and pitched; this time, furniture was torn from its fastenings. Although I silently prayed for the ship to withstand this battering, my body did not betray me, and when at last a day and night had passed, I arose, dry-eyed and calm, shrugging my shoulders at Faith, although she would not smile.

We sat becalmed for two weeks in a still sea under a blazing sun, the sails limp, their rents and tatters now visible. No one had the energy for talk or cards, and the heat made the thought of dancing incomprehensible. The only sound was the teasing lick of the water against the ship's side, and the answering creak of its timbers. The sea looked like a silver plate, untarnished, hard and immobile. The crew was surly, muttering as they repaired the canvas and frayed halyards, casting irritated glances at the passengers who stepped around them in an endless circle of the deck, hoping for even the whisper of cooling air.

And then finally, one morning I awoke to movement, and when I went up on deck, the sails were unfurling, reaching for the wind. The sea was smooth and yielding as the ship cut through it. I felt such a rise in my spirits that I smiled at the most taciturn of the deckhands, the one with bulging forearms and tattoos that shifted with the movement of his muscles. Only the day before he had eerily reminded me of Ram Munt. Now he bore no such resemblance.

It grew even more unbearably hot, and we moved our bedding up to the decks. The ladies slept on one side, the gentlemen on the other, and a sail was rigged between us for decency's sake. That first night on deck I couldn't sleep. Carefully stepping over Faith and the other women, I went to the railing. Standing in the dark, I watched the sea as it reflected the moon, creating a long, winding road of silver. And then the water began to glow with a strange brightness I could not describe, as I know no words for that kind of light. It was as if myriad tiny candles blazed just under the water, as if they floated there, beckoning. I watched, transfixed, until my eyes hurt from the intensity of staring. Was it some underwater creature? Or was it another sign, a sign that this was my true path?

During the day the Indian Ocean was filled with life: flying fish swept past us like narrow silver coins, and, as Faith had predicted, whales and porpoises raced alongside the ship. The sun was clean on my skin, burning deep, seeming to warm the very marrow in my bones, and I wondered if I had ever before been truly warm. As I stood on deck one day, closing my eyes and turning my face toward the glorious burning disk overhead, I realized that I had not had my nightmare for many, many nights—perhaps weeks. It was as though this sun—infinitely stronger than anything possible in England—had burned that terror out of my brain, had eaten into it, destroying it, just as surely as the bold rats scurrying below deck had eaten holes in our clothes.

There was a sudden spray of warm water over the railing. It wet my face. I licked my lips, savoring the ancient, wild taste of the sea. As I did so I turned to the young couple who stood down the deck from me. They had married just before we set sail and were traveling first to Calcutta and then overland to Bombay, where the man had a position with the East India Company civil service. We'd exchanged pleasantries a number of times; now I imagined we would smile, sharing the humor of the unexpected shower we'd all received. But in the moment that I looked toward them, I saw that they were lost in each other, unaware of me. The young man lowered his face and slowly licked the salty water from the tiny hollow at the base of his new wife's throat, and she put back her head and arched her neck. In that instant I felt shock, a deep thudding and sobering emotion. The girl's slight movement and the look on her face brought me down from my moment of giddy hope. That soft and yielding expression, I realized, could only be desire. And I also realized I had never known or felt it, and for this I was filled with sorrow and grieved, suddenly losing all fascination with the sea. It now appeared nothing more than a wearying, endless distance of furrows.

❋

WE DREW INTO NOVEMBER; we had been at sea almost four months. Swallows swooped near the railings, indicating land nearby. Mrs. Cavendish likened these busy, twittering creatures to the dove with its olive branch. But she was right, and within another day villages were spotted along the coast. The water became noisy with dozens of tiny rocking boatloads of Indians. Bumboat men, Mrs. Cavendish called them, shouting to be heard over the cries of the villagers as they boasted of their merchandise, hoping to sell coconuts, bananas, or tamarinds. I hung over the railing, watching as the natives threw ropes with baskets attached over the ship's side. Some of the crew called down to them in a strange tongue that I couldn't identify, putting coins into the baskets. The baskets were lowered, and then came up again, filled with whatever the sailors had requested. I longed to try the strange-looking fruit, but Mrs. Cavendish, with a slight shake of her head, indicated that it would be beneath us to purchase anything in this way.

During the last few days, as we grew ever closer to our destination, excitement grew in me. At first I attributed it to the beauty of the water and sun, the flying fish sending little droplets of water onto the smooth sea, but then realized it was something else. I detected a difference in the atmosphere, and whether it was in the air itself or the degree of heat I couldn't say. Perhaps the smells carried in the wind contributed to the unexplained breathlessness I experienced. My nose filled with the strange smells of an unfamiliar populace, the scents of unknown vegetation. I felt as heady as I had when twirled in my first quadrille.

❦

WE STOPPED AT THE SANDHEADS, at the mouth of the Hooghly River, to wait for the tide to help push us into the river. This last leg of the journey, Mrs. Cavendish cautioned, was very hazardous. Traveling the sixty miles up the dimpled, belching brown water of the Hooghly as it cut through the green Bengal countryside had proved disastrous for many ships because of the dangerous sandbanks and suddenly shifting shoals. "Hundreds of lives lost on one sandbank alone, the treacherous quicksand of the James and Mary," she went on, unmindful of Faith's expression.

Faith had not done well on the journey. Like all of us, she had lost weight. There were new hollows under her eyes and the lines around her mouth had deepened. I had tried to do what I had been brought for—as a companion, to offer company and support—but Faith had grown sullen and uncommunicative. It seemed she had receded into herself while I felt myself growing stronger, more able. I felt as if I had even grown taller, although I knew that was impossible.

"Look, Faith, look there. Palm trees and banana as well, just like in your book," I said, trying to cheer her with the vision of emerald lushness a few hours from Calcutta. There were waving fields of rice. Everywhere the color was so vibrant, so alive. England's watercolor pastels paled in comparison. I gazed idly at a dog on the riverbank, noticing its pathetic protruding ribs and horribly scabbed flesh. It was busily tearing at something surrounded by bits of rotted blue cloth, and I realized that the dog's prize was a human leg and foot at the same time as Faith. She emitted a high, strangled cry, running from the deck. As I made to follow her, Mrs. Cavendish laid her hand on my arm.

"Best let her be," she advised. "India takes some hard. Some never get used to it. And others"—she puffed out her chest, reminding me of a pouter pigeon—"why, others simply do the best they can and are the better for it. Fourteen years—and just look at me. I've survived it all— fevers, heat, monsoons, birthing—two buried in India and three alive back home—heathen customs, snakebite, to say nothing of the things I've seen—stabbings in the market, executions of *thugees,* suttee. Although suttee was deemed forbidden last year. Not many like me, though." She studied me. "You think you have what it takes?"

As I nodded, she shook her head. "Better start learning, then, Linny. Not even a parasol and, I must say, you're quite unfashionably colored from the sun and wind."

THE SHIP FINALLY STOPPED, midafternoon, just before the shallow waters of the docks at Chandpal Ghat. The date I had written on the final page of my voyage letter to Shaker that morning was November 18, 1830. As I looked toward the docks, all I could make out was move- ment, a swarming mass of humanity. The waters were filled with every kind of vessel—fishing boats, rafts, dhows, ferries, and lorchas—so crowded that they chafed at one another. I thought of the coasting brigs and cutters and schooners in the thick fog at the harbor at Liverpool, drawing comparisons to these small vessels, manned by near-naked brown-skinned men.

The outskirts of Calcutta surprised me. Facing the river were white Palladian villas, elegant and stately, owned, Mrs. Cavendish told me, by British merchants grown rich on the East India Company's trade.

After I'd fetched Faith from the cabin, where she sat forlornly in her sling bed, and, remembering Mrs. Cavendish's warning, taking my parasol, we climbed down a rough rope ladder into masoolas—small rocking boats that ferried passengers to shore. The boat pitched and yawed in the brown water, and we held tightly to its sides. Dirty water sloshed over our boots and drenched the hems of our dresses.

Faith had been told that we'd be met by Mr. Waterton, her father's friend who had agreed to be our hosts for as long as we remained in Calcutta. I was actually glad for my frilled pale blue parasol as I sat between Faith and Mrs. Cavendish, watching the crowd swell on the pier as we crossed the short span of water. Voices rose in shouts, cries, and chants.

"Do you see your husband, Mrs. Cavendish?" I shouted into the woman's ear, realizing it was a foolish question. How could anyone discern any one thing in such a throng? Everywhere brilliant colors swarmed; I had to close my eyes for a moment to sort out what I was seeing. Women's saris of bright pinks and oranges and reds, carts heaped high with unfamiliar fruits and vegetables. Dark faces under white turbans. As we drew closer to the pier, I raised my head, breathing in scents that I couldn't identify but was sure, from my reading, must be jasmine and sandalwood and the tang of cloves and ginger. But there was something else. Underneath it all lay a fetid, cloying odor, urine and dirt and decay, a deep smell of rot that I recognized from the seeping cellars, flooded each year, crowded with the most desperate of families in the meanest courts in Liverpool.

We were lifted on to the dock, and the mass of brilliance I had seen from the masoola now became real, and in detail that belied the dreamy beauty I had assumed from the distance. We stood in the dust and heat and babble of the tumultuous crowd, our boots soaked through, trying to say our good-byes to the passengers we had come to know so well over our journey, shouting over the added noise of a tinny band playing to greet the ship. I found it difficult to stand on land after so many months on the rolling sea. My knees felt as if they were still dipping and balancing, and there was a listing in one side of my head. I felt a pressure on my ankle and looked down, thinking it was my body playing tricks on me as it adjusted to land under my feet. But it was a young woman— little more than a girl, really—kneeling at my feet, holding an emaciated naked infant with one arm while her other hand held up a dented tin bowl. Her mouth was moving, but in the terrific gabble surrounding us I couldn't understand whether she was actually speaking or crying or praying. I had no Indian money yet, no rupees or annas in my reticule to give to her, and I smiled uncertainly, pointing at my reticule and shaking my head. But she appeared not to understand, her mouth growing wider. I saw now, with a shock of recognition, that the child's head, which I assumed was covered in black hair, was actually swarming with flies. As the girl shifted the baby in her arm to pull at my skirt with a filthy hand, I saw the tiny scalp to be a mass of running sores. I swallowed, trying to step away from the tugging on my skirt, feeling a tiny ripping at my waist as the girl held tightly to the thin fabric of my frock. I saw that the handful of flowered muslin she gripped was now darkened with dirt, and I knew that the gauzy material on my back must also be growing dark as sweat dampened my torso.

As I continued to pull away, Faith, who stood beside me, looked down and saw the girl and what she held, and her legs gave out. I hooked my arm through hers to hold her up, struggling with my parasol and reticule, feeling, momentarily, a small flutter of panic as I once again looked down at the pathetic creature attached to my skirt. My stays were suddenly too tight, I was too hot, I found it difficult to breathe, and the multitude of strange odors now turned my stomach.

And then the pointed end of a parasol appeared at the girl's ragged shoulder. The parasol—which I recognized as Mrs. Cavendish's—gave the girl a sharp poke. She dropped my skirt and scurried away between trousered legs and flowing skirts.

I tried to drag Faith along. Her skin had the color and consistency of parchment paper, her hair a bright flame around it. Mrs. Cavendish followed, carrying Faith's dropped reticule.

The dock was smothered with human forms: men in the ragged loincloths I knew from my reading were called *dhotis*, carrying bundles on their heads as they pushed their way through the throngs; sweetmeat sellers shouted as they hawked their wares—from water to hot fresh tea to betel nut; beggar children with huge, beseeching eyes screeched, holding out their hands; mangy yellow dogs barked. Everywhere brown-skinned men and women and children sat and stood and wandered about, some eating, some sleeping. It was a mass of moving, jabbering, stinking humanity. My lightheaded listing grew; I had never swooned, thinking women who did to be weak. But suddenly I feared that the immensity of sights and sounds and smells, and the bright heat that encased my body, might squeeze me, like a giant fist, into a limp and senseless being. I took deep breaths, biting down hard on my back teeth to drive away the hazy sense of disconnection.

A series of high squeals rang out above the general cacophony; the urgency of it made me search out this new source of noise. My head cleared at what I saw.

A man on a rich chestnut horse with black mane and tail sat high above the people on the hard-packed dirt and rock of the pier. Man and beast were caught in the shifting, restless crowd, and the horse whinnied in distress, lifting each foot and setting it down, panic in its rolling eyes. The man called out in a loud and demanding voice, but I didn't know whether he called to his horse or the milling throngs surrounding them. He pulled with swift, upward tugs on the leather reins as if to steer the horse in another direction, but the beautiful gleaming animal kept throwing back its head, tossing its thick mane. I knew that if it should rear, the heavy hooves would surely come down on a foot or even a child. The man, seemingly huge on the horse, had long black hair oddly similar to his horse's mane. His white teeth shone in his sun-darkened face, and I could even see the ebony glisten of his long eyes. He suddenly leaned forward, dropped his head, and appeared to speak into the horse's ear, which was pricked forward.

Immediately the creature stopped its frantic head tossing and stood as if mesmerized. They looked as if they had been chiseled from one piece of magnificent stone, and finally the crowd thinned enough for them to move forward. The rider slowly edged the horse along, never glancing down, his eyes fixed on some distant spot.

"Who was that?" I asked Mrs. Cavendish, my arm still tight through Faith's. She sagged against me.

"Who, dear?" Shielding her eyes, Mrs. Cavendish scanned the crowd.

I pointed. "That man. The tall one, on the horse." Whether it was unrealized exhaustion from the journey and the excitement of docking, or the forgotten feel of solid earth under my feet, or the confusion to my senses, or a combination, something about seeing that man on his horse—so alone and distinct in the crowd of hundreds—had somehow settled me.

Mrs. Cavendish followed my finger. "A Pathan—not one of the Indian people. The Pathans are from the northwest frontier, way up beyond Peshawar, on the border with Afghanistan. They fairly often ride down into India to trade horses. Wonderful riders, the Pathans— or Pashtuns, as they call themselves. Rule most of Afghanistan, the blighters. Proud, they are, even noble, I suppose, but the Indians are a bit leery of them. And their women are just as fierce, mutilating their enemies and all that nonsense. Odd, actually, to see one this far south."

"A Pathan," I repeated. "A Pathan from Afghanistan."

"Thank goodness," Faith said, weakly. "Look. That man, with the sign with my name on it. Yes, it's Mr. Waterton."

Mrs. Cavendish and I hugged good-bye, and then I followed Faith as she cautiously made her way through to Mr. Waterton, her shoulders so high and tight I thought they might touch her ears. Mr. Waterton greeted us formally. He was a small man with thinning hair and a twitch under his left eye that made him appear to be continually winking. He'd brought a palanquin for the ride to his home. We climbed into the litter, with its wooden rods and tattered curtains around all four sides. It was carried by four brown men wearing very small, dirty loincloths. Faith was flustered as she climbed into the palanquin, trying not to stare at the men and yet stealing glances at them from beneath her lashes. We sat beside each other on one of the hard wooden benches while Mr. Waterton gave instructions for our luggage, which had been piled beside us on the pier, to be taken in a second palanquin. Then he climbed in and drew the curtains on all sides before sitting across from us. I had the immediate impression of going blind after so much color and activity.

"Oh, please, Mr. Waterton, could we leave the curtains open? I'd like to see Calcutta."

He looked shocked at my request, shaking his head, frowning.

"Of course not, Linny," Faith said. "I'd feel so unsafe, with all those prying eyes, and who knows what diseases might be hovering right outside, in the air. I just want to get to the Watertons'. And not only that," she said, primly, then put one hand to the side of her mouth and whispered behind it. "We'd be staring right at those men. They're nearly naked, Linny."

I sighed, sitting upright on the splintered bench. We lurched as the men picked up the poles and started off at what felt like a trot. While trying to keep my balance, I listened to the bedlam outside the swaying curtains, wishing I could see what was going on just an arm's length away.

"A Pathan, from Afghanistan," I said to myself.

"Pardon me?" Faith inquired.

"Nothing important," I told her. "I was just remembering something."

Chapter Seventeen

WHEN WE STEPPED OUT OF THE PALANQUIN, I SAW THAT WE had come to one of the massive white Palladian villas I had seen from the ship. It was set back on a wide street, which I was later to learn was called Garden Reach. The entrance and portico of the house were transformed into a porte cochere, and this is where we stood now, under the roofed structure that protected us from the sun.

Faith squeezed my arm. "Isn't this the most wonderful house, Linny?"

I was disappointed. I don't know what I expected, but it wasn't a huge and elegant one-story home more extravagant than any I'd ever seen in Liverpool. I turned to see Mr. Waterton sullenly sorting through a pile of coins in his hand. He and one of the palanquin bearers were having a dispute. The man in the ragged dhoti was holding up five fingers, while Mr. Waterton shook his head and held up three. The bearer's voice grew louder and louder, and eventually his companions joined in, creating a high-pitched clamor. Finally Mr. Waterton threw a number of rupees and annas to the ground and turned his back on the men scrabbling in the red dust.

I felt sickened at the sight. Only a year and a half ago it had been me on my knees in the dirty wet streets, collecting my pay.

"Mustn't let them get the upper hand," Mr. Waterton said, looking pleased with himself as he wiped his hands on a large checked handkerchief he pulled from inside his jacket. Then he removed his solar topee and thoroughly scrubbed his glistening forehead and scalp, ruffling what remained of his lank brown hair. "You ladies will get used to wearing one of these," he said, holding out the pith helmet. "We have to protect our brains—they can actually be fried, become quite liquefied, you know. Infernal sun. Our skin isn't thick enough; just not made for this country."

The second palanquin arrived with our luggage, and by the time it was unloaded Mrs. Waterton had come out of the villa, holding a parasol and welcoming us with a kind smile to what she called our "English home away from home." We went inside, and she gave us a dizzying tour of the whole house. My head spun; I was in India, but in the quick and cursory walk through the rooms the furnishings belied this. It was as if I had stepped into a superbly decorated English house. Except, of course, for the brown servants who hovered in every hallway, in the shadowy corners of every room, some waiting, expectant, other moving along the walls with lowered eyes. There was the sensation of being in a giant hive, a sense of humming, of activity and purpose. I could tell from the widened look of Faith's eyes that she was finding it overpowering as well.

"My poor girls," Mrs. Waterton finally said, stopping for breath. "You must be exhausted. And I'm sure the filth and noise of the docks was upsetting. I tend to forget," she repeated. "I've been here too long." She smiled again, and this time the smile was not as pleasant. "Far too long," she said a second time. I would later learn that this tiresome repetition was her manner of speaking. "I'm sure you were frightened and intimidated today. But don't worry. You will not have to witness more sights like the ones you saw. You are safe now and will remain so. Come, I'll take you to your rooms. There you may wash and rest, and at dinner I'm sure you'll feel more like yourselves. We have another young lady, newly married—Mrs. Liston—staying with us as well. She's been accompanied to a dinner elsewhere; you'll meet her at breakfast tomorrow. Now, off you go. I'll send for you when dinner is served."

Faith and I nodded in unison, and after Mrs. Waterton had left me in my room beside Faith's, I stood with my back against the closed door and looked at the four-poster double bed set in the middle of the large open-raftered room, mosquito netting rolled up along the thin wooden frame that was supported over the top of the bed by the four posts. There was a cloth stretched across the top, like a canopy. I thought, briefly, of the beds I'd known—the tiny pallet on Back Phoebe Anne Street, the single mattress I'd once shared with two other girls on Jack Street, the flock mattress in Mrs. Smallpiece's room on Whitefield Lane. I'd never even seen such a spacious, thick-mattressed bed in the finest hotel rooms I'd been taken to in Liverpool.

There was also a rosewood escritoire, a full-length pier glass, a small dressing table covered with bottles of lotions and perfumes, a washstand with a large bowl and pitcher, a deep wardrobe, a chest lined with drawers, and two padded chairs upholstered in flowered fabric. The open window was covered with screens of woven grass, rolled down from the ceiling, obliterating the view.

Overhead, a large rectangular frame of light wood covered with white cotton swung back and forth, stirring the still air. I realized, with a start, it was being operated by a boy sitting cross-legged in a corner, the string from the fan attached to his big toe. A small woman, all in white, squatted in another corner. I looked at the boy and the woman, opened my mouth, but didn't know what to say.

The woman rose and wordlessly came to me, undoing the row of buttons on the back of my dress, still damp with sweat. I stood help- lessly while she said one word to the boy, who took the string off his toe, parted the window screens, and slipped out. When she had pulled off my dress and bodice and corset and petticoats and I stood in my che- mise, she took a sponge from the washstand, and dipping it into cool, rose-scented water, began to slowly, almost languorously, wash my face and neck and chest and arms. I'd never been touched like that by another woman—by anybody, not since the man I remembered only as Wednesday when I was a girl. The pale hair on my arms stood at the unexpected attention, and I felt a drowsiness steal over me in the warm, quiet room. Then she gently pushed me toward the bed, and I obediently lay down on it. She covered me with a thin sheet of muslin, let down the mosquito netting, spoke another word, and the boy returned.

I lay on the huge, magnificent bed, listening to the creak of the fan—which I remembered was called a *punkah*—and the woman's soft humming.

None of the books I'd read on board had prepared me for this grandeur amid the squalor I'd seen on the dock. My head ached and I closed my eyes.

❈

DINNER WAS TOO LONG; tedious. On the way to the dining room with Faith—following a male servant who had tapped quietly on my door— I took the opportunity to look more closely at the house. Although its decoration was English, there were also several things that showed we weren't in England. The ceilings were not enclosed, but open rafters. There were punkahs in every room, and much of the flooring was not wood, but cool stone. I saw a small table whose legs had been made from the curling horns of some large animal, and vases of flowers such as I'd never seen sat on many surfaces. There were animal skins on the floors and animal trophies on the walls; I saw umbrellas in a stand that looked like—yes, it was—an elephant's foot.

Faith and I entered the rather gloomy dining room with its profusion of heavy, dark furniture. The table was covered with a thick, white cloth, and ferns and vines had been laid across it. All the food for dinner was being placed on the table at one time by a tall, imposing man with a hennaed beard and a very high turban.

My heart sank as I surveyed what we were expected to eat: a shoulder of lamb, some type of fowl, sliced finely and swimming in a gluey gravy, a huge bowl of something mashed that vaguely resembled the texture, but not the color, of potatoes, three bowls of vegetables that I couldn't identify, and thick slices of heavy dark bread. My stomach was bloated and uneasy from both the heat and the suddenness of being thrust off the ship and into this strange, contradictory environment, and the ache in my head had not been lessened by the time lying on the bed. Discreetly looking up when I heard a subtle noise, I saw that the entire ceiling was covered by a suspended white cloth. There was a curious movement visible through the thin material, as if something live was creeping about up there.

"Were you able to rest?" Mrs. Waterton asked.

Faith spoke, rubbing her forehead. "I found it difficult to lie still after so many months on the waves. It appears that I'm experiencing the same unease on land as I first did aboard ship."

"How unpleasant for you," Mrs. Waterton sympathized, patting Faith's arm. "It may take you some time to regain your strength." She looked at me. "You appear less exhausted, Miss Smallpiece."

"Yes. I wasn't as troubled by the journey as Miss Vespry," I said, not knowing whether to be proud or ashamed of my evident hardiness.

"Well, I had a *burra khanah*—a grand feast—prepared to welcome you young ladies." Mrs. Waterton beamed. Then she dropped her smile, and her voice dropped as well. "Although I must warn you that these poor ignorant people will never understand how to cook properly. It's often a hodgepodge; no matter what lengths I go to to explain rudimentary recipes to the *bobajee,* his brain simply isn't capable of comprehending. And yet he came with the highest recommendation. It's a curse one must accept," she finished, and I waited for one last phrase. I wasn't disappointed. "A curse." She sighed.

When we were seated, Mrs. Waterton nodded at the stately man. "Khit," she said. "The soup."

The man she called Khit—which I later understood to be an abbreviation of his job, the head server, or *khitmutgar*—stepped forward with a huge silver tureen and ladled out a thin soup that tasted of some nut. As soon as our spoons had emptied the bowls he removed them, and then proceeded to fill our plates with helpings from all the serving dishes. I saw that he cut Mr. Waterton's lamb and fowl, and wondered if we were not to do even this simple thing for ourselves. But Mrs. Waterton picked up her knife and fork and proceeded to look after her own plate. I glanced at Faith, and then we also took up our cutlery. While we ate I heard the scratchings and scurryings of what sounded like large insects and small animals overhead in the white cloth; neither Mr. nor Mrs. Waterton seemed aware of it, and I realized the cloth was there to stop whatever moved through the open rafters from falling onto the table. They also paid no heed to the small flakes of whitewash from the frame of the punkah drifting onto the dinner table. As the punkah swayed, I wondered if the small boy in the dark corner of the room who pulled its rope was the same boy as the one from my room or a different one.

I did what I could with the obscene amount of food piled in front of me, not wanting to insult the Watertons, but I could barely make a difference before I had to set down my cutlery, unable to eat another bite. My stomach was in extreme distress after the very simple and small meals we'd eaten for the last few months.

"My dears," Mrs. Waterton exclaimed, looking from Faith to me and back to Faith—whose plate looked as untouched as mine, "you must be able to nourish yourself. You're both far too thin from the journey. Come now, eat up, my dears. It won't do to languish. Do you not agree, Mr. Waterton?"

Mr. Waterton looked up from his plate, his lips shiny with grease from the lamb. He snapped his fingers, and the *khitmutgar* stepped up and dabbed at his lips with a gleaming white napkin, poured him a second glass of port, then stepped back.

Mr. Waterton took a sip of the port. "Well, they will soon get used to the dining," he said, finally answering his wife, although looking at Faith and me. "I expect Miss Smallpiece and Miss Vespry are looking forward to the social season."

Faith answered. "Oh, yes, Mr. Waterton, ever so much." Her voice was very quiet, almost hoarse, and I knew her to be completely fatigued.

"Of course." Mrs. Waterton either didn't notice or didn't care that Faith's voice carried no enthusiasm. "We'll give you a few days to settle in, yes, two or three days to get your legs back, and have your appetite return, and get some proper rest. There's no rush. My goodness, you girls have at least four full months of delightful entertaining ahead before the end of the seas—" Mrs. Waterton stopped. A large flake of whitewash fell into the gravy. "Well, let's not think that far ahead. My goodness, I'm sure lovely young ladies such as yourselves will be kept far too busy!"

An awkward silence fell over the table, and Mrs. Waterton sharply called out *"Koi-hai?"* Another boy hurried in and took away our plates. "The dessert," she said, and from a long table against the wall the *khitmutgar* brought a lacquered tray of bowls of creamy brown. "I had *custel brun*—I'm sorry, caramel custard—prepared in your honor," she said. "You must have missed your pudding while on board. It's what I always miss when forced to sail home or back again. My pudding."

Faith and I attempted to swallow as much of the sweet, rich custard as we could. Mr. Waterton had waved his hand at the dessert, obviously not as fond of pudding as his wife. Now the server poured Mr. Waterton a cup of tea, and, I noticed, also put in sugar and stirred it for him. I wondered if he would hold the cup to Mr. Waterton's lips, but Mr. Waterton did appear capable of this on his own.

I FELL INTO A DEEP and dreamless sleep almost immediately upon placing my head on the pillow and letting my body sink into the thick mattress that first night. When I opened my eyes to shafts of brilliant sunshine slicing through the window screens I was momentarily disoriented and sat up in alarm, but the woman in white—whom Mrs. Waterton had told me would be my ayah—appeared out of nowhere, pulling back the netting and handing me a glass of something milky and sweet that was very refreshing. I realized, after she had helped me with my dress and hair, that I was rested and excited to discover what the day would hold.

Faith looked better than she had the day before, although the shadows around her eyes were still dark when we met in the dining room. We were greeted by yet another groaning table. I was still full from the night before, and nibbled on a sweet bun and ate a plaintain, much to Mrs. Waterton's disappointment. And, as promised, Faith and I met Mrs. Liston—and I immediately liked her. I guessed her age to be between Faith's and mine. She had dark blond hair in thin ringlets and wide green eyes. She laughed with her mouth open. Unfortunately, her face had been badly marked by the vestiges of a long-ago bout with smallpox, but she appeared unaffected in all ways. She had been born in India, gone home for schooling as a small child, and then returned three years ago to live once again with her parents. She had seen her mother only three times in the twelve years she'd lived in England, and her father not at all, which was, she said, only natural.

"Natural?" I'd asked. "To see your mother three times in all those years?"

"You're too new to know the ways of the English in India, Miss Smallpiece," Mrs. Waterton interrupted. "As it happens, my own four children are living with relatives in Cambridge, having a proper education. I accompanied my youngest two years ago, when he turned five. I do try my best to get to England every third year, but the duration and unpredictability of the voyage are, of course, quite restricting."

Inwardly I wondered at the backbone of these women, that they conceded to this rigid rule of parting with their young children. It was, I was to understand later, only one of the sacrifices—although perhaps the greatest—that the British women in India suffered in order to support their husbands.

"Once you start to socialize, you'll notice there are no older English children here. Mothers in India must face an inevitable separation," Mrs. Liston said. "Children aren't allowed to stay here beyond the age of five or six—they must be sent home for proper schooling. So the mother must decide if she will accompany her child or stay with her husband. Most choose the latter. I lived with an aunt and uncle and three male cousins all those years—and I'm afraid my parents were rather shocked at how I turned out when I finally returned. I wasn't what they had hoped for, I'm afraid." But she laughed as she spoke the last sentence, and her genuine laughter tempered the rather strange comment.

I smiled, glancing at Mrs. Waterton, but she wore a rather guarded expression, and was paying great attention to her rumble-tumble, as she called it. Scrambled eggs. Already I had noticed the obvious household jargon.

"Anyway, Mr. Liston and I have only been married for two months. He's gone ahead to prepare our home in Lucknow, which is in the northeast, where he's been appointed a district officer. And since Father retired from the East India civil service a month ago and he and Mother sailed for England, well, the Watertons have been generous enough to have me stay with them until Mr. Liston returns for me."

"How did you meet your husband?" Faith asked. I was pleased to see she had regained some of the color in her cheeks and she had done her hair in a most charming way. Her rust-colored frock brought out the creaminess of her skin.

"Oh, we met through friends, shortly after I arrived, but there wasn't much romance at first."

Mrs. Waterton cleared her throat, but Mrs. Liston didn't appear to notice.

"No, we were good friends for quite a while. We often went riding—chaperoned, of course," she added, which I felt was for Mrs. Waterton's benefit, "out into the country. We rode through miles of mustard fields or beans with wonderful scents. We'd pass peacocks strutting about, and ride into villages where the dogs would rush out, barking round the horses' legs. The villagers were ever so polite and friendly, offering us refreshments, offering us a seat. He's full of surprises, is my Mr. Liston, and while we were courting he introduced me to all manner of interesting and unexpected adventures, from visiting shrines in the countryside to pig sticking. I'd always known I didn't enjoy many of the pastimes most young ladies enjoy—maybe it was my upbringing in the country with my cousins—and never fully expected to marry. Oh, come now, Mrs. Waterton," she said, at the woman's shocked intake of breath. "Don't look so gloomy. You know it to be true." She smiled back at me. "I play no instrument, my singing causes the birds to fly from the trees, and dancing with me is like lurching about with a drunken goose."

I had to laugh with her.

"Cards have always remained a mystery to me," she went on, "and I find musical evenings and flower arranging and spending hours poring over the goods displayed by the box wallahs so tedious." She faced Mrs. Waterton again. "Now, please, Mrs. Waterton, humor me. Agree that it isn't the end of the world that I have been unable to master the expected accomplishments."

"Of course it's not, dear," Mrs. Waterton murmured, but it was obvious she disapproved of Mrs. Liston's choices, and of her unabashed disclosure of these choices.

"And what of you girls? Are you quite prepared for the social activities which are absolutely endless during the cool season?" Mrs. Liston asked us, putting a large forkful of fried plaintain into her mouth. She chewed and swallowed with a gusto that I knew Mrs. Waterton disapproved of, and yet I found her enthusiasm quite pleasurable.

"I most certainly am," Faith said, daintily cutting her sausage into tiny bites. "After the positively wretched months on that ship I am quite prepared to enjoy myself. I'm sorry to have to admit, Mrs. Liston, that I'm one of those young ladies who *do* enjoy dancing and cards and all the other pleasurable aspects of an active social life." Her voice, no longer weary as it had been the evening before, now had an almost haughty air, which surprised me. I assumed she would like Mrs. Liston. In fact, the other woman's straightforward speech and confidence reminded me of the Faith I had known in Liverpool. I realized then just how much Faith had changed during the voyage, but I knew that once she was rested properly she would regain her excitement of life and make me laugh with her outrageous statements and confidences. I made a pretense of spooning a strange-looking orange jam onto my bun, watching Faith from under my eyelashes.

"I do intend to enjoy myself," Faith repeated.

"As you will, my dear," Mrs. Waterton said, smiling again. "As you will."

I witnessed, that first day, that Mrs. Waterton spoke sharply to her servants and constantly grumbled about them. She didn't call them by name, instead calling them by the name of the job they performed. And yet she did seem to carry almost an underlying sense of affection for them—and they treated her with the utmost respect. In very short order I began to understand the hierarchy of these servants.

The household was run by the *khansana,* or head bearer. It quickly appeared to me that he kept a stern eye on all the other servants. Then there was the *khitmutgar,* the imposing figure waiting on us at the table. There were a number of servers under him. Next came the cook—the *biwarchi,* or, as Mrs. Waterton referred to him, the *bobajee.* He had an assortment of helpers, which Mrs. Waterton simply called the *bobajee's* boys. Then there was the *chuprassi,* or messenger, in his fine red sash, whose job it was to stand at the door all day to open it to admit anyone who entered, and to accept all chits, or calling cards, that were delivered. There was the *dhobi,* in charge of washing and ironing the clothing and linen, the *bheesti* to carry water, the *mali* to look after the gardens, and

the night watchman, the *chowkidar.* Mrs. Waterton shared a *durzi,* or tai-
lor, with two other households. There was a huge cleaning staff, each
with a specific job. The boy who carried the dishes from the dining room
was not the boy who washed the dishes. Another polished the silver.
The boy who swept the house was not the same boy who swept out the
verandah. The boy who dusted could not touch the dishes, and so on.
The youngest servants were the host of punkah pullers and the very
small boys who forever hovered behind our chairs, waving horsetail
whisks over our heads to discourage insects from alighting on us. The
only female servants I saw were the ayahs—each woman in the house
had a personal ayah to help her with bathing and dressing and brushing
and styling her hair.

There appeared to be a litiny of rigid rules, which were overwhelming at first. Over and over I asked someone passing me in the hall, or on
the verandah, or in the dining room, for something, only to be met with
a blank look. At first I assumed it was because they couldn't understand
the few simple commands I learned, but then later realized I had simply
asked the wrong person. As the majority of servants—apart from the
khitmutgar and *chuprassi*—dressed in simple white dhotis, shirts, and
turbans, their feet bare, I found it difficult to distinguish them. But
within a few days I began to recognize faces, and height, and distinctive
manners of walking.

By the end of our third day in Calcutta it occurred to me that there
was nothing for any of us to do. Mr. Waterton—and it would seem,
every Englishman who wasn't in the army—was a civil servant for the
East India Company. Mr. Waterton was a director of land records; he
left after breakfast, returned for lunch, went back to work until dinner.
The household ran itself—or rather, was run by the imposing *khansana.*
From what I witnessed, Mrs. Waterton's role was primarily to meet with
her *bobajee* each morning and discuss the meals of the day. After this,
she might inspect the rooms to see if they had been cleaned to her stan-
dards. There were the flowers—armloads of blossoms cut and laid in an
enormous pile by the *mali,* with vases filled with water at the ready—
that she might arrange. Sometimes she consulted with the *durzi* over
what she wanted sewn up or repaired. Some days a box wallah came to

the back door and spread out his wares, ranging from ribbons and cooking pans to fabric and teapots. Mrs. Waterton would pick what she wanted and hand the required rupees to one of the serving staff, who would in return hand it to the box wallah. She would write out any chits to communicate with or reply to chits left by neighbors. This was done between breakfast and lunch.

There was a large lunch, a nap, and then perhaps afternoon callers, followed by dinner out by invitation, or, if it was dinner in, a visit to the Calcutta Club or to a social event.

❧❧❧

"MRS. WATERTON," I SAID, finding the woman at a small table in the drawing room, studying a book that had illustrations of cakes, "would it be possible to go for a walk?" It was our third day in Calcutta; as Mrs. Waterton had predicted, I felt refreshed. I had continued to sleep well and was now anxious to see some of Calcutta outside the front door. Faith was reading in her room, but had agreed that she would go for a stroll with me if there were a chaperone.

"Certainly, dear. Just follow the path through the garden along the flowers. It is lovely to walk in the garden." She didn't look up from the book.

"No," I said. "I meant a walk outside the garden."

She looked up now, her finger on the page. "A walk? Where would you walk?"

"I—I don't know. I wondered if Faith and I—if we were accompanied by Mrs. Liston, of course, or by yourself—might go for a walk."

"Do you mean on the road?" Her face showed consternation. "Oh, no, my dear. It just isn't done. A lady doesn't walk about the streets of Calcutta. This is not London, or Cheltenham. One simply doesn't walk about," she repeated.

"Oh," I said. "I'm sorry. I didn't realize."

"Well, one wouldn't, would one? It's quite all right. You'll learn how things are done here very shortly." She bent her head over her recipe again.

I stood there. "Would it be possible to go for a ride, then?"

Now she closed the book. Gently, but with a definite purpose. "A ride? At this time of day?"

I glanced at the swinging pendulum of the mantel clock, swallowing. Was I showing complete ignorance? I should have conferred with Faith first. "Oh. It's just gone two. I didn't realize . . ."

"Well, it's not unheard of, I suppose. But I shall have to have the *chuprassi* summon a palanquin. Where did you wish to go?"

I looked down at the carpet. "I don't know, Mrs. Waterton. But I would so like to see some of the city."

Mrs. Waterton's lips formed a thin line. "There's very little of interest to see. There is a possibility of a drive to the Maidan after dinner, to take the cool evening air. I suppose, if you are quite insistent, that we could arrange to do that now, but I hadn't planned for an outing today. I feel I have quite a bit to do with planning for meals right now, as there are more of us in the house than I'm used to. And I have a number of calling cards to answer."

It was obvious by her tone and the steel in her voice—as well as her reference to having extra guests, through her own goodwill—that I should not be asking for anything as frivolous as a ride out. "I understand, Mrs. Waterton, of course. Please. Forgive my uncalled-for request." I backed out of the room. "I'll have a lovely stroll in the garden."

She opened her book again. "Yes. That's best, my dear. That's best."

It appeared that I must wait a while longer to find out about the country I had come to. Mrs. Waterton seemed content to shut out the whole Indian world and concentrate on the one she knew.

❦

WE BEGAN TO SET UP our social calls on the fourth day. A number of calling cards that had been delivered were brought in by the *chuprassi,* and Mrs. Waterton and Faith and I read them over together. There were invitations for dances and dinner parties and evenings of cards. Mrs. Waterton went through the wardrobes we had purchased before leaving England, studying our dresses and admiring the latest styles. "You have a good selection, but you shall need more. It won't do to be seen in the same frock at too many events. We shall purchase some new material, and then have the *durʐi* make new ones in similar styles. They're wonderful at reproducing, down to a stitch, these Indian *durʐis*. One must be careful, though—such is my *durʐi*'s zealousness that if there has been a small rent, patched over, even the patch will be reproduced. Even the patch, bless him!"

I REALIZED, ALMOST IMMEDIATELY, how uncomfortable I was about the complete servitude. I looked away when I witnessed the tall *chuprassi*, in his fine uniform and rigid bearing, go down on his knees to dust off Mr. Waterton's shoes with a tiny brush every time the short, officious man entered the door. I noticed the burned hand of the *dhobi*, and knew how the blistered welt, caused, I deduced, by a heated iron, must ache. And yet he cheerfully salaamed before he accepted still another mound of lightly soiled linen Mrs. Waterton piled in his outstretched arms. I saw my ayah crying when I came into my room unexpectedly. She was straightening the items on my dressing table, tears coursing down her face, but when she saw me she beamed as if overjoyed to see me, gesturing for me to sit on the stool. I tried to question her as to why she was crying, pointing to her face, but she acted as if it was nothing, completely unimportant, brushing at her cheeks with a careless swipe, never losing her smile. I saw that one of the little fly-whisk boys was missing the last two toes of his right foot, and that the amputation was fairly fresh, and that he touched it gingerly when he thought no one watched him. I wondered if he was the son of any of the other servants, or if he had parents at all. I wondered about many things, but dared not mention my observances to Faith or even Mrs. Liston, as it might make them think strangely of me, that I should bother myself so with people who should not be noticed at all.

I WANTED TO INSTRUCT the *durʐi* that all my dresses must have a neckline that covered my scar. I tried to remember my Hindi, but couldn't find the words. Finally, alone with him in my bedroom but for the ayah, I disclosed my scar, then held a piece of fabric over it. The *durʐi*, his face showing nothing, said, so quietly that at first I thought I hadn't heard him, "Missy sahib would like her dresses to cover this? It is possible."

"You speak English?" I cried, smiling, but at the look on his face and the violent shaking of his head, I clapped my hand over my own mouth as if I had done something wrong. Once more he shook his head, this time putting his finger to his lips, and I understood that I was not to let on that I knew he could speak English.

That afternoon Mrs. Waterton had left me alone with Mrs. Liston, who had asked me to call her by her Christian name, Meg, on the verandah. Well, alone as one ever is in India. The *durʒi* sat cross-legged in one corner, stitching my new dress. He held the fabric straight between his toes, and in his turban he had stuck dozens of needles of different sizes, threaded with assorted colors, which he pulled out as needed. A bearer stood at the waiting, should we require something, and, of course, little boys waved their fly-whisks over us the whole time.

The verandah was wonderful; I found it to be the best place in the whole, grand, overdone house. Bamboo trellises, upon which grew masses of creepers yielding reddish yellow flowers that I later found out were called bignonia, screened the verandah, creating a cool, green room. On the floor were grass mats, and there were hanging baskets and flower boxes with pink geraniums, white and red achimenes, rubbery begonias, and fragile violets. Chairs and chaises provided comfortable seating; instead of the hard horsehair settees or overstuffed chairs in the parlor, the verandah had small grass chairs and bamboo couch chairs for the ladies and heavy, dark teak chairs with wide seats and tall curling backs for the men.

When I had the opportunity to be alone on the verandah for a few minutes I sometimes allowed myself the privilege of lolling, leaning back on one of the couch chairs with my arms over my head, smelling the cool green of the plants. Mrs. Waterton had warned me that at the first breath of the hot season all the plants would shrivel and die, no matter how many times a day they were watered, and that I should enjoy them while I could.

"Meg, today the *durʒi* spoke English to me, but seemed frightened that I should let on," I said to her, quietly, so that he wouldn't hear.

She grimaced. "Of course. There's really no way for them to win at all in most households—or at least with petty tyrants like Mr. Waterton. If a servant is perceived as too stupid, he's beaten and dismissed; if he shows he is clever—and one indication could be that he has mastered the English language—he's viewed with suspicion and, possibly, dismissed. It's completely unfair, of course, but a game played by the people of this country in order to survive. Of course, much of the same goes on back home, but the rigidity of master and servant is more noticeable to me here. Perhaps because we, after all, are not *of* this country. We are of England, and yet—" She stopped, as if aware of saying too much. She stood suddenly, causing the boy with his whisk to jump out of her way, and went to one of the hanging baskets, pinching off a dying flower. "Anyway, I can't wait to get to *mofussil*—that's the countryside—and away from all this pompous nonsense and overbearing officiousness. I find it quite intolerable. It's much, much more informal in the countryside." She studied my face. "Do I have to fear you'll report my mutinous thoughts?" Although the sentence was serious, I could tell by her expression that she hoped she had seen in me an ally.

"Of course not," I told her, smiling warmly. "But I do hope you're not leaving too soon."

"I imagine I shall be here another two weeks." She continued to study me, and I felt a prickle of the old fear under her scrutiny. I had long ago stopped worrying about Faith ever finding me out, or questioning my behavior in any way. Although I knew she cared about me, she didn't seem to study me with much depth. I often felt I was a reflecting board for her feelings and thoughts; mine were not of that much interest to her. Of course, this had always worked in my favor. But with everyone else here, as it had been during my time in Everton, I was constantly on my guard, fearful of giving myself away with a sudden wrong word, a lapse in manners.

There was a canniness in Meg's long face that worried me. "Tell me about yourself, Miss Linny Smallpiece," she said now. "I think I would like to know where you have been, and what you have seen. You give the impression of one who knows much more than she cares to say, unlike most people, who say much about things they know little about."

I was unable to think of a proper response. My palms were wet; I hid them in the folds of my watered silk tea gown.

"I'm sorry. Have I offended you?" Meg asked, finally. "My aunt and uncle and cousins—as well as my husband—are all used to my forthright outbursts. They not only tolerate my free thinking, but at times encourage it. And it so happens that I may forget myself in polite company."

Polite company. Here was young Mrs. Liston, apologizing to me because she might be appearing common. It really was quite ironic, and I might have delighted in it were I not so uncomfortable.

"No, I'm not offended," I said. "I'm just not . . . particularly at ease talking about myself."

"Of course you aren't. Most well-brought-up young ladies wouldn't be. Please ignore me and my inappropriate familiarity. I do apologize." She smiled.

"There's no need to apologize." I returned her smile, relaxing then and feeling a rush of gratitude for Meg Liston. By asking my forgiveness, and allowing me to grant it to her, she had endowed me with a feeling that was akin to benevolence.

Chapter Eighteen

AND SO WE BEGAN THE ROUNDS OF SOCIAL EVENTS IN EARNEST. We attended dinner after dinner, and it felt as if every hostess gave the same dinner party. We would have a drink at precisely eight o'clock in the drawing room, where Faith and I and any of the other unmarried ladies from the ship—I refused to use the phrase *Fishing Fleet*—were introduced to bachelors. There was polite chitchat, which I found dreadfully tedious, as I had to keep my wits about me every moment. I despaired of telling the same brief, fabricated story of my past in England night after night, of smiling politely at the same small talk, and of feigning great interest in the stories of the men. A tiresome game that I had played so many times, in so many forms. When I felt I would scream if I had to stand one moment longer, my glass sticky in my glove, we were finally summoned to the dining room by the bearer. We filed to the room in a strict order of precedence, depending on the position of the husband within the civil service. The hierarchy was very much in play here in the candlelit glitter of these fancy dinners, in much the same way as it was with the servants.

At many of the grander dinners a servant waited behind every chair; every place had its array of cutlery and a champagne glass—complete with silver cover to keep insects from falling in—and finger bowls with a sweet-smelling flower floating in them. The seating was planned with the utmost care; the most senior gentleman sat to the right of the hostess, and the most senior lady to the right of the host. The Watertons appeared fairly high up on the seating scale, while Meg—who didn't often join us, giving a variety of excuses, which I knew were fabricated to avoid the formal fuss and tedium—had a low spot at the table. But the very lowest were Faith and I, as we had no man to lift us in rank. We ate variations of the same English food: soup, followed by fish, joints, overcooked vegetables, then puddings and savories. And it appeared to me, that first week, like the table settings and the menus, that in appearance everyone looked similar—the gentlemen in their boiled white shirts and tails, the women in their feathers and long, wrinkled gloves and dresses of surprisingly similar styles, made, I assumed, by many of the same *durzis* who had a limited number of patterns.

There were a few times, I will admit, when my thoughts went back to standing at a high table in a crowded, noisy chophouse, eating a greasy pie with the other girls from Paradise. How the stories had flowed easily, the laughter loud and genuine, the camaraderie honest. I knew I had experienced one sort of freedom there that nobody in these rooms had ever known.

When the meal was over there were port and Madeira poured for the gentlemen, while the ladies gathered in the drawing room with cordials or ratafia, waiting for the men to finish their drinks and join them. Then there might be music played on a piano that always sounded out of tune. And eventually the senior lady stood, and this was an indication that we could all leave. Nobody, it appeared, would dare to depart until the senior lady of the evening had made her silent declaration.

As well as the formal dinners, we attended afternoon teas and more casual evenings of cards and dance salons at the other opulent homes of the affluent areas of Garden Reach and Chowringhee and Alipur.

I found it so difficult, the endless social chatter. The voice I had used since I began my work at the Lyceum—the cultured voice with the same inflection as Shaker and as Faith—came now with little concentration. But it was the energy that I needed to act as if interested, as well as putting on a combination of appearing demure and yet cheery, that exhausted me. I wasn't either. Demure was difficult; cheerful, even more so. It's not that I was bold or glum. I didn't know what I was. I only know that nothing ever felt right in those overdecorated drawing rooms. I was always acting, a player on a stage. Except that the play never ended, not until I retired to my room at the Watertons', and even then I wasn't alone. There were always the servants—the *durẓi* and the sweeper and the polisher and the tiny boy with his fly whisk—in and out, and the ayah and punkah wallah permanent fixtures.

DURING THIS BEGINNING of my time in India I felt as if I were waiting, waiting to actually *see* India. I wasn't allowed anywhere without Mrs. Waterton and Faith, although Meg was allowed time on her own, with other married ladies such as herself. Our only expedition, apart from visits to the other homes, all similar to the Watertons'—on the long road that ran in a straight line from Government House to Chowringhee—was to the Maidan in the center of Calcutta. Of course the palanquin curtains were always firmly shut. I had peeked out the first time we went for an afternoon, and had seen, running in all directions off the good road, fetid alleys and torturous lanes, the twisting underbelly of Calcutta. I was severely reprimanded by Mrs. Waterton for my indiscretion, and from then on sat, like Faith, with my gloved hands in my lap until we arrived at the Maidan. The huge flat esplanade of greenery boasted small orange groves and pleasant graveled paths, and was bordered by an array of flowering trees. There were no Indians allowed in the Maidan except for ayahs with their small charges and those sweeping the meticulous path or picking any fallen leaves or flowers from beneath the trees. We sat on freshly painted benches and chatted in exactly the same way that ladies of society would gather and chat in a park in any part of England. Faith and I were assured that we should enjoy this weather, for it wouldn't last much past the end of January. This brief cool season was free of the intense heat and debilitating humidity which, I was told, brought out an uncomfortable heat rash as well as hordes of flying and crawling, biting insects.

"It will be arriving all too soon," Mrs. Waterton warned, her lips pursed. "All too soon. And then you'll get a true taste of India."

If I only could.

December 15, 1830

Dear Shaker,

India is an education; I am a tabula rasa, ready to be inscribed with all India has to write on me. No matter what the future, I know, with some deep animal instinct, that I am to be marked by this land.

I am amazed by the attitude and role of the English, although I have not been here long enough to have a completely informed opinion. But from what I have experienced in this first month I am feeling uncomfortable, being forced into a position of unnatural importance. Although I have been treated admirably by every white person I have met, there is an obvious underlying hostility toward the Indians. Toward *them*, Shaker—and it is their own land. The East India Company—casually referred to here as John Company—is like a huge and heavy master, forcing the people of India in directions they surely do not want to go. And yet it appears that perfectly ordinary British men and women, shortly upon settling here, don a voluminous imperial cloak as if it is their right—no, their duty.

I cannot imagine bearing this weight.

While Calcutta is, as they say, the "city of palaces," I would call it a city of contrasts. Near to where Faith and I are staying, with Mr. and Mrs. Waterton on Garden Reach, is a world of squared white buildings of classical design, all thanks to the presence of this honorable John Company. But so near the fine shops and beautiful homes are rows of mud-thatched huts and the sight of a body burning on the river's shore. Over the fragrance of jasmine hangs the stench of open drains and rotting corpses.

Shaker, you would not believe the things one sees. I made the discovery that the Watertons employ a servant who stands all day at the riverbank behind their home. He shoves corpses—some with vultures already at work—back into the river before they can pile up on the bank. The man looked frightened when I came upon him and his grisly job. The gamy scent of decaying flesh was in the air. He demonstrated that I was to cover my eyes and flee, as if he were somehow responsible for what I had seen, and would be punished. Poor man.

I wouldn't think there is any source of medical help for the Indian people. I asked Mrs. Waterton, only the other day, why there are so many obviously sick and maimed people at every turn. Do they not have a medical service, I asked her. She laughed at me, Shaker, implying that I was a silly girl, at which I took affront, although I was careful to hide my anger from her as she is, after all, my hostess. Then she told me that these heathens have their own forms of hullabaloo that they consider healing, all noise and nonsense, she assured me. Of course, I'm sure there is more to their methods of treatment than Mrs. Waterton is aware of, but I knew it best not to suggest it. Then I asked if any of them were ever treated by the physicians and surgeons employed by the East India Company. At that she simply shook her head and said, in a very huffy manner, "Really!"

I suppose I had better watch my step.

There is a very interesting woman staying here as well. Her name is Meg Liston. I feel I am learning much from her.

You now have an address should you ever choose to correspond, Shaker.

I hope and pray that you are well.

Yours faithfully,
Linny

It was Meg who filled me with hope for my future in India, for she was full of opinions and questions. She told me she had already started writing a book on the shrines of India, as well as organized a collection of sketches she had made of local customs, both of which she planned to finish while traveling to villages in the Lucknow area. She argued openly with Mr. Waterton.

"It's all very easy when you have no European rivals in India, Mr. Waterton," she announced at the table one evening shortly before her husband was scheduled to arrive for her. "And after the defeat—perhaps I should say the crushing—of the Marathas in the Anglo-Maratha war just over twenty years ago, you have no Indian ones, either. The Company is responsible for ruling ever-larger parts of India, and yet you refuse to learn to communicate with her people effectively."

Mr. Waterton's left eye winked furiously. "We have an earnest desire to teach these heathens what the Almighty has given us. There is only anarchy without us. The good Indian is the obedient Indian, the one with complete dependence on us. We must have faith that our values will put things in order."

"Our values? Ha!" declared Meg. I hid my smile behind my napkin. "And just what have we achieved so far?"

"Meg? May I offer you more fruit compote?" Mrs. Waterton asked, glancing at her husband, a wan smile fixed in place. "The cook has tried so hard to get it right; I've been working with him for the last—"

"What have we achieved?" Mr. Waterton demanded. "Achieved? Why, Mrs. Liston, look around you. Do you not believe in the hierarchy of society? Do you not believe that as British men and women we are at the top, and therefore able to do our job of controlling and bringing enlightenment?"

"Why should we think only we are at the top?" I asked.

All heads turned toward me, and I felt a moment of trepidation.

"Good for you, Linny," Meg said. "You see—she agrees. We are the new generation. Myself, and Linny—and Faith," she added, with only a second of hesitancy, "are confident women ready to rise to a new challenge of being part of the bigger whole."

Faith made a sound that could have been agreement or denial. I wanted to shake her. Why didn't we speak up? She had so many opinions—too many, I'd sometimes thought. And yet, since we'd left Liverpool it was as if she'd left something of herself behind. Could it be that she felt that old Faith had been unsuccessful in securing a proposal of marriage, and now, in what she saw as her last chance, she was determined to fit into the conventional role that might work more successfully for her? I intended to ask her.

"Oh, dear," Mrs. Waterton said, now having completely lost the last vestiges of her smile. "Really, I'm afraid we must move to the verandah, where it's fresher, for our coffee. Please. We must move to the verandah." She stood, and we all were forced to rise and follow her outside. Mr. Waterton excused himself to smoke in his billiard room, and the conversation—aggressively directed by Mrs. Waterton—regressed to talk of the weather and its effect on the flowers. "Just think, all the lovely phlox and nasturtiums will be ruined by the first blast of hot weather," she exclaimed.

I saw that Meg's chest was rising and falling too quickly as she sat stiffly on the edge of a grass chair, not joining in or even appearing to take note of Mrs. Waterton's attempts at a conversation. She finally rose, excused herself, and left the verandah, heading to the garden, her back stiff. I watched the *mali* follow her with a light chair should she wish to sit. Meg turned and waved him away with an impatient flick of her hand. He stood there momentarily as if confused, finally setting down the chair and squatting beside it. His eyes never left Meg, as if hoping she would change her mind and need his services.

When Meg was out of earshot, Mrs. Waterton shook her head. "My. I wonder how her husband will deal with her. She is all too eager to show signs of learning. Not a desirable trait at all. Not desirable at all."

I glanced at Faith, who was absently picking at a loose strand of rattan on the arm of her chair. Wearing a gown of pale rose batiste with matching pink satin slippers, she was lovely and languid. Her pale, long-fingered hand played listlessly with the bit of binding as if unaware of her surroundings.

Meg's husband arrived that weekend, a young, good-looking man with a black eyepatch over his left eye, which somehow added to his air of dashing attractiveness. He and Meg left, full of talk of their upcoming adventures. As we waved good-bye, I knew how I would miss her. And how I envied her. I knew that there would have to be other British women in India who were individuals, who didn't follow the lead of all the others. It just appeared that they were few and far between.

WE HAD BEEN IN INDIA a full month and I had yet to experience anything of what I thought would be the real India. I was living a British life, eating many-course meals of meat and gravy and vegetables and heavy cakes for dessert, being spoken to in English voices, seeing only that which was carefully controlled. I knew that, even with the little I had been allowed to see of it, I could love India. And yet I had begun to despair. When would the time come, and under what circumstances would I be able to venture further into Calcutta, or perhaps the country? I understood now that this was simply not the introduction; this was the whole game, and the rules were that I was more of a prisoner in Calcutta than I had ever been in Liverpool or even in Everton. I was good at game playing, and at waiting, but the troubling sense of captivity grew daily.

Shortly before Meg left I had asked her whether she found it difficult to wait for her husband, to spend such quiet, passive time at the home of the Watertons before she could begin her life. *Her true life,* as Chinese Sally had said so long ago in Liverpool, and I thought that this was what Meg was waiting for as well. "I have learned patience, living in India," she told me. "Something that has helped me is a Pashtu proverb: 'Patience is bitter, but the fruit of it is sweet.'"

Now I repeated the proverb many times a day.

Faith did not seem in need of a proverb. She appeared outwardly content with all of this—the staid visits to the Maidan, helping Mrs. Waterton plan the meals, writing out responses to invitations we received, or sitting in the garden. Or, of course, attending the never-ending circus of social events, where we were introduced to eligible bachelors. Faith had been right; there were more than three men to every woman.

More and more I thought about Faith's behavior. At first I thought she was simply worn out by the long journey and that she would regain her cheekiness after a short while. But instead, as the weeks went by, it was obvious to me that she had chosen—here in Calcutta—to embrace the tight reins of respectability that she had so strained against in Liverpool. She was snappish with me the one and only time I questioned her complete acquiescence to the frivolous and what I saw as shallow lifestyle of our life on Garden Reach.

"One does not come to India for one's health, Linny," she reprimanded. "I thought that was clear to you. It is all about the social season." She pushed back a strand of hair that had come loose. "And I simply will not suffer the indignity of being sent back to England as a Returned Empty."

She was doing her best. I often heard her bright, high laughter from across the room, although it was only I who heard the undertone of desperation. She regularly appeared to be surrounded by men. On our return from each party, she came into my room and sat on my bed, telling me about each young man and what he had said to her. She had a favorite, a dark and shy gentleman named Mr. Snow—Charles, she confided to me—who said little, but seemed mesmerized by her chatter and the lustrous color of her hair.

I personally found it tiresome, the troops of appraising young men, none of whom held the slightest interest for me. I did try, but found fault easily. Some appeared tight-lipped and priggish, although more of them struck me as vain. Strutting about, full of themselves, they reminded me of the peacocks on the lawns, their tails in full display for any peahen about.

I wondered if it was because, unlike the other young women here, I had once known men too well.

IT WAS AT ONE of these parties, the week before Christmas, that I met Somers Ingram.

He was tall and quite handsome in a rather traditional sense, with thick, wavy dark hair and a well-trimmed mustache. He had deep brown eyes and even features—a slightly aquiline nose, full-lipped mouth, and strong chin. His complexion was burnished by the sun. The first time we were introduced he bowed over my hand, holding it just a moment longer than necessary, and gave me a slow smile. How well I knew his type, but perhaps there was something else, some carefully controlled danger under the brilliant smile and guileless expression. I smiled back, murmuring my pleasure at making his acquaintance.

"You arrived on the November ship, then?" he asked.

"Yes. How long have you lived in India?"

"Five years."

"My. You must have had some very memorable experiences."

It was just a game. The same questions, the same answers. Was he as bored as I?

"Yes. And what are your impressions of India?"

I had been asked this question by every young man I had spoken to. I had a small, memorized speech that I'd heard Faith and other women use, about the wonder and strangeness of it all, the exotic difference between India and England, and so on. All lies, in my opinion, since I hadn't been allowed any impressions of India. So far, they were all of England—the endless pressure of proper behavior, the snobbery that showed itself in the ranking of the gentlemen within the civil service, the attempts to dine strictly on English food, the disdain shown to the servants within the household—picked up and set down in another country that was still a tantalizing mystery.

I was weary this evening, and in general bad humor. I sighed, not bothering to launch into my rehearsed speech.

"I wish I could speak to the servants properly," I said. "You must speak Hindi very well after all this time here, Mr. Ingram."

"Only what's necessary. Command and rebuke, mainly."

A moment of silence passed. Mr. Ingram waited for my reply. Should I do the proper thing and agree with him? No. I looked straight into his eyes and thought I saw something of substance then, in spite of our rather quotidian introductory conversation. I deemed that his was not a nature to trifle with. He might even react with interest if I spoke my mind. "Well, I would like more than that. I'm studying the language in some depth, but it's difficult. I try to practice with the servants at the Watertons', but they seem reluctant to respond. I don't know if I'm not pronouncing the words right, or they're frightened to answer."

"Probably neither," Mr. Ingram said, his eyes narrowing just the tiniest bit. "They're not comfortable, you coming to their level. Confuses them. I don't know why you bother; all you need is a smattering, just enough to get them moving. They're like children, really. Best to treat them with a firm hand. And consistency. Their own worlds are so tumultuous, so undisciplined, that it's a comfort to them to be told what to do, and to know what to expect if they don't obey."

I didn't answer. He was definitely like so many of the rest, then, with his plummy voice and arrogance. I tried to think of an answer Meg might have to his prejudiced announcement, and yet knew I must not make my disappointment too obvious. I had briefly thought I recognized something in Mr. Ingram that might have made him different.

My annoyance grew as we stood in the crush of silk and fine wool, the laughter and chatter all around us. I had no further wish to talk with him, and Mr. Ingram quite obviously felt the same way; his eyes briefly roamed the room. But there was no polite way for either of us to escape.

"Have you family in England, Mr. Ingram?"

He shook his head. "There is no one. My mother died when I was a child. I lived in London until five years ago. But after my father's death I decided to venture here. Are you from London as well, Miss Smallpiece?" he asked, his eyes suddenly looking into mine with intensity.

"Liverpool."

"Liverpool? I've never had call to visit Liverpool. Your family is there, then?"

"My parents are no longer living either," I said. "I had been staying with an aunt and cousin." It was easier to give simple answers. Back to boring, safe territory.

"I suppose they live up in Mount Pleasant."

"Actually north of the city, in Everton. I thought you said you hadn't been to Liverpool, Mr. Ingram."

His expression didn't change, but he blinked, and then raised one knuckle and touched his mustache, just under his nose, and in that split second before he responded, I knew he was lying. A good liar usually recognizes another. "Well, one does hear of places, even if one hasn't actually been there."

"Yes, I suppose so," I said.

He cleared his throat, and raised his chin over my shoulder, and in the next moment an elderly gentleman appeared at my side. Mr. Ingram introduced us, then politely took his leave.

Later that evening, as I was preparing to depart with my party, I saw Mr. Ingram in conversation with another young man, glass in his hand, listening intently. As I watched him, he glanced up, and our eyes met. We held each other's gaze for just a second too long before looking away. Neither of us smiled.

I found the handsome Mr. Ingram somehow intriguing. And yet the intrigue was a strange hold, an uncomfortableness that made my heart beat faster, as if I should be ready to flee. At the time there was no way I could understand this combination of attraction and repulsion. It would come back to haunt me in a double circle.

But now I am getting ahead of myself.

Chapter Nineteen

THE MORNING AFTER I HAD MET SOMERS INGRAM I ASKED FAITH if she knew of him; she admitted she had met him and found him to be utterly charming. "And he has a most officious position in the Company, I've heard," she said. "He's quite the talk, to have risen so far for one so young. And apparently there's quite a bit of family wealth. Some have rudely commented that it was his family's influence that allowed him such an expeditious move forward in his career. But one can't believe all one hears."

I nodded.

"Why do you ask, Linny?"

"I had the opportunity to meet him last night," I told her. "He appeared slightly arrogant, I thought."

"Arrogant? He's nothing of the sort, Linny. Now, if we speak of arrogance, it must be in reference to Mr. Whittington. Have you been forced to spend any time with him?" she asked, and then chattered on about other bachelors. I stopped listening, wondering what it was that Mr. Ingram had to hide, and when our paths would next meet.

THE OPPORTUNITY AROSE at an elaborate ball put on at the Calcutta Club to celebrate the ringing in of 1831. Much of Calcutta's elite was in attendance; it appeared to me that the number was over three hundred. My dance card had been filled for two weeks. I wore the ball gown I had had made—at Faith's insistence—before we left Liverpool; it was golden brocade and parchment silk, with a lacy fichu to cover the low neckline. I must admit, as I turned to view myself in the full-length pier glass, candlelight shimmering on the skirts of the dress, that I felt it lent me a look that I dared to call splendor.

I saw how I had changed since I had stared, aghast, into the mirror in Shaker's home after the terrible night he'd rescued me. The constrast was striking; my hair was now thick and lustrous, my eyes bright, and my cheeks a becoming shade.

As the ayah fussed with the last few curls of my hair, I knew Somers Ingram would be there. I found myself watching for him as soon as we arrived. Although I didn't see him at the reception, or as we were seated for dinner, as soon as the dancing began he appeared, bowing before me. "Miss Smallpiece," he said, and again I was struck by his posture, the smoothness of his skin, his full lips. "May I have the pleasure of escorting Miss Smallpiece around the floor, Mrs. Waterton?" He held out his gloved hand to me.

Mrs. Waterton trilled giddily, holding my dance card at a distance as she peered at it. "Why, Mr. Ingram, I don't see your name on Miss Smallpiece's card."

"Come now, Mrs. Waterton," he cajoled. "Depending, of course, on whether Miss Smallpiece will grant me the pleasure." He held out his arm to me.

"Mrs. Waterton?" I asked, looking at her. I realized how badly I did want to dance with him.

"But of course, my dear. I will extend apologies to your disappointed partner when he arrives."

We moved smoothly around the dance floor in a waltz. Initially, Mr. Ingram's patter required little of me. He spoke of the fine organization of the ball, of a problem with his *khansana,* of a sporting event he had recently attended.

"You are an excellent dancer, sir," I told him when the moment was right, my gloved hand on his shoulder, the other held firmly within his own gloved hand.

"Thank you, Miss Smallpiece," he said, smiling down at me, and drew me just the slightest bit closer. I was aware of the feeling of his thigh against mine as we turned. No other bachelor had been this bold with me; when I thought about it, most held me at more than a respectable distance. "But I'm aware of a certain hesitancy in your step. Does dancing bore you, or are you just not terribly accomplished at it?"

I was shocked at his less than complimentary statement, that he might actually speak of my dancing ability—or lack of it, according to him. I stopped in the middle of a turn.

"I find you quite thoughtless, sir," I said, putting as much indignation into my voice as I could. Other couples floated around us. I didn't care what he thought of my dancing, but didn't like the implication that I may not have had many years of dancing in fine salons and ballrooms. I thought of Meg Liston, and her admittance of her lack of interest in dancing. "Not all of us are as talented as you, Mr. Ingram," I said now, and my voice held a saucy note. "There are those of us who may have spent time pursuing more intellectual and cultural interests than the movement of feet against the floor." I watched his eyes widen slightly.

"In fact, by your expertise on the dance floor, I'm certain your talents run to the more mechanical, and that you have little interest in things intellectual whatsoever."

He laughed, an open, delighted laugh. "Well spoken, Miss Smallpiece, and I am humbly chastised. And rightfully so. Of course, you dance lightly and well. I only spoke so boldly because I did sense you were bored by all of this, and wondered how you would react to a statement that was not as safe as the usual niceties we are all forced to utter, dance after dance."

I was charged with a bolt of surprise that he was seeing in me precisely what I'd felt. And that he had the affrontery—no, I decided, the courage—to speak of it to me. It meant he actually had picked up on what I thought I carefully concealed in my words and tone.

As one, we moved into the dance again. "You were testing me, then. Is that it? To see if I would rise to the challenge of your poor manners?"

He smiled. "You might put it that way. And, Miss Smallpiece, I'm delighted to report that you have passed my test. You obviously have nerve, something badly lacking in many young women I meet here. Nerve and spirit, judging by the way your eyes are flashing so indignantly right now. I must compliment you on those golden arrows you send my way."

Now he was flirting openly. He had gone from insult to compliment in seconds. I didn't know how to deal with a man like Somers Ingram.

"What is it you do for the Company, Mr. Ingram?" I asked, breathing deeply, unable to come up with anything else at that moment. I didn't have to think about my body. He truly was a marvelous dancer and led me expertly.

"I am the chief auditor," he said.

I had no idea what that was. "How marvelous."

"Do you think so? Why? I'm interested to know what you would find marvelous about my post."

Was he again reading my mind? How dare he put me in this uncomfortable position? Most other men would accept the compliment with a proud acknowledgment and talk about the position, so I would know what it was. They wouldn't question me on my reaction. As I tried to think of something logical to say, he laughed again.

"You really don't know what a chief auditor does, do you?"

I clicked my tongue and smiled naughtily. I realized I could be as capable of flirting as he. "Really, Mr. Ingram, you are impossible."

"Oh, come now, Miss Smallpiece. It doesn't suit you."

"What doesn't?"

"This false air of injury. Why would you say my position is marvelous when you don't know what it is, and, furthermore, don't really care?"

Before I was forced to answer, the dance ended, and he led me back to Mrs. Waterton.

"Would you be so kind as to consent to allowing Miss Smallpiece a future dance this evening?" he asked her.

"Miss Smallpiece has many young men requesting her company," Mrs. Waterton said, fanning the air with my dance card. "She must not appear rude."

"Of course," Mr. Ingram said, and bowed again. Strangely, I felt a surge of disappointment at not having the opportunity to talk with him again, and at the same time relief that he wouldn't confuse me with his unpredictable and unsettling behavior.

"Although," Mrs. Waterton added, "she may have an opening toward the end of the evening."

Now Mr. Ingram bent over my hand, which he still held, pressing his lips against my glove. "I shall look forward to it," he said, and then left.

But he didn't come back again, and I didn't see him in the crowds. And at that I felt something that was almost akin to loss. No. Not loss. That would make it appear that I missed something. Perhaps the feeling I experienced when Mr. Ingram did not return for a final dance was more of the same frustration that I felt, imprisoned with Faith and the Watertons on Garden Reach, with India just at my fingertips.

I couldn't quite put a name to it.

I found myself wondering when I would see Somers Ingram next—and again, it wasn't longing to be close to this man. It was more something that bothered me about him.

WE MET NEXT at a soirée at the Calcutta Club later in January. His skin was even more darkened, as if he had spent recent time outdoors. While surrounded by others we exchanged opinions on expected subjects: the weather (cool and pleasant), architecture (the renovation of some of the rooms at the Writers Building), Indian politics (the rumors of difficulties with the administration of the rajah of Mysore), and news from home (the exciting prospect of steam navigation).

As others drifted away and we found ourselves alone near one of the high doors, I commented on his appearance. "You're looking very well, Mr. Ingram," I said. "Have you been taking some sport?"

"Yes, I hunted all last week, enjoying the glorious weather, which is not to be with us much longer, I'm afraid. We must take every advantage of it. Do you enjoy riding, Miss Smallpiece?"

I ran my finger along my cuff. "Not terribly." I had never been on a horse. Were we never to have a conversation where I wasn't put on my guard?

"I would think you would like to get out in the sun and wind of the cool season, gallop along and have a look about. Have you had that opportunity yet?"

I shook my head. If he only knew how I longed to have more than a look about.

"Would you care to join a small party? A number of my friends, as well as ladies such as yourself, with Mr. and Mrs. Weymouth accompanying us, are planning an outing next week."

"I think not, Mr. Ingram. Thank you so much for your invitation, but . . ."

"Please put aside coyness, Miss Smallpiece. It doesn't suit you, much as I reminded you in the recent past."

"I'm not being coy," I said, annoyed that he would assume he could judge my behavior.

"Really? Then what is it? Do you know how clearly your expression gives you away? You're almost scowling. I can see you arguing with yourself. What is it that's stopping you from agreeing to join me? Come now, Miss Smallpiece. I'd like the truth. I can tell you are more than a little anxious to be in my company."

Now I was far more than annoyed; I was furious at constantly being pushed into corners by this impossible man. His presumptuous haughtiness that I wanted nothing more than to spend my time with him brought angry heat to my face. "A lady does not need to explain herself," I said, fiercely, leaning close enough to smell the faint apple scent of his hair pomade.

"A lady does not forget herself, either," he said, openly chastising me. "Do I detect a tone of rudeness?" He tut-tutted.

"I do not appreciate your manner, sir," I said, my voice low. "I can assure you I do not forget myself." I leaned even closer. "Ever."

He raised one eyebrow in an infuriatingly cocky manner. "Really?" His eyes bore into mine. Then he whispered, having the nerve to let his lips touch my cheek, "I don't believe you." His breath was warm, his manner far too familiar as he put his hand on my forearm. His fingers gently stroked the sleeve of my dress.

Blood roared in my ears. His face was only inches from mine, a small smile on his mouth as his hand remained on my arm. A condescending smile, one that presumed that I was like all of the other silly girls, that I would grow faint at his nearness, swoon into his arms in shock at his daring. How I found him attractive and yet hated him, with his insolence and his absolute certainty of his charm.

I moved my face a fraction of an inch closer to his, the blood still pounding in my head, my face hot. "Mr. Ingram," I whispered, my jaw tight, and he waited, turning his head slightly, so that I might speak into his ear. I was trembling with a sense of power, of how I would show him that he couldn't toy with me. "Take your damn hand off my arm."

He pulled his head back as if I'd slapped him. And in that instant I knew what I'd done—what Somers Ingram had driven me to do. I had managed to spend the last two months here acting like the lady I was pretending to be every moment—no matter how I struggled with it inside. And now, in such a brief conversation, this man had made me forget who I was supposed to be. He had thrown out a challenge, and stupidly, I had risen to it.

Somers Ingram looked directly into my eyes, and what I saw there made me close mine momentarily. *No. How could I have been so foolish? I had worked too hard.*

"Did I hear you correctly, Miss Smallpiece?" he asked, finally removing his hand and stepping back. There was something akin to triumph in his face. His expression made it clear that he had accomplished what he'd hoped to do, that he'd managed to get what he'd wanted from me, perhaps all along.

"I—I . . ." I raised my gloves to my burning cheeks. Perspiration trickled beneath the tight lacing of my stays.

Glancing around to ensure that we were still unobserved, Mr. Ingram now took my fingers in his hand, lightly, but again, in a manner far too intimate. He ran his thumb to the center of my palm, and even through my glove the pressure of his caress made me shiver. Then he said, in a voice that was low and pleased, "My dear Miss Smallpiece, I do believe the last time I heard such language was in a Turkish bathhouse in East London."

There was nothing for me to say. I looked down at the carpet.

Mr. Ingram let go of my hand and stepped a respectable distance away. "Don't worry about it, Miss Smallpiece. I find your . . . openness of expression, shall we say, refreshing. I'm not above plain talk myself, given the right circumstance. So, I take it that is a definite no to the riding invitation?"

I turned on my heel and left in a rustle of skirts, hoping for the impression of dignity.

ON JANUARY 31 the Clutterbucks hosted an evening of cards to which the Watertons, Faith, and I were invited. I was in good spirits this evening; I had actually persuaded Faith to slip away from the Maidan with me, for a full half hour this afternoon. The usually watchful eye of Mrs. Waterton had been diverted when she ran into an old friend, down from a posting in the north, and she and the friend became lost in conversation as Faith and I sat on a bench facing them. When I politely interrupted, asking whether Faith and I might stroll through the Maidan together, she nodded absently.

As soon as we were out of Mrs. Waterton's view I steered Faith toward the outside path of the Maidan. And then, linking my arm in hers, I pulled her along, between the row of waiting rickshaws and palanquins. Faith was hesitant, but I kept a firm grip on her.

"Linny! Linny, stop. Where are we going?" she asked, her face flushed and anxious.

"I don't know. That's the beauty of it." I laughed.

"We can't, Linny. What if someone sees us? What if something happens to us? What if somebody—"

I ignored her halfhearted cries, and within a minute we found ourselves in a market of sorts. Everywhere were flowers—I especially recognized roses and marigolds—piled randomly together. There were fruit and vegetables that I'd never seen. I stopped in front of one cart, pulling off my gloves to caress the smooth, elongated shapes heaped there, some white as ivory and others a deep purple. The turbaned man who crouched upon his heels beside the cart jumped up, taking a particularly gleaming purple one and pushing it at me. I shook my head, no, no, and hesitantly told him, in Hindi, that I had no money. But he shook his head back at me, gently setting it into my hands and then performing a salaam, and I understood it to be a gift. I bowed my head at him, and he nodded in a dignified manner.

"What is it? What will you do with it?" Faith asked, clinging tightly to me.

"I don't know the answer to either," I said, "but I couldn't insult him by not accepting it."

We followed narrow paths in the market. I breathed in the smell of cooking oil and garlic and tobacco. I recognized ginger and cloves, but there were too many other spices I had no name for. There was the glorious scent of sandalwood one moment, the acrid odor of burning cow dung the next, and Faith covered her nose with her gloved hand as we passed the braziers where women cooked flat, doughy shapes. I realized I was hungry, and I longed to stand in front of a brazier and chew on whatever it was the women were paddling so efficiently about in their hands before throwing into a flat pan to bake. I heard snatches of foreign-sounding music created by unknown instruments, and over all was the tinkling and ringing of all sizes of bells and the creaking axles of bullock carts.

I stopped, Faith bumping into me, and stood still, closing my eyes and listening, breathing, letting it all soak into my skin.

"Why are you stopping, Linny? Do you know how to get back to the Maidan? Oh dear, look at that child. Is he all alone?"

I opened my eyes to see a naked child of about two, tottering about with short steps on the hard-packed mud underfoot. A red string was attached to his wrist. I followed the string and saw it was tied to the wrist of a young mother who held an infant against her sari while she haggled with a merchant over the piece of bright yellow cotton in her other hand.

"No. Look, there's his mother."

The child came right to my skirt, stopped, and looked up at me. He closed his small fist around the dotted poplin of my dress. I smiled and put my hand on his dark head. His hair was silky.

"Don't touch him, Linny," Faith said, under her breath. "You may catch a disease."

"He's just a baby, Faith," I said. "Look how beautiful he is."

"It's shameful, though. He's completely without clothing."

The child now looked at the gleaming purple vegetable in my other hand. He let go of my skirt and reached both hands toward it. His eyes were huge, a luminous black, and he made a small cry that is the same sound that babies of all worlds make when they want something.

I put the vegetable into his outstretched hands. There was a jerk on the thread at his wrist as he took it, and I looked from him to the mother, and saw her watching, her face concerned. I smiled at her, and her face relaxed and she returned the smile. Faith tugged at my sleeve.

"We must find our way back, Linny. Too much time has passed. Mrs. Waterton may start to look for us, and it won't take her long to realize we're not in the Maidan."

"All right, all right," I said, casting one more look at the child, who now toddled on his little bowed legs to his mother, laughing, holding out the vegetable.

I instinctively understood the way the market ran; it was not so very different from the markets I'd hurried through every day as a child in Liverpool. Faith sighed with relief as the tidy, carefully sculpted shape of the Maidan came into view.

"Aren't we wonderfully wicked, Linny?" she'd said, at ease now that we'd survived what she obviously saw as a bold foray. The chaos of the market receded behind us, leaving only a faint memory of sounds and smells. "Mrs. Waterton would have a fit of dyspepsia if she knew what we've been up to."

"Let's make sure she doesn't find out," I said, and smiled at her. In that moment I felt the old Faith was stirring under the tight cover the new Faith wore. I put my gloves back on and raised one to my face. It carried a trace of the smoky, spicy scent of the India I wanted to know. I linked my arm through Faith's and we hurried on.

❦

AS WE ARRIVED at the Clutterbucks' I was still filled with pleasure from the afternoon's unexpected and very minute taste of freedom. There were a number of guests, and within moments Mr. Ingram and I ran into each other in front of the open verandah doors. And even though I felt a tiny jab of pleasure somewhere in my chest at the sight of him, I was nervous about the way I'd behaved the last time we'd met. I didn't wish to speak to him, didn't want him looking at me in that familiar, suggestive way that made me react badly. I was afraid that he would spoil my mood.

All I wanted, at this moment, was a breath of air. The Clutterbuck rooms were crowded and the air filled with the scents of women's perfume and the large vases of oleander branches and jasmine and Queen of the Night that sat on every surface. But Mr. Ingram would not let me pass without speaking, even though I turned my head in the other direction.

"Well, Miss Smallpiece, it is wonderful to see you again," he said, the picture of politeness.

"And you, sir," I said, trying to keep my voice pleasant, not meeting his eyes. A definite tension hung in the air.

A slender young attendant in crisp white pants, jacket, and turban, hovered near us with a silver tray of fluted glasses filled with crimson liquid. He appeared nervous, stepping from foot to foot, and the glasses shivered against one another almost inaudibly. I noticed a fine line of perspiration running from under his turban. Finally he moved forward, holding the tray in my direction but looking at Mr. Ingram.

"Claret? Or perhaps Madeira?" Mr. Ingram said to me.

"No, thank you," I said, and yet the server stayed where he was. Mr. Ingram finally took one of the glasses. Still the boy stayed. Mr. Ingram dismissed him with a quick murmured sentence in Hindi that I couldn't make out.

At that moment our hostess clapped her meaty hands and announced that we would break into pairs for a game of whist.

"If it's all the same to you, Miss Smallpiece, I think I'll slip out for a cheroot. I'm not terribly interested in card games that don't involve a major gamble." He flashed his practiced smile, setting his full glass on a nearby table.

I nodded, not sure of my feelings now, watching him disappear through the open doors. He had acted as if nothing unpleasant had passed between us only ten days earlier. I breathed deeply, reassuring myself that he would have the manners never to mention my vulgar display.

I played a few hands of whist, but was restless and edgy, and felt I might bite through my tongue if Mrs. Clutterbuck, with her low drooping bosom and donkey's bray of laughter, asked what was trump one more time, or moaned that she was destined to receive only the pip cards, never the court. I begged off the rubber, slipped out through the open patio doors, and descended the deep, broad stone steps into the villa's back garden.

The garden was lovely, with its array of chest-high canna, and beyond, a stand of temple frangipani with delicate, almost sculptured flowers giving off the heavy fragrance that always surprised me, coming from such delicate blossoms. The full moon was white, round, and swollen, shining over it all. I stopped in the middle of the garden, putting a frangipani blossom behind my ear, and looked at the sky. I felt odd, suddenly, very light, as if I might rise up into that starry night sky. It was vertigo, a dizziness that was unsettling and pleasant at the same time. I smiled, thinking of the gentle hospitality of the merchant who gave me the vegetable, of the silkiness of the child's hair, and then I held out my arms and slowly twirled, there in the moonlight. I felt that something cold and hard and dark, deep inside of me, was coming undone, releasing. And I realized, with surprise, that what I was feeling was happiness. *I am happy*, I thought. *I am here, in this garden in Calcutta. I am Linny Gow, and I am here, now. I am not waiting, not dreaming of another life. This is my life.* "I am happy," I said, into the tangled beauty of the garden. The words sounded odd in my mouth, full and round, silvery and bright, as if they were catching the reflection of the moon. It seemed that I had been holding my breath all my life, my chest tight with the effort. And now, when I breathed out those words, *I am happy,* my chest was able to expand.

I steadied myself, standing undisturbed on the moonlit grass. I couldn't possibly go back to the loud, stuffy drawing room. I slowly made my way down the path to the servants' quarters, the simply built godowns huddled against the back wall, where there was the constant muffled thrum of voices and the slow beat of a drum. Outside one hut a young woman sat with her back against the rough wall and nursed her baby. She jumped up when she saw me, trying to cover her breasts with her sari and salaam at the same time, the infant losing the nipple and wailing thinly in startled protest. Please, I tried to tell her in my stilted Hindi, please, continue. As I wound my way along the path I passed men and women squatting around rush lights set on the dirt outside their huts, talking in low voices. They all rose and fell silent as I walked by. I smiled at each of them, greeting them, knowing I was making them uncomfortable by venturing past their quarters, but I didn't care. There was one final hut and, as I could see in the flood of moonlight that made everything as clearly outlined as day, a narrow path beside it that would loop back in the direction of the house. I was glad I wouldn't have to retrace my steps and disturb the servants a second time.

The hut sat alone, slightly distanced from the others. As I passed the open doorway, the familiar sounds of coupling made me stop and look in. I instantly made out two figures, moving in rhythm on a mat, and I should have immediately kept on my way. Why didn't I? What human curiosity made me want to watch the couple in this private moment for even an instant? I believe now that it was that loose, bright hold of the joy I possessed at that moment, the realization that I could feel this way, that created my lack of inhibition. I stopped, listening to the harsh quick breath of one, answered by the other, and realized, in that same second, that it wasn't a man and woman, as I had assumed, but two men. My eyes adjusted enough to see that one was on his knees, supporting himself with his elbows, his small slender body gleaming darkly in the moonlight. The other, larger and more strongly built, was kneeling behind him, wearing a white shirt whose pearl buttons winked as he grasped the thin hips in front of him, driving himself in with urgency.

Before I could step away, or even avert my eyes, the man performing on the other turned his head, as if somehow aware of my presence, and I stared into the face of Somers Ingram. He stopped, midmovement, the drumming from somewhere behind me seeming to grow in intensity, and the other person—I recognized him now as the young serving boy from the drawing room—also looked toward the door, and cried out in alarm. Mr. Ingram roughly pulled away from the boy, who rolled onto his side, grabbing his shirt and throwing it over his turban and face.

It was too late to pretend I hadn't seen them. "I'm so sorry for intruding," I said, the words stilted, almost comical, in my own ears. What could possibly be said, given the situation? "I'm really terribly sorry. I . . . was lost," I went on, feebly, and Mr. Ingram simply stared at me, not even attempting to cover himself, his arousal still obvious as he sat back on his heels.

I hurried away from the hut, finding it difficult to breathe properly. I wasn't sure why I felt this unnerving sense of shock at what I had seen—I, who had not only witnessed any manner of perversions, but who had also been a participant. I cursed myself for my boldness in wandering about, my elation of moments earlier spoiled now, my mood confused and sour. I took the frangipani blossom from behind my ear, tossing it to the ground. Was I disappointed to find Somers Ingram acting in this manner, or was I simply angry that he had made me uncomfortable during our conversations, for his own pleasure, as it was obvious that his taste ran to boys and not women? He had never been interested in me in the slightest, and I realized this offended me.

I had traveled only a short way before Somers Ingram strode up behind me, the ground shells of the path crunching under his feet. "Miss Smallpiece?"

I turned to him. He was as composed and neatly attired as he had been in the Clutterbucks' drawing room earlier. "I don't believe we have any business, sir," I said, raising my chin.

"Please allow me to escort you back to the house," he said, and took my arm firmly in his.

When I attempted to pull away, he tightened his grip so that I was unable to withdaw my hand. I tried to walk quickly, but he forced me to stroll at a leisurely pace.

"Miss Smallpiece," he said, "I must speak frankly."

I made a small sound of disgust. "Do you really feel that at this moment I care to speak to you about anything?"

He stopped, removing his arm but now holding my upper arm in his hand, and turning so that he was facing me in the moonlight. "You see," he said, obviously not concerned at all with whether I wanted to speak to him or not, "what has just occurred is part of what's been troubling me about you, Miss Smallpiece. What you just witnessed . . . well, I'm trying to understand your rather strange response. You didn't react as any other young lady of your class when you saw me with my Ganymede. You didn't shriek in absolute horror or faint dead away. You didn't become a quivering, speechless wreck, bewildered at the sight, as would be expected of a young English virgin. A sight, which, by the way, most would not imagine even in their most guilty dreams, such is their carefully preserved innocence. I saw the expression—or perhaps lack of expression—on your face when you saw us—in flagrante delicto, shall we say? It was quite nonplussed. And that leads me to believe you weren't particularly shocked, or even dismayed. As if you've seen sights a proper young lady from home should never have witnessed. Am I not right?" His hand burned through the thin silk of my sleeve.

I knew I was on a precipice and one wrong step would send me off the edge. "I don't understand what you're talking about." A desperate note crept into my voice, unnerving me. Of course I did. He was working it out.

"Now this, coupled with your surprising language the last time we spoke, well, it does make one wonder."

He knows, he knows, rang in my head with a clanging loud as a heavy bell.

"Are you all right, Miss Smallpiece? Perhaps you are indeed suffering from shock after all; you're looking terribly startled." He had the audacity to smile, as if his words were somehow humorous.

I yanked my arm from his grip and picked up my skirts, running through the damp grass, ruining my slippers. I went back to the drawing room, finding a quiet corner where I sat, breathing deeply and fanning myself, trying to catch my breath. I constantly glanced toward the verandah doors, expecting Somers Ingram to appear, wondering how I would manage to stay composed. I had made too many mistakes with Mr. Ingram now. I was terrified.

But he didn't return, and half an hour later I was thoroughly thankful when Mrs. Waterton suggested we take our leave.

Chapter Twenty

IT WAS THE FIFTH OF FEBRUARY. FAITH AND I HAD BEEN INVITED to an evening of light refreshments and chamber music at a home in Alipur, where several of the bachelors—including Somers Ingram— had their quarters. The party was being put on by the Senior Ladies Group from the Calcutta Club. Apparently, this was a proper evening, Mrs. Waterton assured us, chaperoned by this group of ladies who often assisted unmarried men with entertaining before they found a wife to take over the duty. "It's a nice change for gentlemen to be able to entertain in their homes occasionally," she said.

As soon as I had heard that Mr. Ingram was one of the hosts, I tried to find excuses to send my regrets. But Faith was very keen to go, as she had been seeing more of Mr. Snow, and she knew he would be in attendance. "If you don't accompany me, Mrs. Waterton may say I can't go, Linny. Please. You must come, for my sake if nothing else."

I finally agreed, but knew I would be uncomfortable. And yet there was no way I could avoid Mr. Ingram indefinitely; our paths would have to continue to cross at social events. I could not remain within the Waterton home forever.

The home was airy and more sparsely furnished than the couples' homes I'd visited. Apart from the Senior ladies, bustling about importantly, the crowd was all young, the laughter louder, the talk more animated. It was obvious that the mood this evening was less formal than usual.

Charles Snow immediately came to greet Faith. She took his arm and they wandered off, their heads together, intent in their conversation. I chatted with a few of the other young ladies in the drawing room, sipping lime cordial. I didn't see Mr. Ingram and was relieved.

But as we were summoned to the music room, where the tuning of a viola was evident, he appeared at my side as if from smoke.

"Miss Smallpiece," he said.

"Good evening, Mr. Ingram," I said coolly. Now it was up to him to set the tone. His face was unreadable.

"It's good of you to come. Welcome to my home."

"It's very nice."

"Yes. It's quite comfortable." He stepped closer. "I was hoping we would meet again before too long, Miss Smallpiece. In fact, I had this event moved ahead a few weeks so that I would have a chance to speak to you before too much time had passed. I considered sending a card to the Watertons' but thought you might turn down my offer to call. As well, Mrs. Waterton would have been present even if you did accept."

"And why would her presence be a problem, Mr. Ingram?"

Without speaking, he led me down a wide hallway. I looked over my shoulder as we went, wondering whether to draw away from his grasp and join the others, wondering if anyone saw what would be interpreted as very unbecoming behavior. But everyone was filing in the other direction, their backs to us now, and I allowed myself to be led.

We went into a room, Mr. Ingram closing the shuttered doors behind us. It was a bedroom with a four-poster bed, the canopy of which appeared to be moreen. There were doors thrown open to the terrace at the back of the house.

"Is this your room, Mr. Ingram? This is entirely improper." I noticed the punkah wallah in the corner, languidly pulling the rope. "What kind of woman do you think I am, that I can be expected to come into a gentleman's quarters, and—"

He didn't let me finish. "Let's stop all this charade. You and I need to speak in complete privacy," he said. Now there was something in his voice that made me realize that I had been right in my first estimation of him. As he turned to face me in the low light of the room, I saw that he had dropped the mask I knew I also wore when in the company of others. And I saw, in that instant, his true nature, recognizing that he carried within him the knowledge, heavy and solid as a rock, that he would get what he desired, at any expense.

"I see no point in avoiding the subject, Miss Smallpiece. The subject being, of course, your unfortunate discovery on the card evening at the Clutterbucks'."

"Actually, I don't know what there is to speak of," I told him. "What you do—your preference and activity—can hardly be classified as a subject. At least not to me."

Somers Ingram sat on a tufted stool, watching me with a stare similar to the one I had last seen in that moonlit hut. Sitting while I stood was a glaring indication that he was not giving me the respect he should, that he looked on me with an insulting brazenness. Growing uncomfortable under such scrutiny, I finally sat as well, primly, in a small armchair.

Although the evening air outside the open windows wasn't hot, the room was airless, the atmosphere thick as the square petticoat of the punkah waved slowly over us. I heard the distant tinkle and scrape of the music stop. There was muted clapping, and then the familiar strains of a Mozart prelude began.

I waited, although my impulse was to rise with the haughty dignity I witnessed around me every day here, and leave the room, no matter what tactics Mr. Ingram chose to employ. He had no hold over me. I could leave of my own free will. And yet I didn't.

"I know what you girls from the Fishing Fleet are like," he finally said. "It's all desperate speculation. You'll do anything you can to find a husband, won't you? The very idea of going home as a returned empty! Why, I'm assured it's the most terrible threat hanging over your lovely heads from the moment you set your dainty foot on Indian soil. And so I've wanted to speak to you to ask if there's anything I can do to make you forget about this little bit of business you stumbled upon. Could I, perhaps, introduce you to one of the men who haven't yet had a chance to become acquainted with all you have to offer?"

"I need no help from you, Mr. Ingram," I told him. "And, as I told you, how you conduct your life is no concern of mine. So there's no reason to bribe me. I know how to keep my mouth shut. And there's another thing that might interest you. I'm not at all the desperate creature you describe. I may not be as anxious to find a husband as you seem to believe." There was something so condescending in his manner— his mocking tone when he spoke of the Fishing Fleet and Returned Empties—that I wanted to put him in his place, let him know I was not like the others.

He appeared undaunted, now daring to smile. But I saw the gleam of perspiration on his brow, the quick touch of knuckle to mustache that came when he was nervous. And it gave me confidence. He crossed his legs. "There's no other point in coming to India as an unmarried woman, is there? Oh, I know there are those who use the guise of caring for a brother, or as company for a lonely mother, but we all know the truth. No single woman comes here with any other purpose save for an occasional weak-eyed missionary. And could this bold statement—that you *aren't at all desperate*—arise from the fact that it's painfully obvious you haven't been doing terribly well with suitors? One can't help but notice how often you sit alone."

I didn't drop my gaze. "I'm not here for that, I've told you. I came as a companion to my friend, Miss Vespry."

"And you plan to return to England as soon as she's found a likely match, then?"

I hesitated. Nobody had actually asked me what my plans were. "No. I'm not planning to return to England. At least not any time soon." *There's nothing for me to go back to, although I wouldn't admit that to you.*

"And?" His foot bobbed. "You'll do exactly what here, when the busy Miss Vespry becomes a memsahib? Surely she won't want you as a companion when she has a husband."

"I'm not entirely sure. I . . . I've thought about enquiring. About various positions. I once had a very dignified position in a library. Through my own choosing, of course."

He cocked his head. "You have been *employed*? And you would think that it would be possible to carry on like that here, in Calcutta? My, my, Miss Smallpiece. I wouldn't let that get out. Such news would definitely be the end of you. You may as well take out an ad in the *Calcutta Gazette* that you're unmarriageable material. Besides, no white woman is ever employed in India. And no white women stay unless they're married, or have the misfortune to be a spinster daughter or sister. Surely you understand that, don't you, Miss Smallpiece? Whatever are you thinking?"

I stood. "Really, Mr. Ingram, you are too rude. I don't know why I've stayed to speak with you. We'll say no more about—your indiscretion. I would never threaten you with it, even though of course sodomy is, let's not forget, punishable by hanging, and we'll do our best to ignore each other when we're forced together in society."

He shook his head, then tilted it to one side, narrowing his eyes. He hadn't risen when I did, choosing to stay, disrespectfully, on the stool. "There it is again, Miss Smallpiece. You surprise me more with every passing day. How would you know that sodomy is a crime? For that fact, what do you know of sodomy, Miss Smallpiece? Even to know and utter the word—"

I raised my chin and started toward the door.

"There's something about you that's not . . ." He looked toward the open doors. "Not exactly . . ." He paused again. "I can't seem to put it into words." He smiled, but his smile was now little more than a slash beneath his mustache. "I've always considered myself a good judge of character. And now I believe it all ties together. The way the men make a wide berth around you. Your insistence on not being interested. It's almost as if you don't *like* men, Miss Smallpiece. Yes, I believe that's what it is," he said, nodding his head as if surprised by his own sudden intuition. "You may try to cover it, but now that I think about it, it's quite clear. And the men sense it as well. There's no other reason for their reticence, is there? It's not that you don't have a certain appeal, and while you're not the picture of conventional beauty, you're certainly as passable in appearance as any of the others. Let's speak frankly, shall we, Miss Smallpiece?"

I was halfway across the room. "Why is it that you feel you can speak to me in such a rude and familiar way?" There was a warning buzz in the back of my head. I wished Faith would come looking for me. The distant music droned on. The punkah swung lazily overhead, and from the darkness beyond the terrace came the scream of a peacock, followed by the longing answer of a peahen.

Mr. Ingram emitted a barking laugh. "Familiar? Well, it's not as though you haven't seen me in a most familiar way, is it?"

At that moment a gecko fell from the rafters, dropping onto the sleeve of my pale lavender watered silk. I gasped at the surprise of it, brushing at the little lizard, but it clung tightly. Mr. Ingram swung into action; his breeding was intrinsic, and he acted as a gentleman without thinking. He crossed the floor in a few long strides and took hold of the gecko, and as he attempted to pluck it from my sleeve, the tiny creature's claws remained caught in the delicate material, dragging the loose bell sleeve up to my elbow as Mr. Ingram pulled.

And then he stayed still, his hand closed around the fragile green body. I looked at his face; there was a curious expression there. Blinking, he used his other hand to disengage the harmless reptile from my sleeve, holding it gingerly between thumb and index finger.

"Take this," he called, and the punkah wallah appeared out of the shadows and took the gecko from Mr. Ingram.

I arranged my sleeve, and saw that Mr. Ingram was still staring at my arm with that odd, thoughtful gaze. And then he grew pale, in spite of his sun-darkened skin, as if his blood had suddenly been sucked out of him by an unseen siphon. For one incredible moment I imagined he had been frightened by the gecko.

"Let me see that again," he demanded. "That mark on the inside of your arm." A far-off whisper, something that troubled me in his voice, set the faint buzzing still in my ears into a loud bell of alarm. Pounding heat rushed to my head; it was as if there was too much blood coursing through my veins, as if Mr. Ingram's blood had been transferred to me.

While he had blanched the color of suet, I was burning, flushed. My hands continued to flutter over my sleeve, smoothing and patting it as I ignored his request.

His eyes raked my hair, my face, and then, with no warning, he grabbed my hand and turned my arm over, roughly pushing my sleeve back up. He stared down at the smooth skin and my fish birthmark, and then he dropped my hands and took a hasty step away as if he had suddenly become aware of the putrid breath of contagion.

I put my palm on my birthmark, looking at him with consternation. "It's just a birthmark, Mr. Ingram," I said. "Hardly unusual."

"I know that birthmark. I've seen it somewhere before." His voice was low, the words weighted, as if an unseen hand were pushing on his Adam's apple.

"Surely not," I stuttered. And as another moment passed, with Mr. Ingram still scrutinizing me, that odd drawn look about his mouth and eyes, I knew the worst had happened. His next words confirmed the unspeakable fear.

"I've seen you before, I realize that now. Your face isn't overly familiar, but that distinct fish marks you clearly. Although I chose not to speak of it to you, I did travel to Liverpool, and I regularly had the opportunity to keep company with all manner of men—and women. Although many of my memories of those visits are less than clear, some things stay with one, don't you find?"

God, no, I prayed then. His sort didn't usually frequent Paradise. Had he actually ever been a customer? Wouldn't I have remembered him in the vast number of faces and bodies I had known? I always believed I remembered too much, in detail I wish I could forget.

I stood, waiting. I knew by the smile now playing about his still bloodless lips that he was confident that he knew about my past, and he would use it to destroy me. The smile also made it clear that it would bring him pleasure to do it. But why? I had assured him his secret was safe with me. It was true; I had no interest in anyone else's secrets. I had my own to protect.

I straightened my shoulders, and unexpectedly felt the old pull of my scar as if it were a fresh wound. I would have to play it out, deny whatever he accused me of. "Whatever do you mean? I demand to know what you are implying, sir," I said, trying for polite outrage, for genteel indignation, but to my horror I heard my old voice trying to edge its way out. I stopped, swallowing. Although I might, by complete consternation, be forced into a rough phrase, as I had with Mr. Ingram, I had really begun to believe that voice—not just the inflection, but the higher shrillness—was gone. But in that moment, when it erupted involuntarily, I knew that it—like Back Phoebe Anne and Paradise Street, was grimly ingrained forever, no matter how conscientiously I held that part of me at bay.

"I suggest you sit down, Miss Smallpiece. You're not looking well, not well at all."

I could see that the color had snapped back to his face, two hectic spots high on his cheekbones, and there was the heavy-lidded look about him as one sated by too much rich food or brutal sex. "Here. Let me help you," he said.

He held my upper arms, walking me backward until my calves touched the seat of a chair, and I lowered myself onto it.

He watched me. Then he glanced around the room. The punkah wallah had crept back in from depositing the gecko off the terrace steps, and resumed his job from the corner, but I knew that to Mr. Ingram he was of no consequence. "Now I know what secret I've been seeing on your face, reading in your body. Now I know exactly what you are."

There was a dark rushing at the back of my head. I heard, as if from a great distance, "Why, you really are a simple working girl, aren't you, my dear? Although a post in a library is not the position I seem to remember you in." He pushed up my sleeve and stroked my birthmark tenderly. My skin dimpled. "Now I know exactly what you are," he whispered.

Not who you are, but what. A whore.

I had been found out. It was all over.

❧

I DIDN'T FAINT. Something, desperation perhaps, drove me to fight the thickness in my head and to rise from the chair. I ran, stumbling, from the room, and from Somers Ingram. I ran down the deserted hallway and passed the music room, smelling the burst of hot, scented air, hearing the French horns and violas singing sweetly. I ran on, out onto the wide drive, where one of the servants stopped me and understood my desperate pleas to leave. His calm expression beneath the high turban showed no surprise at an English girl running like a lunatic from the house, panting and gasping, and he summoned a small palanquin pulled by one runner.

I don't remember giving the *boyee* the location, or getting back to the Watertons' house. I dismissed the servants who gathered around me as I stepped inside, and fell across my bed fully dressed. It wasn't more than a few minutes before the chill started, my teeth dancing against one another, and I couldn't get warm even though the night was far from cool. I pulled a cover over me but it didn't help. I heard Faith's voice in the corridor, heard the rustle of taffeta as she peeked in my room, and then the reclosing of my door as she assumed I was asleep.

Shortly afterward I became ill, throwing up the light tiffin I'd eaten hours before.

Faith heard me as I retched into the washbasin, and came into my room, laying her smooth, cool hand against my cheek. "We all wondered where you'd got to. I came back early, before they served the evening refreshments, worried over you. I hope it's not malaria, Linny. Have you been taking your quinine?"

I nodded. "It's not malaria," I whispered. "Perhaps—I think I ate something at lunch that disagreed with me."

"Do you suppose it was the pea-fowl pilau? It was a bit oily. Or perhaps you ate too much of the amandine comfit. Can I fetch you anything?" She looked at the empty mat at the foot of my bed. "Where is your ayah?"

"I sent her away. I want to be alone. I'll just sleep, and be fine tomorrow, I'm sure." My teeth started their dance again, and I hugged my arms against my chest.

"I don't care what you say. I'm going to send in your ayah, and she can help get you into your nightdress. You can't be alone when you're ill. And she can alert me should you grow worse in the night."

I nodded, too distressed to argue, and the ayah came in. I let her undress me and take down my hair and slip the nightdress over my head and bathe my hands and face with cool water. But even the quiet rhythm of her breathing in the still room as she fell asleep did little to ease my illness, brought on not by food but by terror, and I knew I wouldn't sleep that night, and perhaps for many more.

Chapter Twenty-One

A DAY PASSED, AND THEN ANOTHER. I STAYED IN MY ROOM, telling Faith I was indisposed. Mrs. Waterton felt we should call for the physician, should it be the start of a tropical malaise, but I insisted it would pass with time, implying that it was simply my monthly discomfort.

I couldn't stay still, though, and endlessly wandered about my bedroom, picking up objects and setting them back, unable to sleep or keep food down or even read.

By the third day I was so agitated, waiting, trying to guess what Somers Ingram would do with his information, that I simply could not remain shut up any longer. I sat at dinner with Faith and the Watertons, trying to focus, to act normally. I felt my mouth smile, felt food, dry as ashes, struggle down my throat, actually heard my own words prattling unimportant nonsense. There was a fête at the Club that evening; Mr. Snow had invited Faith to be his escort, and the Watertons would also be present. I convinced everyone to go, that I would be fine, but didn't feel up to socializing yet. I was terrified of running into Mr. Ingram, and yet thought that perhaps it would be better to face him, let whatever he was going to do surface. Surely it would be better than what I was suffering with now—the unknown.

The Watertons' palanquin had barely pulled away when the *chuprassi* appeared in the drawing room, where I sat at a desk, holding a quill in my hand, the sheet of paper before me blank. I had thought of writing to Shaker, hoping that the act of describing trifling matters would calm me. The *chuprassi,* adjusting his distinctive red sash, announced the arrival of Mr. Ingram.

I stood, the quill falling onto the paper, ruining it with a smear of ink. Had Somers Ingram been watching the house, waiting to ensure that I was alone before he came to call? How improper, I thought, in that one insane instant, that he arrive unannounced and me without a chaperone. And it was followed in the next instant by a small and bitter sound, laughter at my own hypocrisy. I was acting in the same way as the women I secretly scorned. And it was a little late to be worrying about improprieties with this particular man.

He was ushered into the drawing room by the *chuprassi* and followed by the *khitmutgar.* As the *chuprassi* bowed his way out of the room, the *khitmutgar* went to the sideboard and poured out a measure of dark rum into a heavy crystal glass. He brought it to Somers Ingram on an inlaid tray and then bowed in front of me.

"No. Nothing," I said, and the tall man bowed again and took up his place at the sideboard.

"Linny," Mr. Ingram said, smiling as he took a sip. It appeared to be an artless smile, but I knew better. "No point in bothering with Miss Smallpiece any longer, is there? Surely—given what I know you to be—there's no need for playacting."

I stepped closer to him, returning his false smile with an even falser one. "Look. All I care about is staying here, and of course I won't be able to if you disclose what you know of me. There's no point in spoiling it for me, Mr. Ingram." I said his name with the same firmness he'd used with mine. "You don't tell my secrets, and I don't tell yours." At least I had the tiny comfort of thinking I could also hurt his reputation. His next words dashed that comfort.

"So, you threaten me? Do you really think anyone would believe your tittle-tattle? Can you really imagine that anyone would take you seriously—a griffin, fresh off the boat—over me, well established and respected throughout Calcutta? Anything you might say would come across as the hysterics of a bitter woman, rejected by her heart's desire.

It's quite laughable, and rather pathetic, that you actually feel you can intimidate me."

"Have you already begun your campaign of slander, then? Shall I expect to be dismissed from the Watertons' this very night?" The words burst out with an edge of hysteria.

He seemed to be considering my question, enjoying making me suffer. He shook his head, smiling.

"Or will you use your knowledge to satisfy yourself at will?" I cried. "Is that what it is to be about, then? You think you will be able to use me as you imply you had once, at least, in Liverpool—although I must admit that your efforts had so little effect that I have no memory of you. You must have performed in a very lackluster manner indeed."

I saw his jaw clench.

"I was never interested in such common trade then, and still am not. My interest, as you have discovered, runs more fully toward the stronger sex. No. Although I would never have used you myself, I am full aware of recognizing that birthmark, and knowing it is tied in to the various times I spent with the lower end of life in Liverpool."

Still I found it strange that I had no stronger recollection of him than some tiny, disturbing whisper that might have only been created by my current fear.

"Have you had many offers of male companionship of late, Linny? Any prospects? Has any man here ever paid you serious individual attention?"

There was little point in trying to bluff with Somers Ingram. I knew I'd managed to scare away the young men of Calcutta all on my own. Or, if I hadn't actually scared them, I'd made them uncomfortable enough that they weren't approaching me. I knew what they were looking for— a reserved, and perhaps slightly coy, accommodating woman—for was there any other kind in these circles? But that role—coy sweetness— was so difficult for me to play; no matter how interested I appeared in their stories, nodding, downcast eyelashes creating what I'd seen as becoming shadows on the cheeks of other women, I knew I couldn't do it. My heart wasn't in it. Now I shook my head.

"But then how do you propose to stay in India, Linny, if there are no marriage proposals forthcoming?"

"As I said, I—perhaps . . . some kind of position."

"Really, Linny. Stop your dreaming." The scent of rum wafted toward me, strong.

I knew he was right. I think I had known, almost from my arrival, that if I were to stay I would indeed have to find a husband. I had just refused to admit it to myself. Our time at the Watertons could last at the most six or seven months without an announced engagement, and we were into the fourth. Looking at Somers, I knew I would only have to fool one man. At that moment I realized that I didn't care who it was. Faced with the thought of leaving India, of returning to Liverpool, I knew then that I would do whatever I had to. Marry someone. Anyone. I thought of Shaker and my words to him—that I would not marry while in India. But if it came down to the choice of staying as a married woman or leaving. . . . Here, with servants to carry out every domestic duty, there would be no demands on me other than entertaining. I could learn to do it, make endless, tedious talk over the dinner table and order servants about, organize parties and plan meals. And as for the rest—it would certainly be no hardship to spread my legs under the mosquito netting for a faceless husband. These things meant nothing to me; a small price to pay for staying here, in India, where my heart had unclenched for the first time in my life. If I were to be a prisoner, better a prisoner in India, where I might eventually earn some freedom, some time outside of the curtained palanquins and the Maidan and the Calcutta Club.

I thought of Meg Liston, riding off into the wilds with her husband. Writing her book. Free to explore. It could be possible for me, too.

"Are you listening, Linny? I said I had a plan."

I blinked. "A plan?"

Somers sat on the settee, nodding at the chair across from it.

"I'd rather stand."

"As you wish. But this is what I've been thinking about, these last few days." His eyes drifted about the room, then returned to the dark liquid in the bottom of his glass. He was taking forever to say what he had to say. He brushed back his springy dark hair with manicured fingernails. "Simply put, I need a wife. I cannot wait any longer. I had planned to pick someone out of this fleet; in fact, for a while I thought I might choose that little parakeet with the high voice you came with—Miss Vespry. She looked as if she would be easy to put up with, pretty enough to not turn me off my breakfast every morning, although she appears a bit skittish and possibly given to instability. I would venture to guess that she's also scared witless of the touch of a man, and that could help me for the first while—she would have no expectations, of course." He continued to rake his fingers through his hair, gazing into his glass, and then he looked back to me. "Anyway, never mind about that. It came to me, the other night, that not only is the timing perfect, but that we are an ideal match, Linny."

"A match? You and I? We're no such thing. Please don't compare us. I find it an insult."

Somers laughed, a loud and spontaneous laugh. "Very refreshing. That you, a Liverpool doxie, would be insulted to put yourself into my league." He laughed again, gesturing at the *khitmutgar*. The tall man stepped up immediately, the silver tray ready. His hennaed beard trembled slightly as he waited for Somers to set down the glass. Taking it to the sideboard, he refilled it and brought it back to Somers. Then he faded into the recesses of the room once more.

Mr. Ingram took a delicate sip. "But we are a match, my dear, for the simple reason that we both have a secret to hide, and that we can use each other to fulfill our needs. There is the added benefit of both of us having no other attachments in this world."

I watched the *khitmutgar* in his darkened corner, seeing that his eyes never lifted from the floor. "Why must you marry so hurriedly? Why is it so important right now?"

Mr. Ingram drank again. "I'm waiting to come into my full inheritance. My father made his fortune by his instincts and shrewd investments in the building trade. Although in later years much of that fortune was squandered due to his . . . shall we say, ungentlemanly pursuits." He stopped and shook his head in an impatient and angry motion. "I'm the only heir. In spite of a goodly loss, the sum of the inheritance is still pleasing. Not huge, as it won't allow me complete leisure for the rest of my life, but sufficient to allow me some choices.

My father's will specifies that I receive it at twenty-five, if all conditions are met. One of those conditions is that I be married. I turn twenty-five in a mere three months." With a swift motion he drained the glass.

"What I'm saying, Linny, is that you and I are both in a bit of a tight spot. Wouldn't you agree? And the simplest solution is for us to marry. You'll get to stay in India. And I, too, like this country, in spite of its confusion and filth and idolatry. I don't know what you find attractive, but I like it because here I can live in the manner I prefer—every need cared for, with an embarrassment of servants to jump at my slightest whim. To say nothing of the endless wealth of eager and fresh young boys, throwing themselves at the chance to be the paramour of what they see as a pukka sahib.

"India is a wonderful place for someone like me. Had I come of age half a century ago I might have been a freewheeling trader or soldier of fortune. But those days—the ones of straightforward trading concerns—are gone. Now we are responsible for ruling the Indians. No. Not just ruling them—trying to help them. India is a stagnant country." He paused. "My position as chief auditor for John Company gives me a respect I could never acquire in London. And by marrying you, Linny, I'll become wealthy enough to do more or less what I like, and appear exactly as I should. A hot-blooded young man with a wife to do for him, a wife to join the English team in India, cheer it on. It's becoming a bit embarrassing, my staying single as the fifth Fishing Fleet in so many years has come in to shore since I've been here. People may well be wondering why not one of these lovely young ladies has been to my fancy, in spite of all the well-meaning matchmaking set up by overanxious matrons wanting to ensure my domestic happiness."

The *khitmutgar* came toward Somers again, tray raised, but Mr. Ingram waved him away with an impatient flick of his hand. "You will admit that you would be getting the better part of the bargain, Linny. You'd have your wish of remaining in India, while all I would get, in actuality, is a dependent. But one that will allow me the money and freedom to satisfy my needs exactly as I please. And of course you realize there would be no children. I have absolutely no interest in ever touching you. The assumption would, of course, be that you are barren. You will garner great sympathy from the other women on this."

"And if I say no, and do find my own means to stay here? I may find someone else, after all, who is interested in a marriage." I was clutching at frail straws on the wind. He knew it and I knew it.

Mr. Ingram set his empty glass on the polished table beside the settee. He chose a cheroot from the humidor there, sniffing it. "If you say no, why then, my dear Miss Smallpiece, you will be on the next ship home. And everyone who is anyone in Calcutta, and actually much further beyond, since there is nothing more loved here than gossip—will have learned about Miss Linny Smallpiece. Somehow, by some insidiously creeping tittle-tattle whose origin will never be remembered, everyone will hear that you are not what you appear. That you are a whore of the lowest quarter. Imagine the state Miss Vespry will get herself into! The Watertons will be mortified, as well. And the men will nod to each other, realizing what they'd been smelling when they sniffed around you. Why, it would soon be heard that you'd even propositioned one or two of the chaps down at the Club." He put the end of the cheroot in his mouth and rolled it, making a small satisfied sound. "And the women would appear horrified, but even they would admit to each other that there was always something not quite right about Linny Smallpiece, that they'd known there was something odd all along." He shook his head. "And of course the news would arrive home, straight to Liverpool. It might be hard on your family—a cousin and aunt, was it?—or is that a fabrication too? Whatever the case, whatever you came from there would no longer be open to you.

"You've done well, haven't you, Linny, at fooling people?" He didn't expect an answer. "What a long way you've come; I can't imagine the route that's brought you to this level. What you must have done to get here." He shook his head. "Most admirable, I must admit. I think I almost like you for it."

I walked to the wide windows and looked at the darkness beyond. Suddenly the country was threatening, dark and watching. "Even if I were to agree to this ridiculous proposal, how would we keep our true relationship hidden? For there could be no pretending that we could ever care, even the slightest, about each other."

"Quite simple, really. We're both experts at living lies. We'll live as man and wife under the same roof, but spend as little time together as possible. We don't even have to share dinner, unless we have company. My job here"—he smiled, snapping his fingers at the *khitmutgar,* who stepped forward, lighting a flint match—"keeps me very busy. I'm often away for weeks. And I like to go off to the jungle, hunting. So we won't have to see each other for much of the time. When we are forced together while in public, or in the presence of guests in our own home, your life will appear to be that of the proper bride. You'll want for nothing.

"I ask only two things of you," he continued. "Firstly, you must never breathe a word about whatever it is I might do, or with whom. Of course that's understood. And secondly, should you ever, *ever,* revert to your ways, even once, and disgrace me with your whoring, you shall be out of my home in less time than it will take for me to smoke this cheroot. Out with nothing but the clothes on your back. I'll not be cuckolded."

He sucked deeply on the cheroot as the *khitmutgar* held the match to its tip. I watched his handsome face in the brief glow of the match, and in that sudden flare of light I wondered what it would be like to rise to this daring challenge. In the next instant I shuddered involuntarily, imagining what hell he would make my life, and how I would forever be made to dance to his tune. I turned away from him.

"Linny? Do you understand completely?"

"Oh yes. Yes, Mr. Ingram, I do."

"And you're in agreement with the plan?"

When I didn't answer, Somers came to stand behind me. "There's a ship, the *Bengal Merchant,* sailing for home in three days. You could be on it, in disgrace, if you don't answer carefully."

I TOLD MR. INGRAM I'd need time to weigh my decision carefully. And in the early morning of the third day I packed my trunks and sent my ayah to wake Mrs. Waterton and tell her I was leaving. Then I went to Faith's room and woke her, sitting on the edge of the bed as I told her of my decision.

Her face first registered complete disbelief, followed by confusion, then disappointment and sadness. "You're leaving Calcutta? Now? But . . . but *why,* Linny? I don't understand. And—well, I thought our

spoken commitment was that you would be my companion, until . . .
until either I went home or, more hopefully, had reason to stay. It's only
February; the season isn't officially over until the beginning of April,
and there's even time after that." She was still in her bed, now staring at
the floor. "I thought you loved it here. You told me that you loved it,
Linny, loved it. That you'd never felt so wonderful, and now—now
you're just up and leaving. Do you really want to go back to Everton
and your cousin and aunt that badly? Is it that you miss them? You're
homesick?"

I clenched my back teeth, but before I had a chance to answer, Faith
continued.

"No one, but absolutely no one starts the tiresome voyage home
again after such a short time. It's unheard of. You haven't given it a
chance, that's it. And—and . . ." She looked around wildly, as if hoping
to draw reasons for me to stay out of the air. "And my father will be ever
so displeased. He's on his way here right now, aboard a ship that is due to
arrive sometime within the next few months. He only gave his consent
to all of this—to me coming the season ahead of him—because I spoke
so endlessly and highly of you. And now if he comes, and you're not
here . . . he shall report to Mr. Smallpiece, to your guardian, that you've
broken your part of the bargain, and his embarrassment—your
cousin's—will be your burden to bear. So you can't leave, Linny. You
simply can't." She scrambled out of bed, grabbing my arms so that I was
forced to stand too, facing her. "Please. Say you'll stay. Just for me."

I looked at her pretty face. How she had changed, starting the
moment we had left the docks at Liverpool. I had kept waiting for her to
adjust to the strangeness of all that was India. But it seemed she had
fallen out of step, somehow, even with the atmosphere of England
smothering us here in Calcutta. She had become ever more complacent,
less outspoken, perhaps even fearful, while I had found my place in the
world. Faith was out of her element, and I was in mine. Or had been.

"I can't explain to you why I have to go." I prayed that once I left,
without telling Mr. Ingram, he would say nothing. But then again he
might decide, simply out of spite—remembering his expression, that
smug knowledge that he would get what he wanted—to go ahead and
start the stories about me.

"But the season isn't out for another six weeks. Two months or more, as I said. There's still time."

"For what?"

"For someone to show interest."

"I know someone will, Faith. Aren't you seeing Mr. Snow quite regularly?"

"I meant for you, Linny. Time for someone to ask you for your hand. You mustn't despair."

"That's not it," I said. "I came to be your companion. It wasn't my intention to marry here. I told you that before we left. I just thought I might . . . stay . . ." Again, my reasoning was flimsy. I walked out of Faith's room. Crying, she followed me out to the waiting palanquin, wearing her dressing gown. We were followed by Mrs. Waterton, her clothing obviously thrown on in a great hurry; it was clear she wasn't wearing her stays. She wrung her hands, her face a crumpled mask of dismay. I saw Mr. Waterton poke his head out the door, looking mulish, and then he retreated back inside.

"This doesn't look well on us, dear. It's as if we haven't made you happy here," she said. "Mr. Vespry entrusted Faith—and you—to us. And now you're leaving, with no traveling companion for the voyage home. I don't know of any married women on the Bengal Merchant at this point. It's not right, just not right at all. These things have to be planned, with all kinds of arrangements."

"I sent the *chuprassi* to book my passage, and will use the return ticket bought by Mr. Vespry. I promise I can look after myself," I told her, thanking her for her hospitality. The palanquin runners loaded up my luggage, and I left. I looked back at the two women standing outside the beautiful villa, gleaming whitely in the morning sun. Mrs. Waterton fluttered a handkerchief, while Faith covered her face with her hands, her shoulders shaking as she wept.

I left the curtains open as we rode through Calcutta. It was my first and last time to ride through the city, alone, and drink in India through all my senses.

Again, as at the dock that first day, it was the vividness of color that was so astounding. The light was yellow. I thought of the blue light of England, and how it made everything appear slightly worn. A soft, soporific light, creating a life that was standing still, accepting. Here, in this brilliant light, my eyelids felt burned away, making it impossible to close my eyes. We passed the last house on Garden Reach, then turned up a smaller street. Here the houses were still in the European fashion, but smaller and meaner. The roofs were thatched, the walls stained with mildew. These were the homes of the employees of the uncovenanted civil service, the men who were Eurasian, who were born here and tainted with Indian blood, no matter how distant the union had been. That bloodline ensured there could never be any hope to rise above the uncovenanted rank in the Company. Half-caste children ran about— grandchildren and great-grandchildren of the pairing of the native women and men from the John Company, before British women were allowed to come to this wild and dangerous country. Some of the children were startlingly European looking, others darker and more native.

Finally we were at the docks. They were teeming, swarming with life and noise as they had been when we arrived. I thought of the morning Faith and I left Liverpool, how the dull fog had swirled about us, dampening our clothes and skin and chilling us in the silence. I imagined arriving there again, in the same fog, trudging out to find a carriage, and then the ride to Whitefield Lane, past Paradise Street and then Bold Street and the Lyceum. I imagined the look on Shaker's face, the light in his eyes when he saw me. And then I imagined myself years later, still living in Everton, a withered old woman in a black coat and bonnet turning green. I imagined my own face, my eyesight failing and my penmanship losing its firmness as I bent over the recording cards at the Lyceum, obediently hidden behind the stacks.

I stood beside my piled luggage, my ticket in my hand. From nowhere a near-naked sadhu, a holy man, twirled and shouted his way through a crowd of uninterested women in fuchsia, turquoise, and orange saris. The sadhu's body gleamed blue-black under its covering of smeared wood ash, and his dense, wiry hair hung like twisted ropes, the parting on his scalp vermilion dusted. I recognized the three horizontal lines painted with a thick white substance on his forehead, indicating that he was a follower of Shiva, the god of death. As he leaped about, closer and closer, the layers of beads on his chest danced and clattered. He came straight at me, as if he had been searching for me, and I stared into his bloodshot eyes. He shouted something into my face, spraying me with saliva, and his breath was rank with the smell of betel and stomach rot. I didn't understand the words, but I knew the meaning. It was a warning, a premonition. A man in an army uniform and solar topee pushed him rudely away from me, asking if I was all right. I nodded, but couldn't speak.

I understood the portent of the sadhu.

❧

I RETURNED IN A PALANQUIN. When the door was opened by the *chuprassi*, he stared at me, then behind me, with a look of modified horror at my lack of decorum at calling at a gentleman's house, unchaperoned.

"I wish to speak to Mr. Ingram," I said. "Is he still at home?"

He nodded, but stood, immobile, blocking the door.

"Come now," I said, pushing past him and into the entrance hall. "I must see him. Please summon him for me." When the man still didn't move, I started through the house, to the room where Mr. Ingram and I had last spoken. By the time I reached the hallway a small herd of servants trailed, obviously distressed with my boldness.

I stopped in front of the shuttered door, my hand raised to knock. But a breeze rattled the shutter before I had the chance, and there was movement inside; perhaps my shadow had been cast into the room, my presence announced.

"Hazi? Is that you? Have you got my clean collar?"

I pulled open the shuttered door. "No. It's me, Mr. Ingram," I said, and stepped inside the room with the moreen canopy, firmly shutting the door on the concerned servants.

Somers Ingram stood behind his desk. He wore only his trousers and an unbuttoned collarless shirt, the cuffs undone. His hair, lacking its usual pomade, curled about his ears and neck. In spite of what had passed between us, I was still struck by his appearance.

I felt the closed door at my back.

Mr. Ingram came toward me, his face unreadable. "To what do I owe this early morning visit?" he asked.

"I've made my decision."

He came closer. I smelled soap, the starch of his shirt. "And?" I could see now that although he was trying to hide it, there was a shallowness in the rise and fall of his bare chest that belied his attempted nonchalance.

"I agree to your terms."

"To be my wife," he confirmed, and his voice came out with less than his usual surety. When I nodded, he raised the knuckle of his index finger to his mustache in that tiny, quick way I had come to watch for. And in seeing his body's involuntary reaction—his breathing, his voice, the touch of his mustache—I felt a small sense of pride, of accomplishment, for I knew then that no matter how he tried to act as if my decision meant little to him one way or another, that my final answer had been the one he'd actually hoped for.

"You've made the right decision, Linny. For don't you see? We are the same. We both hide something, and we both must stay at the level of acceptance we have attained here. It will go much easier on both of us this way. There need be no sham between us; we understand each other. Do you not see it this way?" he repeated.

I didn't answer, turning my face from his. While it might be true that he found a part of me loathsome, as I did him, there could be no denying that for all his bluster, I saw that I did hold some power over him.

Chapter Twenty-Two

February 15, 1831

My dearest Shaker,

It is difficult to compose this letter, only because it is one I never expected to write to you. I know that by the time you read this you will have only just received my initial packet of letters, telling you about my new life here. I wrote those letters with a heart full of joy, with the lightness of shaking off an old life and beginning one anew. And now this brief page is written in a different vein, with a heavy heart. There is no other way to say it but this: I am to be married within a fortnight. Of course, by the time you read this I expect I shall have been married for months.

It was a completely unexpected and, as you must know, unforeseeable, event. The words I spoke to you last summer, before I left Liverpool, were true. So please dismiss from your imagination romantic trysts, passion, or even the hint of friendship. This is not a marriage that involves any emotion for either the gentleman or myself. It is a marriage of convenience. I can say no more, although I know you are now thinking—a marriage of convenience? Did I not speak this phrase to her myself, suggesting that this could have worked for us? But Shaker, there is more to this, so much more. There are things I can never explain, a hard, linked chain of events from my past that precipitated this union, each link rusted, forever fixed. And it is due to that dark time that I must become Mrs. Somers Ingram. He is a gentleman from London, in the employ of the East India Company.

I can write no more at this time. As is apparent from the appearance of this letter, my hand is far from steady. Please forgive me, and please, please dictate a letter in reply. I await each posting from England with great eagerness. Although you may not have forgiven me enough to wish to correspond, at least my letters have not been returned, and I take this as an agreement to this one-sided correspondence. Should you feel that contacting me is impossible, I will understand. But again I beg you, please, Shaker, do not cast me from your life, for in many ways, I feel that I need you even more now.

With deepest affection,
Linny

Writing to Shaker was the most difficult aspect of marrying Somers, even more difficult that trying to explain my decision to Faith. After I had given Somers my consent and we'd discussed when the event would take place—of course, as soon as possible, as Somers wanted no dilly-dallying or false courtship rituals—I returned to the Watertons'. I found Faith, pale and listless, on the verandah. A servant stood behind her, fanning her with a peacock fan. She sat up straight, her mouth falling open, as I stepped through the doors.

"You didn't go, then? You've changed your mind?" she asked, jumping to her feet.

I nodded.

"I knew you couldn't abandon me, Linny. I just knew it." She gave me a quick hug.

"I must tell you of my plans, Faith," I said. "Sit down. Please."

She lowered herself to the rattan settee. The boy immediately resumed his fanning. "Plans?"

Taking a deep breath, I sat beside her and took her hands in mine. "I'm to be married, Faith."

Her fingers contracted, and I felt the bite of her nails against the backs of my hands. "Married? But . . . but to whom? There's been nobody—"

"I know. It's come about quite suddenly. It's Somers Ingram."

Faith frowned, then shook her head. "Somers Ingram? Mr. *Ingram*?"

"Yes."

"He's never even come to call. I've hardly noticed you speaking to him or dancing with him more than a few times. I . . . I don't know what to think, Linny. What to say."

There was silence, except for the soft swoosh of the beautiful fan.

"The wedding will be in two weeks. February twenty-eighth. Somers—Mr. Ingram—says it must be before the approach of the hot season."

At that Faith wrenched her hands from mine and stood, an odd expression on her face. "Well. You are a sly boots. I see you're capable of doing quite well for yourself, after all. And here I was, pitying you." She was bristling with anger now. "It appears you've been working some black Hindu magic behind my back—behind all our backs. It's well known that Mr. Ingram has been quite unattainable—and he is certainly a handsome and charming catch, as you obviously know. And with his senior position in the service—well, Linny, you will find yourself quite a senior lady, won't you? You will even be above Mrs. Waterton in rank."

I swallowed. I had not for one second thought of my own position as Somer's wife within Calcutta society.

"Apparently a number of girls have tried for a match with him, but he wasn't interested," Faith went on. "There is the usual rumor of course—that he has a black mistress—and then . . . the other rumor."

"Which is?" Was the secret Somers Ingram thought he kept so well hidden common knowledge after all? But Faith's next sentence assured me this wasn't so.

"That he might like a woman with a naughty edge; that he's looking for more. And perhaps there *is* more to you than meets the eye, Linny. What is it, exactly, that has so attracted Mr. Ingram to you where the rest of us have failed? And why is it that you felt you had to hide everything from me? Why have you been so selfish?"

"It isn't like that at all, Faith."

"It isn't? You didn't bother to confide in me for one moment, to tell me you were even interested in Mr. Ingram. And there I was, making a fool of myself with him only a few weeks ago, thinking that if Mr. Snow was too shy to come forward, Mr. Ingram certainly seemed attracted. You must have been laughing at me the whole time." She bunched her skirt around her and swept past me, stopping at the verandah doors. "Well, don't expect me to attend your wedding, Linny Smallpiece, for I no longer consider you a friend. I should have listened to my instincts, and to everyone in Liverpool who advised me that you might not be a suitable companion. Did you know that, Linny? That I was cautioned against becoming too close to you by more than one? And I thought they proved right only hours earlier today, when you told me you were leaving India, and me. But now this? *This?* Showing me up, marrying before I've had a proposal? You, whom I rescued from that dreary library and even more dreary existence in that awful, provincial Everton, bringing you here out of the goodness of my heart and with the purse of my father. You made it perfectly clear that you had little interest in marriage, for some completely unknown and ridiculous reason. And now you dare to be the first of our entire fleet to become engaged—and with a wedding date set in such a hurried, preposterous manner? It's as if everything you've said is a lie. And it's too much for me, Linny. Just too much."

And she swept from the verandah, leaving me with the boy and his peacock fan, the languid rhythm never missing a beat.

❧❧❧

POOR MRS. WATERTON. Still recovering from the shock of my leaving, she reclined on a sofa in her bedroom, a wet cloth on her forehead. I now had to go and tell her the same thing I had told Faith.

She was predictably amazed, sitting bolt upright and tossing the cloth to the floor. She kept repeating, "Mr. Ingram? Mr. Ingram, well. Well, Mr. Ingram," making it clear that she thought it an impossibility that a gentleman such as he could have even noticed one such as myself.

"But why so quickly? Why must the wedding be so immediate?" she asked, when I told her the date. "There's a great deal to go into planning a wedding; why, to enjoy it fully it must be drawn out for months. The end of February is terribly inconvenient. In fact, it is impossible."

"I'm sorry, Mrs. Waterton, but it is at Mr. Ingram's insistence."

"Is there no way you can convince him to extend the engagement, Linny, and be married in the first glorious sweep of the cool season next fall?"

I shook my head. "I'm sorry, Mrs. Waterton."

Mrs. Waterton was silent for a moment, and I saw a veil of suspicion fall over her face. And then she took a deep breath and stood, opening her arms. "Well, no matter what I feel, I suppose congratulations are in order, my dear. I'm sure you'll be very happy," she said, coming to embrace me. Her hug was stiff.

I was grateful to her; I knew how difficult this was, but she was trying her best to be pleased.

She stepped away, her face now composed. Ever true to her class, I knew she would say no more to me about the strangeness of the situation, although I also knew that within hours there would be much tongue-wagging throughout Calcutta society. "There's not even any time to make up proper invitations," she sighed. "Well, I suppose the first thing we must do is have a dress made," she said, opening the drawing room door to shout her usual "Koi-hai?"—is anyone there?—and send a servant running for the *durzi*.

～❧～

FACED WITH THE MAMMOTH TASK of creating a wedding gown, the *durzi*, swaying back and forth in distress, called in a small contingent of his fellows, and they managed, in just over a week of round-the-clock work, to create a wedding dress for me. Mrs. Waterton oversaw the production, not really asking what I would prefer but telling me what would be most appropriate. It was as if she were informing me, with this action, that I was not to be trusted, and since I was her guest, and a most troublesome one at that, I would do her bidding. And of course I was more relieved than she would ever know to let her take over the complete planning of the dress and wedding. Instead of punishing me, as she must have imagined she was doing, she was making it possible for me to continue to carry out my charade, for I had absolutely no knowledge of what a wedding would entail. I had never even attended a wedding. The closest I'd come to a bride and groom was passing by a church in Liverpool as they descended the steps.

The dress was of the most delicate ivory silk with wide-blown gigot sleeves. Because the highly fashionable dress could be nothing but low cut, Mrs. Waterton came close to swooning when I first tried on the dress and she laid eyes on my scarred chest. I had always gone to great lengths to hide the scar with collars and lace and scarves and fichus, right from my first days in Everton with Shaker, and not even Faith had ever seen the horrid mess. The only people who knew of its existence in India were my ayah and the *durzi*.

"Oh, my dear, I didn't know—I don't quite know how we'll . . ." Mrs. Waterton was terribly flustered at the obvious harm I'd once come to, although of course she wouldn't ask, and I didn't offer any information. As I stood in the middle of Mrs. Waterton's spacious bedroom, three *durzis* kneeling around me, Mrs. Waterton fanned herself rapidly as she sank into a chair in front of me. I saw a glimmer of pity in her expression, and hoped this would lessen her anger at me.

Then she conferred at length with the head *durzi*, and between them a bouffant bow was devised for the neckline, which effectively hid most of my scar. Transparently sympathetic now, she raved over the shape and creaminess of my shoulders, telling me that the small evidence of my "trouble" that still showed could be layered with a thick disguise of powder.

She then admired the tight belt and the inverted triangle of the skirt that emphasized the curve of my waist, while the wicker cage tied with straps around my hips held the dress out in what she said was a glorious example of the style in London.

WHAT CAN BE SAID of that loveless wedding? We had been able to forgo the banns, and there appeared no need for any legal papers of birth to be in evidence here in India. The word of Mr. and Mrs. Waterton to my character seemed all that was necessary, and Mrs. Wateron had, in her usual way, taken care of the details. The simple service took place in St. John's Church. When the minister pronounced my name during the ceremony, Miss Linnet Smallpiece, I was aware of Somers's eyes shifting in my direction. He hadn't even known my full Christian name. I thought of my mother many times through that day, and felt ashamed for the falseness of it all.

The social gathering that followed, held in the ballroom of Government House, was in the finest taste, and attended by the closest friends of the Watertons, friends of Somers, and the other girls from the Fishing Fleet. Mrs. Waterton was constantly surrounded by the bevy of matrons who rather grimly swooped in to help her arrange this shockingly sudden event. More than one of those ladies, possibly with hopes for a match with Mr. Somers Ingram for her own daughter or for one of her houseguests, treated me quite coolly, some verging on rudeness.

But in spite of the strange pall that hung over that day, to all outward appearances it was a lovely celebration. The room was resplendent with mirrors and glass chandeliers, and handsome sofas of blue satin damask sat between the rows of shining white *chunam* pillars. An elaborate white cake on a stand was surrounded by a display of presents— vases, cruets, silver serving pieces of every description, clocks, and all manner of home decoration to help set up a young couple. Did it appear strange to anyone that the groom and his bride rarely spoke after the service? While trays of dainty sandwiches and liqueurs were passed by immaculate servers, my new husband was taken off to the smoking room by a crowd of friends. I was surrounded by the other girls, who repeated endlessly how lovely my dress was, what a sparkling array of gifts we had received, and how lucky I must consider myself. All this was spoken in loud and cheerful social voices that barely concealed true feelings, which I knew must run from disbelief that I, the odd Miss Smallpiece, had married the most eligible bachelor in Calcutta, to bitter jealousy that they had not yet had the good fortune to start planning weddings of their own.

Faith did attend, in spite of her vow, but I sensed she came simply to avoid any gossip that her absence might create. She had treated me with a careful distance for the last two weeks at the Watertons', staying in her room while Mrs. Waterton fussed over me, giving excuses that she was resting or had a headache when I knocked on her door. During that long wedding afternoon, her face remained tightly pulled by a smile that never left. Her peck on my cheek after the ceremony reminded me of the harmless nip of a creature who only reacts out of distracted habit.

I felt as if I were somehow floating above the whole scene, smiling and accepting compliments, nodding. Eventually Mr. Ingram was deposited at my side by his cronies. His demeanor indicated that copious amounts of port and brandy had been poured down his throat for the last few hours. He put his arm around my shoulders in what I knew was an inappropriate public display, even at our own wedding, and gave my cheek a rather wet kiss.

"Mr. Ingram," I trilled, for the sake of the others watching. "Please, darling. I believe it's time we were on our way." I cupped my hand coquettishly around my mouth as I spoke into his ear, as if I were whispering something very personal and loving. "Don't overdo the display, Somers," was what I whispered, using his Christian name for the first time since we'd met. "I do have a reputation to keep up."

He laughed gaily at that, and the crowd joined in, uncertain of what they had just witnessed, but assuming it to be a very sweet and touching moment between two people who were utterly in love with each other.

I LOOKED FOR FAITH as Somers and I made our good-byes, but she had disappeared. I had so hoped she might have softened enough to at least wish me well before I set off for my new life as a married woman, but there was no sight of her.

Just before we left, Mrs. Waterton hugged me, pressing her cheek against mine and whispering, "Be strong, Linny. Pray to the Lord for deliverance tonight, and know I shall also be praying for your ordeal to be bearable."

I pulled back and looked into her tear-filled eyes. Did she weep with true concern, or was it fatigue, and relief that such a bothersome house-guest was to no longer be her worry? "Thank you, Mrs. Waterton," I said. "For all of this, and for your prayers. I am sure to need them." Then, because I really did owe her a great deal, I said what I knew she would want to hear. "You have been like a mother to me, and I shall never forget your kindness." She wept openly then, hugging me to her again, patting my hair, and said softly, so no one else could hear, "If you do feel that way, then permit me to speak as your own mother might. Do mind to keep your . . . you know, your . . ." Here she discreetly touched the bow at my neckline. "Covered by your nightdress. It may be dis-tressing for your new husband to view it immediately. Let some time pass, and prepare him, so that it isn't so shocking."

"Yes, Mrs. Waterton, I surely will," I agreed. As if Somers Ingram would be shocked by anything about me now. He would never see it anyway. "That is a very wise suggestion."

And then Somers and I stepped into the opulent, ceremonial silk-curtained palanquin with its curved pole covered in silver, and we drove back to Alipur, to Somers's bachelor quarters—the other young men having moved elsewhere—where we would reside temporarily, until he was able to find us our own home.

I was exhausted, my head pounding from the stressful day, from the ordeal of acting like the excited and demure young bride I must portray. Somers was, actually, very drunk, although managing to retain some dignity in spite of it. As we were ushered into the house by the *chuprassi*, both his *khansana* and a small woman came forward, obviously waiting for us. The woman kneeled at my feet, salaaming. She wore a simple white sari threaded with blue.

"Your ayah, Linny," Somers said, his words running together. "Let me know how she works out. Came with quite a good reference."

The woman rose and stood in front of me, her head still lowered.

"I'm off to bed," Somers said now. "The girl will show you your room. Your trunks were delivered earlier, I believe." His eyes weren't quite focusing on me. They blinked heavily.

I nodded. Although I knew full well that Somers had no physical interest in me, I felt curiously empty. And in that brief moment I think I would have preferred a meaningless encounter to this disconcerting sense of loneliness, if only to be close to another body.

"All right then. Good night," he said, and walked, rather unsteadily, down the hallway. His *khansana* followed closely, arms slightly outstretched as if to catch Somers if he fell.

The ayah and I stood in silence until I realized she was waiting for me to instruct her. "Could you show me to my room, please?"

She turned and padded softly along the hall on bare feet, in the opposite direction of Somers. She opened a door to a bedroom lit dimly by a few candles, and, still without a word, helped me out of my wedding finery, into my nightdress, and took down my hair. She fetched scented water and bathed my face and hands and feet. She turned down the sheet of the bed, and when I got in, she pulled it, very gently, over me, and let down the netting. If she thought it strange that a bride spend her wedding night alone, her face betrayed nothing.

"Do you speak any English?" I asked, finally.

For the first time, she met my eyes through the fine mesh. I saw her hesitate. "Yes, some English," she finally said. Her voice was low and melodic. From the darkness outside came the distant scream of a jackal, followed by the baying of a pariah dog. "Does memsahib wish me to remain?"

I blinked at my new title. "Yes," I told her, turning my head away as my eyes suddenly burned. I wondered, as I had done constantly in the last few weeks, if the choice I had made was the right one. "Yes, please stay," I repeated, keeping my face averted and my voice firm.

As she blew out the candles, I thought that this would be the first time, since I had left Back Phoebe Anne, that I was not sleeping in close proximity to another woman whom I called friend—whether Dorie or

Helen or Annabelle or Chinese Sally or any of the others on Jack Street, or Faith on Garden Reach. Thinking of these women, I felt the gaping loneliness increase.

The ayah settled, almost noiselessly, on a mat in a corner of the room.

"What is your name?" I called.

"Malti."

"Does it have a meaning in English?"

There was a moment of silence, and then she said, very quietly, "Its meaning is a small flower. Very small and very fine."

"Oh."

Silence. And then I said, "Although I'm called Linny, my name is Linnet. A bird. Also small."

"Very good, memsahib."

And so we lay in the darkness, a small Indian flower and a small British bird.

Chapter Twenty-Three

THE MARRIAGE STARTED OFF QUIETLY. RIGHT FROM THE FIRST, Somers told me I was to entertain twice a week, and to accept all invitations that came our way. The couples we had for dinner seemed eager to be included on the invitation list—after all, Mr. Somers Ingram did hold a senior position, and of course now that he was married and could entertain properly, many wished to bask in the glow of that small celebrity.

Somers's position was unimportant to me; I cared as little about how he spent his days as he cared about mine, although occasionally the weariness on his face some evenings made it clear that his responsibility was great.

I found it a simple matter to plan the menu and confer with the cook about it; it required no stamina of any sort. The actual evenings did, however, require Somers and I to act like a blissfully married couple. We were both quite magnificent at acting, I must admit. There were times, when I smiled at Somers across an acre of blinding white damask, the silver winking in the candlelight, hearing the laughter of our guests, that I almost believed, for those brief, make-believe moments, that we were what we pretended to be. He could be absolutely charming in company, and I also felt embraced in the bright rays he so easily emitted. But at the final closing of the front door he turned off his charm and took a bottle to his room, and I retired to my own room, suddenly aware of how stiff my neck was, how my face ached from the tight fit of the mask I must wear.

Occasionally, were I particularly hot or tired, I knew the mask slipped. And Somers was the first to notice, and reprimand me for it later. Eventually I believe others saw it, as well, and there were many times when I sat at my end of the table with all heads turned to Somers, at the opposite end, as if I were no longer there.

After one especially trying evening, as the last of our guests were ushered out, Somers turnd to me, and I tensed, waiting for his reprimand.

"Were you particularly weary tonight, Linny?" he asked, surprising me with the quiet tone of his voice.

I nodded. "I was. Did it show?" Because he had spoken almost respectfully to me, I was willing to meet him halfway. "I did try, Somers. But that insufferable Major Cowton, well, really, he talked so much that it was quite difficult to pay attention after a while."

"I must admit I found tonight difficult as well," he said, sighing, and I felt a rush of something toward him that he and I would agree on this simple fact. I put my hand on his sleeve.

"Must we see so many people, so often?"

"I'm afraid there's no other way. We would be viewed oddly if we didn't follow what is expected." His eyes rose to my hair. "I find your hairstyle tonight attractive."

"It's something new Malti tried," I said, flustered. What was happening? Where was his arrogance, the usual verbal sparring in which we tried to outdo each other?

"Well, good night then," Somers said, but his voice held a slight hesitation, something that I could almost—almost—interpret as loneliness. And I knew, too, how lonely I was, in the midst of the endless stream of events with people who cared nothing for me except my position in the community, and in my moment of unexpected emotion, I put my arms around him and laid my head against his chest.

He immediately removed my arms and held me at length. "Why would you do that?" he asked, his voice tight, the usual voice he reserved for me.

"I don't know," I replied honestly. "I felt—well, was it wrong of me?" Was I so repulsive to him that he couldn't bear my touch?

But he didn't answer, leaving me in the entrance, while behind me began the discreet sounds of the table being cleared.

❧

FAITH MARRIED CHARLES SNOW six weeks after my own wedding. And while hers was a hurried affair, as was mine, it was far less auspicious, a simple exchange of vows at the Registry Office. Poor Mrs. Waterton—she must have regretted the day she opened her home to guests. Within less than a year she had to calm the flames that the untameable Mrs. Liston had fanned, arrange my wedding, and then deal with the terrible social implications that befell her due to the scandal caused by Faith and Charles.

When Faith's father arrived in Calcutta, three weeks after I was married, it was said that Mr. Snow had already proposed, and Faith accepted. I heard all of this news secondhand, as Faith still had not answered any of my invitations to call. Daily my thoughts went to her, missing her, wanting to share my life with her as I had once done. I refused to give up on her, refused to believe she would abandon our friendship so completely. I sometimes found myself thinking how she would laugh over some small incident, or would enjoy hearing about a book I was reading. I had conversations with her in my head at times.

When he arrived, Faith's father forbade her to marry Mr. Snow.

Nobody knew why at first, but then the rumor spread like a river flooding its banks throughout the cloistered English enclave. It was somehow disclosed that Charles Snow was Eurasian, although he had managed to hide it until he and Faith announced their betrothal. He had already disclosed his heritage to her, she confided to me eventually, when we had begun to speak again, but she wasn't aware of the backlash of gossip and discrimination it would herald. It's impossible to know who began to speak of it, and Charles, being an honorable man, did not deny the fact, once confronted. Apart from gleaming black hair, there was nothing in Charles's appearance to suggest that his mother, who died in childbed, had been Indian. Mr. Vespry was enraged at the slur he felt his daughter was threatening to cast upon his family's good name by her union with a half-caste. It was reported that he had shouted at her, on the very steps of the Calcutta Club, that if she chose to marry this man he would disown her.

And that is when Faith came back to me. Without even a prior calling card she stood in my hall, gloveless, picking at her nails, asking what she should do, her eyes tear-filled. Without speaking I opened my arms, and she came into them. It was as if I had been missing a part of myself as I hugged her, and she returned the pressure. I felt an immediate lightening sensation, a heaviness lifted from me, and although I sorrowed for her tears and her trouble, I also inwardly rejoiced.

Once we were seated in the drawing room, and I had sent out the servants and closed the doors, I felt I could speak to her candidly, as we had once been able to.

"Do you really love him, Faith?"

"Linny, I do. I never thought I could feel this way. Of course no one—absolutely no one—supports me in this. And although I so want you to, I will understand if you don't, either." Her bottom lip was flaky and she continually bit at the loose skin with her small teeth. "But somehow I sensed you would understand, and so took a chance on calling on you, hoping you would admit me if you found me at your door. I was afraid to send a calling card and be rejected."

"I will support you, Faith," I said quietly. I knew better than most of the need to follow one's own instinct. "If a marriage with Charles is what you want, then of course," I told her, and her face crumpled with relief.

"I can't bear not to have you as my friend any longer, Linny, even though I will accept your decision if you don't want me back, after the way I've treated you." She wept, and I took my handkerchief from my sleeve and handed it to her, as she appeared not even to have brought a reticule. "I realize how ridiculous I must have seemed when you announced your marriage plans. I was so afraid——" She stopped, as if unsure if she should continue, then took a breath and plunged on. "It was fear, my darling Linny, fear that I would be sent home. I had hoped and hoped that Charles would propose, and was a bundle of nerves, waiting, and then you came along and announced, so unexpectedly, that you would marry, and . . . and I'm sorry, Linny. Please forgive me. Since Charles has asked me to be his wife, and I recognize the true depth of his feelings for me, I feel as if I am a new person. I'm happy, Linny, happier than I've been for—well, I don't remember. I don't care about my father's threats. And I don't care that Charles has been lowered to the uncovenanted ranks, and that our manner of living will be much reduced. I realize, as I look upon his dear face, that I don't give a fig about all of that. I love him, and he loves me." She gave a great shuddering sigh.

I took her hands. "Then you must marry Charles, Faith. How many times, after all, does one feel love, and have it returned, within a lifetime?"

She attempted a shaky smile. "I knew I was right to talk to you about this. I know I've been impossible since we left Liverpool, Linny. I own up to that. It's you who have been so brave, and so strong. And no matter what I might have said to you, in anger, please know that there is no one I would rather have had on this journey. So you do forgive me?"

I smiled, nodding. "I am so very happy for you, Faith," I told her. "And we shall always, always be friends."

"But you are a senior lady now, and Charles . . . well, I will no longer be of your standing," Faith said.

"I won't allow us to be pushed apart because of that." I snapped my fingers. "That's what I care about what anyone might say of our friendship."

She hugged me, quite spontaneously. "Isn't it absolutely marvelous,

Linny, to be loved so deeply and so truly? Just think. Soon we will both be memsahibs in Calcutta. Would you have ever dreamed of this life?"

"No," I told her, honestly. "No, Faith. I wouldn't."

AND SO FAITH CHOSE Charles over her allowance and inheritance and returning to her old life in Liverpool.

I liked Charles. He was unassuming and had a quiet appeal. He had been employed as a commissioner in one of the Company's smaller offices, but immediately after the disclosure of his heritage he had been reduced to a member of the uncovenanted ranks, his salary only a fraction of what he had formerly commanded. As soon as they were wed, most of the English community snubbed Faith, and cards requesting her presence at the finer events stopped. Social rank and the invitations it brought had been terribly important to Faith, but I hoped she could get over that, buoyed by the strength she must now draw from Charles. With him I saw her blossom, although I later realized it was to be a brief season.

I MADE A HORRENDOUS mistake in trying to include Faith and Charles in our own circle. Somers and I had been married four months, and Somers often let me draw up the invitation list, choosing from a roster of names he supplied. Tonight I chose two former Fishing Fleet girls whom Faith and I knew well. They were now betrothed to young men Somers approved of, and who had worked with Charles before his recent fall from grace. There was also an older couple known by Somers for most of his time in India who would act as chaperones for the engaged couples. I selected Charles and Faith without mentioning it to Somers.

As Mr. and Mrs. Charles Snow were announced in the drawing room, where the rest of our party stood with drinks in hand, a hush fell over the room. I hurried to greet them. Faith looked particularly fetching in a flowered poplin dress, the underskirt a deep, rich brown red, which of course emphasized her hair. But her eyes were wide and uncertain; Charles stood, poker-straight, at her side.

"Please, please come in," I said, smiling, turning to look back into the room, and saw that there were no welcoming smiles, no murmurs of greeting. And then Somers turned his back, speaking loudly to one of the other gentlemen of an inconsequential matter, completely snubbing Faith and Charles, and setting the tone for the evening.

It was completely miserable; I struggled to include Faith and Charles in the conversation at the table, but they, too, aware of the atmosphere their presence had created, were stilted and uncommunicative. I saw Charles's dark, intelligent stare across the table, and I was deeply ashamed that I had put him and Faith in this position.

When the last of the guests finally departed, Somers turned on me. "How *dare* you do that to me," he growled. "Of all the asinine, inappropriate—"

"Don't tell me that you go along with the rest of them, Somers," I said wearily. "You told me yourself you had even considered courting Faith when we first arrived. And it was she who brought me here, who—"

But he cut me off. "Those bloody half-castes. They're all alike, you know, with that damn chee-chee accent, bowing and scraping and stabbing you in the back whenever they get a chance. Mixed blood," he sneered. "If you've been touched by the tar brush, you can't hide it. It will come out in one way or another."

"You had no difficulty accepting Charles before you knew," I said. "And he speaks no differently from you."

"I always suspected there was something off about him," Somers said. "Just as I knew there was something hidden about you when I first met you. I've got a nose for deceit. You must know that about me by now." He turned to go to his room, but stopped, looking back at me. "Don't you ever, ever humiliate me like that again. Do you understand me?"

"Yes, I understand," I answered, refusing to acquiesce to his demand.

He stood there a moment longer, staring at me, and then, with long, angry strides, went to his room, slamming the door.

※

I SENT A CHIT to Faith the next day, asking her to call in the early afternoon, after lunch, when Somers would have returned to work. She sent
back the chit with a large *yes* written across it.

When she arrived, I took her hands in mine. "I'm so, so sorry for
last night, Faith. Please forgive me. I could not have imagined you
would be so shabbily treated."

Faith squeezed my hands. "It's all right. Charles didn't want to
come, but I convinced him, pouting and putting on an act to make him
guilty, telling him you were my only real friend in Calcutta, and how I
would never forgive him if we didn't attend. Now I so wish I hadn't.
Like you, I had no idea that our presence would be so inappropriate."

We sat down beside each other on the settee, still holding hands.
And at that moment there seemed little more to say.

June 15, 1831

Dear Shaker,

Thank you, thank you, thank you! When I received your
letter I cannot tell you how my heart tumbled and raced. I
immediately recognized Mr. Worth's distinctive hand. It is kind
of him to scribe for you. Does he still do all the lettering for the
announcements?

I was deeply saddened to hear of the death of your mother.
I can well understand how difficult this last year must have been
for you, with her needing constant attention. How kind that
Celina Brunswick and her mother paid a condolence call. Faith
has often spoken highly of Celina, citing her many good qualities and her musical abilities.

I have been a married woman—a memsahib—for all of
four months. My husband, Somers, has family wealth that
allowed him to purchase a home for us in Chowringhee within
two months of our marriage. The area is one of the spaciously
planned districts of Calcutta, one that attempts to catch the
cooling effect of the wind off the river and shade from natural
vegetation. It is set in a verdant garden compound, and the
house is a stucco villa.

The house is really quite lovely, but too large and echoing.

Somers takes great delight in an ongoing decoration, smothering the rooms in an English scheme of furniture and rugs and artifacts which, frankly, hold less appeal for me.

The thing I love the most about the house is the wide verandahs, front and back. They have proved essential in the hot season, which is full upon us. There are occasional small, blistering winds now, the precursor, I've been warned, to the monsoons that will arrive within the month. The sun, which I welcomed on my arrival in India, has now become a threatening and brutal master. The air is bright, brilliant, and washes out the color from the trees, the roads, the gardens, the rocks, even our faces. Surfaces are impossible to touch; the hurtful edge of the sun is everywhere. I can feel its sharpness against my own skin. There is debilitating humidity. I am covered with heat rash. There are insects that defy explanation. Even my words, when I have the energy to speak, seem to melt as they leave my mouth, dissolving as if made of sugar, and carrying little meaning.

But in spite of this cruel god in the sky, the more intense the heat, the sweeter the fruits, the heavier and more fragrant the blossoms.

I stay inside my lair with all manner of devices to try and stay cool. There are the everpresent overhead fans—the punkahs—although they do little but churn the thick, hot air. The *tatties*—reed screens over all the windows and doorways—are constantly spashed with water in the hope of cooling the hot air that blows through. And I also have a thermantidote—a horribly noisy contraption that is intended to dispense cooled air through the room. For all its deafening roar, it helps little.

When Somers is home, we are kept busy with the endless rounds of unbearable social visits. There is a kind of forced jolliness in all this business of calling cards and daytime visits between eleven and two—when the sun is at its worst—that I find vapid. But when Somers is away—which he is, frequently, pig sticking in the jungle or visiting one of the other Company presidencies in Madras or Bombay—oh, Shaker, my Indian world opens, although I must keep my activities secret. And

perhaps this is how I am, and how I feel the most comfortable. I
see clearly now that much of my life has been a secret, and may
always be so.

With Somers gone I send my regrets to all invitations that
come in and instead stay home, going barefoot, pushing aside
the dhurrie rugs and savoring the coolness of the stone floor. I
read endlessly—there is a small but adequate library at the
Club, and I am a frequent visitor. I give no orders for meals,
which sends the cook into deep sulks, and I know he is terribly
offended. But I prefer to avoid the everpresent meat—venison,
beef, mutton, pork, veal, and poultry—and the endless courses
of rich English food that our poor *biwarchi* tries so desperately
to create, often with strange results.

The servants think me mad, I'm sure, except for my beloved
ayah, Malti (her name means small, fragrant flower, and suits
her perfectly), and they pretend they are not staring at me dancing about the house barefoot, in one of Malti's saris, my hair
down, living on rice and almonds and muskmelon and mangoes
and an occasional curry. They have also grown bold enough to
carry on—at my urging—very minor conversations in Hindi
with me when the "*burra* sahib" is not at home, and my command of the language has grown remarkably.

I have also learned to ride. Again, this activity had to be
done in secret, for how could I explain to the fine British ladies
of Calcutta that I had never ridden? Even the smallest English
child here is set into a ring saddle and becomes competent at an
early age. And so I sought out a stable away from the Club, with
a patient Eurasian handler who doesn't question my inexperi-
ence, and within a few months found myself managing quite
ably in the saddle. I have not yet tackled jumps or anything
more ambitious than a trot or canter or gallop, but I can ride
passably enough to not draw attention to myself.

At other times I creep about Calcutta on the pretext of
shopping. What do I care of shopping, Shaker? You know me
well enough to understand that this pastime, so precious to the
English memsahib, holds no interest for me. Instead, I give Malti,

my confidante, who seems to adore me for no other reason than that she has been given the task of caring for me, a shopping list, a large basket, and a chit. She rides off to the Hogg Market and collects what is needed for the next few meals, or else goes to Taylor's Emporium, with its wide clean aisles of gleaming silverware and sparkling china and crystal and jewelry and all manner of things English. She feels important and happy with these chores, and tells me she is the envy of her counterparts, whose memsahibs would never entrust to them such decisions.

And while Malti does the shopping, Shaker, I explore. I go to the open bazaars. The main one is Bow Bazaar, with its cheerful, although squalid, profusion of stalls, and oh—I have seen items I didn't know existed, items never found in all the books I studied before arriving. There are curious idols and strange fabrics, pungent, aromatic spices, rich gums, and large glass bottles of oil and rosewater encased in wicker. There is pure ivory from Ceylon and there are rhinoceros hides from Zanzibar. I am perfectly safe; there is an unspoken and, I suspect, false respect for all memsahibs here. False because the Indians have no choice. It is not a respect born of admiration, but one that simply is, for no reason other than the color of our skins. This, to me, is deeply disturbing, and yet I have come to understand that India is a country that links worth with the level at which one is born.

Much as life is in England. In this one respect only there is a similarity.

I am assuming that you are aware that Faith married not long after I did. I know that Faith wrote of this wonderful fact to Celina, and I hope she may have passed the news on to you. I do see Faith as much as possible. Her health appears rather fragile, I'm afraid. Her husband, Mr. Snow, is a kind, serious yet thoughtful man, and obviously adores her. In spite of this happiness within her marriage, Faith finds the chaos of the Indian world difficult to manage. She talks about making the journey home for a visit next year, which I think would be a wise choice, although she would have to build up her physical stamina to face that challenge.

Thank you again for writing, Shaker. I tried not to lose faith in hearing from you since I left Liverpool—close to a year now. Your letter makes me feel as if a door has just swung open again.

Again, Shaker, my deepest condolences on the loss of your mother.

> *Yours faithfully,*
> *as always,*
> *Linny*

P.S. For future correspondence, your postings will reach me directly if sent to Mrs. Somers Ingram, which is the name by which I am now addressed.

❧❧❧❧❧

THERE WERE PARTS of my life that I didn't describe to Shaker. I didn't tell him of my visits to the cemetery at St. John's churchyard, for fear he would think me strangely morbid. It seemed that, for some of the Englishwomen, grave visiting was a compulsive pastime. The Glory Here Lies All Buried was written over the gate to the graveyard at St. John's. I found a peacefulness there that brought me closer to the memories of my mother and little girl. There were many, oh, far too many little babies buried in these cemeteries: dead of cholera, dead of enteritis, dead of smallpox, dead of fever, dead of . . . the inexplicable, delicate, yet terrible grasp of India. But in spite of the sadness of all of this, again, I felt at peace there. After the rains started, and the stones had been washed clear of dust so that the lettering stood clear, and green sprouted from crevices in those very stones, it indeed felt a holy place.

I also didn't tell Shaker of other things I witnessed. One was a suttee. Although it was prohibited by a government sanction the year before I arrived, I chanced upon the smouldering remains of a pyre where a widow had lit herself and burned to death. Judging by the two small boys weeping there, at the pile of dark ash and grisly human remains, she had been a young woman. I looked at the boys, wondering whether they were old enough to understand that she had sacrificed herself not only for their father—her death ensuring his successful rebirth—but for them. With their mother gone to take her place at her husband's heavenly feet, they would now be assured that the whole of the family property passed on to the male heirs. I wondered if the boys had any sisters, and, if so, what their fate would be.

Another afternoon, as I stood in the shade between two temples, I watched a crowd of men dragging another man with his arms and legs bound tightly with strips of cloth to a clearing between the shrines. The man was forced to kneel and place his head on a large wooden block. Hearing *"Chore, chore"* murmured through the quickly gathering crowd, I knew him to be a thief.

Next a *mahout* led a docile elephant, ceremoniously painted, bells jangling on his massive ankles, into the clearing. An uncharacteristic silence fell over the assembled people. At a word of command from the *mahout,* the huge wrinkled leg rose over the thief's head. Slowly, almost delicately, with a slight tinkling from the bells, the massive foot descended, crushing the man's skull into the stained wooden block. I couldn't look away. The reverent silence continued as the elephant was led off and the crowd thinned. Immediately two Sudras hurried to drag away the body with only a pulpy mess attached to the neck. The remaining throng made a wide path around the Untouchables in their rags. The Sudras passed in front of me, hauling their gruesome cargo. I vomited neatly and quietly on the macadam, wiped my mouth with the edge of my skirt, and walked past the blood-covered block to the alley that would lead me back to the bazaar.

There I bought a paper pack of *pan* and stood chewing the ground mixture of spices, leaves, and betel nuts, hoping to settle my stomach. As I ate I watched a withered blind man play a sitar with graceful movements. The music he created was unstructured and yet ethereal. When he was done he tilted his head to the sky and I saw tears streaming from his eyeless sockets as a wide smile creased his filthy face. I squatted beside him and pressed what was left of my *pan* into his hand. He took hold of my outstretched hand and gently ran his hoary fingers over my palm and wrist, whispering a toothless blessing, and I felt a shiver of repulsion and yet—and yet, I believe the other emotion I felt at that moment was envy.

Yes. I was envious of this stinking, ancient musician. He wanted nothing more than his sitar and the warmth of this patch of sunlight. At this moment, he knew his place in his world and he accepted it.

For all I felt that the strange shape of my life had brought me to a secure place—a lovely home in which I wanted for nothing materially, I couldn't understand why I continued to feel, often, that I was not right within my skin. Was I to feel this way—this restless questioning— while dressed in fine gowns and knowing no hunger or fear for my life, as I had for all of my former years in Liverpool, both on Back Phoebe Anne and Paradise?

What was this odd, empty ache that clung to me no matter how luxurious my life now proved to be?

As I walked away from the old man, I berated myself heavily for my selfish thoughts.

Chapter Twenty-Four

I WORRIED MORE AND MORE ABOUT FAITH.

She and Charles were forced to live in the rather run-down area for the uncovenanted civil servants that I had often passed through. Their home was at the furthest end of Chitapore Road, in a row of low, poorly constructed bungalows with weedy growth sprouting from wide cracks in the outer walls.

The hot season was growing intolerable when I first visited Faith. The bungalow was small but neat, filled with evidence of Charles's life in India, unlike the homes in Garden Reach and Alipur and Chowringhee I frequented. It was simple and unadorned in a pleasing way with its rattan furniture and small brass tables, the white walls bare except for a few woven hangings, and rush matting fragrant underfoot. In spite of what might be seen as a step down the social ladder, Faith appeared to be blissfully happy in this first flush of marriage with Charles, enjoying playing at house. There was no verandah, and the back of the house opened on to a courtyard. With no chance of any breeze, the house was utterly suffocating.

She had the bare minimum of servants: a thin, rabbity girl of about twelve as her ayah, the girl's younger brother as a general cleaner, and a very elderly man who seemed to shuffle about a great deal without really accomplishing anything. She shared a cook, a *dhobi,* and a *durzi* with three other bungalows.

As time passed and debilitating heat descended over Calcutta, Faith's answers to my chits, asking her to visit at my home during the day, or whether I might call on her, began to hold her regret and apology, citing a variety of reasons, from the heat to her feeling poorly to a problem with a servant. And so, after I hadn't seen her for three weeks, I took it upon myself to visit her in spite of the afternoon sun.

I was met at the door by the ayah, who ushered me into the tiny drawing room. She went to fetch Faith, and as I waited in the unbearably hot room, lightheaded with the lack of air, I couldn't help but notice that white ants crawled within the matting on the floor, and there was a sour odor of unwashed linen. The flounce of the punkah showed a layer of dust. Dirty plates and cups sat on the small round teak dining table, visible through an open doorway. Finally Faith came to the drawing room. She was pale, her clothing rumpled, and her hair fell from its pins.

"Hello, Linny," she said. "I was trying to stay cool by just lying very still." She glanced around. "Please forgive the state of my home. We haven't been entertaining at all; it's too hot."

"Of course, Faith. Who can deal effectively with anything in this scorching air?" I said, trying to put her at ease. We sat, and she had the ayah bring us some cold tea. With the tea the girl sullenly brought out a plate of biscuits and put it in front of us. She smelled strongly of the ghee she used to oil her hair. Faith didn't even glance at the plate, but I noticed the biscuits had a mealy look to them.

We attempted small talk, but Faith seemed somehow confused, giving the ayah instructions to give to the cook for dinner, and then changing them twice over. She ordered the cleaner to spend time on small and unimportant tasks while flies swarmed over the dirty dishes on the table. When I announced that I would be leaving within the half hour, she paced about the room, looking out the windows.

"Are you sure you're all right, Faith?" I asked her. I saw that she wore no stays or petticoats, and her ecru dress hung limply, sweat-stained under the arms and down the back. I changed at least four times daily in this heat, but I had Malti to prepare cool baths for me and have fresh clothes waiting.

She looked at me distractedly. "Yes. Yes, I just thought Charles might arrive home earlier than usual. I hoped so. I don't like being here alone."

"You're not alone. You have the servants and the other women in the courtyard. Do you not visit with them?"

She looked away from the window. "I just meant . . . I hope he arrives before you leave." She came closer. "It's the servants. They're always watching me, and I feel they don't like me."

"Perhaps you could come out more," I said. "I know it's almost impossible in this heat, but it doesn't do to stay shut up alone every day."

"I am not invited to the same events as you, Linny."

"But I often go out with Malti to individual pursuits. They have a small library at the Calcutta Club."

"Charles is not allowed to be a member."

"But I could bring you there as a guest."

Faith shook her head. "It's all too wearying," she said then, and when I left, twenty minutes later, she was distracted, fussing about the littered table and worrying that Charles's dinner would not be prepared to his liking.

❋❋❋

ALTHOUGH THERE WERE aspects of my life in Calcutta that I chafed against, there was much that I loved. I did spend many happy hours at the library. Although the selection of English books was small, there were some lovely volumes. Mr. Penderel, the elderly man who supervised the library, came to know me. I think he was pleased to see anyone come through the doors, as there was never anyone else there when I arrived, every fourth or fifth day, to take out another two books. After a few months he began to put aside the books newly arrived by ship, letting me have first chance at them. The first time he saw me inspecting the binding of a particularly lovely book, he frowned.

"I assure you, Mrs. Ingram, there are no mites in the binding. I check each one thoroughly before I put it on the shelves, and again when someone takes it out and returns it. I care greatly about preserving the books in this blasted climate."

"Oh, I wasn't looking for mites, Mr. Penderel. I was looking at the detail. There's a curious stitch just here"—I showed him the curved detail—"that I haven't seen before."

"Well, now," Mr. Penderel said, his eyes lighting. "Are you interested then, in the world of books for themselves?"

"Oh yes," I told him. "I've studied the manner in which books are created for—well, since I was very young. I've always enjoyed this pursuit."

Mr. Penderel hastened to bring out a variety of books then, and we spent a good half hour discussing the finishing and stamping. I found myself stimulated by that conversation more than any I'd had in a long time.

I must say that between visits to the library, and seeing Faith when I could, combined with Somers's frequent departure from our home for his own pleasures, I began to believe—those first months of my marriage—that I was as close to a quiet contentment as I might have ever been.

July 18, 1831

Dear Shaker,

The end of June brought the red-hot *loo*—the winds from the west. The wind carries dust. This fine silty dust is impossible to escape; it is as insidious as a smell, finding its way indoors around cracks and fissures. It lodges in my eyes, ears, nostrils, between my teeth. It seems my senses, too, are choked with dust. Even the servants appeared restless.

At its most severe the force of the wind is such that flimsy buildings are torn from the ground and trees bent almost in half. It is said that it brings madness for the English; perhaps it does—a temporary madness, for the incessant moaning burns into the brain in a monotony in what I imagine might be similar to brain fever. When it stops, everyone stands very still, listening, for it is the quiet that now appears to carry a threat.

With the end of the winds comes the first monsoons, which descend without warning. It's as if the skies have opened and unceremoniously dumped buckets of warm water over the city. The streets run with muddy rivers, making walking almost impossible for me, with the heavy trailing skirts and layers of petticoats and crinolines I am forced to wear when I leave the house. The daily downpours of solid roaring walls of water last for a few hours, then stop suddenly, turned off as abruptly as they started. The hot, saturated air is difficult to breathe, and at times I feel as if I am trying to catch my breath through a soaked piece of gauze. After a short respite of surprising blue sky and the appearance of a floating, shimmering sun, new clouds sulkily gather, the blue turns an ominous slate gray and within moments the heavy beating melody of the monsoons returns with jubilant renewed force.

Green mold, often as bright and glistening as emerald, grows up overnight and covers anything that is made of paper, cloth, or leather, even in the house! I learned what the mysterious stack of tin-lined boxes I found in one corner of an empty bedroom are for, and store my clothing in them. If no callers are expected, the servants cover all the furniture with sheets. I spend most of my time in the verandah off my bedroom.

Flies swarm through the open windows by the dozens, and an amazing assortment of flying, creeping, and whirring creatures seem born from the wet air itself. Last night at dinner I recognized silverfish, white ants, stink beetles, caterpillars, and centipedes all busily working their way over and around the table. It is difficult, of course, to eat. The fluttering over the food begins the moment it is uncovered, in spite of a horde of boys with their fly whisks. One of the servants stands behind me with a tablespoon, with which he scoops off the larger beetles and bugs that land on my shoulders and hair. Somers has taken to having most of his meals at the scrupulously clean and almost sealed Gentlemen's Lounge at the Civil Service building.

I could never admit this to anyone but you, Shaker, but I find many of the insects fascinating. Some of the moths are graceful and delicate, with wings of spun gold. I trapped a very formidable centipede, green and yellow striped and over ten inches long, and kept him in a huge glass jar for over a week. Every morning I dropped in leaves and watched with respectful awe as he munched through his meal. Even the flies, Shaker— the flies!—are not the common bluebottle of England. Many have bodies of deep burgundy or rich green.

I have learned to swathe the bed in voluminous folds of very sheer muslin, and before climbing in every night, I pull back the sheets and perform a thorough examination to make sure I won't be joining a sleepy scorpion. Then I check the heavy linen canopy over the top of the bed, assuring myself it is firmly in place. I was awakened most unpleasantly one night when a dung beetle the size of a walnut dropped onto my face from the rafters on the first and last time that I was careless in my nightly inspection. I have also discovered, with not a little dismay, that a bath sponge makes an ideal home for a scorpion.

I take my dose of quinine—a horridly large spoonful— each morning, shuddering at the bitter taste. I have been warned that malaria strikes most often in the wet season. Somers fell prey to the disease his first year here (more than five years ago), and is subject to bouts of it.

When he is ill he prefers I stay away, and is attended to by the servants. But I have heard his moans, his hoarse whispers of his bones being twisted by a huge and violent hand, and of the relentless kettle drum keeping up a beat in his head until he thinks he might go truly mad. Although he has spoken little of his parents to me, in his delirium he cries for his dead mother as if still a child. And in the next instant he shouts curses upon a cruel father, whose memory obviously haunts him.

During his last attack he shivered so violently that he chipped one of his own teeth. Poor man!

On that cheery note—!—I shall close, with the promise to write again, dear Shaker.

Yours,
Linny

I carefully avoided writing more than a few lines about Somers, for what is there to say? I didn't believe, at the start, that he was a completely evil man, simply one who was totally self-absorbed. We continued to treat each other as disinterested though polite neighbors who shared the same house. Occasionally he spoke cruelly to me, hurling insults, but usually it only happened after he had drunk more than usual, or perhaps was disappointed in a rendezvous. And the following day he would apologize by way of a small gift—some trinket or bit of jewelry, something impersonal that he could send one of his coolies to Taylor's Emporium to purchase. I saw, at these moments, that Somers did indeed understand that his behavior had been uncalled-for, and although a genuine smile or kind word would have meant more to me than another showy, useless novelty, it seemed to be the only way he knew to tell me he was sorry.

At odd moments I would find him studying me, but he would always look away quickly, denying, when I asked him, that something was on his mind that he wished to speak of. I sensed a deep and underlying unhappiness in Somers, which he covered with his charm and bravado. Once I tried to ask him more about his childhood in London, about his mother and father, but he refused to speak of his past.

It would appear that he didn't wish to discuss any aspects of his life, not only past, but present as well. And likewise he wished to know nothing of how I spent my time. When I asked him about his work, he said it would be of little interest to me. When I tried to tell him of the books I was reading, and of my conversations with Mr. Penderel at the Club's library, he appeared bored with my prattle. And so, on the odd evening when we found ourselves alone together—when we did not entertain or Somers did not go out on his mysterious assignations, or we did not find ourselves at yet another evening at the Calcutta Club or the home of another couple—we spoke of household and servant issues, of the plans for entertaining, and of social events we had been invited to. We spoke of no matters of the mind, or of the heart.

It was after the monsoons abated, and we were into the delightfully temperate cool season, that the downward spiral of our marriage began. I had been in India almost a year.

Somers had taken advantage of the weather to go with a few other men on a hunt, and had been gone almost three weeks. He came home burnt a plethora of shades and immensely weary, sullen at the lack of a trophy, blaming the incompetence of his coolies to beat the bushes. He recounted that although there was a rich assortment of game—tigers, panthers, sambars, pigs—the coolies had been easily spooked after one was killed by the unexpected swipe of an injured tiger.

"Damn cowards," he added. "Clambering up trees at the first answering rustle to their beating after that. Letting the big game get away."

"But surely they had reason to be—"

"There's no excuse, Linny. It's a job they're paid to do." We were in the drawing room, with its hushed and formal atmosphere. He paced in front of the damask sofa, where I sat with the book I had been reading before his arrival. He was in the worst temper I had ever witnessed, and I kept quiet while he ranted about the miserable time he'd experienced. Finally he shouted for the servants, and many came running. He demanded bath water be brought to his room and gave instructions for a hearty English meal to be prepared for dinner, ordering many courses, which included a saddle of lamb and roast beef and gravy with Yorkshire pudding. He took a bottle of port from the cabinet and disappeared for the rest of the afternoon.

In early evening he invited me to join him for dinner, and the meal was served with its usual pomp on Sèvres dishes and fine polished silver. Somers kept a glass of watered Madeira beside his plate, sipping from it with every bite, and summoning the *khitmutgar* to continually top it up.

As he rather clumsily cut his meat, chewing slowly but with obvious relish, I took a sip of water from my delicate crystal goblet and shoved my slab of pink beef around.

Eventually Somers looked up. "Meat not done well enough for you?" His words were slurred; I had never seen him quite this intoxicated. I wondered if it was the beginning of another malaria attack.

"I ate a late tiffin. And I find this a heavy meal."

"Well, call for something else. Rahul," he said to a boy passing through the room carrying a stack of clean napkins, "take Mrs. Ingram's plate away."

The boy looked at the table. His eyes widened and he lowered his head.

"Take her plate, Rahul," Somers instructed again, slowly and loudly. His head still down, Rahul backed away.

"Somers, you know he can't," I said. "Call for someone else to—"

But instantly Somers pushed back his chair with a loud scraping and jerked toward the boy. He grabbed the thin arm roughly, and the napkins fluttered to the floor like released doves. "When I tell you—"

I ran to Rahul's side, prying Somers's hand off his arm. "Leave him alone."

"He must obey when I give him an order." Somers's neck and face were a dull red, and his grip tightened even further. "This one doesn't like to take orders. I found that out earlier today, didn't I, Rahul?"

So it was more than the issue of the plate. My heart went out to the boy, no more than fourteen, his whole body shaking in fright. I hated to think what might have happened to him only hours earlier, when I imagined Somers to be resting. "Somers," I said, quietly. "Leave him."

"You stay out of this," Somers said. "How dare you go against me in front of the servants?"

"He's a Hindu. He can't touch a plate that holds beef. You know that," I said, my voice still low, my fingers working at Somers's hand. "You could beat him until he was senseless and he still wouldn't take it. Fetch Gohar, Rahul. Gohar can take the plate. Somers. Let him *go*." I said the final word with more force than I had ever used since Somers and I had married.

In the next instant Somers smiled at me. An odd, unnatural posturing of his lips. Then he dropped Rahul's arm. Rahul fled, his shirttails flying, and in seconds another boy emerged and silently took my plate. The rest of the servants in the dining room—the punkah wallah and *khitmutgar* and boys with their fly whisks—continued as if nothing had happened.

We both sat down. Somers methodically shoveled in forkful after forkful of his dinner. I picked a fig from the plate of fruit and nuts sitting under the soft candlelight of the huge brass candelabra in the middle of the table. I took a bite, but the fig was overripe, mealy, and my throat wouldn't work properly. I looked at the fine spray of bloody juice from his meat on the front of Somers's cream-colored silk waistcoat, at the perspiration trickling from his sideburns.

We sat there, in silence but for the clinking of the punkah, the flutter of a moth over the candelabra, until Somers finished his meal with a large bowl of lemon custard, and then he left the table without a word.

I thought the incident was over as I prepared for bed. But just as Malti helped me into my nightdress Somers came in and, leaning against the doorjamb, dismissed her with one barked word. She slipped away, having to turn sideways awkwardly in the doorway to avoid brushing against him. He had never come to my bedroom, nor I to his, at any time during our marriage.

"Somers," I said. "Why . . ." I stopped. From behind his back he pulled a riding crop.

"Should you ever—*ever*—humiliate me in front of anyone again, you'll think back to this night and pray for it, for this will only be a warning."

"What do you mean? You're not going to whip me, Somers." I said it with confidence. There were at least twenty servants within hearing distance.

"I'm not?" he asked. He waited a heartbeat, then stepped closer, smiling as if reading my mind. "You think the servants will help? Do you? Have you learned nothing about this country? Are you so blind as to believe that anyone cares what happens to you? That any of these subservient curs would stop me from controlling my own wife?"

I opened my mouth, but before I could say anything he had grabbed the front of my nightdress and yanked me against him. I struck his chest with my fists, but I was no match for his strength, driven by an alcoholic rage. As he threw me onto the bed, an unlit lamp crashed to the floor, spilling coconut oil, filling the room with its odor. The bench of my dressing table was overturned. He effortlessly flipped me over, his knee in the small of my back, pinning me against the mattress, and holding my wrist with one hand, used his other to whip me with the stinging leather thongs of the crop. I felt the thin fabric of my nightdress shred, and then my own skin split. He whipped me as I screamed at him, cursing him in the worst language I knew—the language of my old friends Helen and Annabelle and Dorie and Lambie and Skinny Mo. He stopped, suddenly, and I turned to look over my shoulder at him. I saw his heaving chest and twisted, contorted face, running with sweat. The odd, glazed look in his eyes was, I realized with a shudder, one of sensual intimacy as he stared down at my flayed, bloody back. And then he flung down the crop and unbuttoned his trousers and pulled up my hips so I was forced onto my knees. I struggled, wrenching myself violently away from him as he fumbled with his clothing, and then I crouched, facing him as I held the bedcover against me. He looked down at himself. Then he muttered his own curse and turned away. The mattress dipped as he half-fell off the bed.

"I can't be bothered to spill my seed in you," he said, getting to his feet and tucking in his shirt, buttoning his trousers, smoothing his hair. "And I'd never dirty myself in such a filthy hole. That tight little black Hindu arse of Rahul's is a hundred times cleaner than you'll ever be. I should use the end of my riding crop instead, although I wouldn't want to pollute it, either."

His words were no more than a false boast, for I'd seen that although he was aroused by my anger and fear and the sight of my torn back, he couldn't maintain it. He left, and I knew then that the bargain we had made was more than I had foreseen.

I was his prisoner, as surely as I had been Ram Munt's.

✦

THE NEXT DAY Somers offered an apology in the only way he was capable.

I was sitting on my verandah when he appeared in late afternoon. It had been difficult for me to move before noon without furious pain. I knew the deep lashes would leave scars. Malti had hurried into my room after Somers crashed out. She wept, moaning in Hindi as she washed and dressed the wounds. Her hands were tender and soothing, working with a salve that smelled of almonds. Once she had settled me she sat on the floor beside the bed and sang softly to calm me enough so that I fell into an uneasy sleep. She was still there, her head against the side of the bed, when I awoke in the shadowy early morning. Now Somers carried in a large wicker basket and set it down in front of me.

"What is it?" I asked, not wanting to look at him. The basket trembled, and there were wet, snuffling sounds. In the next instant the lid was pushed open, and a young dog looked around, his wet tongue flopping out of one side of his mouth. I took his small, bony black head in my hands and stared into his liquid amber eyes.

"He's a crossbreed of sorts; I can't even being to pronounce the Indian word, meaning a complicated mixture of hand-picked sire and bitch. Apparently they thrive in India, with their sturdy disposition and short hair. They're not subject to mange as our dogs here. They're ferocious but loyal." Somers's voice was quiet, tinged with a tone I didn't recognize. Was it embarrassment or remorse?

"They don't breed well," he went on, "and it's difficult to get one without a wait. Got lucky with this one. Quite a bit of terrier in him, I would think, judging by his wiry build. There's a half-caste who raises them for the English here."

I pulled the dog out of the basket and into my lap, wincing as I moved. Even though the dog was small, he was leggy and awkward, his hind legs scrambling and clawing for a foothold in my skirt as he put his paws on my chest and licked my face.

"He has some sort of awful Hindu name, but you can call him what you want. He's been weaned for a few weeks now and will learn to obey easily, the breeder assured me." He leaned in and scratched the dog's ears. "They've wonderful tracking abilities."

The dog's stub of a tail wiggled with furious intensity. I looked at Somers. His eyes were veined with pink, and the skin around them pouched. I suddenly saw that he had gained weight since we'd married, and his face was bloated. And I saw that he looked truly miserable, a misery that was not only a physical cause from the alcohol he'd consumed. He looked away, and I knew he was ashamed for what he'd done.

Still, I didn't thank him for the pup. I would never thank Somers for anything again. I wasn't grateful for anything he had to offer, and had decided, after the last minor altercation the week before, when I had refused to accept a tiny flagon of toilet water, to never take anything from him ever again.

But I was surprised at how I wanted the pup after those first few moments. I had never had anything of my own.

I named him Neel, Hindi for *blue*, for his glossy coat was so black it had a blue sheen.

Chapter Twenty-Five

March 12, 1832

My dearest Shaker,

Thank you so much for your last letter. I was so very interested to read of your growing interest in the new homeopathic approach to healing and pleased to hear that it is being embraced in England. There is much use of natural vegetation for various ailments among the Indians here. If you would be interested, I could ask Malti to give me more specific information about those she considers to have healing qualities.

I am leaving for a hill station in a few days and want to put this letter in the post before I depart. I'm making the journey to Simla, far in the Himalayan mountains, and will stay there for the duration of the hot season. My first experience with it last year made me very grateful that Somers suggested I spend the next few months away from the dust and heat of Calcutta. This time at a hill station, I was instructed, is the thing we memsahibs "must" do, if one's husband can afford it and the lady's constitution is hearty enough to withstand the difficult journey—traveling 1,200 miles north, first on the Hooghly and Ganges and Yamuna rivers by budgerow, and then a long slow march up into the mountains by *dooli*. Summer in the cool greenness of the mountains is, obviously, most desirable. From what I have gathered, memsahibs apparently think little of leaving their husbands to swelter in the cities and plains while they enjoy the thin, fragrant air.

I am very pleased that Faith has agreed to come. I am grateful that she is able to join me, as Somers was insistent that I travel with a companion. There is a certain amount of irony in these circumstances, is there not?

But I am troubled for Faith, Shaker. She appears unwell in a profound sense. At times I wonder if she has inherited a form of melancholy from her mother, although she refuses to speak of it when I gently question her health. Although Charles is dear to her, the circumstances surrounding their marriage have only added to the considerable strain of her malaise. When I think of the lovely, laughing girl I first met in Liverpool my heart is heavy. I really do fear for her and wish there were something I could do to help her.

I am hoping this time in Simla will revive her.

Your faithful friend,
Linny

P.S. Guggal (Indian bedellium) has a fragrant resin that is extracted and used for those bloated with their own fluids, and also for painful swelling of the joints.

When I had first suggested that Faith accompany me to Simla, convincing her and Charles with the facts that Somers had already rented a bungalow (true) and arranged and paid for the journey (true) and was in agreement that Faith come along (a lie), Charles urged Faith to take the opportunity. It was unspoken that he couldn't afford to send Faith. She said she couldn't bear to be apart from him, but I knew that Charles didn't want her spending another hot season in Calcutta. She had fallen victim to a strange ague as well as nasty conditions, first boils and then shingles during that time last year, which had only worsened during the wet season. Her body was covered in sores and wracked by a fever that left her weak and wordless.

She recovered physically, but had lost the ability to chatter and smile. Instead, she sat, wan and unmoving, in her chair by the window for hours at a time.

Charles had confided in me, after the invitation to Simla had been accepted, that he feared she might not survive the approaching hot season, having so recently recovered from the ills of the previous year. Now he was jubilant at the thought of her spending months in the cool comfort of the Simla hills. He wanted her to be happy again, to smile and clap her hands and read and argue and sketch the birds she loved to watch. I also suspected he thought that she might be more accepted in Simla without his constant presence. A perfect, albeit temporary, solution, he called it.

But Somers was furious that I'd invited Faith. I'd known all along that he would be, and I would suffer the consequences, but I accepted that fact. I purposely didn't tell him about Faith joining us until the night before we were to leave. He was on his way to the Club when I stopped him at the door and informed him.

He frowned, then shook his head. "No. As you well know, I've already arranged for Mrs. Partridge to accompany you," he said, fuming, turning his hat in his hands. His thumbs made deep imprints into the soft fabric. "You had no right taking this upon yourself. You know I spoke to Colonel Partridge about it a good month ago, and Mrs. Partridge was going anyway, and so is quite willing to share a bungalow with you, and be your—"

"Minder? Somebody to watch my every move, Somers?"

"Your companion. That was the agreement, that you go to Simla with a companion. And now you're muddying the Ingram name by keeping up your association with that woman. You'll just have to find some way to cut her out." He put his hand on the doorknob as if the matter was concluded.

I pulled at his sleeve. "No. It can't be done. I've invited her, and she's agreed to come, so it's settled. It will have to be the three of us, and you have no further say in it." I held my breath, then, having learned that now I need only provoke Somers with the smallest thing to bring out his violent behavior toward me. And for some inexplicable reason I sometimes found myself goading him purposely. I knew full well what I was doing as I corrected him in mixed company, or went against his wishes with some domestic request, or some other equally simple action. It was as if I wanted to see how far I could push him before he would react; I knew by the look on his face when he was reaching his limit, and yet I kept on, finding a perverse pleasure in baiting him. I think now, looking from afar on my strange behavior, that it was a way of drawing Somers's attention—even if it brought me nothing more than trepidation and fear of physical pain. I wanted to reach him in some way, in the confusing push and pull of our relationship, and perhaps this was the only way I could make him respond to me.

Now he grabbed me by the arm and swung me around. He punched me in the jaw with his knuckles, and as I fell he left, slamming the door so hard that a gilt-framed painting of King William IV also fell from the wall, its glass smashing on the stone floor beside me.

THE NEXT MORNING, March 15—the ides of March—was hazy and warm. Faith, Charles, Muriel Partridge, and I stood on the muddy riverbank, watching the trunks and boxes being loaded onto the long, flat barge that would carry the servants and supplies for the next three weeks. A makeshift tent toward the back of the barge would serve as a sleeping shelter for the servants and bargemen. Faith and Mrs. Partridge and I would ride on a smaller budgerow, a flat combination of houseboat and barge.

Mrs. Partridge was a sour and affected woman. But she had been to Simla for the last two years, and although I found her bossy and unlikable, she had been helpful in advising us what we would need for the journey as well as during our stay. Her husband was as fussy and snobbish as she, as if his past position in the army—he'd retired the year before—entitled him to his pompous righteousness. We'd entertained them occasionally, and I'd taken an immediate dislike to both of them.

We had three travel trunks apiece, with our clothing packed neatly between flannel and wax cloth. We shared a huge chest of bed linens and towels, two cases filled with cooking and kitchen utensils, and a large case containing my books and writing portfolios and Faith's sketch pads. We had also organized a trunk of warmer clothing for the servants to wear in the thin mountain air. We had brought our own ayahs, our own *dhobi*, and two household sweepers to accompany us to Simla, and hired a cook and two coolies for the journey itself.

"Looks like an awful amount of paraphernalia," Charles said. "I can't imagine conveying it uphill on those narrow mountain paths."

Mrs. Partridge sniffed. "This is only half the amount most women take."

"You will send a message back as soon as you can, saying you've arrived safely, won't you?" Charles asked Faith. His blue eyes looked young and worried.

"I said I would," Faith said. "Please try not to fret over me. Everyone goes to the stations now; there's really no danger." I saw that her gloves were buttoned improperly, and her hair had lost all of its shine.

We all looked at Mrs. Partridge, standing at the edge of the bank shouting at a small man sitting on one of the loaded trunks.

"Off! Get off there! You mustn't sit on our luggage!"

The man ignored her, crossing his arms over his chest and looking the other way as Mrs. Partridge continued to bluster and rant.

"Besides," I said, "no one would dare bother us with Mrs. Partridge along."

Charles laughed boyishly, the smile leaving as his eyes settled on my bruised jaw. He said nothing more, but cupped Faith's chin in his hand. I bent and fiddled with Neel's leash, but watched discreetly while he kissed Faith a final time. Charles's mouth was gentle on Faith's, and after they'd kissed he lowered his face to the crook of her neck, as if breathing in her scent one last time before they were separated. I saw Faith's arms tighten around Charles, and as they stood there, uncaring that they embraced in plain sight of anyone who might care to see, the love they felt for each other was clearly visible. I felt a brief stab of something like sorrow as I thought of how Somers and I had parted.

He had stopped by my room before he left for the office early that morning. I was still in bed. He stood at the doorway, making a great show of buttoning his jacket.

"Well," he finally said. "Safe journey."

"I'm sure it will be."

"Right, then."

"Right," I echoed, and he was gone.

Standing on the slippery mud of the Hooghly now, listening to the cries of the sweating men loading barges all along the bank, I took a deep breath, then let it out slowly, pushing away that last image of Somers. I would be away for five months—a month each way for traveling and three months at Simla. I was almost as excited by the prospect as I had been when we'd first arrived at the docks in Calcutta a year and a half ago. Now I would truly be discovering the India I longed to know more of.

<hr/>

FOR THE FIRST FEW DAYS, when the riverbanks weren't too covered in tall coarse grass as high as two men, I asked the agile bargemen to pole close to the bank so I could jump off and walk along briskly. Neel loved to frisk at my side, although I kept him on his lead after the first time he dashed into the bush after a rodent. I begged Faith to walk with me, but she wouldn't, seeming content to sit on a small rattan chair tied to the barge and gaze at the river going by. I sensed her retreating further and further and was desperate to have her come back to me. She was my one true friend, and even though I'd kept my past life a secret from her, in an odd way it made me feel even closer to her. She had always believed in me, in who I was—or had become—and this complete trust gave me a sense of pride that I had never known. I couldn't imagine my life without her; where once she had been an anchor for me, now I felt that it was me keeping her steady when she was in such obvious danger of drowning in some unseen darkness. I was determined that our time in the cool green of Simla would rouse her from this state of sorrow. Simla was sure to remind her of home, and then perhaps I would once more recognize the vibrant, funny girl I had met at the butterfly lecture, which now seemed such a long time ago.

We had left the Hooghly and were traveling through the delta of the Ganges, a vast ragged swamp forest called the Sundarbans, which I learned from one of our bargemen meant *beautiful forest*. There was a different smell to the river now, something deeper and more earthy as we traveled north, and the breeze would occasionally carry the smell of a dung fire from an unseen village. I continued to walk along the riverbank when I could, but Mrs. Partridge noticed a bamboo pole with a bushy branch tied to it sticking out of the marshy ground I stepped through.

"You! You!" Mrs. Partridge shrilled, pointing at the man working the pole at the front of the barge. He was the obvious leader, able to speak some English. He turned, and she redirected her finger at the bamboo. "What is that?" she demanded.

The man glanced at it. "Oh, lady sahib, that is merely a sign."

"A sign of what?"

"Others are telling us that on that spot a tiger has taken a man for his dinner," he replied nonchalantly.

"Stop the barge!" Mrs. Partridge roared.

I smiled at Faith, rolling my eyes. From her chair she returned my smile with a tiny one.

"I am sorry, lady sahib, we cannot be stopping. Barge behind will run into us. We must always move ahead."

"Mrs. Ingram!" Mrs. Partridge screamed, her small eyes wild. "Get back here immediately." At her shrieking, a huge flock of tree bats that had been resting in a large jungle thorn near the bank flapped up in alarm and glided away.

I picked up Neel and ran alongside the barge, easily leaping onto it. "Mrs. Partridge. That bamboo looked as if it has been there for months. I'm sure we were in no danger," I said.

"You're not stepping off this barge again," Mrs. Partridge said. "What have I been thinking? Of course, the Sundarbans are home of the royal Bengal tigers. I will not have you fall prey to some wild beast while you're under my supervision."

"Your supervision?" I asked.

"Mrs. Ingram," Mrs. Partridge said, puffing out her bosom. "I am the senior lady on this journey and I have taken it upon myself to ensure that the voyage is a safe one. You young women, relatively new to India, may have difficulty accepting that behavior you employed while at home in England does not work here. Now there will be no more said about it. You will stay on the barge. And please, Mrs. Ingram, pull your solar topee further over your face; your nose is quite pink."

There seemed little recourse.

We continued on the twisting, turning Ganges. I watched the wiry men gracefully poling hour after hour, seemingly tireless. Passing villages and meager towns, the river would briefly become a busy highway of barges and boats, always crammed with men and boys.

When away from the population, we slid by small and humble rice fields, walled with mud to keep in the water necessary for the plants' growth, and I watched women with their saris tucked about their hips, ladling each tender plant with clumsy wooden scoops. There were larger cultivated fields, yellow with mustard, and always jute, growing high and wild. Here, the brown river was deserted and lonely under the glaring sun. I sometimes saw the pointed, blunt-nosed head of a *mugger*—a crocodile—poke up, watching our progress with filmed eyes. For much of the time the river's still surface was broken only by bubbles from a hidden water creature or sudden groups of furiously paddling water beetles.

Faith occasionally read, but didn't bring out her sketchbooks. One afternoon, while Mrs. Partridge slept in the shade at the far end of the budgerow and Faith and I sat in our chairs, she turned to me.

"When do you expect you will have a child, Linny? You and Somers have been married over a year now."

I reached down to rub Neel's ears. "I don't know."

"Are you not anxious about it?"

I thought about the English children—those who existed in spite of the adversity of first their birth and then the heat and disease. The ones who survived were often too pale, listless. They wore their little solar topees and were shrouded in layers of clothing as they went for their riding lessons, their polo lessons, as they learned to order their ayahs about. There were no English children beyond the age of six to be found in India, as Meg had first informed me shortly after our arrival in Calcutta. I thought about all those tiny graves in the churchyard at St. John's. I thought about baby Frances, under the holly bush. I knew, by the choice I had made, that I would never know the feeling of a baby's movement within me again.

"Linny? Do you long for a baby?" Faith went on, when I didn't answer immediately.

"I suppose it is in the hands of Fate," I finally said, and was thankful for the distraction of the sudden appearance of a village as we rounded a bend in the river.

❧❧❧❧❧

AT THE END of each day, when we stopped for the night and anchored the barges, the bargemen lined up in front of Mrs. Partridge, and she placed the agreed-upon number of rupees into each man's calloused hand. The paid men would jump off the small barge and wade to the larger servants' barge, where they would be given a wooden bowl of curry, some chapatis, and a plate heaped with fruit. If the night found us stopping in the country, the men would simply curl up on the open deck of the servants' barge and sleep, keeping the mosquitoes at bay with smoking braziers. For our safety there were a few *chowkidars* who were posted to keep an eye on the little flotilla during the night hours. If we stopped near a town, some of the men would silently slip away after their meal. The next morning, although the right number of men in dhotis would be patiently standing in position at the sides of the budgerow, I eventually noticed that, except for the lead man, they were not always the same men who had so deftly maneuvered the long slender poles the day before.

At the junction of the Ganges and Yamuna rivers, our barges were directed onto the Yamuna. Eventually the sun played on the gilt domes and pointed spires and towers of the temples and mosques of Delhi as we floated by. I heard the sounds, muted by the distance, I knew so well from Calcutta—bells and chants and cries and laughter. The *ghats* that led down to the river held crowds, some sitting, some standing, and in the water others bathed or washed clothes. A child on his father's shoulders waved at the budgerow; I waved back. The ivory of the buildings gave way to shades of yellow and orange in the lowering sun as the city disappeared from view.

The river grew ever more quiet, eventually leading us to a tiny village, where the budgerow stopped. The village had carts and animals for hire, as well as men to carry us. We had been traveling on the water for three weeks and were finally ready for the last portion of the journey— this one on land.

An hour later we stood on a narrow road that appeared to lead straight up into the hills, the servants loading the heavy trunks and cases onto hackeries pulled by lumbering bullocks.

"Get yourself into one of the *doolies*," Mrs. Partridge instructed. She climbed onto the straw-filled mattress of a one-person palanquin and firmly buttoned the curtains. Faith did the same. I got into my own *dooli* but pushed my curtains aside. I was immediately thrown backward as a *boyee* picked up each corner. The ride was mainly uphill, so it was impossible to sit up. I lay back, Neel beside me, his head resting on my bodice, and I watched the rough rock that formed a low wall alongside the path. Tiny red flowers and lichen grew out of the cracks, a sure sign of cooler temperatures.

Near a dry *nullah* the *boyees* started a chanting song, their voices broken by their huffing intake of dusty air. As I listened, I realized, with a start, that it was about Mrs. Partridge. The song consisted mainly of comments on her spreading backside and voice like that of a hyena in heat. I wondered how much Hindi she understood.

❦❦❦

WE SPENT SIX days being conveyed mile after mile up the precarious mountain paths and six nights of camping in primitive tents or the simple *dak* bungalows constructed out of thatch along the way by earlier English visitors.

I loved the nights, sitting outside our tents or thatched huts before a fire. The twilight descended in one fell swoop, and the birds quieted and the forests around us grew quiet. The smell of woodsmoke was sweet and drove away the mosquitoes. The simple food tasted more flavorful than any I'd eaten in the grand dining rooms in Calcutta. I slept, deep and refreshing sleeps, awakening in the morning with a vigor I didn't know I could possess.

And finally we approached Simla. We stopped at the bottom of the serrated foothill, breezes filtering down to us, and once the *boyees* had rested, began the climb up. I couldn't stay in my *dooli;* I got out and walked. Trees with blooms of scarlet rhododendrons blazed, bright as fire, all across the hills. When we reached the edge of the town, on a mountain road sheltered by dark pine trees, I stared in fascination at the majesty of it.

Seven thousand feet above sea level, the hill station's houses had been built on a high, crescent-shaped ridge running along the base of Mount Jakko. They resembled English houses, some half-timbered cottages, and yet had an Indian flavor. Chattering monkeys scrambled along the tiled roofs, and mynahs and magpies called from the thick copses of trees clustered about. I could see the spires of a church and the covered stalls of an Indian bazaar. Mrs. Partridge knew exactly where to find our rented bungalow. Like many of the homes, it bore a strangely displaced English name—Constancia Cottage. Unlike the fussiness of our home in Chowringhee, it was small, built of lathe and plaster, with a thatched roof. Inside were three bedrooms, a dining room, and large sitting room. There was a fireplace there, the first one I had seen since leaving England. The kitchen, as usual, was a separate small building behind the house, close to the huts for the servants. I ran to each window, throwing open the wooden shutters. From the sitting room and the tiny front bedroom I looked up at the gigantic Himalayas, snowcapped and regal against a soft blue sky. The dining room and two larger back bedrooms looked down through sloping tree-covered hills to brown plains, and glinting like thin ocher ribbons in the far distance were the Sutlej and Ganges.

"Isn't this marvelous?"

"Yes, yes it is," Faith agreed, and spontaneously I grabbed her arms and tried to dance with her. But she stood, rigid, her eyes fixed on the view of the mountains. Mrs. Partridge gave me an annoyed look and limped into the largest back bedroom, closing the door firmly, and there was a heavy groan and the creak of a wooden bed. Faith moved, as if the pressure of my hands on her arms hurt her, and I let her go. She went to the other back bedroom and noiselessly closed the door.

Chapter Twenty-Six

May 20, 1832

Dear Shaker,

How shall I describe Simla, Shaker? I have written at great length about it in my journal and I pray you will be able to see and hear and smell it as I try to explain this queerest of places to you by copying out sections I have put down—so that I will always remember it—and in this way try to show you the shape of my life now.

Perhaps it is simplest to say the whole town is a curiously distorted vision of England, as if a wavering reflection in an Indian mirror. It is most definitely Chota Vilayat, little England of India, as it is often referred to here.

But in spite of this familiarity in a place so utterly foreign, I love the beauty and freedom it affords. If I wake early enough, I rush to my bedroom window to watch the distant line of peaks of the Himalayas catch fire, one after another, as they are touched by the rising sun. During the day I roam the promenade, a wide center street known as the Mall, built on the one flat stretch of ground in the area. All along the Mall are scores of English shops and the bustling Indian bazaar. There is even a small bandstand, where once a week an enthusiastic, if slightly off-key, orchestra plods through its repertoire for anyone who gathers to listen.

During the day, the Mall is filled with ponies and rickshaws waiting for hire. There are sidesaddles available should any of the memsahibs wish to go riding. The *jhampanis* pulling the rickshaws are to be pitied on the steep village streets, Shaker, and often it requires a joint effort of one or two pulling and another behind, pushing, to maneuver some of the more hefty women up the hills. Some women choose to ride in a dandy, a strong cloth strung between bamboo poles. It became apparent to me, after my first few days in Simla, that the ladies don't change their habits when they leave the cities; they are determined not to exert themselves. I personally believe this inactivity is the cause of many of their ills, real and imagined.

I have taken to renting a pony early every morning. There is a wide, pine-framed field called Annandale, where all manner of sports and picnics and fairs take place. Beyond the field are low hills, and it is here that I set out for my ride. When I return I often sit on one of the park benches positioned along the Mall, listening to the blackbirds and cuckoos and watching Simla's population.

Well-dressed white children in proper English sailor suits or long fancy dresses scamper freely about, attended by ayahs in snowy saris. Every day after tiffin a kindly old elephant with a magnificently decorated howdah is paraded into the Mall, and the children, in squealing groups of two or three, are carefully placed into the canopied chair and led around, waving proudly to their ayahs.

The British women, busy shopping and taking tea or cherry brandy in the sidewalk cafés while their children are entertained, put away their hated solar topees and fight to outdo one another in the splendor of their hats. I personally find the flowered and feathered bonnets monstrous compared to the unadorned heads of the Indian women, gleaming with oil of the *eclipta alba*.

Because of the cooler air, the fine ladies are also able to discard the limp muslin dresses of the city and wear their cotton and calico with heavily starched ruffles from neckline to hem. With the huge bustled skirts, broad-brimmed hats, and lacy parasols, each memsahib takes up three times as much room on the crowded boarded walkways as the Indian women. In comparison to the undulating ease of the Indian ladies, who slide by gracefully, bracelets and anklets jangling with a quiet sensuousness, ours are fettered in their armor of stays. They appear inflexible, as if frozen between neck and hip. I sometimes think their faces take on the same strangled expressions as their bodies. And perhaps also their souls?

There are a number of gentlemen present, although the vacationing women far outnumber them. Some are the men who work in Simla, and some are married men whose wives are currently at home in England. I have seen that these men, taking their own little vacations, are often looking for the company of bored wives anxious for a holiday flirtation while their husbands toil in the heat of the cities. It appears that the hill station, with its carefree festive air, makes these ladies much more susceptible to the attentions of gentlemen than they would dare to show in their usual domestic setting.

Soldiers, on leave from the King's regiment of the Indian army stationed all over the country, are striking in their scarlet uniforms. In Simla for the recuperative climate as well, it is quite apparent that they are the most notorious for leading the ladies . . . astray, shall we say. As in Calcutta, there is a constant and tiresome round of formal affairs and full-dress balls, as well as less ceremonious dances and picnics.

I have made my own Simla friendship, Shaker—although it is not the sort of the other memsahibs. The relationship I have forged is with our cook. He is a swarthy fellow from the west coast, given to much muttering. I know he was not at all happy with me visiting his kitchen at first, casting angry looks at me as he scoured his pots with sand in a big tub.

And now, instead of spending hours lingering over tea and cakes at the popular Peliti's, which Mrs. Partridge—who shares our bungalow—adores, or browsing in the English shops, I go to the Indian market and buy as many tempting foods as I can find. Now I am familiar with the strange fruits and vegetables that I had no names for when I first arrived. There are days when I stagger home, my basket filled with okra, aubergine, yams, mangoes, and lychees, and triumphantly deposit them on the dirt floor of the lopsided kitchen hut presided over by Dilip.

It's taken a few weeks, but Dilip has finally agreed to show me some of his tricks. The fact that I can now speak Hindi quite fluently was, I believe, the final straw in winning him over. And I am careful to not show surprise or dismay at anything—not the acrid smell of the mustard oil he cooks with, nor the sweet reek of the *daali*, the cow-dung cake hearth. His stove is simply a square of bricks with a hole on top to set a pot and an opening for the smoke on the side. If an oven is needed he has a tin box to place over the opening.

He eventually told me that everyone knows that memsahibs cannot cook, so he assumed my reason for such interest could only be to spy on him. Did I suspect him of atrocities? he asked me, with narrowed eyes. Did I believe he was an uppity cook who stirred eggs into the rice pudding with his fingers, or did I suspect him of straining the soup through his turban? Or was it worse? Did I believe the story of the offended *bobajee* who sprinkled the curry with ground glass or the one who inserted minute portions of belladonna into the kedgeree?

I laughed at his stories, picked up a brick, and began pounding a slab of lamb on a board, and he watched me for a long while. Eventually, after a number of visits, he agreed to show me how to prepare Indian dishes—but only if it remained a secret. There it is again, Shaker. My life of secrets.

And so I now make peppery mulligatawny soup, goat curries, and fish kedgerees, with Dilip instructing as I stir ingredients into the handleless shining *dechis* made of indigenous brass and cook the food over that brick stove.

Faith and I eat what I prepare (when Faith can be persuaded to eat)—I did confide to her how I was spending my time—but of course we don't breathe a word of it to Mrs. Partridge. She frequents the shops that sell prepared English food and makes her own shopping forays daily, bringing home cold game pies, bread sauce, and roast chicken and tongue. She carefully hides away her packages of Indian sweets; she can't admit to us that she has a weakness for cakes filled with cheese and almonds, or the delicate pastry babas full of mashed dates, and she hotly denied that the large box of *jallebis* found under the settee by the sweeper belonged to her.

A certain peacefulness has washed over me here, Shaker. There is simple freedom. In the afternoons, alone in the garden, I wear only a simple cotton frock; if truth be told, I have given up wearing a corset and crinolines. Although Mrs. Partridge appears disgusted with me, what do I care? Swinging lazily in a hammock with Neel tucked beside me, I read or watch puffy white clouds gather low over the Himalayas, then blow away in long scattered wisps. Overhead, fresh breezes rustle the cool green leaves and scarlet blossoms of the huge rhododendron trees, and a resident blackbird scolds me with the three warning notes of his trill. A disdainful peacock struts through the shady garden at least once every afternoon, a scaled foot raised daintily before each step, and I must keep my hand tightly on Neel's quivering back.

It took me a few weeks to understand part of the reason for feeling, for the first time in my life, this peacefulness. Then I realized that it was the lack of noise, Shaker. I have always lived in noise. First Liverpool, and then Calcutta. Calcutta! There is no louder place on earth, I believe. The chants, the constant gonging of big bells and clanging of smaller ones, high-pitched tuneless reedy horns, the pounding of drums, and over it all the endless human voices. My first night here I lay in bed, wondering what I was listening for. And then I realized it was the creak of the punkah—of course, unnecessary in Simla—that has accompanied me every night since I arrived in India.

I have always lived amidst the sounds of life, and much as I love the heartbeat of Calcutta, here life hangs suspended. I am peaceful, but under it all, there is a sense of waiting. For what, I don't know.

Thank you for your patience in reading this overlong letter. I have written it under my favorite rhododendron. I try to imagine you receiving this at Whitefield Lane in Everton and how you will look up at the English sky as you read and see me under this Indian one.

Always,
Linny

P.S. *Eclipta alba* is sometimes known as the false daisy. As well as keeping the hair dark and lustrous, eclipta is also used for inflammation of the skin caused by fungus and for eye disorders. I also discovered *manjith*—Indian madder. The root of this plant is powdered, then used as a blood purifier and to battle internal inflammations.

<hr>

I SAW A prisoner today. There is a small and miserable hovel at the end of town; it seems derelict and unused, and I have never paid it much heed. But today, as I rode my pony back into town, I witnessed a group of soldiers jerking and dragging a man toward it. He was a Pathan; I recognized him by his long eyes and his height, the golden earrings glinting in his ears. His hair, loose about his shoulders, was coated with thick dust, lightening its deep color.

I instantly remembered my first view of a Pathan at the docks as we landed in Calcutta. I remembered, too, Mrs. Cavendish's warnings about how fierce they can be. In a manner similar to that Pathan, this man was indeed striking. What I also saw was that although he was being treated with terrible disdain, he somehow maintained a dignity that should demand admiration. His face was not the pinched face of a simple thieving *dacoit* or cowardly thug. What could he be accused of? Surely something serious, judging by the hard kicks of the soldiers' boots into the man's ankles, the sharp jabs of their rifles in his back as they forced him along. I wondered how he managed to appear as though he was unaffected by it all, as though he was above their humiliation.

Another soldier led his horse, a huge black Arabian covered with foam, snorting and whinnying as it tossed its head. Spotting Mr. Willows, one of the shopkeepers from the mall, I stopped my pony and inquired what had happened.

"I'm sorry. I simply can't speak of his crime to a lady," said Mr. Willows. "But hopefully he'll be hanged. Although even death is too good for him," he added. "Now you get yourself off home, Mrs. Ingram. One of ours should never have to set eyes on a fellow like that."

As I nudged my pony forward, Mr. Willows called out, "Mrs. Ingram? Do your best to forget you ever saw that man, for he is the stuff of nightmares."

A Pathan, from Afghanistan, I chanted inside my head, as I had on that first day in India. *A Pathan, from Afghanistan.* "They call themselves Pashtuns," Mrs. Cavendish had said.

I HEARD THE STORY about the Pathan—actually, two stories—that evening. Mrs. Partridge told the first one. She considered herself an authority on all the Simla gossip.

"It's too horrible, simply too horrible to recount," she told Faith and me, although her eyes gleamed excitedly and she repeatedly licked her lips.

"Did he . . . did he . . . murder someone?" Faith asked, glancing at me.

"Oh, worse than that, dearie, far worse."

"What could be worse than murder?" I asked. *What could be worse than murder?*

Mrs. Partridge raised her eyebrows and leaned in. "He violated young Mrs. Hathaway."

Faith covered her mouth with her hand, shaking her head. "Do you mean . . . ?" she asked, her voice muffled.

"Yes." Mrs. Partridge nodded. "She's destroyed, of course. He caught her behind the picnic grounds, although what she was doing there alone I don't know. I've been told her body will recover, but of course her soul will never be able to forget what that beast did to her. Let's just hope a child doesn't result. That would surely be the death of poor Olivia. Can you imagine bearing a half-caste, a black *baba*? And think of her husband! Oh, it sickens me to imagine what he'll feel, knowing his wife has been desecrated by a native. Is there anything worse?"

I couldn't look at Faith. Had Mrs. Partridge forgotten about Charles, or did she simply not care, titillated by the excitement of the unexpected and lurid situation? "Now this will be an end to those lonely pony rides you take on your own, Linny. It could have been you. Obviously he was just lurking about, waiting to catch one of us alone."

I had no intention of stopping my rides. "Has it happened before? A Pathan causing trouble? I thought they were quite respected."

"They come through at times, but usually they mind their own business. And although they have some nonsense about personal honor, they're also capable of terrible violence, as is obvious in this case." Her nostrils pinched and her jaw tightened. "I suppose the temptation was just too much, seeing a lovely young white woman with no one to protect her. They all want one of us. Dark is always attracted to white, you know. Never the other way round."

"Really, Mrs. Partridge," I said, snicking my tongue. Poor Faith, to have to listen to this. I thought of Olivia Hathaway. She was a flighty thing, pleasant enough but always overexcited and overdressed. "What will happen to him?" I asked, wanting Mrs. Partridge to move away from the topic of color. "Mr. Willows suggested he would be hanged."

"Of course. There'll be no bothering with any kind of judgment. It's clear that he did it, and there is no alternative but to put him to death. He shall be hanged, and his body thrown into the forest for the jackals and hyenas."

Faith stood then, and as she passed to go to her bedroom, I saw that her face was completely drained of color.

※※※※※

LATER, AS MALTI BRUSHED out my hair, she leaned close to my ear. "It is not as Memsahib Partridge tells it," she whispered.

I looked at her in the mirror. She continued brushing—slow, long strokes of the silver brush. Her oval face was creased with worry. "Tell me," I said.

"Memsahib Hathaway's ayah knows the true story. She was witness."

"Witness to the rape?"

Malti shook her head. "There was no such deed. Not by the Pashtun, and not by any man."

I had heard the theories—that the thin air caused delusions in some. I reached up to stop the brush and turned around on my stool. "What do you mean, Malti? Is all of this Mrs. Hathaway's imagination?"

Malti gracefully lowered herself to the floor at my feet. "I know you are fair, Mem Linny. I want to tell you, for Memsahib Hathaway's ayah, Trupti, is my sister."

"Your sister?" Malti never talked about her family, even when I asked her pointedly. She always shrugged, telling me that her life should be of no importance to me. "Does she live in Delhi? That's where Olivia Hathaway is from."

"Yes."

"When did you last see your sister?"

"Five years ago. But we had imagined we would never see each other again, at least not for many, many years. So you can imagine my joy when we arrived and . . ." She stopped, swallowed, and then continued. "And now, because of what has happened, Trupti has serious trouble. So serious. I am the older sister, Mem Linny. It is my duty to help Trupti."

"Of course. Tell me what happened."

Malti never dropped her gaze. "Memsahib Hathaway has a business with a soldier. The man-lady business. They meet in the woods beyond the picnic grounds. Trupti always sits some distance from her memsahib, ready to warn her if anyone approaches as she lies with the soldier." Malti fingered the silver brush, picking at the few blond strands caught in its bristles. "But today Trupti was not careful enough. Her lady and the soldier stayed together so long. She fell asleep, to awaken only as a small party of sahibs walked with their rifles, looking to shoot something, perhaps the round walking birds with the piercing cry."

I nodded.

"They did not see Trupti, and she tried to hide herself as she hurried through the bushes to warn her lady. But she was too late; the sahibs spotted the movement in the woods, and raised their rifles, thinking perhaps a bear had come down from the forest. They fired, and at their shots,

Memsahib Hathaway screamed. The cowardly soldier, covering his red jacket with the blanket he and the lady lay on, escaped on his horse, riding further into the forest and leaving Memsahib Hathaway in disarray, her clothing unfastened. Trupti stayed hidden, afraid, and watched as her lady continued to scream, partly in fear but, Trupti believes, more so in panic at her disclosure. The sahibs hurried to her, helping her to cover herself as she sobbed uncontrollably. They asked her, over and over, what had happened, who had done this terrible thing to her, and finally she told of her ayah abandoning her as they walked by the woods, and of a man riding a black horse. She said the man had grabbed her and taken her for his pleasure. She pointed out Trupti, crouching in the bushes, saying she had seen it all but had not helped. The *burra* sahib beat my sister soundly with his fists and his rifle.

"It was the great misfortune of the Pashtun to be in the bazaar today, buying cloth as he passed through on his way back to the north-west frontier." She stopped, and pleated the fold of her sari between her fingers.

"Did Olivia specifically say it was a Pathan?" I thought of the face of the Pathan: the set of his jaw, the narrowed eyes, the way he took the blows without flinching.

"No, Mem Linny. She said that she had swooned during the misery and could not describe him."

"So they based everything on the black horse?"

Malti nodded. "It would appear so."

We sat in silence for a few minutes.

"Why have you told me this, Malti?" I asked. "I cannot bear to think of the Pathan being killed so unjustly."

"Memsahib Hathaway blames Trupti for what happened. She has already dismissed her in disgrace, saying it was because Trupti did not help her in her time of need. Tomorrow she starts her return to Delhi. The Memsahib wants her away from Simla for what my sister knows, even though Trupti would never speak of what she saw—except to me. And now she will not be able to feed her children, living in Delhi with our mother."

"What can I do, Malti?" I said gently. "I don't believe anyone within the English community would doubt Olivia's story. And obviously the soldier was more worried about his own reputation and future than he was of Olivia's, Malti. Oh dear, what is to be done?"

Malti's face closed. "I see I should not have revealed the truth to you. It was unfair of me, Mem Linny. I told my sister I would help her, but I didn't know how."

I picked at the raised bump of darkened skin on my third finger, caused by the constant pressure of the quill. "Let me try and think of something tonight, Malti. Maybe by tomorrow I'll be able to see it all more clearly."

Chapter Twenty-Seven

I COULDN'T FALL ASLEEP. I THOUGHT OF OLIVIA, A WEAK WOMAN looking for romance, and her soldier, a man so low he would run from the woman he had just finished jiggling, rather than risk being caught. I thought of Trupti, being sent back to Delhi in disgrace, her days as an ayah—or working for the English in any capacity—over. I thought of the look in Malti's eyes as she told me about her sister, the way her eyebrows had risen in the hope that I could somehow intervene. But mostly I thought of the Pathan and his proud struggle with the soldiers. I thought of his death here, in this town created for our pleasure, and how his family might never know what had become of him.

As I lay there, my mind racing, there was a soft knock on my door. I sat up. "Yes?" I whispered, in case Malti was asleep, although from the sound of her tossing on her pallet I doubted it. The door opened, and

Faith stood in the moonlight in her nightdress, her arms wrapped around her.

"Linny? Did I wake you?"

"No. I couldn't sleep. Are you ill?"

"No. But I—but I need to talk to you." She came to the edge of the bed, and I saw the glint of tears on her face.

"You're cold. Come. Get under the covers." I put Neel on the floor, and he padded over to Malti's pallet and curled up there.

"Oh, I couldn't," Faith said, her face registering shock, and I realized she had probably never shared a bed with anyone but Charles.

"It's all right, really. There's lots of room." She looked tiny and frail, her red hair a tangle on her white cambric nightdress.

She sat down, her back to me. "I'll just sit here. I don't want to look at you when I tell you this."

I waited.

"It's about what Mrs. Partridge was saying this evening," she said.

"It was very rude of her, Faith. I'm so sorry. She's a blunt, thoughtless woman."

"I'm frightened, Linny."

"Frightened? Of what?" I could see her shoulders trembling through the thin nightdress.

"I'm carrying a child, Linny," she said then.

I moved closer to her. Relief flooded through me. This, then, was the problem, was the reason for Faith's inertia, her lack of interest, her troubling vagueness. "But that's wonderful, isn't it? Charles loves you, and—"

"We said we wouldn't have any children. We agreed it would be unfair to a child. They say the next generation is always born black, Linny. And I still hoped to reunite with my family. I was sure if I took Charles home, even once, and they met him properly—my father refused any contact with him in Calcutta—they would see the same things I see in him, and would relent. But if there were a child, a dark child, Linny . . ." Faith's head shook slowly. "No. Charles even took me to an Indian woman, Nani Meera—I believe she's his aunt or a distant relative of some sort. He explained, and she gave me . . . things. To use—before, and after—to stop a baby from starting. She's a midwife."

I nodded, even though she couldn't see me.

"But they didn't work," she whispered needlessly.

"Surely Charles is pleased, though, after all. And perhaps the child . . ." I wasn't sure what to say.

"There is no perhaps, Linny. Charles doesn't know. I hoped that I would lose it on the trip here, and he would have never known." She put her face in her hands. "I've tried not to think about it, tried to pretend it isn't happening. But tonight, when Mrs. Partridge went on about the horror of a black *baba* . . ." She wept. "There is no point in anything anymore, Linny. No point. My life at home was meaningless, and my life here feels no better."

I pulled her down beside me, and although she wouldn't turn to face me, she let me put my arms around her. Her bones felt like those of a bird, and her hair smelled of jasmine. I hadn't slept with my arms around anyone since my mother had died, although of course I had crowded with the others on the dank mattress on Jack Street. But how different it was to share a bed with Faith, here, in comparison to those other girls, with their smells of cheap powder and sweat and semen, in a room rank with damp mold and cold ashes and greasy clothes.

"Meaningless? How can you say that? You have Charles, and now—"

"Don't speak of it, Linny. I can't bear to think. I can't bear to think about anything anymore."

I stayed quiet. I breathed in the scent of Faith's hair, comforted by her warmth and closeness, and felt myself finally spiraling toward sleep.

❈

I AWOKE BEFORE FAITH and Mrs. Partridge in the morning. I had fabricated my own plans and lies while lying in bed in the early morning light. First of all I called Malti and told her that when we returned to Calcutta her sister could come to our house and work there, that no matter what Sahib Ingram said I would make it so. Malti kissed my hands and then my feet, much to my discomfort. "Go and find her, and tell her we'll retrieve her on our way back, past Delhi," I said, not wanting Malti to see where I was off to. As soon as she was gone I dressed and hurried through the quiet town, all the way to the windowless hovel on the outskirts.

As I approached I saw a soldier slouching against the wall, but as soon as he saw me he stood at attention beside the open door, which looked surprisingly heavy. Through the opening I could see a damp dirt floor and a pile of old straw. And I also saw a foot in a high black boot.

"Ma'am? M . . . May I help you?" the soldier asked, stuttering slightly, as if nervous. "This is a temporary jail, and no place for a lady." There was a tin plate of half-eaten food on the ground beside him. I wondered if the prisoner was being fed.

"I do mean to be here," I said. Then I told him my name, and that my conscience had been playing up all night, that it wasn't my affair, but as a Christian I felt it my duty to tell the truth. These lies came to me easily; my whole life was a lie. It was only when I was forced to be truthful that I stumbled. I went on to tell the soldier that I had been in the market at the very time that Mrs. Hathaway was brutally defiled, and had seen the Pathan there. Then I had seen him ride off in the opposite direction of the picnic grounds. "Where was he found?" I asked.

The soldier didn't answer immediately, and that gave me courage.

"It was on the other side of Simla, wasn't it? Because as I told you, I saw him nowhere near Annandale. He was going off toward the western hills."

Now a shadow passed over the soldier's face. "Why is it, Mrs.— Ingot, did you say? Why is it that you care what happens to this bas— pardon me, ma'am, to this filthy Arab?"

"Ingram," I said, standing as tall as I could. "Mrs. Somers Ingram, of Calcutta. My husband is with the convenanted civil service. Although my heart does indeed go out to poor Mrs. Hathaway, there are, you must admit, a number of black horses in this vicinity. Did she say specifically it was a Pathan?"

The soldier looked even more uncomfortable. "Mrs. Ingram. Ma'am," he said. "I'm only in Simla on leave. I have been asked to stand guard here, although not in an official capacity." He was very young, with a pale downiness over his top lip. In all probability he was only a year or two younger than I, but I had purposely dressed in a suit of navy silk, a dark blue bonnet whose navy ribbons ended with white egret tips, and black kid gloves. I kept my chin raised and spoke to him with my eyelids lowered.

"And who is your superior, then? To whom may I speak about this matter?"

"That would be Major Bonnycastle, ma'am. But he's not here; as I've explained, we're not here in a military sense, ma'am. There's never been any need for that in Simla before now."

I glanced at the open door again. There was the clink of a chain, and the boot was no longer visible. "And so the Pathan will remain here until a commanding officer arrives?"

The soldier looked even more uncomfortable, blinking rapidly. "I don't believe so, ma'am."

"Then what would you do with him?"

The young man's Adam's apple bobbed in his scrawny neck. "Please, Mrs. Ingram. This is not a matter for you to concern yourself about. He will be taken care of by those of us here, and none of the ladies will have anything to fear from the likes of him ever again. Now I must ask you to leave. This is no place for a lady." And as if to prove his point, at that moment an aggressive black crow flew onto the roof of the hovel with a great coarse flapping. It opened its metallic beak and tilted its head, looking down at the plate. Then it let out a gasping croak and swooped low, grabbing a meat-covered bone in its menacing beak. Carrying it triumphantly, it flew over the head of the black horse, who shied, its flanks quivering.

I TRIED TO TELL MYSELF I had done all I could for the moment. I didn't like to think that the soldiers would simply take matters into their own hands and hang the Pathan, but the young man's blinking uncertainty had not been encouraging. Surely Olivia would never retract her story, or admit the horse wasn't black after all, but brown or gray, that it hadn't necessarily been a Pathan. I doubted she would say anything more, and she would never be questioned further.

Faith was sitting in the back garden when I arrived. She was clutching a sodden handkerchief, but I saw a new glow around her. There was something different in her expression that cheered me, although she was desperately pale. Mrs. Partridge had commented on Faith's pallor only a few days before, asking her if she'd been eating clay for the purpose of whitening her complexion.

Neel lay on the grass at Faith's feet, beside a pile of her books. The sight of the books encouraged me further.

"You're looking better, Faith," I said, truthfully, in spite of her paleness. "You mustn't worry about the baby. No matter what, you know you have Charles and his love."

"Yes," she said, studying Neel. "Yes. I do believe, now, that everything will turn out for the best."

I smiled at her. "Oh, Faith. I am terribly glad to hear you say that. I've been so worried about you."

She finally looked into my face. "I want you to have these books, Linny," she said, touching the leaning stack with the toe of her slipper.

"What do you mean?"

"I shan't read them. You love books. You take them."

"I couldn't, Faith. Of course you'll read them. Come on, come for a ride with me." I stood and held my hand toward her.

"I don't feel like riding, Linny. I have a number of things to do."

What could she possibly have to do? "Please, Faith. We'll take tiffin with us, and I know a place we can go. I have a map."

"Not today."

"Tomorrow, then?"

She was silent, but finally smiled. I realized I hadn't seen her smile for a long time. It looked unnatural, more of a rictus. "Can we ride far, Linny? Into the mountains?"

"Perhaps."

"All right, then. Tomorrow."

"I promise you, Faith, we'll have a lovely, lovely time."

꧁꧂

THAT NIGHT I DECIDED that when Faith and I returned from our ride I would again go to the jail. Perhaps there would be a different soldier on duty, and I would plead my case to him. I felt a tiny surge of hopefulness about Faith and the slight enthusiasm she had shown when she talked about riding far into the mountains. Perhaps everything really was going to be all right for her, after all.

※

WE WOKE JUST AFTER DAWN. I left Neel with Malti and went out to the kitchen. Dilip was waiting for me, clutching a woven basket with leather straps. A warm wheat fragrance filled the hut. He must have been up in the middle of the night to make fresh chapatis.

"I told you it didn't have to be anything special, Dilip. Just some cheese and fruit would have been fine."

He tucked back his chin as if insulted, holding out the basket. I looked inside and saw the chapatis, saffron rice, a jar of melon and ginger jam, and a container of goat cheese with mushrooms.

I thanked him once, knowing he grew annoyed if I said too much. And then I fetched Faith and we walked up the hard-packed road to the Mall. The morning was beautiful, its stillness broken only by the shrill cry of a lone black-and-white hoopoe.

Because it was so early, the only person at the stables was the *syce*, wearing a threadbare tweed jacket over his long white dhoti. He had been squatting under a leafy tamarind but jumped up when he saw us and led out two ponies, flowers woven into their manes. He tightened their saddles and I tied the basket on the side of my pony, Uta, a pretty brown filly with white spots. Faith's was a gray colt, Rami.

We led the thick-haired ponies toward the outskirts of town, and once we were on our way, I pulled a wrinkled scrap of paper out of my sleeve.

"What's that?" Faith asked. She appeared composed, calm. The tightness of her features had relaxed. I marveled at the change that had come over her in a few days.

"It's a map. A boy I know—Merkeet—who works in the spice bazaar drew it for me. I talk to him every time I buy food. Once, when I admired a hill woman's burka, he told me that the women made beautiful beaded ones in Ludhiana, and they would sell them. Ludhiana, he claims, isn't far at all. I thought we could go and visit it, then have our tiffin and ride back." I studied the paper. "It looks like we follow this main ridge until we come to a stream."

Faith spread her yellow skirt neatly over her knees on the leather sidesaddle. "Are you sure?"

"Yes—look. Here are the Himalayas, this is the road back down to the river. We can't go wrong." I felt similar to the way I had the time Faith and I had slipped away from Mrs. Waterton in the Maidan and ventured through the bazaar. This time we were to be away from the stern face of Mrs. Partridge, free to explore. To gallop and not care that our skirts blew up or our hair was tangled. Free to laugh out loud or to sing into the wind.

BUT AFTER WHAT FELT like close to two hours, I began to doubt Merkeet's cartography skills. We had followed the ridge to a shallow stream, then let the ponies amble through the pebbly water until thick copses of trees on either side reached in closer and closer. Overhead, the sun grew warmer. Faith hadn't spoken since we'd left Simla.

"I have a feeling that we'll see Ludhiana just around the next bend," I called back, not yet willing to admit that I may have made a mistake in going so far from Simla.

But the stream only trickled to a damp gully after the next turn, and with nowhere else to go, I steered Uta up into a narrow opening that I hoped was a path. We had to push thick scratchy branches away from our faces as the horses plodded along. And then, with no warning, we broke out into a daisy-covered field.

"It's beautiful," I shouted, gazing at the wide clearing. Trees enclosed the field on either side, but on one end it dipped down too low to be able to see where it led. The other end was edged with a jumbled pile of huge rocks. "Let's stop here and eat," I said to Faith, as she trotted up beside me on Rami. "And then I suppose we'll follow the stream back, for I don't think we'll find Ludhiana after all."

"All right," Faith said, staring at the rocks. "You set out the food. I'm just going to have a look around."

"Uta loves the daisies," I called as she left, but Faith didn't answer, urging Rami toward the rocky end of the field. I unpacked the food while my spotted pony snuffled happily, pulling up bunches of the flowers and munching them loudly. Faith rode back and sat beside me while I ate. It was windy in the field.

"Please, Faith, try to eat a little. You must," I begged.

She took a chapati, but I saw that she only crumbled it into smaller and smaller pieces, distractedly making a small nest of it on the ground beside her. The wind lifted her skirt in a golden circle about her; her bonnet had become untied and slipped back, and her hair was tossed in all directions. She occasionally glanced toward the rocks.

"What's beyond them?" I asked, wondering at her fascination.

"Nothing. There's a sheer drop over the edge. Nothing at all," she repeated.

I shrugged and lay back in the sweet-smelling flowers, looking at the blue sky and listening to the steady tearing rasp of the grazing horses. I felt a slight tremor under me, and as I sat up to ask Faith if she had felt it, a high whinny broke the stillness. It was Uta. She bolted toward the rocks at the far end of the field. Rami trotted anxiously in a small circle.

"Uta!" I shouted, jumping up. Faith had grabbed Rami's reins, and pulled herself into the saddle. "What's scaring them?" I called to her.

But Faith took off, first at just a trot, but then the pony was galloping. She lost her bonnet; it swirled in an updraft and disappeared.

Something made me turn away from the puzzling vision of her, galloping toward the rocks. A man on a horse rode up the field from the dip of the valley on the far end. The ground shook with the heavy pounding of hooves. He stood in his stirrups every few seconds to look behind him. In a shock of recognition I realized it was the Pathan. I looked back to Faith, her skirt billowing out behind like a ship's sail.

I was in the middle. The Pathan rode toward me, Faith away. Uta veered suddenly—was it because of the sudden ringing explosions somewhere behind me?—but Faith didn't follow. Instead, she rose in her saddle in a parody of what I'd just seen the Pathan do. But Faith did not look behind. She appeared fixed in a straight line, heading toward the rocks she had ridden out to earlier. And then she urged Rami on with her crop. Rami tried to turn aside as they neared the rock outcropping, but Faith must have held his lead. I saw her, saw her forcing him toward the outcrop. I didn't understand. And then she let go of the reins—I saw them drop as she raised her hands in the air, and Rami tried to stop before the edge of the outcrop, skidding, tipping sideways, and Faith went over his head in a graceful arc as if pushed by an unseen hand. But she hadn't been pushed. She had thrown herself from the saddle. My mind couldn't comprehend what I'd just witnessed. Faith had flung herself over the rocks.

Her full skirt wafted, and I saw a slice of the white of her petticoats and then the scissoring of her legs. The whole image of her flying into open air was like a pantomime, a yellow and white spinning disk, and then she was gone from my sight. I closed my eyes in horror, and in the same instant a terrible pain exploded in my shoulder.

The Pathan thundered down upon me, my legs gave way, and I fell like a broken doll in that meadow, an odd screaming echoing in my head. In the next instant I realized the scream came from my own mouth, a long and terrible cry, because I knew that something disastrous had just occurred, and whatever happened next could only be worse.

Chapter Twenty-Eight

I WAS ON THE SHIP THAT HAD BROUGHT ME TO INDIA, IN MY SLING bed, being tossed in a storm. All my bones ached. From the passageway outside our cabin I heard voices calling something unintelligible. There was a pounding from under me as if great boulders were hitting the hull; I feared they would break through and I would be drowned. I tried to hang on to my bed, but my left arm was somehow pinned; it wouldn't work. The waves were relentless in their rocking rhythm, and my ribs banged painfully, driving the pain back to my left arm and up to my shoulder. It was difficult to breathe; my face pushed against the unyielding surface of the bed. I struggled to lift my head and fresh cool air stung my cheeks. I opened my eyes, seeing my left arm hanging oddly above my head as if I were suspended.

And then it grew clear. The pounding rhythm was the beating of horse hooves; I was thrown over a horse's back and saw the ground rushing by. There was nausea from the sight and from the growing intensity of the pain in my shoulder; I turned my head to the side, and my nose pressed against something warm and hard, moving with the rise and fall of the giant animal. It was a leg.

I looked up at the broad chest and carved face of the Pathan and the last terrifying image of Faith flying out into the air came back to me. Faith. Perhaps my eyes had tricked me. Perhaps she landed before the rocks, on the grass of the meadow. Perhaps she hadn't intentionally committed the act I thought I saw, perhaps she wasn't . . .

I couldn't even think the word. I had to go back and find her. I struggled, kicking my legs, and there was a stinging lash against my calves. And that made me more distressed and furious; I must get away, must go to find Faith. I lifted my chest, pushing under me with my right hand, but the Pathan lifted his own hands—which I saw were bound together with thick, frayed rope—and slapped my head down as effortlessly as one swats absently at a mosquito, and I heard a popping noise as my nose smashed against the horse in a shocking burst of pain. And then something warm and sticky ran into my mouth. I felt I would smother; I couldn't breathe, my nose and mouth filled with blood, and once again, I fell into rocking blackness.

I WAS SHAKEN into consciousness as I was dragged off the horse. I opened my eyes but all was dark, not even the hint of a shadow. The Pathan held me against him, his tied hands in front of my face, one arm over my mouth. His body was so still and hard that if it hadn't been for his heat and his heavy breathing in my ear I might have been leaning against stone. I heard the horse beside us, its own breath whistling and wet. As we stood there, I eventually made out a thin strip of faint light far ahead of us; from the smell and dankness I knew we were in a cave. The filtered light came from an opening in what must have been heavy bushes that hid the high entrance. The horse let out a low whinny, and the Pathan took his arm from my mouth—to soothe the horse, I suppose—and I took the opportunity to try to struggle free. I know I shouted. But the Pathan yanked me back against him, his arms crushing my ribs, and then he slapped his joined hands over my mouth, bumping my throbbing nose, and there came a rush of fresh blood. The horse now wheezed softly, and the Pathan quietly hissed; it fell silent. I breathed through bubbles of blood in my nostrils.

Hoofbeats thundered by, and that bit of light at the entrance was cut off abruptly. There was a second of light, then another shadow. I counted seven shadows; there were seven men after the Pathan. I made a growling, deep in my throat, as if trying to call out, knowing, as I did, that it was as useless as the buzz of a fly. Finally there were no more hoofbeats, no shadows.

We continued to stand motionless for so long that I lost track of time. And then the Pathan took his hands from my mouth and I slid through the circle of his arms, to the ground, my legs useless as pieces of stretched India rubber.

WHEN A DIM LIGHT hit my face, I sat up, shakily, the moving of my left shoulder making me cry out. The Pathan, who was standing so that his body held back the bushes that covered the doorway, gnawed at the knotted rope that held his wrists together. He looked at me and uttered a few terse words.

"I can't understand you," I said. Then I repeated it in Hindi, and he responded in kind.

"Come here."

"No."

He stormed toward me and pulled me up by my hair.

"Let me go. Take me back to the meadow. I need to find my friend." I twisted under his grip, my scalp burning.

"Untie this rope," he said, taking his fingers from my hair and holding his joined hands toward me.

I looked at them and saw that his wrists were chafed and bleeding.

"Untie it," he said again. When I still stood, unmoving, in front of him, he said it a third time.

His voice was not the voice of a madman, a murderer or rapist. It did not carry the superiority of Somers's voice or the threatening tone of Ram's growl. It was simply a man's voice, raspy with exhaustion. Besides, did I have a choice? I worked at the knots, although my left hand refused to obey properly. Finally the rope pulled free.

He breathed deeply, rubbing his wrists, then led the black horse to the entrance. He pulled out long handfuls of the grass that grew there, and rubbed down the horse with them.

"My friend," I said. "My friend . . . I must go to see what happened. Just let me go now."

"We cannot go now. The *ferenghi* still search for me."

"But I'm no use to you. Let me go," I begged.

"You would lead them to this spot."

"I wouldn't." I grimaced and looked at my shoulder, and in the light saw blood, too much blood, both dried and fresh, covering the blue calico of my dress.

"Their bullet hit you," he said, glancing at me, his hand, filled with the sweat-soaked grass, still for a moment. "They shot at me but hit you."

I looked at him. "Why did you take me? Why didn't you just leave me there, in the meadow?"

He rubbed again. "I thought you might be of use to me."

"Use?"

"For a bargain. If they caught up with me. And your friend is dead." He murmured to the horse, and it stamped its front foot.

"Dead?" Why did my voice shake with such horror, such surprise? I think I had known, from the minute I saw Faith heading toward that rocky outcrop, rising in her saddle, what she was about to do. Perhaps I had known, for an even longer time, that what Faith suffered from had no cure. "But are you sure?"

"I am sure. There is only rock there. It is a long drop to the stones below, an empty riverbed."

"Let me go now, then." My voice was weaker than I wished it. *Faith. Why didn't I tell you I had begun to think of you as a sister? Why didn't I do more to comfort you?*

"Not yet. When I know they have returned to Simla, then you can go. It will take you most of a day to walk back. I will be too far by then for you to help them." Dried blood flaked around his ear and down his neck. His earlobe was torn where there had been an earring.

How had he escaped, I wondered. "I told you. I wouldn't help them. I know you didn't do it. What they said you did."

He turned and we looked at each other for the first time. He had been beaten; one eye was swollen shut in a puffy purple pouch and his bottom lip was split. His shirt was torn down the front, and there was a cluster of dark bruises on his chest. I saw the glint of the gold hoop, still in his other ear, through his hair.

"I know you didn't do it," I repeated. "I know." Why was it so important to me that he understood this?

"How do you know what I have done or not done?"

"I know the woman created a story to save herself and her cowardly lover. I went to the jail. I told the soldier there. I told him you weren't guilty."

The Pathan turned back to his horse, and I lowered myself to the floor, leaning against the wall. Finally he threw down the wet grass and let the bush close over the opening. "It grows late. We will stay here tonight. In the morning you will go back to Simla."

I turned away. The pain in my shoulder grew to a steady pitch. *Faith. Oh, Faith.*

✾

I REALIZED I HAD cried out. I opened my eyes to see the Pathan kneeling over me. He held a small branch, its end flaming, in my face. I turned from the heat. One small corner of my mind wondered how he had made fire. The floor of the cave was damp and cold.

Earlier I had tried to curl up into myself, tried to find a level spot, but the pain in my shoulder was unbearable. A sickness came over me, a heat and thirst so strong that I couldn't stop the small sounds that came from my lips. I sat up at one point but sensed I was alone in the cave. It was too dark to make out any form but I couldn't hear breathing from either man or horse. Had he left already? I heard my teeth chattering; in spite of the heat from my body, I shivered. And then he was there, with his flaming branch.

"Water," I said, in English, but there was no water, only a tugging on my left shoulder, and the sound of tearing fabric, and a strange sizzling, and then it was as if a huge beast had attacked my shoulder, and I screamed as it tore and chewed at the flesh, and the flame grew brighter and brighter until I was lost in its light.

❧

"Come. You must awaken now," I heard, and opened my eyes. There was a smoldering pile of twigs in the cave, throwing off a dim light.

"It is almost morning. I must go, before they begin to search for you again," the Pathan said.

I stared at him, unable to focus, partly because of the near darkness, but also because my eyes wouldn't work properly. I kept blinking, trying to clear them, but the lids were weighted. They closed.

"I removed the small ball from the back of your shoulder. It will heal."

I opened my eyes again, turning my head to look at my shoulder; even that slight movement brought a fresh pain, but not the same burning of the night before. A muddy poultice was smeared on my bare shoulder, front and back. My sleeve hung in torn strips.

"Come," he said, and led his horse out of the cave.

I followed him, stumbling. I put my hand to my face and felt dried blood. The sun hadn't risen, but the sky had lost its blackness. "You must walk that way," he said, pointing. "Your people will find you."

He leapt onto his horse with one easy movement. "There is a stream, not far from here. You will come to it if you stay in the direction the sun moves."

I nodded, my head so heavy that even that slight movement was difficult, and walked away from the Pathan. It was difficult to keep my balance.

"No," he immediately called. "Look at where the lightness comes into the sky. You go in the wrong direction."

I looked back at him, trying to understand where he wanted me to go, but in the cold dawn he and his horse shimmered as if underwater, or being consumed by flames. I saw the ground come up to meet me. Time buzzed in my head, the noise finally receding as the Pathan lifted me, putting me on his horse as easily as if I were a child. My skirt bunched up about my thighs as my legs stretched wide over the bare back of the black Arab. I grabbed hold of its thick mane, the hair coarse in my fingers. And then the Pathan swung up behind me, his arms, on either side of me holding the rope tied through the horse's bit, prevented me from sliding off.

WE RODE AT A STEADY gallop for what felt like hours. I was so relieved to be taken back to Simla that I allowed myself to relax against him, squinting against the burning light of the rising sun, which cast an orange light over everything as we rode. My head was strangely light and yet so heavy it was an effort to keep my chin from falling toward my chest. And the thirst was worst of all; my tongue was too dry to even lick my lips. I tried not to think of Faith, tried not to think of how all this would be talked of back in Simla, or worse, of Charles, who had trusted me with his wife. I grew aware of wetness on my cheeks, and I wondered at this. Tears? I didn't cry. I disgusted myself with my feebleness and closed my eyes tightly, willing myself to be strong. *You have survived worse than this, Linny. Much worse.*

And then we stopped, and I opened my eyes, expecting to see the familiar landscape around Simla. Holding me by my right upper arm, the Pathan slid me off the horse. My legs were wobbly, and there was a painful numbness between them.

We were in a long, lush valley. Flowers bloomed everywhere—wild tulips, purple and white irises, yellow mustard. The mountains, enormous and powerful, rose beyond the pine forest at the border of the meadow. And a narrow strip of river lay in front of us, glimmering in the sun. I walked unsteadily to it, falling to my knees on the muddy bank and scooping water into my mouth with my right hand. When I had drunk as much as I could, I gingerly patted water around my tender nose, flaking away the dried blood. Then I bent lower, wanting to wash the cracked poultice off my shoulder.

"No. Leave it," the Pathan said, leading his horse to the water. "It will heal faster if covered."

I stood while his horse drank and he squatted and splashed water into his mouth and then over his neck and face and hair. Afterward he turned to the east and performed the prayers I had seen our Muslim servants carry out.

"How near is Simla?" I asked when he had risen, although instinctively I knew if we had ridden this far we would have been there by now. But perhaps the strange fever and unrelenting pain in my shoulder had confused me. Perhaps we had been riding for only a short time after all.

"I have not brought you to Simla."

My legs would hold me no longer. I crouched on the hard, damp earth of the riverbank, closing my eyes. "Faith," I whispered, rocking back and forth, closing my eyes. "Oh Faith, what have I done?" I sat, heavily, on my bottom, and put up my knees. I rested my right arm on them and lowered my forehead to it. "Where are we, then?" I asked, speaking to the ground.

"We are near Kulu."

"Kulu," I said, trying to remember if I had ever heard of it. But I realized my only knowledge of India this far north was of the Himalayas, the northwest frontier, and the Afghan border. "Is it still India?" I was whispering now.

"Yes," he said. "Kulu is on the border of Kashmir."

"Why have you brought me here?" I raised my head and looked up at him. The sun was behind his head, and I couldn't make out his features.

He didn't answer, and I lowered my head to my knees again.

"I know you speak the truth," he finally said. "I heard your voice, while I was prisoner of the red-coated *ferenghi*, although I only understood some of your words." He stopped, as if unsure of how to continue. "You tried to save my life. And so I could not be responsible for you losing yours."

I looked at him again.

"I could not risk taking you any closer to Simla. But I could not leave you, so weakened and unable to help yourself. You need water, and you are ill from the injury caused by the bullet. If the *ferenghi* did not find you within a day, or perhaps two . . ." He brushed at his horse's mane with his fingers. "So I will take you into Kashmir, to a camp there. We will ride the rest of today and tomorrow. At the camp you will gain strength, and I will arrange for you to return to Simla with someone who can lead you safely."

I did not know what to say. Kashmir. What did I know of Kashmir? I could only think of reading of high, snow-covered mountains, of thick pine forests.

"You have nothing to fear," he said.

"I'm not afraid. I'm not afraid of you," I repeated, louder than was necessary.

He dipped his head, then led his horse to a small thicket and secured the rope. I heard him call the horse Rasool. He disappeared into the bush, returning eventually with wild mushrooms and berries caught in the bottom of his torn shirt. I saw that the shirt, although torn and filthy, had been made with tiny, careful stitches. He wore a brightly embroidered open vest over it. The sash around his waist was thick, woven with bright red and orange threads. His full black trousers were tucked into high leather boots.

I considered not taking the handful of mushrooms and berries he held to me, his fingernails broken and dirty, the hands covered with scars, but then wondered why I would refuse. What good would arrogance, stubbornness, do me now? None. Better to drink water and eat what he offered, for I was far from anyplace safe and familiar, feverish and in pain. If I was to have any hope of returning to Simla, it would be because of this Pathan.

❊❊❊❊❊

AFTER WE HAD RESTED and Rasool had grazed, the Pathan put his hands around my waist and swung me up again. This time he rode in front of me. As he urged Rasool to a gallop, I grabbed his sash, hooking my hands over it to keep from falling. I tried to look around as we raced through open fields and along gentle hills, but I had to concentrate on gripping my knees and keeping my fingers digging into the sash. Only my thin skirt and even thinner petticoat and lawn drawers were between me and Rasool. We stopped at rushing streams to drink every few hours, and I slid off the horse, walking a bit to try to keep my legs from stiffening. They were rubbery and uncooperative, my inner thighs chafed. Once I went behind a bush to relieve myself, not caring about the Pathan's nearness.

Finally we stopped at the edge of a dark forest. The Pathan raised his chin at a huge conifer, and I sat under it. The moss was spongy and cool. I put my head on it and slept. When I awoke a fire crackled in the small clearing. The Pathan came to me, holding out a small steaming bird on a stick. It was well cooked, its skin brown and crackly.

"What is it?" I asked, not really caring, not knowing why I asked.

He said a Hindi word I didn't know. I saw a second bird, lying beside the fire; it was still feathered, and a heavy vine was wound tightly about its neck.

"I think it's a grouse," I said in English. I bit into the savory flesh, grease smearing my lips and running down my chin. I chewed, watching the Pathan expertly plucking the second bird. By the time he was roasting it over the fire, I felt myself falling asleep again, the bones of the bird still in my hand.

I awoke some time during the night, my legs stiff and cramped but my shoulder, for the first time, not paining with the same intensity. The Pathan sat behind the flickering fire. The small, dancing flames heightened his cheekbones and accentuated the fullness of his lips. He appeared to be staring at me, but perhaps not. Perhaps he only looked at the fire, the blaze reflected in his eyes.

I closed my own eyes again, falling once more into a deep motionless sleep, and when I awoke again the next morning, I wasn't sure whether I had really seen the Pathan looking at me or whether I had dreamed it.

***

AS I STIRRED in the dappled sunlight coming through the low branches of the trees, every bone in my body screamed. All evidence of the fire was gone, and neither the Pathan nor Rasool was in sight. For one second I panicked, and tried to stand.

My legs threatened to buckle at my sudden awkward rising, and I had to grab on to one of the spiky, fragrant branches to keep from falling. As I straightened, slowly, I gingerly flexed my left arm. I could lift it now. I explored the crust of mud on the back of my shoulder with my right hand and felt the tender wound. When I pulled my fingers away, there was no fresh blood.

My clothes felt as stiff as my body; they were encrusted with dirt and pine needles, and the whole front of my dress was spotted with grease from the grouse I had devoured. I tried walking a few steps. The insides of my thighs were bruised and tender, and my drawers pulled against my body in a sticky, distressing way, as if my courses had come, but it was too early for them. I went behind the conifer to relieve myself, and realized my drawers were stuck to me with pus and blood. The skin of my bottom had been rubbed raw from riding the horse.

I hobbled back to the clearing, and the Pathan suddenly appeared from between two trees, leading Rasool. "We will find water in two hours," he said, "and will reach the camp by nightfall."

I nodded, coming toward him. I saw him watch the way I walked, my legs stiffly held apart from each other. I didn't look at him as he put me on the horse.

By the time we reached the next stream, I didn't know how I would ride any farther. I slid down and walked to the water, barely shuffling my feet. When I tried to squat at the water's edge to drink, I couldn't stop the moan that came out.

The Pathan said nothing. But as he swung me up, and I spread my legs and came down heavily on Rasool's hard, wide back, I felt blisters break open and weep. I involuntarily and loudly sucked in my breath and tried to shift my weight.

"Why do you cry out?" he asked. "Does the pain of your shoulder worsen?"

"No. It's not my shoulder," I said.

"You can ride?"

I nodded, but saw him studying my face.

"We have many more hours. You must tell me if you cannot ride."

I nodded. "Could I—I need to sit . . ." I knew no Hindi word for sidesaddle. I swung one leg over, wincing. "If I can sit like this, it will be better."

He shook his head, looking at the sky. "We have not made time as quickly as I hoped. Because of the extra weight for Rasool. Ahead is a difficult trail. You cannot stay on in that position, with no saddle. Why do you wish this?"

I slid off. I didn't want to have to admit to this dark stranger that my flesh was oozing with unbearable blisters. I put my hands on the back of my skirt. "I have never ridden—so. Like a man. It hurts my skin."

He made a sound of disgust in his throat. "Take this, then, and sit on it." He unwound his sash. "There is no time for this behavior, this *ferenghi* modesty," he said when I hesitated. He pushed the sash into my hands.

Staring at him, I folded the sash into a thick bundle, and hiking up my skirt at the back, tucked the padded wool into my drawers. Then I nodded at him, and he put me back on Rasool.

The sash protected my torn bottom enough to ease the worst of the discomfort. No longer having the sash to hold, I had no option but to grip the Pathan's waist. He urged Rasool on at a gallop, but only for a short while. Soon I saw the peak of a mountain against the brilliant blue sky. Its base was hidden in mist. Dots of huge fir trees and boulders grew visible. Rasool was forced to a slow climb up a stony hill, higher and higher. The air grew cooler. And then the descent was steep, although brief, and as Rasool picked his way down, his legs stiff and his hooves loosening pebbly chunks of earth that rolled down in front of us, gravity forced me to lean against the Pathan's back. I put my cheek against his vest; I felt the vibration of his heart. He smelled of sweat and pine, horse and air.

I saw a patchwork of land in the plateau in front of us and beyond another set of foothills rose, their edges trembling, unformed. Finally the Pathan pulled Rasool to a halt. We were beside a lake ringed with willows. There was the sound of splashing, and I turned to find its source: a small waterfall at the far end of the narrow lake. Beneath Rasool's feet the ground was sheeted with wild strawberries and columbines. The western sky flamed with orange and pink streaks behind green ranges. I thought of sketches and paintings of Switzerland I had seen in the travel books at the Lyceum. Even Simla's beauty could not rival this. And yet this glorious scene was darkened by my endless thoughts of Faith. The pain of losing her shadowed my every moment. What was happening back in Simla because of my foolish desire to have an adventure?

"We will go no further tonight," the Pathan said, interrupting my thoughts. "It is still a number of hours, and the route too treacherous in the dark."

I clambered down.

"Wait here," the Pathan said, then rode away.

I drank at the river, washing my hands and face, and as I stood, looking at the reflections of the rolling foothills in the still water, the Pathan returned, carrying a saddlebag embroidered with porcupine quills. He brushed leaves and twigs from it, and I assumed this was a familiar spot for him to camp, and he had left a cache for himself.

Leaving Rasool pulling at long grass, he crouched near me and pulled a clean white cloth out of the bag. He unwrapped it; a lump of hard white cheese was in it. He also pulled a knife out of the bag, and, cutting the cheese in half, gave one piece to me. He ate the other in a few bites. "The water is shallow and full of fish. You gather fruit," he told me. Then he dug in his bag again and pulled out a small skin, folded and tied with a thong. He handed it to me, saying a word I didn't understand. I looked at the small square. He took it and untied it, and I saw a dark gleaming substance. "It is for the horse, for cuts and injuries. Use it." He pointed at my shoulder, and then my skirt.

I took it and walked toward a grove of low fruit trees. Some were blossoming, while others already bore small fruit. There was a gentle curve in the lake where the willow branches, with their tender young leaves, swept low over the almost transparent sapphire water. The verdant branches made a natural screen.

I looked back at the Pathan, but through the lattice of leaves all I could see was a flash of his white shirt as he moved about the shoreline. The cool water lapped quietly on the grassy sand. I unbuttoned my dress and stepped out of it. It was so covered with dirt and blood and grease that it was hardly recognizable as the simple crisp periwinkle frock I had put on—when? Two mornings ago. Two days ago . . . It was as if I had lived a lifetime since then. I stood in my chemise and petticoat, unbuttoned my high leather boots, and tugged them off with a sigh of relief, rolling down my stockings and pulling them off, too. I wiggled my toes in the warm loam, luxuriating in the softness.

There were still a few pins left in my hair, although it was a tangled mess. I yanked them out, dropping them into the sand. Then I pulled off my drawers and eased the Pathan's sash away from my body. As I stood at the edge of the water with the warm evening air on my skin, a king-fisher swooped down over my head. I picked up my dress and drawers and stockings and put one foot into the water, then the other. The bottom of the lake was covered with small slimy stones and soft mud. I walked in, slowly. I had never been in a lake, or a river. I had never had more water on me than what a zinc or copper tub could hold. I went deeper, seeing my petticoat float up around me, a white disk. The cool water burned my raw blisters. When I was waist deep I let my dress and drawers and stockings drift on the surface of the water and ducked my head under, trying to pull the knots out of my hair with my fingers. Then I took my dress and scrubbed it as thoroughly as I could. I did the same to my stockings. The drawers were harder to clean, stiff with dried blood and pus.

At last I walked back up to shore and dried myself with the Pathan's sash. I spread the smelly ointment on the crusted scab on the back of my shoulder as well as the open sores on my bottom. I wrung out my dress and got it back on with great difficulty over my wet chemise and petticoat. I left off my drawers and, carrying them along with my stockings and boots and the sash and the ointment, I walked back around the willows.

The Pathan was standing on a small boulder in the water a few feet from shore, working at the end of a narrow branch with his knife. Several fish already flopped senselessly at his feet, and as I watched, he suddenly raised the sharpened stick over his head, then stabbed it into the water with great force. Just as quickly he pulled it back, and on the end was a large wriggling fish, its iridescent scales smooth as metal. Then he gathered up the fish and nimbly hopped back over the rocks to the edge of the water.

I set down what I carried and quickly went to the spreading branches of the trees covered with small hard dark plums, gathering handfuls of them in my wet skirt.

The Pathan was now crouching, slicing the scaled fish into fillets on a flat rock, burying the heads and entrails in the sand. He glanced up as I walked nearer and watched me shake my skirt. The plums rolled onto the sand like small, hard stones. He reached into his boot and pulled out a flint. He set twigs and small bits of brush around the rock and lit a fire.

Later, we silently ate the flaky fish and the plums, as well as the tiny sweet strawberries that grew all around us. The Pathan built up the fire, and darkness fell around us. I held my feet to the fire, then put on my dry stockings and my boots.

I realized, suddenly, that I wasn't hungry. I wasn't filthy. My shoulder throbbed only if I moved my arm too suddenly. I could sit almost comfortably by leaning on one hip. The only real and terrible pain I had was thinking about Faith. It was all my fault. If not for me she wouldn't be dead. She would be in the garden of Constancia Cottage, reading. It was I who had allowed her to carry out her plan. I put my hand over my eyes. I had had one true friend in life and I had betrayed her.

Strange sounds were around us: small animals rustling in the underbrush, something larger circling us with cautious steps. There was the far-off warning cry of a jackal and the murmur of a night bird high overhead. Rasool gave a shuddering whinny, and the Pathan said something to him in a language I didn't understand. The horse quieted, and I took my hand from my eyes.

"What do you speak?" I asked.

"The language of my people. Pashto."

"But you know Hindi as well."

"Hindi, Dari, Uzbek, Urdu, Kashmiri, Bengali, Punjabi. I have traveled widely within this country and my own. I can speak to anyone I might meet. Except the *ferenghi*. The foreigners. I choose not to learn their language, although some of their words collect within me, unbidden." He raised his eyes from the fire. The swelling of his eye and lip were diminishing. "Your language." He dropped his eyes again, but not before I saw something in them. Something that made me unafraid. Had I been afraid all this time, even though I'd boasted to the Pathan that I wasn't? I don't know. The haunting thoughts about Faith, the fever and pain, the uncertainty of what would happen—all had been part of my existence for the last few days. What did I feel now? If I could stop thinking about Faith, berating myself for not seeing the depth of her despair, for not recognizing her long and slow decline as more serious than a failure to adjust, I believe now that I would have realized that I wasn't frightened at all.

The Pathan spoke again, his eyes still on the fire. "You have been in India long? To know the language."

He was making conversation with me. How strange, I thought. I am sitting before a fire somewhere near Kashmir, talking with a wild man of the northwest frontier.

"Not so long. A year and a half."

He nodded.

I needed to stop thinking about Faith, needed a diversion to take my mind from her.

"Tell me about your people—the Pashtuns."

He threw a stick into the fire, where it crackled and hissed. "There is little to tell. I am of the Ghilzai. My own tribe numbers about one hundred and fifty. We live in no one place but spend our summers in the coolness of the mountains and our winters sheltered in protected valleys. My tribe herds sheep, and we sell or trade the wool for what we need."

He stopped, and finally looked up at me. "My people love music and poetry and games. We live a simple life."

His words belied what I saw in his eyes. There was nothing simple about this man. I pulled my heels up and wrapped my arms around my knees, resting my chin on them. "What were you doing in Simla?"

"I catch the wild horses of the plains. When they have learned to take the rein, I sell or trade them, sometimes in Kabul, sometimes in Peshawar or further south in India. I had sold a small herd in Rajpura, and was passing through Simla on my way to collect another herd that waits in Kashmir."

"I'm sorry," I said, surprising myself.

"Sorry? Why are you sorry?"

"For how you were treated. It was unjust."

He nodded, his face grim.

"How did you escape?"

"They took me out. To hang me."

I heard my own intake of breath.

"Rasool stood nearby. I made the sound he knows and obeys. He broke free of his bindings and came upon the men who held me. They scattered to protect themselves from his striking hooves; I leapt upon him. By the time they collected and mounted their own horses I had a good lead."

Silence.

"Do you have a family?" I finally asked.

"I have two wives." He bent forward to pile additional branches on the fire, and his face was hidden by the curve of his hair. Then he leaned back and his hair fell away. "Both have given me a son. Allah has smiled on me." And then, completely unexpectedly, his teeth flashed in a quick smile, thinking, I suppose, of his children. In that moment his face changed, showing him to be younger than I had first thought. His teeth were white and even. The smile was gone as quickly as it had come.

There seemed little more to say, then. We both studied the fire. Finally I spoke. "I have a husband." I don't know why I chose to tell him that.

"Of course," he said, and then he lay on his side, his head propped by his hand, and through the wavering heat I could see only the outline of his body, the rise of his hip and the thrust of his shoulder.

"What is your name?" I called across the heat.

"Daoud," he said. "Chief of the Ghilzai."

Chapter Twenty-Nine

I RAISED MYSELF ON ONE ELBOW AND LOOKED ACROSS THE SMOL-dering remains of the fire. In the first light the man named Daoud slept, his lashes dark against his cheeks. His face was shadowed with stubble.

I lay back and watched the sky with its shades of layered pink. A waft of scent from the blossoms came to me, and I breathed deeply. At a quiet rustle in the leaves of the overhanging *chenar*, I watched a pair of golden orioles silently groom themselves, pulling at their feathers with their tiny sharp beaks, fluffing up their breasts, and admiring each other with bright eyes. They flew off in a sudden rush of beating wings, and in a moment I saw why—the arrival of a large green woodpecker with a crimson head. He landed on a branch in the same tree, looking down at me with an arrogant proprietary glance, then attacked the hard tree limb with his long, pointed bill. The instant the loud drilling sounded, Daoud was on his feet, knife in hand. He stared around the campsite with jerky alarmed twists of his head.

I sat up, wincing at the pressure, and wordlessly pointed to the branch. At the sight of the bird's gleaming, busy head, he shrugged as if annoyed, then tucked his knife back into the top of his pants. He turned and looked at the still water, and with one swift movement, pulled off his vest and drew his shirt over his head as he walked to the edge of the lake. I saw, with surprise, that his skin not burnished by the sun was much paler than I would have imagined. He wet his face, hair, chest, and arms, then stood and shook, sending tiny pearls of water flying in all directions. He pulled out his knife and scraped it across his cheeks. Then he walked along the shore, disappearing behind boulders, and I went behind the same lacy screen of leaves where I'd bathed yesterday, tentatively touching my blisters. They had dried in the night. I put on my drawers, washed my face, and raked my fingers through my hair.

We ate the cold leftover fish and handfuls of strawberries standing beside the blackened fire. Daoud covered it with sand, then whistled, and Rasool immediately walked to him. He motioned to his sash, which I'd left beside his saddlebag. I took it and folded it into a thick pad and tucked it into my drawers, this time without even thinking.

Then he lifted me onto Rasool and we traveled quickly for the next few hours, through the foothills and into a valley. As we rode, I grew aware of my breasts pressed against Daoud's back, the feel of his hips under my hands. Just that, but it was an odd awareness.

Daoud stopped to let Rasool drink at a small pool, and I looked out at the valley spread before us. It was a paradise of lushness, spring flowers blooming everywhere—tiny blue gentians and purple violets fought for space with larger showy, multicolored anemones.

"Are we in Kashmir?" I asked, and Daoud turned his head and nodded.

"You see it at its height of beauty," he said, with a touch of pride in his voice. "Further north, winter can be very long, very cruel. The Kashmiris wait for spring as the hawk for the hare. The birth of warm weather passes very quickly, but it is a sight to soothe the emptiest spirit. Every year I hope to be in Kashmir in the time of its awakening." He pointed to a low hill, bordered with trees. "Beyond the trees is a small Kashmiri settlement. I have my horses there, and some of my men. That is where I will leave you."

He turned to face forward, but before he urged Rasool away from the water, he glanced back at me. "What are you called?"

"Linny," I said, and then added, "I am Linny Gow." I said it without thinking, although in the next instant realized I had used my old name. Here I was Linny Gow. I was not Linny Smallpiece, or Linny Ingram. It was here, I realized, that there was no need at all for pretense. For the first time in a long, long time, I was who I was.

He repeated it, *Linny Gow,* and it sounded strange and full of music as it came off his tongue.

IN A GROVE OF TREES beside a small stream, the camp was a combination of black tents and animal enclosures built of stone or wooden rails. One of the larger fenced areas held a number of majestic horses, and small pastures held single mares and their foals. In the smallest field, surrounded by a rough stone wall, a mangy, bloated, and limping goat bleated loudly and mournfully as Rasool splashed through the rushing stream.

We had arrived. It had taken us four days to reach this camp, only four days, and yet we had traveled to a world far different from the one I'd left behind in Simla. My breath quickened; what would await me? What if the people here treated me with hostility? Would Daoud protect me?

Once the horse stepped up on the low bank, men, women, and children immediately gathered, talking and pointing. The men were dressed in a manner similar to Daoud—dark pants, white shirts, and embroidered vests, although some wore a white turban. They were all strongly built. Some had well-trimmed, thin mustaches. The women were lighter complexioned, their skin a soft toffee and their eyes light brown, although their hair was very black, hanging down their backs in one tight plait. They wore long, loose, cotton tunics of faded blues, greens, plum, or crimson, and underneath the calf-length robes, full black trousers gathered in at the ankle. Their shoes were of soft material, embroidered, the toes turned up. Most had small, dark blue caps with a loose veil. On some the veil hung behind; others had their faces covered with it. They were all adorned with an abundance of silver jewelry—bracelets, anklets, earrings, and the Muslim nose ring of the married woman.

A hush fell over them as Daoud dismounted, then reached up and swung me down. A child in his mother's arms repeated something over and over in a shrill reedy chirp until he was shushed with one sharp word. I didn't know where to look. Nobody smiled at me, or came forward. They all simply stared. I dropped my eyes to the ground, conscious of how odd I must appear to them, afraid to stare back, as if too bold, while at the same time not wanting to show them how uneasy I felt.

Daoud spoke in an unknown language, and I looked up again. A boy of twelve or thirteen, in muslin jodhpurs, a shirt, embroidered waistcoat, and cap, scurried forward and Daoud handed him Rasool's reins. The young *syce* proudly led the huge horse away, and when he was gone one of the older men approached Daoud. They greeted each other in a chest-to-chest embrace. Then the man asked something, his tone questioning, and all the eyes in the crowd came to me, then went back to Daoud. Daoud spoke at length, and the eyes pivoted to me again. I longed to know what he told them; I prayed it would not turn them against me. He spoke again, and I saw some of the women nod, not unkindly, and my fears were diminshed.

And then Daoud looked at me. "The women will care for you," he said, in Hindi. "They are the women of the *gujars*—the Kashmiri herdsmen. Their men are driving the goats to pasture, and the women are hired to feed my men. Mahayna!" he called.

A young woman with a baby in a sling on her hip stepped forward. "Mahayna speaks many Indian dialects," he said, gesturing at the tall angular girl in the deep plum tunic. He addressed her in Hindi. "This *ferenghi* is called Linny. She speaks Hindi. Give her food and fresh clothing, and let her share your tent." He walked away with long strides, and his men followed.

The sloe-eyed woman nodded at his back, then turned to the rest of the women and chattered in a high-pitched voice. The crowd of about twenty surged forward, and I clenched my hands at my sides. The women's own rough, reddened hands reached out to touch my dress, my hair, my skin. They spoke to one another in a low murmur, as if I were some strange animal they were assessing. I thought that perhaps they had never before seen a white woman.

Finally the girl called Mahayna quieted them. The baby on her hip looked to be close to a year old, with huge liquid eyes and a fringe of curly dark hair. Mahayna stood in front of me for so long that my heart beat hard and fast. Was she waiting for something? Finally I reached out and took the baby's pudgy hand. "Your baby is very fine," I said. "A boy or a girl?"

I had obviously done the right thing. Mahayna's face split in a large grin, showing several gaps in her teeth. "A son. My first living child."

I smiled back at her. "A son. You are very lucky. Allah has blessed you." The baby played with my fingers, and instinctively I put my lips to his little fist.

Mahayna continued grinning, and once more chattered to the women. They all nodded, letting out long breaths that seemed to say "ah—aha" in agreement with my comment. Babies appeared as if by sleight of hand—from under tunics, from slings on hips and supports on backs. They wore tiny muslin shirts, embroidered with delicate flowers, and miniature cloth caps decorated with fine needlework. The infants and toddlers were thrust toward me, one by one.

"Touch them, please," Mahayna said. "The touch of a *ferenghi* woman is said to be good luck."

I obligingly stroked downy cheeks and dimpled hands, smiling at each mother. I patted the heads and shoulders of small children prancing about my feet. Then Mahayna took my hand and led me to a small tent. The throng of women and children followed closely. Mahayna motioned for me to sit, and I did so carefully in the trampled grass beside the patched tent. All the women lowered themselves to the ground.

Mahayna bustled in and out of the tent importantly, stirring at a small fire over which hung a battered black pot. Using a dented tin cup, she ladled a concoction I recognized as *dal* into an earthenware bowl and presented it to me with a flourish. I brushed back my hair, then, using my fingers, spooned the mashed lentils and rice into my mouth. Mahayna watched, and when I looked at her and said, "Good, Mahayna. Good *dal*," she clapped her hands happily, and the women smiled and began to talk quietly until I had finished. When I handed the empty bowl back to the Mahayna, she made a curious whistling sound. The women fell silent and got to their feet, taking their children and heading toward different tents. Mahayna set the baby on the grass beside me.

"They will not get their work done if they sit and look at you," she said. She pointed to the child, who stared solemnly at me. "His name is Habib," she said, looking at my abdomen. "How many children?"

"None. I have no children," I answered, and Mahayna's face showed sorrow.

"It will be soon, with Allah's will," she said with a confident air, her face clearing as she stirred the steaming *dal* in the black cauldron with a skinned stick. "The chief's women bear sons easily."

I thought I had misunderstood her strangely accented Hindi at first. But as she continued to stir, I shook my head. "No. I am not—his—Daoud's—not his woman. No." The baby whined, crawling toward his mother.

Mahayna smiled, opening the front of her tunic. She pulled out a heavy breast and picked him up. He immediately began to suck contentedly, reaching up to swat at his mother's dangling earring. "I have been here for three years, since I was a bride. Every year Daoud and his men come. I have heard many stories of Daoud's Ghilzai." She smiled, but it wasn't the open smile of earlier. Now it held a teasing quality.

"I will return to my own people," I said. The thought of even attempting to explain what had happened was wearying. "I will not stay here," I simply said.

She nodded, looking down at her baby. His eyelids blinked heavily, and his sucking grew shallow.

"Your husband is—with the goats?"

She threw her head in a vague gesture toward the hills. "Some come down once every week, for fresh food. There must always be men with the goats at this time of birthing, otherwise many are lost."

I watched her gently set the now sleeping child inside the tent opening.

"Why are Daoud's men here?"

"They keep the horses they catch here, readying them for selling or returning to Afghanistan. We feed them and clean their clothes. They do not touch us, or our men would not allow us to do their bidding. Our husbands are rewarded handsomely by the Pashtuns for our work."

I found it hard to believe she had been married for three years. "How old are you, Mahayna?" I asked.

"I am sixteen years old," she said, "but many of the women look up to me." She told me this with simple honesty. "I am not born of the *gujars*; my husband bought me from a village near Srinagar, the largest city of Kashmir. My father was an educated man and very wise. He instructed my brothers in the languages of India, and I also learned. He beat me when he found me listening, for it was not right that I learn as my brothers. But it pleased me, so I continued to hide, and learned against his wishes. The saying is "A daughter's intelligence is in no way helpful to the father." This was not so for my father. He was not unhappy when I commanded a large price because of it. I am useful to the *gujars*, for I am called upon to deal with the peoples of the south who come to buy our goats."

She pulled a half-woven basket from the side of the tent and began to twist the tough reeds over and around in an intricate pattern. "Soon," she said, "you will dress in fresh clothing. The women arrange it."

I watched the shape of the container emerge in her capable hands.

WITHIN AN HOUR, four women came to Mahayna's tent. They carried a pile of clothes and pulled at my arm, talking loudly. Mahayna had taken the pot of *dal* off the fire, and now a large tin of water bubbled merrily in the flames. She pulled two small gathered bags from within the folds of her tunic and emptied a small pile of tiny leaves into her palm from one of the bags, then dumped the leaves into the water. As if this were a sign, the women all sank gracefully to the grass and produced a small cup from their own tunics. The tunics seemed to be the equivalent of a lady's reticule.

Each woman dipped her cup into the boiling water, and Mahayna opened the second skin bag and passed it around. She handed me a cup of the steaming amber liquid, and I copied the other women, taking a pinch of the white substance that I realized was coarse sugar. Like the others, I blew on the hot liquid, then cautiously stirred it with my right forefinger, finally taking a sip. It was an unfamiliar but delicious blend of sweet tea. We were taking afternoon tea. The ladies chattered quietly among themselves. What a strange parallel, I thought, remembering the afternoon tea parties in Calcutta or Simla.

Immediately I cursed myself for letting my thoughts go back to those places. The last tea party I had attended in Simla had been with Faith. We had been invited to the home of a young woman from Lucknow. Faith had been so lovely in a peach-colored crêpe de chine gown. Her delicate cup had rattled in its saucer, I remembered now.

I had to set my own cup in the grass and breath slowly, for the pain of Faith was reawakened, fresh and new. I realized I had forgotten for the last few hours.

By the time the ladies had finished their tea, wiped their cups on the hem of their tunics, and tucked them away again, Habib was stirring. Mahayna picked him up and motioned for the women to enter her tent. I followed, and the minute we were all inside the small space, the oldest woman began pulling at the buttons of my dress.

"You must give us your clothing," Mahayna instructed. "We will repair and wash it."

I took off my dress and boots and stockings and stood in my chemise and petticoat. Mahayna picked up the edge of it, admiring the delicate lace. The other women waited expectantly, their hands outstretched as I took off the petticoat, and finally my chemise. There was silence as they looked at what was left of my breast, with its crazed and crooked stitching, and at the fading lash marks of Somers's riding crop on my back, and at the new wound on the back of my shoulder. I wanted to explain to them, and so I pointed to my breast.

"A knife in the hand of an evil man," I said, and they nodded, ah-ahaing as Mahayna translated. I turned to show my back. "My husband's anger." They nodded again, and I touched my shoulder. "By my own people. A mistake."

It was so simple.

And then I took off my drawers and pulled away Daoud's sash with small involuntary intakes of breath as the freshly formed scabs were torn off. "From the big horse," I said, turning to Mahayna. The women clucked in sympathy at the sight, and immediately one dug in her tunic, extracting a tiny muslin bag.

"Daoud gave me his horse medicine," I said, trying to appear nonchalant as I stood completely naked in this small clutch of women. I saw some of them looking at my feathering, pointing at it and then the hair of my head, comparing the color.

"Layla has a similar medicine, but for people," Mahayna said. She nodded at the hook-nosed woman, who sprinkled some herbal-smelling powder over the sores, talking to Mahayna in Kashmiri the whole time. "Layla makes many medicines from the flowers and leaves of the forest," she said. "This powder, if shaken on three times in a day, will heal the sores very quickly. But you must not bind yourself, as the air will dry and close the openings sooner."

Layla handed me the bag, and I put my hand on her arm to thank her.

They had brought me clothes to wear. One woman held out a pair of voluminous black trousers, and I stepped into them, pulling the drawstring tightly at the waist. Another slipped a soft burgundy tunic—a *kamis*, they called it—over my head, and still another began working through my hair with a comb intricately carved from scented wood. Finally the oldest woman, her face badly pockmarked, knelt in front of me. I looked down to see her holding out two pairs of low boots. I slipped my bare feet into the flexible warm inner shoes of soft chamois leather, and the woman laced them. She set the strong outer sandal, with its turned-up toes, to one side.

"You wear the second shoes over the first if you walk away from camp. They protect your feet from the sharpness of the stones," Mahayna said.

As the women adjusted my clothing, Mahayna, with Habib back in his sling, burrowed in a large cloth bag in the corner of the tent, then approached me with a pair of delicately patterned, long, silver earrings. I thought of the garish jewelry I'd bought myself on Paradise, of the genuine jewels Somers had given me in Calcutta, usually after some unpleasantness toward me. But this last straightforward gesture of kindness made my eyes burn. I took the earrings and attached them with strange silver clips to my ears. "Thank you," I said.

Mahayna flashed her disarming gap-toothed smile. "Now you look like one of us," she said. "At least from the back." She repeated her joke to her friends. They all laughed, and little Habib clapped his hands.

I SAW DAOUD later that day as I walked with Mahayna to the stream to fetch water. He was sitting with two men, and they fell silent as we passed. He nodded at me, and as I saw his eyes take in my altered appearance, I unexpectedly felt heat in my face. Something was happening, something I didn't understand, and yet wanted to think about. There was a peculiar stirring in me at the sight of him. The same feeling I had when I felt my breasts against his back, felt his hipbones under my fingers. You know what it was, of course, and are probably laughing at my oddness, my naïveté. Me—a girl who had known hundreds and hundreds of men. But this was new, and both curiously exciting and uncomfortable at once.

That night I slept on soft quilts in Mahayna's tent. The tent flaps were left open, as the air was warm. Occasionally there was distant baying; the camp dogs perhaps, hunting in the nearby hills. I heard Habib's sleepy demanding snorting, and after a quiet rustle of clothing his fussing was replaced by deep gulping and swallowing, and then the tent grew quiet again. I thought of Faith, and of Charles, when he received the news. I realized I had never once thought of Somers. Would he think me dead as well, if news traveled to him in Calcutta before I returned to Simla? He would outwardly show grief and despair, but I wondered if he would rejoice inwardly. For wouldn't it be so much better for him if I *were* dead? He had his inheritance, and could go on as the grieving widower for many years, with the sympathy and respect of the English contingent. *Poor man,* the matrons would whisper behind their gloves. *So in love with that strange little wife of his that he never got over her death. Chooses to live a solitary life; we could never interest him in another woman. No one could compare to his dear departed.* How disappointed he would be when he heard I was back in Simla; how he would wish it were Faith who had returned, and me lying dead on the cold rocks.

I turned my face toward the open door flap. I let myself think of Daoud, the shape of his bare back as he stood at the water's edge, the look of his thighs as they pressed against his horse. His smell. Here it was again, the strange, restless feeling.

⁂

THE NEXT DAY I helped Mahayna with the food and played with Habib. I didn't see Daoud. Would I see him again? Surely he would come, soon, to tell me when and how I would return to Simla.

Late in the afternoon, tickling Habib's double chin with a long blade of grass, a shadow blocked the sun. I looked up to see a short, stocky man in a dirty blue shirt and even dirtier pants. He had a half-grown beard, and his lined brown face and red-rimmed eyes looked tired and drawn. He stared down at me and Habib, then ducked his head inside the empty tent.

"Mahayna!" he roared, although it was obvious the tent was empty. Habib screamed at the unexpected sound, and I picked him up and held him against me.

"She brings water from the stream," I shouted over the baby's howls, but the man stared at me blankly, and I realized he didn't speak Hindi. He dropped a sack he held over his shoulder. A woman sitting in the doorway of the tent across from us yelled something at the grizzled man, and he turned his back to me and crossed his thick arms over his barrel chest, standing with his legs apart and his eyes fixed in the direction of the stream.

In a few moments Mahayna swayed into view, gracefully balancing a dripping earthenware pot on her head. Seeing the man, she quickly set it down and reached out her arms to Habib.

"It is my husband, Bhosla," she said, her voice slightly breathless. "He has not been down from the hills for two weeks." Settling the baby in her sling, she immediately stooped over the black pot and dished up a huge bowl of fish and wild mushroom stew. She handed it to her husband with downcast eyes, and he barked a sentence at her, tossing his head in my direction. She answered in a quiet current of sentences, her tone curiously flat as it never was when she spoke to me or the other women.

Her answer satisfied Bhosla. He squatted, his back still to me, and finished the stew in a few enormous slurps.

I felt the strain. "I will go for a walk," I said, seeing Mahayna's expression. She nodded, distractedly, already pulling a pile of clothing from the grimy sack tossed on the ground. I could smell the greasy sweat that rose from it.

I walked through the tents until I came to the low stone wall that contained the sick goat. I leaned on the wall, idly contemplating the flea-bitten creature. A boy climbed up and perched atop the wall not far from me, whistling to the animal. It was a strange, high, trembling sound that reminded me of both a flute and the cry of a hawk. Every time the boy whistled, the goat turned its dull sulphur eyes toward him and circled feebly, first in one direction and then another, in confused obedience.

I looked to the gently sloping green hills surrounding this valley. Beyond them were the mountains, their tops hidden, the clouds that floated by caught on those snowy peaks. Were these the same mountains I had seen in Simla, viewed from another direction? I thought of the marking on the maps I had studied back in Calcutta, wondering exactly where I was, and if I would ever know.

I left the boy and the goat and wandered to an open patch of grass where a group of children raced about. It was a cruel game of some sort. All the children chased one boy or girl, and when the victim was caught, he or she was subjected to cruel slaps and hair-pulling by the others, who laughed loudly. From what I could see, the object of the game was to fight back, withstanding as much pain as possible. One small boy burst into angry tears after a particularly hard poke in the eye by a larger girl, and at the sight of his red squalling face the group walked away from him. Ostracized, his fist pressing his eye, he tramped to a rock and plunked himself down, forlornly watching the continuing game from a distance.

When the children lost interest and scampered off in different directions, I walked to the horse enclosures. One held a milling pack of horses, and in another, a lone figure stood in the center of the flat stony area, a short-handled whip in one hand and, wound around the other, a rope attached to the bridle of a plunging, pulling, wild-eyed golden stallion. As the man turned, I saw that it was Daoud.

He wore only his trousers and high leather riding boots, and his chest and back were wet with his exertions under the warm sun. He had tied his hair back with a leather thong, and with the black waves away from his face, I could see the strong clean line of his jaw, the long smoothness of his neck. He had put larger, wider hoops in his ears. He called commands to the snorting animal as he worked with it. His face was changed; not only had much of the swelling gone down, although it was still discolored, but it was the expression. It was not the strained, disdainful countenance I had first seen as he was dragged to the jail in Simla. It was not the guarded face he had worn for much of the time I was with him as we rode to Kashmir. Now it was alive, free. I believe it was his true face.

He didn't see me. I rested my arms along the top of the rough log of the fence and watched. Eventually the horse exhausted itself and stood with its head low, blowing noisily through flared nostrils. Daoud, crooning softly, approached the heaving animal, putting his palm against the broad forehead. The animal's head snapped up, sending off clots of bubbling foam, but it didn't run. Daoud stared into its eyes, and very slowly, let out a long, low whistle, as he had to Rasool when the horse trembled with fear in the cave. The stallion lowered its head again. Daoud also lowered his, until his own forehead was pressed against the golden one. They stood unmoving for at least a full minute. Then Daoud lifted his head and gave a mild tug on the rope, walking toward the gate. The horse followed. At the gate, Daoud slipped the bridle off, and the horse turned and ran across the enclosure, kicking behind him with coltish pleasure. Daoud watched, smiling, then opened the leather latch and slipped through the gate. As he retied the latch, I called out. "A magnificent horse."

He looked in my direction. "Yes," he answered. Something closed over his expression, and I was sorry to see that my presence had done this. He wound the thongs of his whip around his hand. "You are well treated?"

I nodded. I wanted to say something, but was confused by the anxiety that overtook me.

"You have the clothes of a *bakriwar,* a goat woman, but your face and your hair—they do not fit," he said, and, like the fool that I felt, I simply nodded.

He came toward me, and my breathing quickened, but he walked by, and I smelled his glistening sweat-soaked skin.

"Wait," I said, and he turned back to me. "I—when will I go back?"

Daoud studied the clouds over my head before he spoke. "If you wish, I can arrange that you leave tomorrow."

When he didn't say any more, I realized he was waiting for me to answer. Why didn't I say yes, yes, I must go right away, tomorrow, as soon as possible? What stopped me?

"Although it would be difficult if you do want to leave immediately," he added unexpectedly.

"Difficult? Why?"

He played with the soft rawhide plaits of his whip. I watched his hands. "There is only one *gujar* boy here who can be trusted with the task of leading you through the mountains, and he is also our only *syce.* The journey to Simla and then back again will take seven to eight days. It will take us those eight days—maybe ten—to finishing training the horses here before we take them to Peshawar. The *syce* will be most important to my men at this time. But I gave my promise that I would see you returned to Simla. If you are most anxious to go, then I will arrange—"

"No." Had I said no?

Daoud's face now wore a curious expression. He tapped his whip softly against his thigh. "Will your people not worry?"

I didn't answer.

He held the whip still. "So you will remain for a while longer, here, at the camp? This is your wish?"

Perhaps ten seconds passed before I answered. "Yes. It is my wish."

"So be it," Daoud said, then turned on his heel and strode away, leaving me alone in the still, fragrant late afternoon air of Kashmir. With him gone I felt a loss.

And as I watched him walk away I knew now the name of this emotion I was struggling to understand.

Desire.

Chapter Thirty

WHAT HAD I IMAGINED DESIRE TO BE? I HAD THOUGHT IT must be a small thing, a thing that arose momentarily and settled only in that part of the body that was to be used; when satisfied, it returned mindlessly to its deeply hidden lair. I didn't know that it had its own life, that it would fill all of one's being, that it would infect even the brain. That it was impossible to push away. It took me close to twenty years to learn this, even though for seven of those years—between the ages of eleven and seventeen—I was used as an object of desire. No. That is wrong. I was used as an object of lust, and it was at this same time, when desire came awake in me, that I also learned the difference between the two.

And why did it take this seemingly uninterested man, this man who had no connection to me or to any part of my life, to make me understand—finally see what drove men and women, men and men, women and women—together? Perhaps it is this very inexplicable part of desire that renders its victims helpless.

Daoud walked away from me at the enclosure. He had never touched me other than placing his hands around my waist as he lifted me on and off Rasool. I knew he had rubbed mud—it must have been carefully, softly—around the wound on my shoulder to stop the bleeding after he had dug out the bullet with the smouldering end of a stick, but I had been unconscious. He probably cursed his momentary decision to pull me from the meadow, especially when his conscience made him keep me with him, slowing his journey back to Kashmir. His eyes had showed mild surprise at my appearance in the *bakriwar* clothing. I knew what I must appear to him—small and weak, insignificant compared to the strong, capable women surrounding me now. But something about the way the ends of the whip played through his long fingers, the way his ribs gleamed faintly from his breastbone . . . I felt a strange movement within some deep part of me, low, in my abdomen, growing soft and pliant. I stayed at the enclosure, wondering at these feelings, as the air turned cooler and the rich smell of cooking meat sent a rush of saliva into my mouth. I didn't remember when I had last felt hunger like this. I had, daily for years, known the aching, burning gnaw of a hungry belly, but this was something different.

And I looked forward to eating with an anticipation that was also new and good, a yearning that matched the rest of my turbulent feelings.

I returned to Mahayna's tent. She was sitting by the fire, holding a small bowl to Habib's mouth. "Bhosla sleeps," she said. "He has gone without proper food and rest for many days. Some of the goats fell ill from eating a poisonous shrub, and he and the other men have worked night and day to save them."

"Is he angry about me sharing your tent?" I sensed she was explaining her husband's behavior.

"No," Mahayna said, shaking her head so that the long earrings slapped her cheeks. "You are welcome in our tent." She said the words with confidence, but didn't look at me, picking at something in the baby's scalp. "Eat," she said then, and I pulled stringy strips of meat from the pot with my fingers, tearing at them, feeling juice and grease run down my chin. I ate and ate, as if insatiable.

"I saw Daoud training a horse," I said, when I had finished. I wiped my hands on the grass, then ran my finger over the etched surface of the silver bracelet Mahayna had given me to wear that morning. I thought of the sweat on Daoud's smooth chest, how I had wanted to put my hand out and press my fingers against it.

Mahayna made a sound in her throat, a small sound, amused. I looked at her.

"You will go to him, I think," she said.

I shook my head, feeling my earrings swing against my cheeks the way I had seen Mahayna's earlier. My face grew hot. "Why do you say this? He is a chief and I a *ferenghi*. He has two wives. I have a husband."

Mahayna shrugged. "Your husband has not given you children. He beats you. This is reason enough to seek comfort elsewhere."

She said it, as she said everything, so simply. Seeking comfort. That coupling could be comfort was an odd concept. Sex meant release, I understood, for men. For women it meant children. Comfort? I looked at the distant silver of the sun, hurrying to rest behind the mountains. Mahayna and I sat in silence as the night sky grew black, and after she had nursed Habib until he fell asleep I followed her inside the tent and bundled myself in my quilt in the crowded space. Mahayna put Habib in a pile of skins in one corner and lay between me and Bhosla.

I THOUGHT IT WAS the camp dogs that woke me, although this wasn't their usual thin yapping in the distance. It was a hoarse, rhythmic barking. I turned over, pulling the quilt around my ears, when a sudden stifled whisper made me tense and waken fully in the darkness. I opened my eyes, making out the curve of the tent wall. The whisper came again, now angry, from behind me. It was Mahayna. Then the guttural sound started again, and I realized it wasn't the dogs at all, but Bhosla with Mahayna. I listened as his grunting grew louder and more urgent, culminating in a hissing groan. In only a few moments there was a muffled thump, followed by rumbling snores.

I lay stiffly, aware that my shoulder was aching; I was lying on my wounded one. Sleep had gone. I waited until I heard Mahayna's quiet, even breaths between the rasps of Bhosla's snores. Then I threw back my quilt and silently crawled through the tent opening.

Millions of stars shone brightly in the clear night sky. The light from a gibbous moon outlined the edges of the still camp; a breeze that carried the deep green smell of the mountains stirred the leaves of the tall birch and graceful poplars. I took the goatskin cover off the large earthenware pot of water beside the tent, splashing some of it on my hot cheeks and taking a long drink.

I walked through the camp, realizing I was not the only one awake. In one tent a child whimpered, in another men's voices rose in angry bursts. I heard muffled weeping in another. A small white dog soundlessly charged at me from the shadows, its hackles standing straight, but after a few concerned sniffs at my feet it trotted away, tail high and rigid with its own importance. Something about the dog's acceptance of me gave me a heightened sense of my own belonging such as I had never felt in Liverpool or in Calcutta or even Simla.

Finally I arrived at the horse enclosure. It was the only place I knew to come, the only place that called to me. I pressed my forehead against the hard roughness of the wooden fence, thinking of the press of Daoud's forehead against the golden stallion's earlier that day. The stallion and three smaller horses raised their heads in the air, alert in their far corner. I wanted to say his name. "Daoud." It was little more than a whisper, but there was a sudden rustle behind me, and I whirled around.

He was sitting on a thick quilt, his back against a huge red-barked deodar. A *chapan* was thrown beside him. Had he heard me utter his name?

"You pray for your friend?" he asked, and I was first filled with relief, and then burned with shame. Him thinking I was mourning Faith, praying to a spirit, when my thoughts were base, and all too human.

I stayed at the fence. I couldn't see his face. Just his boots and legs, stretched out in front of him.

"And you long for your husband," he stated. Not a question.

I was so tired of lying, of secrets. "Yes, I miss my friend, and mourn for her. Her death is like—like a heavy rock, here." I put my hand on my chest. *But I don't care if I ever again see my husband,* I wanted to say, the exhilaration at being able to speak my thoughts growing ever stronger. "But it is not true that I long for my husband."

I had never longed for another person, except my mother. I knew the feeling as it related to her. But had I longed for Shaker the night he wept as I let him take me in his narrow bed in Everton? For any of the young men I had danced with in the Calcutta salons? For Somers, even when I felt an unsettling confusion at the wrath I was able to stir within him? Had I ever longed to be near a man, to smell the scent of him? No. I moved closer to the edge of the quilt, trying to see Daoud's face.

Suddenly he stood, and I took a step back. "You should return to Mahayna's tent," he said, and I knew I didn't want to. I wanted to stay here. This is what I had hoped to find when I came to the enclosure.

I crossed my arms over my chest. I was trembling, although not cold. "Why are you here, and not in a tent?" I asked.

"I am happier sleeping under the sky. And I like to be near the horses," he said. He stepped forward, picking up the *chapan*. He handed it to me.

I took the cape and put it around my shoulders. It was warm, thickly woven in myriad colors, heavy with the smell of woodsmoke.

"It is best if you go," he said, and when I continued to stay, he came even closer. I looked up at him.

"Go, Linny Gow," he said, and at the sound of my name from his lips the feelings that were confounding me swept in with such force that I turned and ran, rushing through the scattered tents in my soft shoes, making the dogs bay.

❦

THE NEXT DAY I worked beside Mahayna, my hands moving in the proper ways. I was thankful Bhosla was there, as Mahayna didn't speak to me while he was present. I didn't want to talk, afraid that if I did I would say things that I didn't fully understand yet, afraid I would give away my yearning. To speak it aloud, giving it a name, frightened me.

Finally Bhosla left, dressed in clean clothing and carrying a sack of more clothing and an enormous pack of food on his back. Within minutes Mahayna was humming, chattering. I answered, but couldn't stop thinking of the power Daoud held over me.

All the men I had known had wanted something—the endless stream of customers; Ram, using me for the easy coins he didn't have to work for; Shaker, wanting love in a needy way that was smothering; Somers, wanting his inheritance and a cover for his lifestyle. And perhaps someone to bully. They all made use of me for something they wanted or needed. And by using me, they made me into an object.

Daoud wanted nothing. He appeared to need nothing; he appeared complete—a complete human being. This realization, coming slowly to me as I worked alongside Mahayana, was like warm water on my soul— he expected nothing of me, asked for nothing, and there was no need for me to fabricate any part of my life, as I had since Shaker had brought me to his home on Whitefield Lane. I was so weary of the lies I had to keep up with every single person I had met since then—first in Liverpool and then in the false image of England created in India.

Here, in this Kashmir camp, I could be who I actually was. Nobody cared what had been done to me, and what I had done, least of all Daoud. I felt myself opening, unlocking, the hinges rusted and giving way with a tearing sound like the wings of birds as they startle into flight.

I was open. My mind, my heart, my body. I knew what I would do. All the past choices in my life had been made for safety, for survival, for concealment and acceptance. All of them had been difficult, bound in twisted wire with consequences that could cost too much should they become unraveled. This choice felt easy, and carried not even the shadow of a doubt.

❦

I RETURNED DAOUD'S *chapan* to him the next afternoon, also bringing food to him at the horse enclosure. By offering him the rabbit stew from Mahayna's pot, the flask of water from the stream, I felt strong, since I was giving him something. He took the bowl and sat on the top rail of the enclosure, eating it. I simply stood there, watching the horses. When he finished he drank from the flask, putting his head back to drain it. I watched his throat swallowing. I felt stretched, as if there were a bright, high singing in my brain.

As he handed the bowl and flask back to me, he jumped off the fence and looked into my face. "You are comfortable here now?" he asked.

I nodded. I wanted him to say my name.

"You do not behave as I imagined a *ferenghi* woman."

I took a deep breath. "I am not like the other memsahibs. I only pretend. I am not one of them."

He leaned one elbow on the rail. "Why do you do this?"

"I did not grow up as they did. I have a shameful past, kept hidden."

He hadn't stopped looking at me. A horse neighed, children shouted. "I have seen a sadness in your eyes," he said. "I wondered at it. This is the heavy gift of your past?" His own eyes were almost black.

"Yes. I hate it. I'm ashamed of my past." It was so easy to say these things to him.

"Perhaps you must let those old lights go out. It requires much effort to keep them burning. Let new ones take fire. Today it is not what you have done, but what you will do that matters. That is the new light."

We both looked at the horses then. I was suddenly shy, and I sensed some feeling—similar?—from him. This gave me courage to say what I had wanted to say. "Will you sleep under the sky again tonight?"

He turned to me, and I saw his throat move as he swallowed. He nodded.

"I will come to you," I told him, and he nodded again, and my heart thudded so loudly behind my ribs that it brought a strange and beautiful pain.

———— ❀❀❀ ————

I UNDERSTOOD, THAT NIGHT, more than I had ever understood. I came to see what I didn't know existed. The first time we came together, only moments from when I lowered myself beside him on the quilt, was rapid, almost desperate, our clothing merely pushed aside. And then, while we rested and our breathing slowed, he reached out and stroked my face with a delicacy I didn't know his scarred, hardened hands could possess, and it was this touch that made me shudder with some combination of joy and grief so huge that I wept. Me, who was not a girl for weeping, brought to tears by the touch of a hand on my face. And he looked at these tears, and then soundlessly pressed my face against his chest by cupping the back of my head in his one huge hand. He kept his other arm around me. And I thought of Mahayna's words as she spoke of comfort.

When my tears stopped I sat up in the moonlight and drew my *kamis* over my head, and he made no sound as he looked at my scar, and then his eyes moved up to meet mine and he put out his hand. It was so large that it covered the entire scar, covered what still remained of my left breast, and I felt the heat of his flesh against mine. And then he lay me down again on the quilt, and he gently lowered himself onto me. And this time our joining was slow and quiet, and the quietness grew inside me until it blocked out all sounds. I no longer heard the movement of the tree's branches, the tumbling stream beyond the enclosure, the snarls and yips of the dogs, the night cries of hungry babies. There was only silence, except for the quaver of Daoud's breath, and it was this sound that I would remember, later and always.

Afterward, my mind and body heavy, languid, Daoud pulled his *chapan* up over both of us, and I fell into a half-sleep, his body warm against mine.

It was still dark when I felt him brushing my hair back from my face, and I sat up. He handed me my *kamis.* "Perhaps it is best if you return to Mahayna's tent now." He said it softly, but I knew it wasn't a question.

I got to my knees, smoothing down the soft folds of my *kamis* and retying the string of my trousers.

"Tomorrow I must work with the horses in the day. And at night," he stopped, wrapping his sash around his waist, "I will sleep here again."

I nodded, and made my way back to Mahayna's tent, stopping once to look at the stars.

※※※

FOR THE NEXT ten days every nerve in my body seemed to be stretched to a breaking point. I would bring Daoud food during the day, and he would come out of the horse enclosure, going to the stream to wash, and then return and eat. Sometimes we didn't speak, but other times we talked of our lives. I told him of my childhood—all of it—and he told me of his. He didn't speak of his wives or children; I didn't speak of Somers. We didn't speak of leaving—of his going to Peshawar, or my returning to Simla. At night I would go to him, and stay for a few hours, always returning to Mahayna's tent before dawn.

On the eleventh night he and his men gathered around a fire and two of them beat goatskin drums. Some of the children whistled a melody, and two of the men danced around the flames. The women stayed back, in the shadows, watching. Habib had been feverish, pulling at his ear all day, and so Mahayna stayed in the tent with him, but I sat with the other women.

When the men put down their drums they all took turns speaking. I couldn't understand their words, but from the rhythm I understood it to be poetry. Daoud spoke, too, in Pashto, and then suddenly switched to Hindi.

"When your face is hidden from me, like the moon hidden on a dark night, I shed stars of tears, and yet my night remains dark in spite of all those shining stars," he said, looking at the flames. And then he switched back to Pashto, and in a moment the man beside him was reciting.

Such was my emotion at his words, spoken in the language only he and I understood, that everything else was shut out, the words singing in my brain, and I could remember nothing else of the evening but them, and the shape of Daoud's lips as he spoke them.

WHEN I GOT to the enclosure an hour after the camp had settled, a breeze blew sweetly. Daoud was waiting with his horse. "It is a night for riding," he said, and, as he had those days on our way to Kashmir, he put his hands on my waist and lifted me onto the soft blanket on Rasool's back. Then he swung up behind me, and Rasool walked away from the camp.

"Do you remember the first time we rode together?" I asked.

"Yes." He urged the stallion ahead, and gave him the lead, so that the beast galloped freely over the territory he seemed to know, into the broad hills, his pounding feet sure of the way. And then Daoud pulled on the reins, and Rasool walked, and we swayed on his back, me leaning against Daoud, his arms around me, the reins slack in his hands. I felt his breath against my hair. After what felt like an hour, maybe more, we returned to the camp. Still without a word, Daoud dismounted, and I slid off.

After he had put Rasool into the enclosure he took my hand and led me to the quilt spread under the tree. We sat together, our backs against the tree, his arm against mine.

"What were the words you spoke at the fire tonight?" I finally asked him.

"They were written by the Persian poet Jami," he said. "His tomb is in Herat." And then we lay down together, under the *chapan*. Although he didn't touch me, I could feel the hum of his body, so close to mine. Heat came from him, and with it the smell that I had grown to love, horse and leather and woodsmoke. After a while I realized he wouldn't reach for me, and I put my head on his chest and slept.

When I awoke I heard Daoud's relaxed breathing. I sat up and lifted the edge of the *chapan*, but Daoud softly caught my arm.

"I thought you were sleeping," I whispered. Even though his face was only inches from mine, it was unclear, his eyes shadowed. "I will go back to Mahayna's now."

At last he spoke. "Stay with me tonight," he said. And then we came together, and this time, for the first time in all the nights we had been together, he spoke my name as he moved with me, his voice a muffled cry against my neck.

I OPENED MY EYES in time to see the sudden swift beauty of the Himalayan dawn as it flashed over the treetops, turning the sky into a blur of sapphire. Daoud was not on the quilt, although his *chapan* was tucked snugly around me. I threw it aside and sat up, running my fingers through my hair as I glanced at the enclosure.

The horses were gone.

I looked toward the camp. One woman squatted in front of the fire, poking at the contents of a pot. A bony camp dog, tail curled protectively between its legs, snuffled with mild interest at a large horse dropping near a tent. A bold crow swaggered around a cold fire, stabbing at morsels of last night's supper that had fallen to the ground.

The camp looked different. Smaller. Some of the tents were missing. I jumped to my feet, clutching the *chapan*, and ran through the maze of existing tents, finally pushing aside the door flap of Mahayna's tent. She was putting a clean shirt on Habib.

"Where are they?" I panted. "The Pashtuns—where are they?"

"Their time here was finished," Mahayna said. "They returned north, very early this morning."

"No!" I cried the word so loudly that Habib looked at me in alarm. "Daoud wouldn't go, not like that, just leave without telling me."

Mahayna put her hand on Habib's head. "Did he not tell you in some way, perhaps in a way you did not recognize? Without saying the words? This is often the way of men, is it not?"

I looked into her keen eyes, then sank to the floor, putting my arms on my knees and burying my face in them. "Yes," I said then, thinking of him asking me to stay with him, his strange silence, his gentleness, and the way he had murmured my name. And of course, of course. The poetry. "Yes, he did tell me."

"You know he had to leave, and you know your place is with your people," Mahayna said. "I have seen you become a different woman since you arrived. I know you now possess a kernel of happiness. But you must bury it deep within you and let it rest. You can open it and touch it, but let it remain a tiny seed. Do not break open the pod and let it grow, become a weed to spread and choke your feelings for your husband—for this way leads to discontentment."

I stayed where I was, not looking up, and felt the whisper of Mahayna's clothes as she brushed past me. Eventually I lifted my head and pressed the *chapan* against my face, breathing in its smell. And then I went out of the tent to help Mahayna.

Outside sat the young *syce,* a small but rugged boy with calm sorrel eyes. He jumped up as I came out of the tent, and Mahayna told me his name was Nahim, and he would accompany me back to Simla.

"Nahim has traveled throughout all of Kashmir and northern India with various groups of *gujars* since he was a very small child. No one knows of his parents or where he comes from, but he arrives at different camps and helps with the horses. He is known for his uncanny ability to find his way about. Daoud has given him one of the tamed mares in return for your safety on the journey, a very handsome payment, and more than Nahim would have ever dreamed. He is happy."

The dark-skinned barefoot boy bowed low, then stood, waiting for me to tell him what to do. He couldn't speak Hindi, so we made our plans through Mahayna. He ran off and within minutes returned, proudly indicating that I would ride his new horse while he trotted alongside on a strong-legged pony, loaded with two packs filled with food and sleeping quilts, all strapped onto either side of the pony's round belly.

I put the *chapan* around my shoulders and swung up into the soft leather saddle, settling comfortably in the molded seat. My sores were completely healed, although there were bright pink scars. Mahayna handed me Daoud's embroidered saddlebag. "Inside are your clothes and shoes," she said.

I knew the time had come for me to go now. And I had always known it had to end, that it was only a dream. And yet I had, so briefly, felt that I was in my true life, as Chinese Sally had once said. No. Not my true life, I thought, but here I was my true self. And now I would return to the false one, the English enclave, Somers, and whatever hell awaited me.

I pulled off the long earrings.

"No, please, keep them."

"But your bracelet . . . ," I started, but Mahayna shook her head.

I put the earrings back on and opened the saddlebag, yanking out my lacy white petticoat. I handed it down to her. "Perhaps you can make something for your next baby."

Mahayna smiled. "My head will pray to Allah for another son, but my heart wishes for a daughter, even though it would displease Bhosla." She took the petticoat and smoothed it against her chest. "I will make a special ceremonial dress with it."

The horse pawed impatiently.

"Now you must leave," Mahayna said. "Nahim will take the shortest route, and you will be back to your home in perhaps three days, maybe four. He is a good boy; you can trust him," she said. Then turning to Nahim, who was not much younger, she made a menacing face and instructed him with a few sharp-sounding sentences. "May Allah go with you," she said finally to me.

"And may He be with you," I said, then followed Nahim out of the camp, looking back once to wave to the girl who was now surrounded by a small knot of women. I slapped the reins lightly to catch up with the trotting pony ahead of me.

~~~~~~

FOR THE NEXT three days I followed the *syce*. When he dismounted to eat or water the animals or relieve himself I did the same. When he tilted his head to the sky, watching a golden eagle swooping overhead in lazy circles, I watched, too. Turning to follow his gaze when I saw his face break into a sudden smile, I spotted a pair of little red-brown marmots, sitting on their hind legs on the sun-baked earth in the mouth of their burrow, reminding me of arrogant landowners. Nahim whooped and they immediately responded with a whistling reprimand.

He stopped his pony when the small animal's ears pricked forward longingly and its skin dimpled and shivered, and I reined in the responsive gray mare. Nahim pointed to a cloud of dust on the far side of the immense meadow we were crossing. As the cloud came nearer, I saw a herd of long-maned wild ponies, mostly mares, with their knobby-legged foals prancing beside them.

In the evening, Nahim cooked tough slabs of goat in a smoky fire, and I methodically chewed the sinewy meat, although I had no desire for food and could hardly taste what I swallowed. As we lay under the stars, wrapped in quilts, I held the *chapan* and fell into a deep dreamless sleep. It seemed I felt little; everything was reduced into a smallness that had nothing to do with the hills and forests and meadows I traveled through with unseeing eyes. I was still living in that other world of flesh and heat, of anticipation and release. The panic and loneliness had not yet begun to surface. I did not, in those first few days after Daoud left, fully understand that I was changed, and did not understand that I would never be the same. That I was richer, and yet for that richness, would feel pain in a new and terrible way. What I had left behind was still large; I clung to its broad surface as a child to the wide and comforting skirt of its mother. That which lay ahead was unreal, far off and blurred as the waves of heat that rose from the plains under the Indian sun.

~~~~~~

FOR THE SECOND and third days we ambled through shadowed forests of cedars, concealed by the damp, dense trees, breathing in the honey fragrance of the tiny yellow flowers that bloomed in the spongy moss. We would wind upward for hours, the plodding of the horse and pony steady in unbroken rhythm over the pathways Nahim seemed to find instinctively. Some of the paths were dry and covered with twisting, protruding roots, others slippery with the damp overflow from shallow, serpentine streams. We would emerge from the darkness of the forests with unexpected suddenness into dipping, sunlit valleys.

By late morning of the fourth day we stopped at the base of a rocky hill with only a narrow stony path through dense thornbushes, and Nahim climbed off his pony and took the horse's reins. He motioned for me to climb down as well, then, slapping the pony's rear, urged it up the path ahead of him, carefully leading the nervous horse. I scrambled behind, sometimes grabbing hold of the mare's coarse tail when my feet slipped on the steep incline.

After an arduous climb, we emerged onto a grassy knoll, and Nahim untied the embroidered saddlebag from the horse. He opened it and pulled out the clean, wrinkled periwinkle dress. Shaking it once, he handed it to me.

I was panting from the uphill struggle, and looked at the dress, puzzled, then back to Nahim. He pushed it into my arms, dug into the bag again, and held up my high boots and dropped them and the bag in the dust at my feet, then pointed down the hill.

I followed his dirty finger, and saw the familiar church spire and thatched roofs of Simla. Nahim was already leading the tall horse and the pony toward the bushes we had just come through. "Wait," I called, and he stopped at the sound of my voice. I ran to the horse and pulled the colorful *chapan* from its strap on the horse's saddle. Within a second he had moved on, and the bushes closed behind him, leaving me alone on the hill.

I pushed the dress and boots back into the saddlebag, and clutching it and the *chapan*, slowly made my way down the winding spine of the hill toward Simla.

Chapter Thirty-One

HALF AN HOUR LATER I STUMBLED INTO THE OUTSKIRTS OF town. The streets and gardens were quiet; it came to me, from the height of the sun, that most families would be at tiffin. As I passed through the almost empty Mall, a few women standing outside the shops stopped their conversations to turn and look at me, and although I recognized them, and knew they knew me, my sudden appearance after all this time obviously shocked them into silence. One did say, "Mrs. Ingram?" her hand to her throat, and took a few steps in my direction. But I didn't respond, and she remained where she was. I felt dull surprise at what I'd forgotten in these weeks—how pale they looked, how tightly they were held in by their armor of clothes. And their reactions to me—the expressions of disbelief, the murmurs to one another, began the first tiny tear. It was a rip of only a few stitches that would, all too soon, widen into a gaping hole of reality where I could see that I was more alive than I had ever been. In their faces I saw my own, and this was the jolt that brought me back not only to Simla, but to my life as Mrs. Ingram, and all it represented.

I tried to plan what I would say when I reached the bungalow, but I seemed incapable of forming logical thought. Would Mrs. Partridge still be there? As I turned into the side street that would lead me to Constancia Cottage, I felt a hand on my shoulder.

"Ma'am?"

It was a soldier in a spotless red uniform. "Do you need help, ma'am? I saw you walking through the Mall, and you looked . . . I thought you might be in trouble."

I looked down at my dusty Kashmiri clothes and turned-up sandals, realized my hair hung in a tangle to my waist. "I . . . no, not really. I'm just . . ." I gestured at the bungalow.

The soldier said, slowly, "May I assume you're the other young lady who . . ." He stopped, and I nodded.

"Well then, let's get you home, shall we? I imagine there will be a number of people very pleased to learn you're safe." He tried to take the saddlebag and *chapan*, but I held them tightly against me, shaking my head.

We entered the quiet house. I thought perhaps it was empty, but Malti suddenly appeared out of Mrs. Partridge's bedroom carrying a flowered china basin. At the sight of me, she stood motionless for a fraction of a second, then screamed loudly and dropped the bowl. It smashed into a few large pieces, and Malti drew her head scarf over her face and ran shrieking from the room, out the back door.

"I expect she thought you a spirit, ma'am," the soldier said. "They're so superstitious." He turned at the sound of a whimper.

I looked to see Neel sitting in the doorway of my bedroom. "Neel," I said, crouching and holding out one arm, the other still cradling the saddlebag and *chapan*.

Neel's mouth relaxed into a wet grin, and he dashed across the slippery floor, his toenails clattering and his whole rear end wiggling in delirious joy. He had almost reached my outstretched hand when he slid to a halt, whined, and backed up a few steps.

"What's wrong, Neel?" I asked. He came toward me again, crouching low, his stubby tail now still and curving toward his hind legs. As he drew near enough for me to touch him, he suddenly drew back his lips and bared his teeth, then let out a short, nervous bark.

"Don't you know me, Neel?" I asked.

The soldier cleared his throat. "Begging your pardon, ma'am, but it would be the smell of the things you're wearing and carrying. Those dogs can detect nomad blood; they're bred for it. They'll tear a gypsy to pieces, given the chance."

I looked down at the saddlebag and *chapan*.

"Once you burn those gypsy clothes and bathe he'll be back to normal, I guarantee it." He looked away from Neel, who still rumbled, deep in his throat, as loud voices came from the back door.

I stood as Mrs. Partridge stormed in, followed by Malti and the other servants, hanging back and peering nervously. Mrs. Partridge slowly looked me over from head to foot.

"Where have you come from?" she asked. No joy, no relief, just a matter-of-fact question. Actually, a suspicous matter-of-fact question.

"I was . . . in the hills . . . I don't know. Really, Mrs. Partridge. I don't know." I was suddenly so exhausted that it hurt to speak.

"It doesn't appear you've come to any real harm," she finally said, her voice uncertain now, as if she didn't know whether to be relieved or dismayed by this fact.

I felt as if a cord were being drawn around my throat. The silence stretched, and I saw Mrs. Partridge's flat brown eyes filling with tears, her lower jaw trembling, although I knew her sympathy wasn't for me. I envisioned soldiers bringing Faith's broken body back to the cottage. A sudden rush of words tumbled from my mouth.

"We just went for a picnic, Mrs. Partridge. A picnic. I didn't know she would—"

"Stop it," Mrs. Partridge said, all traces of distress put firmly in check now. Her low voice was far more deadly than all the loud blustering and ranting of the past. "I don't want to hear anything you have to say. We all know Faith would never have gone off like that without your urging. That poor girl," she said again. "And now she's dead, dead and buried."

Even in my state, I realized the falseness of Mrs. Partridge's put-on grief. She had cared little for Faith, and had been just as horrified as Somers at having her join us. I knew with certainty then that whatever matters of skin color she referred to in front of Faith had been done spitefully, to hurt her.

Now she pressed a handkerchief against her nose. "She didn't stand a chance, apparently." She took away the handkerchief and stared at me. "After they retrieved her body, the soldiers, joined by all the men in Simla, spent the next week searching for you, Linny, but finally gave up. None of us ever expected to see you alive again, I can assure you." Her eyes were hard and dry as they traveled down my body. "Well, here you are, looking none the worse for wear. Except for that heathen getup."

"Charles?" I asked. "Has he been notified?"

"I sent a message to the John Company offices at Delhi immediately, of course, to both Mr. Snow and Mr. Ingram. The Company would get word to them. I wrote to Mr. Snow of Mrs. Snow's tragic death, and I reported to Mr. Ingram that you were missing, and that's all. No point in them coming up here; nothing to be done now, is there?" She studied my clothing. "I don't want to hear where you've been for all this time. Don't speak of it, do you hear me?" She started to her room.

How I hated this large, pompous woman. "You weren't there," I said quietly. "You don't know what happened. Nobody does. Nobody but me."

Mrs. Partridge turned back. "Do you think I didn't see the state Faith was in? How unhappy she was? She needed caring for, true friends who wouldn't drag her out into the wilderness, who wouldn't think more about their own needs than hers. What she needed from you, Linny, was quiet companionship, walks through the Mall, tea at Peliti's, encouragement with her sketching and embroidery. Not some crazy pony ride into the hills. And now she's dead. Thrown over the cliff by that wild man. Oh, it's all been such a terrible business."

I opened my mouth. "Is that what you were told? That he threw her over the rocks?"

She ignored my question. "Well? How did you convince the Pathan not to kill you?" She sniffed, then shook her head as if she couldn't bear to imagine. "The sooner we leave, the better." She started through her bedroom door.

"Leave?"

"I had made plans to leave tomorrow. First to Delhi," she said, over her shoulder, "where Colonel Partridge is currently working. I'm going to stay there with him until his job is done, and then we'll return to Calcutta together. It's too distressing to stay here. The season has been spoiled for me, with all that's happened. First Mrs. Hathaway, and then you and the dear Mrs. Snow . . . So you may as well come along, and go straight on to Calcutta from Delhi. I can't imagine you'd want to stay here on your own, nor would your husband wish it." Did she stress husband? Perhaps the word sounded strange because I couldn't think of Somers at this moment; I hadn't thought of him for so long. "To say nothing of the reception you would be sure to receive here. I can't imagine anyone here would choose to include you in their plans at the moment. I would think you'd be viewed as quite a . . . well, I cannot think of a polite expression for what others might think of you. When one considers that you're responsible for Faith's death, and tries to envision where you've spent all this time doing whoever knows what— would you blame anyone for being horrified at having you present?" She shook her head once more, then closed her bedroom door firmly.

I looked at the huddled servants. The soldier was gone.

"Malti," I said, seeing her bulging eyes. "Don't be afraid. It's only me. I'm the same as I was." Although of course I wasn't, not in any way.

But Malti continued to stare at me, still covering her mouth with the soft folds of her mustard-colored sari. Finally she lowered the material. "But where have you been, Mem Linny? And your clothing . . ."

"Please prepare a bath for me, Malti," I said, rubbing my forehead. "I'm very tired, and I want to lie down after I bathe." I went into my bedroom; on the little desk in one corner lay a book, a slim volume of Shelley's poetry. I recognized it as one of Faith's favorite books. She must have put it here before we left. I held it, running my hand over its soft morocco cover, touching my finger to the pages with their fine gilt edging. There was a ribbon marker; I opened the book to the page. The poem marked was *When the Lamp Is Shattered*. Faith had written, in her small, spidery script, on the top of the page:

> *For Linny, dear friend, whose strength I have admired from*
> *afar. Always keep your lamp burning. Forever your humble*
> *companion, Faith.*

I closed my eyes tightly, then opened them and tried to read the poem.

> *When the lamp is shattered*
> *The light in the dust lies dead—*
> *When the cloud is scattered*
> *The rainbow's glory is shed. . . .*

I could read no further. I dropped to my knees, hugging the book to my chest and rocking back and forth until Malti quietly knocked on my door to tell me the bath was ready. I realized, as I rose from my knees, that I had been crying.

It appeared that tears came with ease now.

THAT EVENING I WENT to the graveyard at Christ Church, accompanied by Neel. He had come into my arms, licking my face and whimpering, once I had bathed and dressed in my own clothing and carefully hidden the *chapan* and saddlebag at the bottom of a trunk. I had also kept the silver earrings Mahayna had given me, although Malti had taken away the clothes I'd been wearing.

Faith's grave was covered in stiff, dying floral arrangements. I planted a small, perfect laburnum that I had dug up from the garden of the bungalow. It would flower every year with Faith's favorite blossoms, the long drooping sprays of yellow flowers that cover the small tree in clouds of gold.

I thought about the other graves I had left behind me—my mother's, in the damp, crowded graveyard of Our Lady and St. Nicholas Parish Church, and my baby's, with its holly bush and pink stone. I sat beside the mound and the little tree in the advancing evening, the breeze fragrant, the sky growing silver, the birds settling. In that lovely hour, I felt that those I loved were destined to die or disappear from my life. And again, I wept.

MRS. PARTRIDGE AND I didn't speak to each other on the journey to Delhi. I suppose she thought she was punishing me with her silence; I was thankful to be left in peace with my thoughts, which swirled between sadness and a strange, burning glow that never left. I thought constantly about Daoud, and I also thought of Charles, and how I must immediately see him once I was back in Calcutta.

After her trunks were unloaded onto the *ghats* at Delhi, I thanked Mrs. Partridge for her companionship and again apologized for all that I'd caused. She simply nodded, once, in an imperious manner, and I thought she would remain silent, but she couldn't leave without one last remark. "I hope that by the time Mr. Partridge and I return to Calcutta the furor surrounding your activities will have died down. If there is one thing I can't abide, it's scandal."

Now it was my turn to say nothing, although I found it difficult. I glanced away so she wouldn't read the look I knew was there, brought on by her hypocrisy.

And then she disappeared, shouting at the bearers as she made her way laboriously up the slippery steps and into the crowd. I sent Malti to collect her sister and return as quickly as possible. When she was gone I went inside the hut on the budgerow and waited in the dim light, alone, rocking with the movement of the barge and listening to the voices— the laughter and chatter of those descending the *ghats* to bathe.

Malti returned with Trupti and Trupti's eldest daughter, Lalita, who looked to be twelve or thirteen, and the budgerow set off again. The ride back down the Ganges was long and tedious. The water was a milky coffee color, the air muggy, as if the sky were an inverted copper bowl, trapping me in its damp, smothering heat. The fruit on board was overripe, buzzing with flies, and the sizzling spiciness of the curries the bargemen prepared at night was overpowering. Malti and Trupti and Lalita spoke in tones too quiet for me to hear. They treated me with gentle solicitation, as if I were an invalid recovering from a serious illness.

I had no interest in walking along any passable banks, as I had done on that other voyage that seemed years ago now. I didn't read, but sat, much as Faith had, on a chair on the budgerow, watching, with little interest, the passing countryside.

It seemed we would never arrive in Calcutta.

But finally, almost four weeks after leaving Simla, I was returned to my old life, back at the house in Chowringhee.

⸙

I ARRIVED HOME while Somers was still at work and was relieved that I had time to rest and gather my thoughts before I had to face him. When he did come home I was on the verandah, Neel in my lap. He stood in front of me, immaculate in a pearl-gray suit and tie, a dazzling white silk handkerchief blossoming from his breast pocket. He had grown muttonchops. I had forgotten how handsome he was, sleek as a weasel.

"It would seem that you're all right, then?" he asked, unsmiling. Without waiting for my answer, he continued. "A bit thinner, I would say, and your skin is an unflattering sun-baked shade, but you seem none the worse for your little escapade." He almost spat the last few words.

"Escapade? How can you call what happened to me an escapade?"

He leaned against the stone balustrade, casually crossing one ankle over the other and clasping his hands in front of him, watching me. "I want to hear what happened in more detail," he said.

I found it hard to breathe properly. In my head were images of Daoud, his hands on me, his weight, surprisingly light, on my body. "But didn't Mrs. Partridge write to you about——"

"She wrote that you were seen visiting a makeshift jail, where a Pathan, waiting to be hanged for the rape of a young woman, was held captive. This was the day before you convinced Faith to leave Simla and go off to some Godforsaken place."

"My visit to the jail isn't important. I took Faith on a picnic. A simple picnic. And we were caught in the middle of the soldiers chasing the escaped prisoner." I didn't trust myself to even say the word *Pathan*, afraid my voice would tremble. "And Faith . . . she . . . her pony . . ." I stopped. I had promised myself during the endless voyage from Simla back to Calcutta that I would never tell what I had seen, Faith sailing out into the air by her own volition. Better that Charles—and everyone else—believe that Faith was a victim, not of her own desires, but of a terrible accident. "Faith fell over the cliff. And I—the man who was being pursued took me with him."

"Why?"

I stroked Neel's head. "I suppose he would use me as a ransom. I don't know. I couldn't understand him." And so the lies continued.

"And where were you, for the good part of a month?"

I pushed Neel to the floor and stood. "Why are you questioning me like this? So coldly, as if I chose—*chose*—for this to happen. Do you think I *wanted* to be shot—did you even know that I was shot, in the back of my shoulder?—or to be taken on a wild ride into a gypsy camp in the far hills?"

Now Somers's silence was making it more difficult; I felt his eyes boring into my brain, seeing the images of Daoud and me on the quilt under the deodar tree.

"What did you do, all that time, in the camp?"

"I stayed with a girl, in her tent, and helped her prepare food and wash clothes and look after her baby. After a while one of the gypsy boys led me back to Simla." My voice sounded unnaturally loud.

"And what of this particular Pathan who captured you? And of all the other gypsy men?"

"What of them?"

"They must have been highly excited to have you in their midst. You, with your light hair, your skin soft and white." Now he came close to me. "Did you like it, Linny? Did they pass you around, night after night?" He put his hand on the back of my head and closed his fingers in my hair. "Tell me about it. Were they as well endowed as their horses? Do they like it rough?" His fingers pulled back on my hair, so my face was tilted up, forcing me to look into his eyes. His voice was husky, his breath in my face smelled of tobacco and whisky. He pressed against me, and I felt him harden.

I twisted away from him. "Stop it, Somers. Nobody hurt me. Nobody touched me."

"Are you sure, Linny? Once a whore, always a whore. Surely you had to do something to persuade them to let you live."

"*No,*" I shouted, and he raised his hand, open palmed. "No," I said then, immediately dropping my voice and lowering my head. "Nothing happened, Somers. Nothing," I whispered.

I knew what he wanted. He was building up to beating me; he was already provoked, excited. Or perhaps he wanted me to live up to his expectations of what I was, so he might find a way to be rid of me. It would be easy to convince a few people of what he imagined me to have done in that camp, with as many men as he chose to count, and carry out his long-ago threat to throw me out in disgrace. I knew that nobody would have sympathy for me if Somers could find a way to convince them that I was a fallen woman. Surely the gossip about me had already started; I had seen a few white women at the docks when I arrived. I would imagine the story of Faith's death and my disappearance was already common knowledge throughout the community. It was sure to be a topic of conversation at dinner parties for at least a month. And if Somers were to add fuel to the fire . . . Oh, yes. Somers had his ways, and his friends. And I . . . I had no one, now that Faith was gone. I readied myself for the crushing slap.

But it didn't come. He must have sensed defeat, felt my lethargy, and knew I would accept his cruelty without a fight. And in this there was no pleasure. His hand returned to his side, and I to my chair.

"It does go to show, though," he said, not quite finished with me, "that you can never be trusted. I should have realized I'll have to watch you all the time. You go off to Simla, and because of you, an English girl is dead. When you're here you fraternize with the Indians. You really think I wasn't aware of all your sneaking around since we married? I have people who tell me everything, Linny, who have seen you in the most unsavory places."

I looked down at Neel.

"From now on only supervised activities, the ones I approve of. You obviously need discipline and boundaries at all times. I've allowed you to go quite tropo, and there'll be no more of that. As it is, I'm sure many of the women will probably avoid you after what's happened." And then he left.

I went back into my bedroom, opened my trunk, and unrolled one of my flowery cotton dresses. Inside the folded skirt was the *chapan*. I took it out and briefly pressed it to my face. The smell of it brought me comfort, but also grief, grief so overwhelming that it made me rise and hurry back out to the balcony, my feet stumbling as if in one of the malarial fevers that plagued Somers. I bent over the wide stone railing and retched dryly. And then I fell to my knees, allowing myself to feel what I had held back since that last morning in Mahayna's tent.

I lay on the stone floor for some time, unable to move, sobbing, curled around the *chapan*. I was filled with grief for that which had been found, and for that which was now lost. And for all the years I hadn't cried, it seemed that since my time with Daoud, I couldn't stop.

❦

A WEEK AFTER arriving home, I awoke from an afternoon nap feeling particularly heavy-headed. I had fallen asleep on the wicker settee on the verandah, the hot wind overwhelming. All of Calcutta awaited the rain, watching the sky hopefully. I was slow moving, my skin sticky. I thought of the coolness of Simla and then, naturally, of Kashmir.

I was unable to bear the thoughts that came then, so I rose and walked through our back garden, although the lacy shade of the neem trees could not stop the driving arrows of the sun. Under the trees were tended beds of nicotiana and portulaca, hardy enough to bloom even in this weather. I glanced at the servant's godown, the simple building almost obscured by the luxuriant growth of the jasmine hedges I had instructed the *mali* to leave wild.

I wondered how Malti's sister was faring; I had given her a job pressing our clothes. Her daughter Lalita was responsible for the flat household linens—the bedsheets and pillowcases and tablecloths and napkins.

Restless, prickly, I wandered to the godown. It was a well-built wooden structure separated into a few rooms, its open windows covered with freshly watered *tatties*. There was a small ivory statue of Ganesh on a cedar shelf over the doorway. I reached up to touch its smooth surface for good luck and heard a low groan from inside.

Looking through the open doorway, I saw Lalita curled on her side on a string charpoy, her forehead beaded with perspiration.

"Lalita?" I said, addressing her in Hindi. "Are you ill?"

The girl struggled to sit up. "No, memsahib," she said. She pressed her hands against her abdomen.

"Shall I fetch your mother?"

"No, no. My mother sent me here." Her face was miserable. She fidgeted, nervous or embarrassed. "I will return to work now, memsahib. It will pass soon."

I realized then that it was her courses. "No, no Lalita, stay and rest."

"Thank you for your understanding, memsahib. Please be assured, mistress, that my mother does my job while I rest." Her round brown eyes widened suddenly. "But you will not tell Sahib Ingram?"

"Of course not. Stay until you feel well enough to work."

I headed back to the house, but halfway up the slope I stopped, thinking of Lalita. I looked back at the godown, then toward the house. I picked up my skirt and hurried through the steamy air, going straight to my escritoire and fumbling in the top drawer, pulling out my social engagement calendar bound in soft calfskin. I opened it to the current month, then flipped back one month, and then another.

The book slipped from my fingers as I lowered myself into the padded chintz chair in front of the desk. I realized my hands were shaking as I pressed them against my flat stomach as Lalita had done moments earlier.

I was carrying Daoud's child.

THE RAINS STARTED that night. I sat on my verandah looking out at the fine mesh of moisture, rain, coming so softly at first that it was almost invisible, almost inaudible. And yet as darkness descended, its intensity grew slowly, steadily, until it was a drumming presence, making channels in the hard, baked earth. I walked out into it, still in shock. What would I do? How would it be possible to keep this child? I fell to my knees in a widening puddle, its surface shaking with the fury of the rain. I looked skyward, letting the stinging drops beat against my eyes, my lips, my neck. I thought of Faith, killing herself and her unwanted baby. I thought of Meg, and her embrace of life. I thought of who I had been—not Miss Linny Smallpiece, or Mrs. Somers Ingram, but Linny Gow, back on Paradise—and the fierce determination to create my own destiny.

I stayed on my knees for a long time, until the lashing rain slackened, became finer, and then was only a steady drip from the leaves. The air was washed and pure, and a moon came sailing through the dark ruffled monsoon clouds. It shone on the tiny pools caught in the little pockets of hollowed earth, and it was as if precious stones glittered around me.

Malti came looking for me and stood in front of me holding a candle. The slight breeze made the flame dip and sway. "Mem Linny?" she said, almost a whisper, and put out her hand to help me up.

I put my hand into hers and lifted my chin. I would find a way to have this baby, and to keep it. It was my connection to my awakening. In the few short hours since I had learned of its existence, I knew that I could and would love it, and that it would somehow be my salvation.

Chapter Thirty-Two

I CLOSED THE WIDE DOUBLE DOORS OF THE HOUSE AND STEPPED into the noon blaze of Calcutta in late July. I wore a wide solar topee wreathed with thick tulle and pulled low on my forehead so that the upper part of my face was shadowed. I carried a sun parasol. Malti followed.

We stepped into the palanquin that now waited outside our house every day. Somers had hired the palanquin and four *boyees*; whether Malti and I went out or not they waited, hour after hour, day after day, in our front garden. They were only allowed to take me to the locations Somers instructed them—the Maidan, Taylor's Emporium, or any of the English homes. I could also attend ladies' activities put on at the Club, and still withdraw books from the library. Today I instructed the *boyees* to take me to the Club for a scheduled meeting of the Ladies' Botanical Society. I told Somers I was thinking of joining the society, but this wasn't true.

Since I had returned from Simla I had attended one meeting, but was unnerved by what I knew to be the curious stares of many of the other women. A few girls I had known from the Fishing Fleet smiled hesitantly at me, asking politely if I had recovered—nobody would give a name to what had happened in Simla. I was startled to see what appeared to be genuine concern in the eyes of one woman as I responded that I was quite fine now. And that made me wonder if perhaps some of the smiles, the attempts at small conversations, and the invitations I'd received since since I'd arrived in Calcutta had, indeed, been earnest endeavors toward acceptance and friendship. Perhaps there was a woman here—or maybe more than one—who would have been my friend, but it was I who pushed her away.

It seemed everything I looked at now appeared different, and I knew it was because something had fallen away from me, some fear that hadn't allowed me to look at the English here with anything but suspicion. I realized that much of the barrier I felt between them and me could have possibly been built by me, protecting myself, sure my every move was being watched and judged.

But now was not the time to wonder about the English ladies. I had a much more serious matter to consider.

When we arrived at the Club, Malti settled down to wait for me in the palanquin. "The meeting should last an hour, and then with the refreshments, another hour," I told her.

Malti nodded, and I went through the doors, hurrying along the main hall and then through a long passage, finally emerging at the back door. I had searched for and found the door a week earlier when I went to the library. Opening my parasol and keeping my head down, I went out onto the street behind the building and signaled a passing rickshaw. The *jhampani* was a skinny little man glistening with sweat, his face as wizened and brown as a walnut shell. When he trotted over, I spoke a single Hindi sentence, then stepped into the rickety box and sat on the hard board nailed between the sides. The bearer picked up the shafts and ran, carrying me down narrower and narrower roads, avoiding the buffalo carts and sacred bulls, *kumkum* on their broad foreheads, garlands of jasmine around their bloated necks. The ancient streets twisted and turned, their paths constructed as an intended labyrinth to confuse evil spirits that might wander into Calcutta's center.

The old man ran through reeking alleyways, nimbly dodging other rickshaws, goats, dogs, and hens. Babies screamed, children laughed and cried, women shrieked, and men called in a barrage of languages and noise. Beggars and cripples jammed the narrow passages; some tried to grab at my skirt as the rickshaw rolled past. The gutters ran with food slops and animal and human excrement. I saw a naked child of no more than three tenderly cradling a dead, stiffened kitten, alive with maggots. My whole body bounced with the rhythm of the man's short steps.

You will not be sick, you will not, I commanded myself. The rickshaw had no cover, and the scorching wind stirred up choking clouds of red-brown dust whenever we emerged from an alley into a cross-section of street, making it impossible to keep my parasol open. The sun beat down on my solar topee, and my stomach roiled and churned. I wished I had eaten one of the fresh pappadams Malti had brought me on a tray with my cup of camomile tea before we left. But at the time I couldn't face anything, not even a sip of the cool tea.

Finally the man's veiny pumping legs slowed, and I saw that we had emerged from the squalor and were in a quieter area. Small wooden houses with tiny individual gardens in front looked refreshingly clean after the filthy confines we had passed through.

I looked at each house carefully, and when I saw one covered in a tangle of Japanese honeysuckle, I called to the *jhampani*. He slowed to a stop, panting heavily, and I slipped out of the rickshaw, but had to steady myself by clutching the splintered side of the rickety cart.

When the ringing in my ears abated, I looked at the *jhampani* standing between the shafts of his rickshaw, and he hesitantly quoted a price. I saw how tightly the flesh was pulled over the bones of his face, the yellowed whites of his eyes. I paid him without bargaining, and he stared down at the extra coins I put in his palm, then back to me, confusion on his face.

I approached the house and quietly called through the mat covering the doorway. "Nani Meera?" There was a soft reply, and I pulled aside the mat and entered. The room was shuttered, dark and almost cool after the heat. For a moment I was unable to see anything but detected a slight movement on one side of the room. As my eyes adjusted to the dim light, I saw a beautiful young woman in a sari of brilliant orchid and turquoise sitting cross-legged on the clean matted floor. In her lap rested a chubby baby girl, naked except for the charm string around her waist. Her huge brown eyes were ringed with kohl, making them enormous in the round little face. She lay quietly as her mother rubbed her body with gleaming oil in lazy, circular motions. The woman looked quizzically at me.

"I'm hoping to find Nani Meera," I said in Hindi. "I was given directions to a house covered in honeysuckle on this street."

"You are in the right place," the woman answered in English. "Nani will return in a moment. Please sit down and wait." She turned her gaze back to the baby.

"Thank you," I said, sitting on one of the two huge wicker chairs filled with soft cushions, wondering how this Indian woman spoke English so flawlessly.

I smelled the faint odor of sandalwood, and a chime made of long, thin rectangles of brass and blue oval beads hung beside one of the many narrow windows. Whenever a slight current of air whispered through a half-opened louver the chimes emitted a fragile tinkle.

A low teak chest carved with birds and flowers sat in front of the two chairs. On its ornate lid was a simple white clay bowl filled with smooth gray pebbles, and from the pebbles narcissi bloomed in orange splendor. A doorway hung with rows of amber glass beads led into another room. Beside the doorway stood a tall, spare cupboard, also of teak, but devoid of any ornamentation except for the two ivory handles carved in the shape of tiny, long-tailed monkeys.

The baby was growing heavy-lidded with pleasure, and as the woman looked at me I could now see that her eyes were a remarkable lilac, with the same milky opalescence as the panicles of blossoms that hung from the chinaberry tree in her garden. I smiled wanly, still fighting nausea, and was about to ask for a glass of water when the doorway beads swayed softly, creating a cascade of melody. A very tall and slender woman, wearing a blinding white sari with a thin gold thread running through it, came through the beads. Although she was not young, she carried herself regally, her chin high and her back straight. Her black hair had one single thick wave of pure white over her forehead, and her large brown eyes were soft.

I stood, pressing my hands together perpendicular to my chest, and bowed. The woman responded to the ritual *namaste*, and I saw that the palms of her hands were dyed with henna.

"I am Linny Ingram," I said in Hindi. "You are Nani Meera?"

The woman nodded. "I am," she answered, like the younger woman, in English.

"Charles told me of you," I said, reverting to English.

Her face lit. "Ah." She smiled, but it was a sad smile. "He has had so little happiness. And Faith. His poor little red nestling. I saw the sickness of the spirit in her. I tried to speak to Charles of it, but he would not listen." Her voice carried the soft whisper of wind as it stirs long grass.

I closed my eyes for a moment. Hearing this woman say that she, too, knew Faith was ill comforted me.

We stood in silence for a few seconds, as if paying tribute to her memory. Then I spoke again. "I saw Charles only yesterday."

"He suffers greatly. He comes often, although there is little I can do to console him."

I had found it difficult to see Charles without Somers knowing, but through elaborate planning, with many chits back and forth, we did manage. Charles met me at the door of a near-deserted tearoom used specifically by the uncovenanted civil servants. We simply looked at each other, tears running from our eyes.

Charles had grown thin, and his rumpled clothes hung loosely on him. His hair looked as if it had not felt a comb that day, nor his face a razor. Once we had composed ourselves Charles steered me to a table near a window, and we made small and trivial comments for the first few moments. But there was no use for pretense. He took my hands in his and asked me to recount every moment of my time with Faith in Simla, every detail of what she'd said, how she'd looked. I tried to cheer him with happy memories, but realized, very quickly, that in actuality my presence only brought him pain. I did tell him that she'd spoken of him daily with great adoration, planning their lives, which she said would be forever together. I had to say it, to tell that half-truth, for Charles's sake. I knew I must not divulge the secret Faith had kept from him—that she had carried his child—for I knew that would only add to his terrible distress. He pressed me for the details of her death, saying he couldn't rest until he knew, and I fabricated more, saying Faith would not have suffered, that the fall was quick and her death instant, that she had been singing happily, enjoying the pony ride, only moments before the accident.

When finally Charles had no more questions, and I had no more to say, I asked him how to find Nani Meera. He didn't ask how I knew of her, or inquire as to my reason for wanting to visit her.

And then we parted, and Charles looked into my face with glimmering eyes. I knew—and saw that he did, as well—that it would be better for both of us if this were our one and only meeting.

Now Nani Meera turned to the other woman. "Yali, could you prepare some melon for Mrs. Ingram, please?"

The woman rose wordlessly, lifting the child, who was on the verge of sleep, and disappeared through the amber beads. Immediately there was soft humming and the chink of crockery.

"Will you tell me the reason for your visit, Mrs. Ingram?" Nani Meera asked, sitting in the other wicker chair and motioning for me to sit again.

"Please, call me Linny," I said, as I perched on the edge of the chair and played with the black silk fringe that bordered the cushion. "It is difficult for me to speak of this," I said finally. "I have told no one of—" I stopped as Yali returned, carrying a white plate of thick, crimson watermelon slices, another of sugar-coated flat biscuits.

"You may continue. Yali is my assistant. And my daughter," Nani Meera said with a smile. The woman returned the smile and set the tray on the teak chest and left. The quiet humming on the other side of the beads began again.

"Please be assured, Linny, that I have heard every story, and I make no judgment." She studied me. "Is it that you wish to be rid of the child growing under your heart?"

My mouth opened, my hands flying to my stomach. "No." I looked down, then back at the woman. "But it doesn't show. It can't. Not yet."

"Calm yourself. It is my life's work; I see what others do not. So. The child is wanted?"

"Yes." Instinctively I trusted her. "But it is not my husband's child."

"Can you be certain of this?"

"Yes."

"Your husband knows of the child?"

"No. No, he mustn't. Not yet."

"Then how may I help you?"

"I want my husband to think the baby is his. It's the only way."

"And the father of the child? Will he not present a problem?"

I took a deep breath. "He is of . . . another world than mine. We will never be together again. My husband doesn't have any knowledge of his existence."

"If your husband knows nothing of this other man, what is the difficulty? Why will he not assume the child is his?"

I stared at the ivory monkeys on the cupboard door.

"My husband doesn't touch me. He turns to other men for his pleasure. Our marriage has never even been consummated." Something about Nani Meera made the truth slide out much easier than I had thought would be possible.

Nani Meera looked at my hair, at my face, then at my hands. I realized they were twisting in my lap. I held them still.

"His *lingam* is powerless with you?"

"Yes. Except . . ."

She waited.

"When he hurts me. When he beats me, only then does he want to take me in a brutal way, but he can never . . . achieve it."

She nodded, tapping her chin with her forefinger. "I believe I can help in one way. But the rest will be up to you." She crossed to the high cupboard and opened the doors, then ran her finger down the rows of small drawers, each labeled with indecipherable markings. "There are many common herbs and sacred plants in India. Some can be used for either benefit or detriment." She stopped at one drawer, pulled it out, and removed a long flat tin, and then took a white linen square from the top of the cupboard. She slid open the lid of the tin and put a large pinch of fine brown powder into the middle of the material.

"What is that?"

"This one is *bhang,* a mild aphrodisiac made from hemp, which also promotes endurance." She opened another drawer and repeated the process. "Crushed seeds from the banyan tree, also an aphrodisiac. And one other." As she added a third fine powder to the mixture, she said, "Only a minute quantity of the powdered leaves of the *dhatura,* for it is a powerful intoxicant with deep sedative powers, to be used with extreme care." She gathered up the cloth, tied it in a small tight knot, and handed it to me.

I stared at the tiny cloth bag.

"You must make sure your husband consumes all of this at one time. I assume, as an Englishman, that he drinks alcohol?"

I nodded.

"Sprinkle the powder into his drink and stir it well. He won't detect it, and the alcohol will intensify the effect. Shortly after he has finished it, you must do what you have to do to bring him to the level you have spoken of. He may act slightly confused, but he will not weary at his task, and may even perform successfully more than once."

I nodded.

"You are in the very early stages of your pregnancy, are you not? Six to seven weeks?"

"Yes."

"You must be careful not to exert yourself and bring it on early, as so often happens to British women. You can fool your husband by a month or slightly more, but if this little one makes a healthy arrival too much ahead of schedule, even the most unquestioning male brain may start to wonder." She looked into my eyes. "One other question. You said the child's father is of another world. Will there be the issue of color? For if he is an Indian, you must be prepared that the child may bear the appearance of—"

"He is not an Indian," I interrupted. I thought of Daoud's black hair and dark eyes, but also of the paleness of his skin not exposed to the sun. I could only pray for the baby's physical attributes not to be too revealing. I concentrated on the fortunate fact that Somers, too, possessed dark hair and eyes.

"Good. How did you come to my home?" she asked.

"Rickshaw. It was all I could find. My visit here must be a secret one."

"An open rickshaw is not wise in midday heat. I will have Yali summon a curtained palanquin." She went through the beads and I heard low murmurs; she reappeared carrying a large glass of thin white liquid. "Coconut milk."

I sipped at the sweet drink. "Your daughter is very beautiful. Her eyes are unlike any I have seen."

"Yes. Her father was the English owner of a tea plantation outside Darjeeling," she said.

"He was your husband?"

Nani Meera smiled. "No. Like you, Linny, I loved a man of a different world." She sat down again, and I did, too, holding my glass with both hands. "I was ayah to his children, although I was already gaining the knowledge of a woman of medicine. His wife . . . she had fallen victim to the illness so many English women suffer in India—much like Faith. Over time I grew to be his . . . companion."

The sound of Yali's baby in the next room made Nani Meera blink, and she looked at my glass of milk. "Drink. It will help settle your stomach." Her hands were still in her lap. "I gave birth to Yali. On the plantation lived an English overseer and his Indian wife; shortly after Yali's birth a son was born to the overseer, but the birth killed the mother. I took the child as Yali's milk brother, and grew to love him as my own." She smiled at me. "It was Charles, of course."

She looked toward the doorway at the jingling of bells. "Come," she said, rising and extending her hand. "Your palanquin is here."

I set down my empty glass and took her hand in mine, holding it firmly. "Thank you, Nani Meera," I said, letting go and opening my reticule. "Tell me what I owe you." I tucked the cloth bag inside and took out a square of folded bills.

But the woman shook her head. "It is my gift to you, for you are a friend of Charles. I wish you success with your husband," she added, pulling aside the mat at the front door. "I am hopeful it will work."

"I hope so, too," I said. "My future—and the future of my child—depends upon it."

Chapter Thirty-Three

As I rode back to the Club from Nani Meera's, then onward to my home with Malti, each jolt of the palanquin was a moment wasted. Time was my enemy. For all I knew, the next day Somers might announce that he was leaving for a few weeks, and my plan would then be useless. I had to act that very evening, after dinner.

I entered the dining room as Somers set down his large glass dessert bowl, leaving only a trace of currant pudding clinging to its sides. I carried a tray with a glass three-quarters full. Somers pushed away from the table as I approached.

"The *khitmutgar* prepared your brandy *pawnee*," I told him, handing him the glass. At the crotch of his tight trousers I saw his outline, sitting like a stone. I knew what I'd have to do to bring it to life. I felt as if a similar stone were lodged in my throat, a stone of dread at what physical pain awaited me if Somers reacted the way I needed him to, a stone of terror that he wouldn't.

He took the glass, glancing at me. "You acting as servant, now?"

I made a *tsk* of annoyance. "I passed him in the hall. I'm simply making an effort, Somers."

He took a generous swallow. "An effort at what? Playing the dutiful wife? You haven't bothered before."

It would be simple, I knew at that moment. He had been itching to beat me since my arrival from Simla. "You idiot," I said, putting my hands on my hips as I spoke loudly, letting the Liverpool whore in me come out. "You'll never give me a chance, will you? You're nothing but an arrogant fool, berating me no matter how hard I try."

He drained his glass and banged it back onto the table. I saw his eyes brighten in the same way Neel's did when I picked up his favorite ball. "You dare to sling names at me? You? Are you forgetting where you came from? What I did for you?" He brushed back a strand of hair that had fallen across his forehead, ran his fingers over his mustache. I saw that his hand trembled, ever so slightly. *Could the drug work this quickly?*

"I'm tired of your bullying ways, Somers. Telling me where I can and can't go. I can do whatever I want." Here was my Paradise voice, coming so easily at my bidding.

He narrowed his eyes, but not before I saw the dilating of his irises. *Yes. It could.* Now his hands were balled into fists.

"Don't you dare touch me," I said, shaking my head at him, smirking. "Don't you dare."

Handing Somers that particular challenge was the key. I backed out of the doorway and ran down the hall to my bedroom, slamming the door and leaning against it. "Out," I barked at the punkah wallah, and he ran through the verandah doors. Somers shoved viciously at the door, and the force knocked me down. He stood over me.

"Think you can talk to me like that? Do you? You sweet little ungrateful bitch," he murmured. He took off his jacket and lay it over the back of a chair. He took his gold ring from his hand, carefully placing it into his waistcoat pocket, and slowly rolled up his sleeves. Then he came toward me, picking up Neel's long leather leash from my dressing table bench.

I forced myself to cry out with a terrified wail. "No, Somers, don't. Don't hurt me," I begged, as he wound the end of the leash around his hand. Then I threw myself facedown across the bed, and he kept coming, the leather strap lashing through the air. He was muttering, but I couldn't make out his words. He brought the leash down across the back of my thighs, its sting deadened by my clothes. The more I cried and begged, the more violent became his blows. Finally he roughly threw me over, onto my back, and I saw that he already had his trousers unbuttoned. In the next instant he forced my knees open with his, shoving up my skirt and petticoats and ripping at my drawers. And then he gripped himself with a look that was a combination of surprise and triumph and lust, and in the next instant rammed himself inside me. I felt my flesh tearing. "Is this how you like it?" he asked, his hands pinning down my shoulders, looking into my face as his hips jerked. "This is what you've been wanting from the first time you laid eyes on me, isn't it, whore?"

He closed his eyes and raised his chin, rutting then with such urgency that I worried about the baby, but knew I mustn't stop him. He went on and on, seemingly tirelessly, as Nani Meera had predicted, his arms eventually shaking with the effort of holding himself above me for so long. I closed my eyes, waiting for it to end, trying to go to the place inside my head that I had always found all those years in Liverpool. But I couldn't reach it anymore. I couldn't make myself float away, disappear from my body. I was no longer sheathed in that imperceptible internal armor that had kept me from going mad, that had allowed me to continue to live as I had to, first as a child and then as a young woman.

Now I knew what this act could mean. I had been touched by its tenderness and shared joy, with Daoud, in such a sweet and splendid way that the bestiality of Somers's act was, indeed, the most horrific of rapes. Not since my first time, with the man called Mr. Jacobs, had I felt so violated. It was as if Daoud's lovemaking had made me clean again, had taken away all the unspeakable memories. What was happening to me now was unbearable. I bit my lips until I tasted blood, bearing Somers's frenzied pounding for what felt like an eternity. At long last he tensed, and then, groaning, collapsed heavily on me, his body twitching and his breath harsh in my ear. Finally he lay still and his breathing grew soft and steady. And then I didn't hear it at all.

I tried to shift under him; he had grown heavier, and oddly limp, although I could still feel him, slighty stiff, inside me. *What if he's dead? What if Nani Meera put in too much of the dhatura, and I've killed him?*

"Somers," I said, getting my hands under his chest and pushing. "Somers!" I pushed hard enough to roll him off me. He lay on his side. I slapped his face, hard, and at that he made a sound and his eyelids fluttered. "Get up," I said, my voice low and cold. "Get up and get out of here."

"What?" he whispered, then opened his eyes. His pupils were huge and black, his face an unnatural shade of red. The leash was still wrapped around his hand.

"I said to get out of my room. You've had your pleasure. Now leave."

He sat up, looking at my dress and petticoats bunched around my hips, my drawers torn and hanging off one leg. My hair was plastered against my cheeks.

He eased himself off the bed, jerkily unwinding the leash and dropping it, forcing himself into his underdrawers, pulling up his trousers and buttoning them with shaking fingers. He tried to speak, licked his lips, and cleared his throat. "So you aren't made of steel, after all," he said. "I have actually managed to make you cry."

I put my hand to my face. It was wet; I tasted salt on my lips.

"You shouldn't anger me, Linny," he said. "Perhaps eventually you'll learn."

I yanked my skirt down and turned on my side. "I want Malti," I said quietly. "Send Malti to me. I want a bath, to rid myself of your slime."

And then he left, and didn't return until late the next day, his eyes red-rimmed and his clothing wrinkled. We didn't speak for the next week.

IN THE FIRST WEEK of September, I sat in the cracked leather chair in front of Dr. Haverlock's desk. He was a rheumy-eyed old man, his jacket and tie spotted with grease. His high color suggested gout. He picked under his nails with a small scalpel. He had been one of the English enclave's physicians for more than twenty years, Mrs. Waterton had told me when I confessed to her that I needed to visit a doctor.

She had grasped my hands, her face beaming. "Is it . . . ?"

"I believe so," I said, with a confidential air.

She looked so pleased, nodding her head. Actually, Mrs. Waterton was one of the only women who still often invited me to her home for an afternoon call. For all the grief I had caused her, I believe she had a soft spot for me now. "I was becoming quite worried about you. But this climate makes it hard for some. You must be very careful not to overdo in any way. I'd get right into bed and stay there for the duration, if I were you."

Now Dr. Haverlock leaned back in his well-worn chair, completely uninterested. "How can I help you?"

"I've been feeling wretched every morning for quite a while, now," I said, looking at my skirt and speaking in the most modest voice I could manage. "And sometimes I feel dreadfully lightheaded for no reason at all. Only this morning, when I smelled my husband's bacon, I——"

"Quite," he said. "Child on the way, I expect." He took a large pinch of snuff from a small lacquered box on his desk and inhaled it noisily, looking at me sternly. "Your first?"

I nodded my head.

"Any questions?"

This time I shook my head. "But—you won't have to . . . examine me, will you?" I asked, forcing a look of embarrassed fear onto my face.

"No reason for that. Symptoms are quite clear. We'll just see when it should arrive. Date of last flow?"

I lowered my eyes again. "The beginning of July," I lied in a whisper.

The old man studied a grimy calendar, flipping the pages ahead. "Right. Watch for signs in late March." He stood, slowly straightened his back, and took a round silver watch out of his waistcoat pocket. He clicked open the cover and eyed the dial. "That should be it, then, Mrs. . . . sorry, what was it?"

"Ingram. Mrs. Somers Ingram."

Dr. Haverlock's face brightened, and he looked at me with interest for the first time since I'd entered the room. He brushed snuff off his sleeve. "Ah. Somers Ingram. Well, well, I expect he'll be a happy fellow with this news, then, what?"

"Yes." I gathered my gloves and reticule and walked to the door. Dr. Haverlock followed me.

"If you experience any major discomforts, let me know," he said, his manner remarkably warmer now that Somers's name had been mentioned. "Just rest as much as you can, no spicy foods, no upsets or hysterics, and in about seven and a half months it will all be over." He smiled in a fatherly way, patting my shoulder. "Messy business, birthing, but a necessary evil, I'm afraid."

I forced a smile. "Thank you so much, Dr. Haverlock."

He reached in front of me and opened the office door. "One more thing, Mrs. Ingram. When your confinement begins, make sure you call for one of our women to help. Don't trust an Indian midwife."

"But of course, Dr. Haverlock," I answered sweetly. My smile disappeared at the dull thud of the closing door.

⟨~≈≪≪≪⟩

WHEN I TOLD SOMERS that evening, a range of emotions crossed his face. Surprise, dismay, and then suspicion. "What do you mean, a child?"

"Have you forgotten, Somers? That night, with Neel's leash, when you—"

He put up one hand. "All right, all right. Damn."

"Damn? That's your reaction to this?"

"I don't want a child, Linny. It will add a complication to all of this. I said there would be no children."

"You also said you'd never touch me in that way."

He sat down, his legs stretched in front of him. "I'm not interested in being a father."

I waited.

"Well," he finally said. "We can't do anything about it now. Perhaps it will settle you."

I nodded. "Perhaps it will."

September 18, 1832

Dear Shaker,

Heartiest congratulations to you and Celina. I was truly delighted to learn of your betrothal. You didn't mention the date of your forthcoming marriage. Is it to be soon?

I returned from Simla much sooner than necessary; I am sure that the news of Faith's tragic death is well known in Liverpool. It is a terrible thing, Shaker, and I am not sure that I will ever fully recover from the unbearable circumstances. I think of her every day and have spoken to her husband. He is constantly in my prayers, for he is a kind and good man who was completely devoted to Faith, and is now naturally numbed by grief.

How fortunate that you are able to travel to London to spend a time of study with the most renowned Dr. Frederick Quin. I will be anxious to hear of the success of his planned homeopathy practice on King Street (do I not recall it was to open this very month?) and what you have learned. Please keep me informed.

In spite of the pall of sadness that hovers over me—and I'm sure over Celina as well—because of Faith, I know that dear girl would want us to look for happiness within our own lives. You sound excited and pleased at the prospect of this new world of medicine, and Celina will be, indeed, a wonderful companion. And I, too, have been buoyed by my own small news. A child is expected, and in this I am very happy.

> *My fondest wishes,*
> *Linny*

P.S. An infusion made from the leaves of the *asagandh*—known in English as the winter cherry—a small and modest shrub, is given to those suffering from unspecified fevers and anxiety.

Somers and I never spoke of my pregnancy, although I sometimes saw him looking at my growing belly with a hint of alarm.

I had Malti go to Nani Meera with a chit, asking her to help when my time came, and to arrange for her to come regularly to Chowringhee, although of course she went to the servants' godown. It was there, in one of the small, clean rooms, that we visited and she touched me with warm, dry hands, telling me the pregnancy went well. I told her I had already given birth once, and she told me it would only make this birth easier.

I was strangely peaceful as the months slowly passed. I sent notes of regret to the social invitations Somers and I received—although he often attended without me—using my pregnancy as an excuse, and instead spent my time sitting on the verandah. In the quick Calcutta twilight, waiting for the first breath of the evening breeze to stir the leaves, I listened to the whirring of the crickets and the frogs' croaks, placing my hands on my abdomen and wondering if the baby was hearing the same sounds. With the heat less intense as we went into the cool season, I could hold a needle without it slipping, and learned to sew, with Malti's help. I worked on clothing for the baby, making intricate minute stitches in tiny yoked shirts and vests and petticoats.

I brushed Neel, who was ever at my side. We sat, Malti and Neel and I, and I rejoiced over the first tiny flutterings and stirrings, content to know the child Daoud and I had created was growing. I refused to imagine what would happen if the baby was too dark; if it had a shock of black hair and long black eyes. I held tightly to the memory of Daoud's skin, no darker than Somers's, of his strong white teeth, his capable hands, his body, hard and muscled. I knew that if the physical attributes of the child shouted my deceit, I would have to take the infant and disappear. Where, or how, I didn't know, and I refused to let it haunt my thoughts.

As the air grew cool I grew heavier, and I summoned my *durʒi* to make comfortable clothes, flowing and unstructured.

Somers hated them, telling me I was a disgusting sight, lolling about uncorseted in loose tea gowns. He forbade me to wear them. I continued to wear them when he wasn't home.

One morning shortly before the new year he watched me heave myself out of a deep armchair and try to stoop to pick up Neel. "We're invited to celebrate 1833 with the McDougalls. I told them I'd come, but that you weren't leaving the house these days. You're frightfully large," he chided. "You still have another, what—three months? Doctor Haverlock did say the end of March?"

I studied the underside of Neel's ear. "Yes. But of course, the baby will probably come sooner. He assured me it's unusual to carry a child for the full term here in India, what with the extreme climate. And because I'm small, I probably appear larger than a tall woman—" I stopped myself. Somers was clever. I couldn't appear to be making excuses.

❈❈❈❈

ON THE MORNING of February 26, 1833, I waited until Somers had left for work before summoning Malti to fetch Nani Meera.

"It is a good day for a birth," Malti said, smiling. "As I arose this morning I saw a flock of *satht-bai*, the seven brothers. This is always a sign of a boy child." She clasped her hands. "I will inform all of the servants, and have them do *puja* for you."

Dear Malti. She was my only ally, doing what I asked with unquestioning faithfulness. After she left I lay alone, frightened by the remembered intensity of the pain. When Nani Meera and Yali hurried in an hour later, I cried out in relief.

Within moments Yali was massaging my temples with something cool and sharp smelling, while Nani Meera laid out cloths and a sharp knife and an assortment of herbs and oils. By early afternoon I pushed my son into Nani Meera's waiting hands.

"It is a healthy boy," she said, deftly cutting the cord and holding up the glistening baby. "From the sound of him it appears he will be brave and headstrong, like his mother."

I raised my head and studied him anxiously, afraid of what I might see. But he simply looked like a newborn, skin reddish, his face screwed into a tight, angry scowl, wailing thinly as if complaining about the discomfort of his journey. And his hair was a wet slick of dark gold.

Malti clapped her hands, laughing as the baby's first cries turned to indignant howls as Yali rubbed him firmly with a warm, damp cloth. "Listen to his cry," Malti said. "No one will argue with him." She took the baby, loosely wrapped in soft flannel, from Yali, and when Nani Meera had finished helping me into a fresh nightdress and I was propped against the pillows, Malti put him in my arms.

While Malti took away the soiled bedding and Yali packed the bag they had brought, Nani Meera pulled a chair to the side of the bed and stroked the baby's damp head.

"He has your fair hair," she said. "Look, it already shines like Surya's first bright rays."

I took her hand. "Thank you, Nani Meera," I said. "You've given me—and him," I added, touching my lips to the baby's velvety forehead, "a chance at happiness."

Nani Meera squeezed my hand. "I have given you nothing, Linny. You create your own destiny."

Yali set a small packet on the table beside the bed. "Dissolve this in water and drink it tonight," Nani Meera said. "You have no damage from the birth. Do not listen to the urging of the English memsahibs who will come to see you, puffed full of advice. They will tell you to remain in bed for a great while, but you will only become weak if you do. They will say the child should not be handled excessively, but this is also wrong. The baby has known only your body's warmth and the beating of your heart. To so suddenly lose this comfort must be a great sorrow for even a tiny spirit. I know it is the way of your people, but perhaps it is the cause of the hesitancy of the English to respond to others, to back away as if burned when touched. Hold your son, Linny, hold him tight against you and rock him and sing to him and let him feel your love. This I did with my Yali, and with Charles, and, in return, they are unafraid to show their own love and feelings."

The baby stirred and turned his head toward my breast.

"You have hired a wet nurse?"

I shook my head. "No."

Nani Meera smiled. "I suspected as much. All the more reason for the English ladies to whisper about you."

"I don't care."

"Good. You must be strong with these magpies. Yali will instruct Malti to prepare a daily boiled drink containing cumin and the climbing asparagus; it will increase your milk flow," she said. "And now you must do one more thing that requires strength."

I looked up at her.

"You must help your husband believe it is his child. It may be difficult, when you look at this boy and think of his father." She touched the baby's head once more, and then laid her palm on my forehead. "May I say a blessing?"

I nodded.

"She is become the light of her house: a red flame in the bowl of a shining oil lamp. She has given birth to his son, whose lands are made lovely with flowers by the pattering rain."

My eyes were damp. I leaned into her warm hand.

"It is an ancient saying—Ainkurunuru," she said, keeping her hand on my forehead, and I felt heat and strength flowing from it through me. "Do you have a name for your son?"

I picked up the baby's loosely curled fingers and kissed them. "David. His name will be David."

Chapter Thirty-Four

SOMERS STOOD IN THE DOORWAY WITH HIS HANDS IN HIS pockets. "It went all right, then?"

I nodded. "Come and see him," I said. At this moment I felt such happiness that it extended even to Somers; I patted the bed beside me.

He came to the bed but didn't sit down.

"Would you like to hold him?"

He shook his head. "He looks fine, I suppose."

"He is fine. Small, because he came early, but healthy."

"Well," he said. "It will be Somers, I suppose."

"Pardon me?"

"His name will be Somers." His voice was curiously flat.

"I thought we'd call him David."

"David? Why David?"

"I don't know, really; I've always admired it as a name. It means *beloved.*" I stared at the baby as I spoke, hoping not to appear too determined. If Somers knew how important it was to me that this child be called David—my only connection with Daoud—he would fight me on it. And win.

"I suppose so. David Somers Ingram, then," he conceded.

"Fine."

The baby made a face, yawned, and opened his eyes, squinting.

"He's got my hair, Somers, but his eyes . . . at the moment they're dark blue, like so many newborns. But they're murky." I raised my own eyes and stared at Somers. "I have a feeling they'll end up quite dark, like his father's."

Somers stood. "I suppose they might. Well." He kept looking at the baby, the same noncommittal expression on his face. I waited, my heart pounding, to see what he would say. "I may as well go on to the Club for dinner, if you're fine here."

I smiled, nodding. He was thinking about his dinner, not whether the child in my arms looked unlike any other English child.

LATER THAT EVENING, after I'd fed David, Malti let Neel in from the back garden. He ran to the bed, jumping on the end. He stopped, raising his nose in the air.

"Hello, Neel," I said. "Come and meet David." I folded the light flannel back from the baby, who had fallen asleep as he'd nursed. Tail curiously stiff, Neel crept up beside me. His kind ocher eyes looked at me, then he sniffed at the blanket. Immediately, a low growl started in his throat, and his black lips twitched.

I grabbed David, pressing him against me. He cried out, woken at the sudden movement, and Neel barked in short, angry bursts.

Somers came to the door. "What the devil is all this caterwauling?" he shouted over the noise of the baby and of Neel. "Neel, stop it."

But the animal kept barking, his legs spread and rigid as he backed away from me.

The words of the soldier in Simla came back to me with a heavy thud. *Those dogs can detect nomad blood. They'll tear a gypsy to pieces, given the chance.* "Take him out, Somers. Take him away." My voice was high with terror.

"For God's sake, Neel," Somers roared, grabbing Neel by the scruff of his neck. "Settle down." He carried him away, returning in a few minutes.

"You're looking awfully green," he said. "Nothing to get that upset about. I suppose Neel doesn't like playing second fiddle."

"Where is he?"

"I tied him up out back and gave him a mutton bone. Give him a few days; he'll be fine."

"No. Tomorrow I want you to give him to the Lelands. Ivy's been wanting a dog for her Alexander. They're leaving for a new posting in Barrackpur next week."

Somers blinked. "I thought you had an affection for him."

"I do. But I don't want him to be near the baby. Of that I'm certain. I don't trust him."

"You can do what you like with him," Somers said, shrugging. "I'm off to bed."

An hour later I left David with Malti and slowly walked out to see Neel. I stroked him and held him, kissing his bony head. "You won't be happy here anymore," I whispered to him, crying into his fur, and he wagged his tail and licked my face.

I stifled my sobs, sitting on the cool stones with him in my lap. I loved him and he me, and now I must lose him.

February 1, 1834

Dear Shaker and Celina,

I trust you are settling into your married life with ease and joy. I thought of you over the holiday season, imagining your Christmas wedding.

Your ongoing study of homeopathy sounds intriguing, Shaker, and I wish you continued success.

David's first birthday approaches. It is difficult to believe almost twelve months have passed since his birth. I find that the year has gone quickly, although the days go slowly.

I hope it won't be too long until you both know the joy of a child, as I have.

My love to you both,
Linny

P.S. The *gadahpurna* is known by the English as *hogweed*. It flourishes at the beginning of the rains and is also known as "the rain born." It is used for those suffering from snake poisoning, rat bite, and jaundice.

The year had passed in a tolerable way. I was caught up in the physical and emotional demands of David, not letting Malti help me except in the most minor ways. I couldn't get enough of my pretty baby, and had him sleep in my bed with me. I never let him out of my sight for that first whole year. He helped me forget my life with Somers, the suffocating presence of the English enclave, and enabled me to remember my time with Daoud.

But as he passed his first, and then his second birthday, and was by then running about, less needy of my endless presence, I found loneliness yawned. There were longer and deeper times of restlessness, of despair, when David's smile made me hunger so much for Daoud, for the time I had spent with him, for the feel of his arms around me, that I developed an odd, inexplicable pain under my ribs that never left.

I was an outsider in my own home and an outsider in English India. I spent my time now, like the other women, shopping at the English shops, and taking quiet walks around the Maidan, pushing David in a pram with Malti in tow.

That and palanquin rides to the homes of the other Company employee wives. They seemed to have forgotten about my "ordeal," and there were always new wives from each year's Fishing Fleet, wives who knew little about me except for my senior position, and that I was not overly sociable. But still, I found their judgmental outlook stifling. They were determined to reinforce the English traditions and rules much more strongly in India than they would have at home. Their narrow-mindedness, their unforgiving attitude, frightened me when I thought about my dark-eyed son. I dared not imagine the ramifications should anyone ever find out. I grew careful with them as I had become with Somers, cautious not to draw attention to myself, not to upset the fragile confines of their narrow world.

Somers no longer found reason to beat me, although he still struck me occasionally, for the sheer pleasure of it. I realized, after thinking about it, that he was no longer interested in intense beatings because of the difference in me. The excitement had gone out of the game; he considered me broken. I remembered how Daoud, with a gentle hand, broke his horses' wildness. And I knew that people can also be broken, although Somers's tactics were on the opposite end of the spectrum from Daoud's. I had grown submissive through fear for the well-being of my son.

And so I lived quietly, in near isolation, finding joy in David, but gradually realizing that I couldn't go on indefinitely, living on the razor edge of my nerves.

WHEN DAVID WAS CLOSE to three I heard, quite by chance, about a handful of women who got together regularly in a house on the other end of Garden Reach. They put together small booklets for the newly arrived English women in India. The booklets ranged in topic from basic Hindi to use with servants to recipes that incorporated Indian with English foods to dealing with minor ailments caused by the climate. I was welcomed into the group, possibly because I came with such enthusiasm, for here was something I was excited about and interested in—creating books. I began working on a booklet that dealt with the information I'd been collecting for the past few years—the healing properties of many of the indigenous plants. The pages were created on an ancient printing press, sent up from Madras when a new printing company opened there. A gentleman named Mr. Elliot—the husband of the woman who held the gathering in her home—ran the press for us. The last time I'd been at the Elliots' I had showed several of the ladies what I remembered from the bookbindery in Liverpool so many years ago, and we'd worked on simple covers of floral cotton and drawings on white vellum. I had been experimenting on a piece of red silk, embroidering it with gold and colored threads to create a pleasing cover.

Those afternoons were very precious to me. It was the first time in a long while that I looked forward to something and felt useful.

I found myself humming one evening as I sat brushing my hair at my dressing table, thinking about the meeting the next afternoon. It was the beginning of the cool season, and as always at this time, spirits rose. I breathed in the fresh air from the open window, looking at myself in the mirror. I pinched my cheeks to put more color into them and thought about the richness of the red silk cover.

But then Somers came to my room. He stood in the doorway, and I saw his reflection in the mirror. I turned on my chair to face him.

"I've heard of your involvement with these people, Linny. The book people."

I put down my brush, standing. I smiled. "Yes. I think the booklets are quite useful, especially to new wives. I wish I'd had something similar when I—"

"You're not going back."

I took a step toward him, my smile gone. "But . . . but why ever not? It's a function for the ladies. You said I could—"

He interrupted again. "It's a function that includes Indian women, Linny."

"Yes, some of them are Eurasian, but—"

"They're all half-castes. As is that Elliot, who works as a clerk in the public office."

"Mr. Elliot is highly educated, very quiet and gentlemanly. His wife is lovely. What does it matter that—"

He wouldn't let me complete a sentence. "Did you not learn your lesson with the Snow woman?"

"Her name was Faith, as you well know."

"Well, you seem to have forgotten that I do not allow you to associate with anyone unless they are of pure Norman or Saxon blood."

"Do you think their color rubs off on the pages, Somers?"

His jaw clenched. "We've taken over this mess that is India, and we're all working together—and that includes you, whether you like it or not—to make this land as proper a place as is possible. In spite of its tremendous downfall. We are the superiors. It's our moral obligation."

"But I do feel as if I'm helping in this way—creating booklets for English women new to India, to help them understand the culture. And help them adjust."

"It's not the booklets. It's the company. As I've said, it's out of the question." He crossed to where I was standing.

I looked into his face, my pulse pounding with anger. "So. You expect me to share in this obligation, yet have no responsibility for it."

"Say it any way you wish, Linny. The point is you'll do those activities I see as fitting the wife of a *burra* sahib, not the wife of a lowly uncovenanted clerk. You won't embarrass me again."

"Why would you be embarrassed by what I create? Mr. Elliot said—"

"I'm quite aware of what he said."

"You've spoken to him?" I looked at Somers's sullen face. "Are you jealous, Somers? Jealous because I'm doing something worthwhile? Perhaps you just can't stand the fact this work has given me something to do. And they respect me, did you know that? That's it, isn't it?"

He laughed. "Work? You call the worthless way you've spent your time there work?" His voice grew louder. "And I won't listen to any more of this," he said, and before I had a chance to move he hit me across the cheek with his open hand. At the sound of the damp smack, there was a small strangled cry. We both turned to the doorway to see David, his hands over his eyes.

"David. Darling, Mummy's all right. Look," I said, trying to smile as he uncovered his eyes.

He ran towards Somers, throwing his small arms around Somers's legs. "Don't hit Mama. You mustn't. It's bad to hit."

I reached down and pulled him away, holding him against me, staring into Somers's face as if to ask what he would do now.

He tugged at his cuffs. "Mama's been very naughty, David," he said. "She must be punished when she's naughty."

David struggled to break free of me. "Mama's *not* naughty," he said. "She's not." He turned to face Somers, his small body rigid, his lips set. There was no fear in his face; what I saw was anger.

"It's too bad you haven't been disciplined properly, either, David," Somers said now, dull red staining his cheeks. "That is not a proper way to address your father."

I held David tighter, trying to shield him from the blow I expected Somers to inflict on him. He hadn't struck David yet, or touched him in any way. In fact, he went out of his way to avoid seeing the boy, or be near him. I felt it was only a matter of time, though, until something terrible might happen.

But now Somers simply strode past us. For the first time since I'd known him, he had the grace to look abashed. It had taken a small child to do this.

⁂

WITHIN A YEAR I found something else to occupy my time, something that involved neither the wrong people nor the wrong area of Calcutta. I found my comfort in the substance derived from the *papaver somniferum*—the beautiful poppy.

⁂

IN 1836, SHORTLY AFTER David's third birthday, I was pleased to hear that Meg and Arthur Liston had returned to Calcutta after their posting in Lucknow. I hadn't had a chance to see her before an invitation for David arrived, asking him to the second birthday of Gwendolyn Liston, Meg and Arthur's daughter.

Perhaps, I thought, we will resume our friendship; I remembered feeling that Meg had much the same outlook on life as I had back at the Watertons' in those last days of 1830.

But I was shocked at the change in Meg. She was gaunt and sleepy looking. The pockmarks on her face appeared more visible than I remembered; perhaps it was the paleness of her complexion that emphasized the deep scars. I wasn't even sure that she remembered me; after greeting me politely she told me she had asked Elizabeth Wilton for the names of the children in the vicinity, and Elizabeth had passed along David's name. I was disappointed in her apparent confusion over who I was; she appeared vague about her time at the Watertons' six years earlier. I was sure that if we had a chance to talk alone I would again find the irreverent, confident, and single-minded woman I remembered.

During the party, the children and their ayahs gathered under a large striped tent in the huge garden and were entertained by performing monkeys and talking birds. Later, after the cake, the children were given rides around the estate on a frisky little pony, the smallest girls and boys—including David—firmly ensconced in a ring saddle.

The mothers remained inside the shuttered drawing room, eating dainty petits fours and drinking lemonade. As I looked around the over-decorated room, I noticed a large hookah sitting amidst small potted palms and ferns on a round, marble-topped table. It had a brass jug and attached cup, with a long snakelike tube wound around it. The tube ended in an ivory mouthpiece. I ran my hands over the jug's smooth round surface. It was warm.

"A pretty hubble-bubble, Meg," I said, when she came over to me. I found myself using Hobson-Jobson more and more often now with the other women, even though I had told myself I wouldn't slip into the nonsense language created by the English in India. "Does Mr. Liston smoke it?" I asked, picking up the mouthpiece.

She laughed. "No. It's mine. The water makes it so much easier," she said, touching the round container. "It cools the smoke by the time it reaches your mouth. Oh dear, here's little Gwendolyn, and she's torn her frock!"

She rushed to her daughter, who was sobbing loudly and holding up her torn gingham skirt. Left alone with the hookah, I tentatively put the molded ivory mouthpiece between my lips. It was smooth and carried a faint sweetness.

After Meg had comforted the distraught child and sent her back out with her ayah, she came back to me. The other women had broken into small groups, intent on their conversations. "Would you like to smoke it with me sometime?" she asked, smiling in a distracted manner.

"Oh, I don't smoke," I said. "I don't even like the smell of Somers's cheroots."

"Foolish girl," Meg said. "You don't have to smoke tobacco in it." She opened a small drawer under the table's white marble surface and removed a wooden box. Made of mangowood, the box had a tiny hinged lid. Meg pressed the lid, and it sprang open. Inside lay six black balls, each the size of a large pea.

"What are they?" I touched one sticky sphere with the tip of my forefinger.

"It's White Smoke. Opium. Quite harmless. You know—the ingredient in laudanum. And what would we do without our laudanum." It wasn't a question. "It saved me through three births."

"Three?" I said, and then immediately clamped my lips together. Gwendolyn was Meg's only child.

"Didn't you rely heavily on it?"

I shook my head.

"Surely, when you had your little fellow . . ." She studied my face. "Nobody goes through childbirth without great quantities of it. Why would one?"

I made a noncommittal sound.

"Well, you simply must, the next time. You give some preparation of it to your boy, for his aches and pains, though. Godfrey's Cordial, or Mother Bailey's."

"The herb teas that my ayah makes for him when his stomach is upset from too many treats seems to do the trick," I told her.

Meg frowned. "He's never suffered from boils, or prickly heat, or earache? What about fevers during the hot season?" Her voice was slow, insistent.

I shook my head, wondering why I suddenly felt guilty for having such a healthy child, and why she kept going on about it in a repetitious and tiresome way.

"I've always dosed Gwendolyn with it to settle her. You know, when she's overexcited or won't settle down at bedtime. Much healthier than gin, as some do. I find Godfrey's works like a charm, just like it says on the bottle—'A Pennyworth of Peace.' She goes straight to sleep, and is dozy for ages, even after she wakes up. I'll give you a bottle; I brought a small crate with me."

I remembered Elsie's baby, back on Paradise, dead from an overdose of Mother Bailey's Quieting Syrup.

"David's always been an easy child," I said. "I realize I've been very fortunate."

Meg touched the hookah. "Never mind, then. But listen—this isn't medicine, but sport. Sometimes I have a few puffs in the afternoon when everyone is napping. It's lovely and relaxing. Lots of my friends in Lucknow used it. We called it Dreamer's Delight. Why don't you come over one day next week and try it with me?"

"I'm not sure . . ."

"Come on, Linny. Aren't you the memsahib who's the recluse, stuck over there in that great big shut-up house? Wouldn't you enjoy some fun?"

I looked at her heavy-lidded green eyes. I felt a strange pull from their unblinking stare.

"All right. Next week. But Meg," I warned, "I'll only try it one time. Just the once."

As she slowly nodded, I saw that Meg was no longer the bold creature I remembered, given to wild flights of impulse and outspoken in her ideals. Now she appeared as worn and listless as all the other women who had been too long under the Indian sun.

Chapter Thirty-Five

THE NEXT TUESDAY I SAT IN MEG'S DRAWING ROOM, LISTENING to the *plunk, plunk, plunk* of the ruffled punkah overhead. *I shouldn't have come.* But our house was even more stuffy and quiet than usual today. Somers was on a two-week hunt. David spent most of his time on the verandah with Malti these days. Today he had played with his small set of drums and tom-toms, and each whack of his little stick on the tightly stretched goatskin pounded painfully against my skull. Even the ticking of the clock on the mantel was unnaturally loud, and I had felt an overpowering urge to flee from what I saw now as a dark prison.

I'd sent our *chuprassi* with a chit to Meg, and she'd replied immediately that she would be delighted to see me. Now she came into the parlor with slow, elastic steps, her smile making her bony cheekbones even more prominent. Today it was the smile I remembered from the Watertons', and I was genuinely pleased. Perhaps I had been wrong in my first judgment of her. She seemed different today, more aware and responsive.

"Linny! I'm so pleased you decided to come," she said, her eyes glowing.

"Are you sure you're not busy?" I asked. "I realize I should have sent my card yesterday, but—"

Meg waved a hand. "Busy? What is there to be busy with? Here, sit next to me."

"Meg, I have so much to ask you. About your travels with Mr. Liston. You must have been able to see so many sights."

But again she waved her hand through the air as if what I said were unimportant. "One can't spend one's life running about; surely you've realized that it takes all our efforts just to keep going here, haven't you?"

"But did you not pursue your book on shrines? Or your sketches of local customs? You seemed so passionate . . ."

Meg looked pensive for only a moment. "I'd almost forgotten. How is it you still remember those silly ideas?" She shrugged. "I was young and impressionable all those years ago."

"It was only six years."

"Six years in India—for a woman—is like twelve at home. Surely you've changed as well, Linny? Are you the same person you were when you arrived?"

I shook my head.

"Well, then," she said, almost triumphantly, as if she were pleased at this.

She pulled a small bamboo table close to the horsehair settee, then set the hookah on it. She placed the mangowood box next to it, taking a small oil lamp from a corner table and lighting it. "Now we're ready," she said, clapping her hands at a boy standing near the door. "Tell the cook to prepare some tea and have it brought in shortly," she ordered, and the boy bowed and scurried away. "This makes one terribly thirsty," she said.

"Just watch me, if you like, then you can have a turn," she went on. "Some people feel a tiny bit funny, at first, as if they're back on the rolling sea, but it quickly passes. Just ignore it," she said, smiling, "and relax."

She pulled a long hairpin out of her carelessly piled dark blond hair, then scooped a tiny globule of the black opium onto the tip of the pin. She held the pin over the lamp for a moment, and when the opium was soft, fit it into the small opening of the pipe. Putting the mouthpiece to her lips, there was a loud hissing as she sucked deeply, then silence as she held her breath for a long moment. She suddenly released it in a long plume of vapor that burst from her nostrils. The smoke swirled slowly around my head, and I breathed in its dark, sweet, slightly decayed odor.

Meg rested her head back against the shiny horsehair cushion of the settee, the mouthpiece still in her hand. She looked at something far beyond my sight.

I waited as long as I could. "Meg?" I finally whispered.

The woman's eyes blinked once, then slowly swiveled in their sockets. Only a rim of green showed around the black centers.

"Shall I try it now, Meg?"

Silently, and with obvious effort, Meg prepared the hookah for me. I put the mouthpiece between my lips and sucked up the warm air through the bead of opium. The smoke went softly into my lungs. I immediately felt dizzy, but it wasn't unpleasant.

After a timeless period I heard myself say, as if from a distance, "Yes. I see."

Time emptied into a shadowy twilight, emptying and then folding inward on itself in a gentle pattern, emptying and folding, over and over, without end. I was one of the loose bits of colored glass caught between the two flat plates and two plane mirrors in the instrument I had held to my eye as a child in Liverpool, standing in a dusty aisle of Armbruster's Used Goods.

I was nothing but a tiny piece of a larger sliding, changing, endless pattern. I thought I felt the very beat of my life in my veins and embraced that false signal.

※

I FELL INTO the habit of stopping to spend an hour or two with Meg and the hookah every other day. After the first few puffs, we fell silent, and I reveled in the peaceful, dreamy lethargy that spread warmly through me. I learned to set the pattern for my visions, letting myself hover, then float, up and away, back to the beautiful Kashmir valley. That's how it was at the beginning. I could direct the shape of my dreaming.

Sometimes I would be astride a horse in front of Daoud, with the assuring broad warmth of his chest against my back; at other times I felt his arms around me, the hardness of his body against the length of mine. But these sensations aroused no bodily passion in me. It was just a wonderful timeless reverie that blended and deepened. Daoud seemed to tell me things, flowing, poetic statements, and yet he never spoke. In the communication I felt totally happy, my mind floating in a sea of warmth. Eventually the dream faded, and I returned to the couch in Meg's drawing room, riding on a favorable breeze of euphoria.

I was grateful to Meg. I thought, in those early courtship days with the poppy, that she had saved my life.

Going home in my darkened palanquin, curtains drawn, I felt that my blood had been replaced by a lighter-than-air, buoyant fluid, and I knew that if I opened the curtains I would fly out, weightless, into the still, muggy air of Calcutta.

But best of all, Daoud's face didn't disappear for a number of hours after my visits to Meg. He seemed real and alive, just in the front of my forehead, like a portrait in the secret compartment of a brooch.

AFTER A FEW WEEKS, I knew that it was unfair and impolite of me to visit Meg simply to smoke her hookah, although she didn't seem to mind. I knew she smoked it every afternoon, whether I was there or not.

"Meg," I asked her one day before we took up the hookah, "would it be possible for me to get some opium for myself?"

"Certainly. There are large English companies that cultivate it in the fields in northern India. Patna produces the best variety. Mr. Liston made a trip there, to Patna, on business, and he says that they have a tremendous factory there, with halls for drying the opium juice, and then balling it—with each ball the size of a small room. Can you imagine? There's also a storage hall with shelves going up to the roof, five times the height of a man, where tons of it can be stored. Most of it is eventually processed into cakes and then sold in vast quantities to China. The Company's way of leveling a deficit, actually." She poured the tea she always had waiting. "Has your husband never talked to you about the problem with the Chinese?"

I shook my head. Somers and I didn't talk about anything anymore. In fact, we didn't speak to each other at all, unless we were in the same room, with David.

"To meet the enthusiasm for Chinese silk and tea at home, England had to pay in silver bullion. Now we want our silver back, and while the Chinese don't want our textiles in exchange, they're all too eager to pour it back out for opium. Arthur says several thousand tons of opium go up to Canton each year. All quite aboveboard. After all, the results of opium are no more than the pleasure derived from a glass of wine, or, for the men, their cigar after dinner."

"Is it sold here, in Calcutta, then, or did you bring it from Lucknow?"

Meg shrugged, studying me. "It's as easy to buy as tea, Linny. You just don't get out enough. Goodness. I'll have my box wallah bring some over, and you can arrange with him the quantity you want, and when you'd like it delivered. It is quite dear, mind. You can't pay with chits; it must be rupees. Are you allowed your own money?"

I smiled tightly. "I'll have rupees."

"All right, then. Look for my man on Friday morning. His name is Ponoo. That's his day to visit me; I'll ask him to go on to your house afterward."

✺✺✺

PONOO WAS A SQUINTING, neckless little man, missing all the fingers from his left hand. As well as opium, he carried tinned anchovy paste, French hair ribbons, and cooking utensils. I had occasionally used one of these peddlers when I didn't want to leave the house because of the raging heat or a debilitating monsoon.

Ponoo arrived just after ten on Friday, holding out a small can and naming a price. I quickly placed the rupees I had taken from the safe in Somers's room into his fingerless hand. Somers didn't know I knew about the safe, but of course I did. The safe and where he kept the key. Did he really think I never ventured into his bedroom while he was away? The safe was behind a false wall in his desk; I had discovered it out of sheer boredom one long rainy afternoon the first year of our marriage. He never gave me any money; I had to rely on signed chits to pay for everything, as did all the other wives. The chits were all sent directly to him, so he would know exactly what I had bought.

In the safe were documents and business papers and a locked strongbox. It didn't take me long to find the key to the strongbox in the pages of a book in Somers's bookshelf. I had been stealing from Somers since the first few months of our marriage, hiding the money away in a place it would never be found, in a tin box to protect it from insects and damp. I don't know why, except that it made me feel good. Every time I took a few bills from the stacks of rupees in the strongbox I felt the same power I had as a girl, slipping tiny objects under my bonnet and down my boots while a puffing man turned his back to wash himself and redo his buttons. Obviously Somers didn't keep track of the amounts he put in and took out. I knew after the first time that he didn't count—if he had, I would never have been able to steal any more, as he would have blamed either the servants or me, and I couldn't have let any of them be punished for what I'd done. I would have been beaten, and Somers would have made sure I never saw the strongbox again.

After the box wallah left I gave Malti more rupees and sent her to the bazaar to buy a hookah, ignoring her puzzled look. She returned with a small but splendid one, the stand and cup gleaming silver embossed with intricate dragons, and the mouthpiece an exquisitely carved piece of green jade.

I promised myself that I would have only an occasional puff, when I was feeling particularly low. I stuck to my resolve for a week, but then smoked more and more. Ponoo became a regular Friday caller.

I was careful to use my hookah only when David was asleep or outside with Malti, and never when Somers was home. Even with Meg's assurances about the popularity and acceptance of the magical black balls, I felt uncomfortable about the enjoyment I derived from my White Smoke.

Eventually I switched to a pipe. It was much easier to smoke than a hookah.

June 24, 1837

Dear Shaker and Celina,

The Manchester-Liverpool Railway indeed sounds fine, as does your new home in the countryside of Cheshire. It must be lovely to be away from the noise and bustle of Liverpool, and enjoy the fine air and peacefulness.

I am sorry I have not written as much of late. Time seems to stand still here. The quill slips between my fingers in the heat. The watered *tatties* and thermantidote are no weapon against the heat of the forge that masquerades as the sun. It brings on a lethargy that is impossible to describe. It makes even thinking difficult, a sad statement since the only real weapon to fight the climate is, it appears, the mind.

The heat spreads, covering everything in its path as water over stones.

I feel as if I am one of the leaves of our neem trees, dust laden, faded, hanging by a thin strand of a former steady stem. And should I submit, and drop to the walk below, I would instantly be swept aside by the waiting broom of a sweeper.

David is growing. He is a lovely child.

With my love,
Linny

P.S. There is something about the use of cinnamon I meant to tell you.

Chapter Thirty-Six

Hot Season, 1838

I LOOKED DOWN AT DAVID, ASLEEP, AND CROONED TO HIM. *"Nini, baba, nini."* Sleep, baby, sleep.

He stirred restlessly, his golden hair plastered to his forehead. I smoothed it back, then wiped his face with a damp cloth and began again. *"Nini, baba, ni—"*

"Linny! Stop that foolishness!"

Somers leaned heavily against the doorjamb. His own hair was damp with perspiration, his shirt soaked down the front. I rose and pulled the netting down over the cot and nodded at the punkah boy, who pulled more vigorously on the fan.

"Don't wake him," I whispered, once I was out in the hallway. "It's hard to get him to sleep in this heat."

Somers shook his head. "Singing those damn Indian baby songs to him, like he was still an infant. Bad enough that Malti coddles him."

"All ayahs coddle their charges, Somers. That's why they're ayahs."

"And that's why it's a damn good thing the children can't be with them any longer than their first five or six years. It's not good for him."

I turned my head from Somers; the words sounded obscene coming from him.

"He's a great strong lad, past five now, and should be treated as such. The best thing that can happen to that boy will be when he goes home within the year."

I stopped breathing. I had refused to think about this fact. It was too overwhelming. What would happen? I could never bear to be parted from David, but I doubted Somers would allow me to accompany him back to England. He had made it clear, over and over, that I must always be under his supervision, and could have no freedom, implying I would immediately embarrass him.

"Yes," Somers went on now, "he needs some decent schooling, and to learn how to behave in a proper manner. The way you let him run around barefoot with the servants' children is deplorable. And allowing him to chatter in Hindi . . . the natives' tongues are peppered with improper words and immoral ideas. I don't know how much longer I can tolerate his errant behavior."

How dare he call anyone immoral? Preaching about the servants and my own child when he himself was . . . the way he was. A brute who relished hurting young boys, who thought nothing of raising his hand to me.

"At least he's healthy and strong," I retorted. "Isn't that what's most important? The graveyards all over India are full of English children."

I thought of Malti's words, only yesterday, as we had stopped cutting flowers in the garden to watch David, babbling excitedly with the *mali*'s seven-year-old daughter.

"My David-*baba* is not like an English at all," Malti said, following his every move.

David was darkened by the sun; he often forgot to wear his hated solar topee, yet his skin didn't burn. He had a mass of shining blond curls and his black eyes sparkled as he chattered in Hindi about the huge toad he and the little girl had caught in the garden. She held the squirming creature firmly in both hands as David touched it.

"Yes, David-*baba* is more like a little native, strong and unafraid, is he not, Mem Linny? He does not fall prey to the usual illnesses of the English *babas* here, and is not listless and nervous as they are. Come, my *choti baba*," she called, "come. Give your ayah a kiss."

David frowned at us. "I'm *not* a little baby, Malti. Am I, Mother? I'm a warrior and I shall ride my horse to battle. The toad is our prisoner, the Emperor of China!" He and the girl ran off, and I thought, as I did each day now, how David was like his father, straight and proud and kind-hearted.

I blinked now, looking at Somers in the dim hall. He'd changed so much in the seven years I'd known him, his once good looks completely gone now. He had put on ever more weight from overeating rich foods, his face was bloated from constant drinking, and he had grown a full beard, which aged him. What would happen to David—and to me?

"MEM LINNY," MALTI CALLED quietly at the bedroom door. "Your ladies are come now."

I opened the door. "Did you seat them in the drawing room?"

"Of course. You are looking very pretty today, Mem," Malti added, eyeing my ruffled gown. "You must wear your fine clothes more often."

I took a deep breath, then fixed a smile on my face and walked to the drawing room. "Hilda. And Jessica. How lovely to see you."

My visitors rose, taking turns pecking my cheek. They were wives of men in Somers's office; it was a wearying game of polite visits back and forth simply because our husbands worked together.

"Are you feeling better now, dear?" Hilda asked, her mouth a concerned moue. "Somers said you were poorly last week. We did so miss you at the Sawyers' musical evening. It was quite a jolly affair, although of course the upper registers of Frederick Jewitt's viola are still frightfully squeaky."

"I'm fine, thank you," I said, trying to remember when the Sawyers' party had been, or if I had even heard about it. Somers didn't tell me about events anymore, preferring to go alone. I knew he would pop in and then hurry away on the pretense of my being ill, although of course he rarely came home directly.

"I must say, Linny, if falling ill would keep my weight down, I wouldn't mind. How do you keep your waist so small? No amount of corseting can do that."

"She's only had one baby, that's what does it, Hilda," Jessica retorted. "Believe me, there's no such thing as a tiny waist after six confinements." She looked down at her massive bulk, a rueful expression on her face, then immediately helped herself to a cream bun from the tray beside her.

"Well, you must get busy, Linny, and give David a little brother or sister," Hilda said, tapping my knee with her closed fan. Then she took a tiny hinged mirror from her handbag and inspected the frizzled fringe of orange hair that rose from her high forehead. "He's, what—five now?—and before you know it he'll be sent home, and you'll need more children to keep you from being too lonely." She snapped the mirror shut and returned it to her bag. "With my Sarah and Florence gone, I'd go mad without little Lucy. And by the time she leaves, Sarah should be finished school and hopefully returning to us."

"Yes," I agreed, shaking my head as the *khitmutgar* offered me a glass of lemonade.

"Did you hear what happened in the Maidan yesterday?" Jessica asked.

Grateful for the change of subject, I leaned forward.

"It was the oddest thing," she continued, licking thick white cream from her thumb. "This . . . dark man, not an Indian, mind you, but dark, was on a huge horse and circling the Maidan. Some say he was peering at English women. I didn't observe that, but can you imagine? The cheek. Quite upsetting."

Hilda took over. "I was there," she said, triumphantly, as if she had performed a heroic deed. "None of us had any idea what he was looking for. Can you imagine? A big ruffian, having the audacity to take an interest in us. Guess he's seen enough of his own sort, and was—what shall we say?—titillated by the look of white women. I tell you, I was quite shaken when he looked in my direction." She touched her faded hair coquettishly. "Of course, he was driven away quickly, but—oh, what is it, Linny?"

I stood, clutching my abdomen with trembling hands. "I suppose I haven't quite recovered from whatever it is that's been bothering me recently."

"Sit down, Linny. Breathe deeply. Hilda, finish the story."

"Well, he was bold as brass, not at all a gentleman. Of course, he couldn't be. After all, he was one of those foreign breeds. And sitting on his horse as if he owned the square." They both looked at me.

"I'm sure you'll excuse me." I hurried out of the room. Faintness overtook me just outside the door, and I leaned against the wall, wishing to extract even a fraction of coolness from the plaster.

"She'll not last here much longer," I heard Hilda say. "That frail, nervous sort never do. She's worn to fiddlesticks. And there's something odd about her eyes, don't you think? Very dark. Too dark."

"I tell you, it's her husband I pity. She must not be any sort of company for him at all, always so poorly. It's no wonder there are no more children. He probably knows another one would kill her. Poor man."

I steadied myself and went to my bedroom. *When had I become one of India's casualties, one of the frail, nervous sort? They could have been describing Faith. Or the woman Meg was now.*

✺

AFTER I HAD TUCKED David into bed that evening, I walked out into the front garden. I slowly approached the acacia tree beside the gate, running my fingers over its bumpy bark. In the air I thought there might be a mild suggestion of rain. Could the monsoons be coming early?

At the sudden bark of a jackal from the darkness beyond the houses, there was a rush of rubbery wings. I tilted my head back to watch as bats, big as crows, rose from the acacia, their black ribbed wings cutting the fading sky. Leaning against the tree, I looked down the darkening, empty street, straining my ears for the sound of hooves. I knew I was being ridiculous. Every so often a Pathan rode through Calcutta. It meant nothing.

I stayed there, my eyes fixed on the street that led to the Maidan. Finally the fireflies were dancing spots of light and the sky dark and furrowed, the moon resting heavily, and Somers called sharply from the doorway that I was to come inside.

✺

THE NEXT MORNING I sat in the verandah fingering the same page of my book over and over. I hadn't been able to sleep more than an hour or two, and my head ached in a tiresome way. Malti arrived home from the daily shopping, and I saw that her face was dark with dismay, and she was muttering to herself as she placed a new bottle of ink on the escritoire.

"What is it, Malti?" I said, coming through the flung back doors into the bedroom.

Malti gave me a sideways glance. "Nothing, Mem Linny," she answered, rearranging the paper and quills and books on the desk. She stopped and looked at me.

"There's something, Malti. You must tell me." I licked my lips. "Did you . . . see anything today? Anything . . . unusual?"

"I saw nothing," she replied, her tone strangely curt.

"Was there any new gossip, then?"

Malti pushed the bottle of ink back and forth on the polished wood. "You do not usually inquire about the wagging tongues in the square."

"Well, today I'm asking. Did you overhear anything?"

"It is not worth repeating, mem. Many of the ayahs have allowed their voices to grow as sharp as those of their mistresses. They do not have enough work to do, it appears, and so devise stories to pass the time."

I lowered myself to the chair beside the desk. "What are these stories, Malti?"

There was pain on Malti's gentle face. "It is just more silly talk of the man, Mem Linny, from the northwest frontier. The ayahs say he continues to ride about the Maidan, looking at the English ladies. It is said he has spoken a name." She shook her head, her brow furrowed. "Can you imagine such nonsense? He will shortly be arrested. This kind of behavior is not acceptable, and—Mem Linny. What is it?" She looked down, and I followed her gaze. I saw that I was gripping her dark hands in my own.

"Did anyone tell him where I live? Does he know where I am?"

"Oh, Mem Linny, be still. Hush, hush. Do not be worried. It is only the bad memories of your troubled time at Simla which frighten you now. And surely the bitter hens simply wish to stir up trouble with their simple tale, for . . . Mem Linny? What are you doing?"

I flew to the dressing table, pinning up long loose strands of hair, my shaking hands scattering hairpins over the floor. I buttoned the collar of my dress and whirled around to Malti. "Do I look presentable?"

Malti's face closed. "You are fine, Mem Linny, fine, as always." Her voice was careful. "But come now, sit down. I will prepare your pipe. That will calm you. And then I will bring you a cup of your favorite tea."

"I don't want my pipe. There's no time. Come, come with me. David . . . David, where is David?"

"He plays with the Wilton children until late afternoon, Mem Linny. Do you not remember?"

"Take my reticule, Malti, and come, follow me." I ran down the hall, turning to urge Malti to hurry. She trailed slowly, clutching the small taupe bag to her chest. As I approached the front door the *chuprassi* appeared, ready to open the door for me. He put his hand on the brass doorknob.

"Please, Malti! There may not be much time. Can't you walk any faster?" I gestured to the *chuprassi*, but before he could open the door it swung inward.

I gasped.

Somers stood in the doorway, his blocky frame filling the entrance. "Hello, Linny." He was very still.

I backed away, bumping into Malti, who dropped the reticule. Somers stared at it.

"Just on your way out, were you, Linny?" He still hadn't crossed the threshold.

"No . . . well, yes, Malti and I were just going to take a turn around the Maidan . . . we often do, at this time, don't we, Malti?" I turned to her. She stood with her mouth open.

Somers stepped in, leaving the door open behind him. "You were going for a stroll, at the hottest time of day, without your solar topee, or sun parasol—and in this apparel?" He had two hectic spots on his cheeks.

I looked down at the wrinkled cotton of my limp frock, seeing the spattering of grease along one cuff, a button missing at the waist. "What—what are you doing home?"

"Fever," he said tersely. His old enemy, malaria, poking his spine with its cold, bony finger. "I'm going to bed. Malti, you're not to allow your mistress out of the house. Do you understand?"

I grabbed his sleeve. "But Somers, I just want—"

He threw up his arm to shake off my hand, catching me across the bridge of the nose. Bright lights burst behind my eyes. "I forbid it.

You'll not make a fool of me, parading around in public like a harridan. Like the whore that you are."

I heard the sharp intake of Malti's breath, and the rustle of the *chuprassi*'s clothes.

"In fact, I'm sick of the sight of you. Dirty whore."

I wanted to spit in his face, to put up my chin and tell him that yes, yes, I was still a whore. It was tempting, so tempting to scream at him that David wasn't his at all, that I was indeed what he always accused me of, that I had joined with a man joyfully, for my own pleasure, and that David was a child of love, and not of his brutal rape. But of course I wouldn't tell him this, for what I had kept hidden for these five years was my trump card. I shook with the effort to keep my lips sealed. I tried to push past him.

He grabbed at the front of my dress and as I moved forward, he pulled at the fabric with all his force. There was a terrible ripping sound, and I stopped, shocked. Somers looked down at the clutch of poplin and cambric—he'd even torn away my chemise—then back to me, and his eyes riveted on my exposed chest. The blood drained from his face, leaving him parchment white. He stumbled back, and the *chuprassi* caught him.

Malti stepped in front of me, trying to hold her own head scarf over my nakedness.

Somers dropped the fabrics and pointed, his finger shaking, at me.

"What's the matter, Somers?" I hissed his name, in a low, shaky voice, pushing Malti away, standing in front of him so that my scar was fully visible. "Don't like what you see? Thought you knew all there was to know about me?"

"Mem Linny, Mem Linny," Malti cried, "please. Do not make him angry. Please." She covered her own face and wept.

Somers shook off the *chuprassi* and straightened, his face still bleached, his forehead beaded with perspiration. "What is that?" he whispered, his finger trembling.

"What does it look like? The touch of an old lover?" I didn't care any longer how I sounded, what I said. The pure hatred I had for him at this moment flooded all my senses.

But before he could respond Somers groaned loudly and doubled over, and the *chuprassi* helped him down the hall to his room. And at that I lurched through the open doorway. I ran, as best as I could, down the drive, my boots crunching in the crushed shells. I heard the gasp of my own breath, loud in my head, felt the tightening of my chest at the accelerated and unaccumstomed pace. I had not yet reached the end of the drive before large, gloved hands gripped my arms from behind.

It was the *chuprassi*, sent, surely, by Somers to fetch me back. I struggled against his hold, twisting and straining. "Let me go," I muttered. "You must do as I say." But the hold remained firm, and his face, as I looked over my shoulder at him, showed nothing as I squirmed like a helpless kitten. Malti was beside us, still crying, reaching up to wipe the spittle from my chin with her fingers, pulling at my dress to cover me, trying to soothe me as I was swept up and carried back to the house in the arms of the *chuprassi*.

The small flurry of activity had weakened me; I could no longer fight, and leaned, defeated, against him until he deposited me on my bed.

LATER, IN MY BEDROOM, I dismissed the punkah wallah and Malti.

"I don't want to leave you, Mem Linny," she said. "You should not be alone. You are very troubled."

But eventually I convinced her I was only going to sleep, and she left, leaving my door ajar. I knew she would remain in the hallway, listening to my every move through the half-open door. I sat at my mirrored dressing table, looking at my hands on my lap, curled into each other, still and white as dead doves.

Was it really Daoud, here, in Calcutta, looking for me? I had to know. I would go to the Maidan, no matter what Somers said or did to me. I would somehow sneak out, and walk all the way there, if necessary. I took a deep breath and looked into the mirror.

Long strands of dull hair fell around my shoulders. I saw how thin my face was, the bridge of my nose purple and swollen from the knock Somers's arm had given it. The skin over my bones was translucent and taut, as if there were hardly enough to cover my nostrils. I had a sudden horrifying impression of my skull beneath the flesh. My lips had grown thin, and lumpy discolored pouches stood out beneath my eyes. I thought of my image in Shaker's mirror, nine long years ago. If I had been shocked then, it was doubly worse now. What had I been thinking? Of course it wasn't Daoud. What was I dreaming of? That Daoud would pull me up on his horse, and we would ride away together? I was a fool, a complete fool. David was here, my child, my life. My fantasies about Daoud were nothing more than that—fantasies. I had known him, almost six years ago, for less than a month. He was, as I had told Nani Meera, of another world, a world that could never be mine.

I looked at myself in the mirror again. I had lost all sight of the bright hope that had brought me to India. I had lost sight of the woman who called herself Linny Gow.

I prepared my pipe and smoked it until I could smoke no more.

Chapter Thirty-Seven

THE MALARIA THAT HAD PERIODICALLY HELD SOMERS IN ITS terrible grip had indeed returned, and this was the worst episode of the string of his recurrent paroxysms. He had terrible headaches accompanied by nausea and vomiting, followed by chills that were more violent than ever before. The fevers were raging, leaving his skin hot and dry, and sometimes there was delirium. And then suddenly the sweating began; his body was drenched and his temperature fell. Weakened, he sank into deep, deep sleeps that lasted hour after hour. Dr. Haverlock visited every day to check his progress. I was not allowed to leave the house; although Somers might not be aware of where I was, the servants he had paid handsomely to mind me were watching at all times. Even as I passed the front door the *chuprassi* would step in front of it, arms crossed over his chest, and when I walked in the back garden Somers's *khansana* followed me closely, stopping when I stopped, walking when I walked.

On the fourth evening of his illness Somers sent for me. He was propped up on pillows, alone in the room. He had lost his fevered color, and his skin had a sticky look in the glow of the lamps lit in his bedroom. The smell of sickness lingered, its stale miasma almost overpowering, but I knew Somers was through the worst, and his eyes glared at me with clear disgust. I felt that he was destined to rise from each attack with renewed strength and venom.

"As soon as this bout is completely past I shall put together preparations for you to leave here," he said.

"Leave?"

He flapped a hand, weakly. "You've become too much of a burden. That last episode, with you ready to run out into the streets of Calcutta behaving like a madwoman, ready to do who knows what, made up my mind. Do you really think anyone would be surprised—or even care—if you simply disappeared? Who would even notice, Linny, apart from the servants?"

I tried to swallow, but I had no saliva. I knew my future depended on the next few minutes. "Will you send us back to England, then?"

He stared blankly. When he didn't answer, I thought it was due to his illness. Then he spoke and his voice was clear and firm. "Do you realize you're using Hindi, Linny? Are you even aware that you're no longer speaking English?"

"I'm sorry." I repeated my question. "I asked if you would send us back to England."

"Us? What do you mean by us?"

I spoke slowly, carefully. "Why, David and myself, of course. As you said not long ago, soon it will be time for him to begin his education. I could live with him wherever you choose—in London, perhaps. He could attend your old school."

He gave a dry cough, then attempted a smile. "You really think I'd trust you to bring up my son? You're an addict, Linny. Among other things, of course."

The floor tilted, and I put out one hand, holding on to the bedpost so I wouldn't fall, lowering myself into a chair beside the bed.

"I would stop, Somers. I can stop if I choose."

"Everybody knows you're nothing but a wasted ruin. I sense that most think you quite mad already, you know. They don't even ask about you or seem the least curious that you no longer accompany me to social events. So my plan is to find a pleasant place for you to . . . rest, shall we call it? Someplace—perhaps an isolated post in the Indian plains— where you would be cared for properly, and couldn't hurt anybody—or yourself. Or maybe I could consider another option, if you would really like to go home."

I nodded vigorously, standing, my head still light. "Yes, yes, Somers. That's what I'd really like. To go home." If I could only get back to England, I would find a way to be near David. Shaker would help me.

"Yes. I agree that's the best plan. There are a number of places in London that could keep you restrained for—well, for an indefinite period of time."

"Restrained?" It took thirty seconds for his meaning to become clear. "A . . . a lunatic asylum?"

"A lunatic asylum, my dear? Is it necessary to use such a harsh term?" He actually managed a smile this time. "Let's just say you'll be under care. Having a nice long rest. It's well known that India has the ability to do this to some, you know. You wouldn't be the first memsahib who proved unable to bear the strain. Everyone would understand, and not a soul would question my motives. In fact," he went on, as if very pleased with himself now, "who, besides David and perhaps Malti, would even care what becomes of you? And David is a child; he'll quickly for- get. Malti will be dismissed. She's of no importance anyway."

My dizziness returned, and I felt behind me for the chair and sat on its edge. I needed my pipe. I shivered, and sweat rolled from my hairline down my face, onto my neck, giving the unpleasant sensation of minus- cule insects scurrying under my skin. Without thinking, I pulled the gauzy scarf I wore tucked into the bodice of my frock, and swabbed at my cheeks and neck.

There was silence, and then an odd, strangled cry from the bed. Somers was sitting up, pointing a shaking finger at my chest as he had days earlier when he'd torn my dress.

I looked down at my scar. "Once again, I'm surprised at your reaction, husband dear," I whispered with sarcasm. I cleared my throat, finding my voice. "Surely you aren't concerned over an old injury. I didn't think my body would be of any interest to you after all this time."

He slumped back, his mouth opening and closing as he struggled to breathe. "I know," he croaked. "I know now. When I first saw that," he said hoarsely, his eyes fixed on the scar, "there was something . . . something. I didn't know what. But yes, I think . . ."

I hardly listened to his raving. I thought of never seeing my son again, of him growing up learning his mother lived out her life huddled on a pile of putrid straw in a darkened stone cell in some Bedlam. Of Somers distorting any memories of me David might retain from his childhood, and, worse than all of that, of trying to impart his own twisted values on him.

The fierce need to protect David from this future gave me a strength I hadn't felt in a long time. I threw the scarf onto the ground, pulling my bodice lower as I leaned toward the bed, so that Somers would see the whole of the destruction. "Done by one of my old customers in Liverpool," I said. "Quite the picture, isn't it? And yet I survived. I survived a madman's blade once, and I'll survive whatever you think you can do to me, Somers. You will not win."

He made a retching sound, putting his fist to his mouth.

"Will you be sick?" I asked, no concern in my voice. "Surely the sight of my ruined flesh would bring you pleasure, not discomfort. After all, my pain is the only thing that *has* brought you any joy in our miserable marriage."

"I know," he said again, speaking through his fist, that same strange agitation in his voice. "I know now why I recognized the fish."

I sat back, letting go of the front of my dress, trying to understand. The fish? And then I remembered that time in his bachelor's quarters, and how his seeing my birthmark had been the reason he knew me to be a whore.

He put his hand down, his fist still clenched. "I'd almost managed to forget my last sojourn to that black spot on the Mersey," he said. He spoke slowly, as if thinking out loud. He struggled to sit up again. "And you're right. You did survive. How, I can never guess. You should be nothing but softened bones by now, the crabs using your eye sockets as a home."

I put my own fist to my mouth as Somers had done seconds before. In the quiet that followed his strange statement, a terrible, shocking sense of knowledge began to form. An understanding too horrific, too unbelievable, dawning slowly at his words. I shivered uncontrollably in the stifling room, my teeth clenched so tightly that my jaw ached.

"Didn't I instruct my man to dump your body in the Mersey?" Somers had regained some of his composure; his voice was low but strong as he stared at me. "And didn't Pompey swear to me that he did it, and assure me there was no one left to speak of what happened that night on Rodney Street?"

And suddenly I heard it, the same cold, rational voice that had ordered my death as I lay, a thirteen-year-old girl made blind and help- less, on a thick rug in front of a trunk of glass jars filled with floating hair. The hair of dead girls. The old man with the shears planted in his eye beside me. The stench of rot coming from him, and then that of burning hair. I gagged, my mouth filling with acrid saliva.

This was not what I had expected. Ever. Rodney Street. The old nightmare came to life, reared up huge and even more terrifying when fed by the light of the glowing lamps in this room. I felt a spinning, a flying apart; the fearful old vision flooded back: my body, with its bro- ken neck, tossed into the murderers' pit of quicklime. I leaned forward, choking as I spat out what my stomach heaved. It splattered the toes of my slippers. I lowered my head to my knees.

Young Master, Pompey had called him.

"I had to relieve Pompey of his services not too long after the inci- dent in Liverpool. Too many slipups. But I suppose it can't all be blamed on Pompey. I saw you, too, that night, and believed you to be dead. You were torn open, right down your left breast. I saw muscle; I swear I even saw your heart, lying unbeating, but of course that couldn't be."

Wiping my mouth with the back of my hand, I raised my head and looked at him.

He licked his lips, then smiled, as if reliving a fond memory. And that smile chilled me even more than his calm words. "If I remember correctly you were little more than a child, your hair gone. Totally unlike the self-possessed woman I first met in Calcutta—but for that telling fish on your arm. No wonder I couldn't remember where I'd seen it. I put that night and its troublesome mess out of my head as quickly as I could."

I kept my mouth open now, sucking in the muggy air, trying to draw it into my lungs, envisioning the illustrations from Shaker's medical books, all those years ago, Albinus's drawings of the two sacks situated behind the breastbone. I knew my lungs weren't plump and full but flat and deflated, shriveled. They wouldn't pump, wouldn't fill with the drenched air. My mouth gaped as a fish out of water. I knew I was drowning. The image of that ravaged face, the horror of the flickering tongue, the senseless eyes, stood in the front of my mind as if lit by rows of candles.

Somers was the son of the man I had killed.

"It's too late," I whispered, finally finding the strength to speak. "You could never prove it. It's too late to have me tried for murder." I must protect David from a future with Somers, and from the knowledge of my past.

A sound like laughter came from Somers's throat, a ghastly crackling noise. "Tried? For murder? I hardly think so. There was no record of murder, after all. Simply the death of a man riddled with syphilis and driven to insanity. It seemed he would never die; I imagined him living on for years and years. In fact, you did the job I wish I'd had the nerve to do much, much earlier. Even before he grew so ill he was a bastard, a cruel, heartless bastard. I left England shortly after you killed him, Linny. I wanted to leave it all behind, to forget."

Silence grew in the room. I took short, shallow breaths as if just learning to breathe.

"Nobody was happier than I to see him buried at long last," Somers finally continued, when I knew we had both gone through the details in our minds—the ones each of us knew—of that night, "where the worms could do their final job on what was left of his stinking body. As for his soul—I don't believe he had one.

"From the time I was twelve—"

"No. I don't want to hear any more," I whispered, but he ignored me.

"—he took me with him on his prowls. At first he just had me watch while he mounted each bitch. He had a penchant for lower-class women.

Like you, Linny. After a while I came to enjoy watching the humiliations to which he subjected them."

I kept shaking my head, wanting him to stop. But it was as if he were enjoying it all, seeing my misery as he recounted the ugly details. I put my hands over my ears, closing my eyes and lowering my head.

"Eventually he tried to force me to join in." He spoke loudly and clearly; it was impossible to shut out his words. "My father kept me at his bidding like a pet monkey, stroked occasionally, thrown a tasty morsel now and then, but impossibly shackled. And he wouldn't, even in death, allow me to live as I wished. He knew from an early age I had little interest in women. In fact, he first supplied me with the boys I grew to hunger for. But he stipulated in his will that I must be married in order to receive my rightful inheritance. Quite like him in every way to have a final laugh from the grave.

"And so it appears that you really have had a remarkable impact on my life, Linny. First you killed my father, and then you made it possible for me to receive my inheritance. In reality you allowed me freedom. Twice." With that word he stopped, and was silent.

I removed my hands and opened my eyes. Now mosquitoes buzzed around my ears and sweating hairline. Somers was looking at me in a manner that was almost jaunty, his head tilted and eyes bright, as if surprised at his good fortune.

I dropped to my knees at the side of the bed. "Then repay me, Somers. Set me free, in turn. Let me take David and disappear." I grabbed his hands. They were icy. "You'll never hear from us again. I'll ask for nothing."

He shook his head gently, as if I were a naughty child caught stealing sweets. "You don't understand, do you, Linny? And yet you've always been such a clever girl." He pulled his hands away from mine. "You can't be trusted to leave me, and you can't be trusted with our son. There is no other way but for you to be put away, properly, lawfully, so there can never be any future questions about you." His eyes were unblinking now, like a snake's. "I'll have the papers drawn up by Dr. Haverlock as soon as possible. He won't need any convincing, of course. One look at you would be assurance enough that you need caring for. As for David . . . I'll bring him up as I see fit. It won't take me long to have him trained into

the shape he should be." He attempted another of his horrible laughs, but
it brought on a fit of coughing, and a chill suddenly came over him.

As I stared at him, his body trembling, his mustache sprayed with
cloudy beads of saliva, I imagined his face settling into the leering
specter of his dead father. I rubbed my eyes, trying to clear away that
old and horrific vision, but the haunting wouldn't leave. It seemed that
in the most terrible twist of fate, the evil hand that had brought me to
Rodney Street had led me to this room. I got to my feet, stumbling away
from the bedside. I looked, in absolute horror, at the man who was my
husband. Knowing the power he wielded. Knowing that his twisted
hatred, his lecherous ways, and his truly vile nature would continue to
grow with each passing year.

This was the man who would finally destroy me, and who would
raise my son.

I had to stop him from what he was about to do to me. I had to protect my child.

<hr/>

I KNEW THE TIMING must be perfect. I didn't sleep that night but nevertheless arose early in the morning and bathed. I had no weariness. I
smoked my pipe, but only to prevent my body from going into painful
spasms. I had Malti pay special attention to my hair, and I chose my
dress carefully. I sat at my dressing table and studied myself. Now I
understood how Faith had felt in her last days at Simla. There is a
tremendous lifting, as if a heavy yoke has been taken from one's shoulders, when one knows with complete certainty what one must do. That
there can be no other way.

Malti looked at me strangely. "Mem Linny? I don't understand."

"What don't you understand?" I swiveled so I was facing her.

"Last night you appeared so distressed when you left Sahib Ingram's
room. And yet today you appear more at ease than for a long, long time.
What is it, mem, that I see in your face? It appears to be happiness. But
that cannot be, with the sadness of this house."

I smiled at her. "It's not happiness, Malti. Not yet. But there is the
future. We must light new lamps for the future."

Malti shook her head, confused. The rest of that day I sat on the verandah and played with David, my mind whirring, planning. At one point I looked toward the windows of Somers's room and saw Dr. Haverlock staring at me. He turned abruptly when I met his gaze.

I went to Somers's room. Dr. Haverlock sat at the desk there, writing. Was it the commitment report he worked on? He stopped when he saw me, and looked at Somers, lying on the bed.

"Do you want something, Linny?" Somers asked, his voice deceptively concerned. "Or have you forgotten something?"

"I thought you might need fresh water."

Somers gestured to the full pitcher beside his bed. "But Linny . . . it was you who brought this in just before Dr. Haverlock arrived."

"No. No, it wasn't. It must have been one of the servants." I hadn't been to Somers's room that day.

Somers shook his head, smiling gently, and, raising his eyebrows slightly, looked at Dr. Haverlock. *You see?*

Dr. Haverlock studied my hands. I realized I was lacing and unlacing my fingers. I stopped, but he had already turned back to his paper and continued writing. I left the room, but lingered in the hallway. I heard Dr. Haverlock tell Somers it was done; I heard Somers assuring Dr. Haverlock that he would receive what had been promised when all matters had been taken care of.

He was making his plans. It was time to finalize mine.

❧❧❧

IT WAS EASY TO acquire a supply of *dhatura* from a box wallah that very day. The shrub's English name was thorn apple. It was one of India's indigenous plants, growing wild in rank soil and wasteland. I remembered Nani Meera's caution about using it. In the right amounts it could be useful in limiting the coughing fits due to pertussis, as well as problems in the bladder. Although the large white corollas of the flowers had narcotic and sedative properties, these properties were found to be even stronger in the leaves when powdered.

The entire plant had elements similar to those of belladonna, only stronger, and overdose caused fatal poisoning.

❧❧❧

ALTHOUGH EVER GAINING in strength, Somers was thankfully still weak, and there were sudden moments of extreme fatigue and feebleness. While recuperating he enjoyed cooled tea, much sweetened, and called for it many times a day. I took it upon myself to fetch it from the cook and carry it to him each time he requested it, as any concerned wife might. By the way he looked at me the first few times I appeared at his bedside with the tray, his lip lifting in a sardonic, quizzing movement, I knew he thought I was trying to prove to him that I wasn't mad, that I was attempting to appear normal. I allowed him to think this of me.

I started with very minute amounts. I had to be extremely careful; it must look as if he had finally succumbed to his oldest and truest Indian enemy.

Within two days he had regressed considerably, his face dry and flushed. He had difficulty swallowing, and was given to muttering and restless, purposeless movements. On the third day he fell into a sleep so deep it was impossible to wake him for many hours; I knew it could eventually lead to coma. When he finally did stir and open his eyes, which had grown gummy, the pupils were dilated and fixed. I continued to get him to swallow a few sips of tea each time he was conscious, crying to the servants that he must have fluid.

As I wrung my hands in front of Dr. Haverlock, I said a silent prayer of thanks that the old man was so lacking in medical knowledge. "He appeared to be rallying," I said. "What has caused this turn?"

Dr. Haverlock shook his head. "One never knows how these foreign diseases will work on their victims." I stared, wide-eyed, into his face. "I fear it's become much more serious. My diagnosis, Mrs. Ingram, is brain malaria."

I put my fingers to my lips in consternation. "Brain malaria?"

"His slipping in and out of consciousness, as well as the mental confusion, are both symptoms. Should he start showing signs of jaundice, or perhaps convulsing . . ."

"But—but he *will* recover, won't he?"

"Now, my dear, you mustn't distress yourself unduly. Your state is quite delicate—"

"Dr. Haverlock." I stood tall. "I'm not in any state, delicate or otherwise. Are you telling me that Somers may not recover from this bout? Tell me the truth, Dr. Haverlock."

The old man took both my hands in his and shook his head, an insincere expression of sympathy on his face.

———❦———

WHEN DR. HAVERLOCK RETURNED the following day, he made a cursory check of Somers and then led me into the study. "Please prepare yourself, my dear," he said.

I waited.

"I'm sorry to have to tell you that your husband's death is imminent. I doubt he'll survive the night."

I allowed myself to crumple to a chair, lowering my head and covering my face with my hands. "Please dismiss the servants," I said through my fingers, "but stay with me." When we were alone, I looked up.

"I wanted to speak to you in complete privacy, Dr. Haverlock," I said, no longer putting on a show of distress. "About unfinished business."

"Now, now, Mrs. Ingram. You mustn't worry. I'll take care of everything here. And very soon you will be back home, where people who know how to care for you can help you through the difficult times you're facing. And you mustn't concern yourself over the child. Mr. Ingram left strict instructions as to—"

I stood, coming straight to him, stopping so close to his face that he took a step back. "Do you really believe me to be mad, Dr. Haverlock?"

His eyes shifted. "Your husband knew what was best for you. There are many ways, many new developments in caring for those unfortunates, such as yourself, who—"

I interrupted. "And there are many ways, I assume, that a man such as yourself may be . . . how shall I word it? May be persuaded to see the truth."

Dr. Haverlock's chin jumped once, encouraging me. He was so transparent.

"I know you must be weary of working. You've devoted your life to helping people, Dr. Haverlock." The words swam out warmly, slippery, clean. "You deserve to spend the remainder of your years in pampered luxury, either here or at home. Whatever sum my husband and you

agreed upon for writing your . . . recommendation with regard to my
future and that of my son, I will double. If you put that letter in my possession, and we speak no more about it."

His chin jumped again, and by that subtle twitch and his hesitation, I
knew I had him. He took my arm and had me sit beside him on the sofa,
glancing around, although the room was empty. "I may have been hasty
in my estimation of your condition, my dear," he said. "Your poor husband made his request out of concern for you and for his son."

"And you realize that Somers has been deeply affected by his constant battle with malaria all these years," I said. "You also know that due
to this he may have been lacking in clarity this last while. I understand,
Dr. Haverlock"—my voice grew low with a shared conspiracy—"how
well I understand what an awkward position he put you in. Please. I
insist you tell me what sum you are owed for the strain this whole
unpleasant situation has caused you. Come now, what will it be?"

He gruffly cleared his throat. Sly old goat. He was afraid of naming
the price in case it was lower than what I was prepared to double.

I went to the desk drawer, took out the wrapped package I had put
there this morning, and brought it back to the sofa. I set it between us and
untied the string. The paper fell away, revealing my huge pile of saved
bills, the amount I had been pilfering from Somers for years and had kept
so safe and hidden. Now it gave the impression of a king's ransom.

The physician licked his thin, dry lips, his breath quickening. I could
almost hear the greedy ticking of his brain. "Oh my, Mrs. Ingram. Dear,
dear. I don't wish to appear grasping, but, in reality, all of this has
caused me a great loss of time and, as you say, a considerable strain on
my own constitution, which hasn't been well of late. I've grown quite
bilious. It wouldn't be gracious to speak of the sum Mr. Ingram and I
discussed, but . . ." Again, his eyes longingly caressed the money so
close to his thigh.

I patted his sleeve. "I understand, I'm sure," I said, pity in my voice.
"Would you be carrying anything with you, Dr. Haverlock, that we
might exchange?"

"Well," he said slowly, "I'm not exactly sure what you're refer—"

"The commitment report, Dr. Haverlock. Do you carry it?" My
voice never lost its sweetness. I moved the package an inch closer to him.

Still studying the lakhs of rupees, Dr. Haverlock reached into his inside breast pocket, and I heard the reassuring crackle of folded paper.

He gave it to me, and once I read what was written there, I passed him the package of money, then held out my right hand.

He looked down at it, took it as if to bow over it, but I pulled back slightly. He then understood, and shook it, firmly. And then we stood, each holding our reward, and exchanged a pleasant smile.

We were each as good as the other at this game. We both had acquired that which we wanted most.

※※※

It was over in the next few hours. And in Somers's last painful moments on earth, I knelt by his bed and stroked his hollow face, appearing to the servants and to Dr. Haverlock to be the dutiful wife comforting her dying husband with final gentle gestures. I kept my own face composed, but in my head I spoke to Somers. *I have tricked and deceived you in ways you will never know. And now it is over; the nightmare is over. I have saved my life and the soul of my child.*

In spite of the depth of his illness I sensed his comprehension of this unspoken fact, that in spite of my past I was the stronger of us. That he was unable to control my future. I knew this from the way his unfocused eyes skittered in their sockets, how his lips shook loosely, as if he needed to speak. I put my fingers against his mouth and brushed back his hair, kissing his cold, dry forehead. "It is all over, Somers. All the hate and hurt you have subjected me to," I whispered, so quietly that the only sound the others in the room would hear was a breathless murmur, the last few pledges of love from a wife to her husband. "I have made it so," I whispered, still more softly, little more than a sigh, and I saw his eyelids move ever so slightly, and I knew he heard me. I knew he understood.

A low rattle came from somewhere within him, and then his eyes rolled upward, to the limp ruffles of the punkah, and stayed there, unblinking.

Epilogue

1840

I T IS ONE OF THOSE GLORIOUS SPRING DAYS WHEN THE AIR CARRIES the scent of the earth warming. The light from the open window falls across the floor in soft, buttery squares; the rustle of the birches that surround our home is a soft whisper. I rise and go to the window, looking out at the new growth in our lovely garden—the delicate bluebells and irises, flowers too fragile to ever have survived India's heat. I have grown to see the beauty in England's misty weather. The colors of the garden, without the vibrancy of India's hues, are delicate, tender. I find them beautiful in a way impossible to me before. I marvel at them.

WE LIVE, DAVID AND I, in a home that shares its garden with Shaker and Celina's.

Shaker has opened a small dispensary in the village of Marigate in Cheshire. Known all over the county for his quiet, trustworthy manner and acute ability to diagnose ailments, he discusses symptoms and possible healing herbs for the treatment of many of these physical and mental complaints. The rooms of the dispensary are always full, and Shaker is often referred to as a physician, although he always gently corrects the misapprehension: he is a lay practitioner of homeopathy. Most days I help him in the dispensary, pulverizing and weighing and measuring, discussing particular cases with him.

I have been amazed at the difference in Shaker since I returned to England last year, after the settling of Somers's will. Shaker still often trembles, but at other times—when he sits and watches David play, or listens as Celina reads aloud by the fire—he is perfectly still. I have seen this but do not comment on it, afraid that if those perceived moments of peace are spoken of they may disappear.

Celina, too, displays a sensitivity I would not have predicted. I remember her as sharp faced and quick tongued, but of course that was only because she saw me as a rival. Now that fear has long fled; I believe it is the simple and powerful act of loving and being loved wholly in return that has changed her. She now has a quiet beauty, her eyes filled with a glow I never saw when I first met her in Liverpool almost a decade ago. She welcomed David and me when we arrived at their door, helping me adjust to the life I had so long been away from. It took some time for me to regain my energy and health, but she seemed to find joy in aiding and watching my recuperation. Whether it is learned from Shaker, or a natural talent that Shaker has brought out in her, she does possess a healing nature.

Neither Shaker nor Celina knows of David's true paternity; their grasp of my time in India will rely forever on the letters I wrote. It is all that is necessary.

Sundays, after church, David and I walk home, hand in hand, along the quiet, tree-lined road from the village. Shaker and Celina walk a few steps ahead, their heads together as they discuss the sermon or whatever news we have heard at church. It is at these times that David and I talk about India, and the difference of life here. He remembers Calcutta clearly, and knows no other place but that and the village here. And so I describe Liverpool—the buildings, the bustling streets, the train. I have promised him we will soon visit Liverpool together and take a journey to Manchester on that huge, steaming beast.

A month after I returned to England I journeyed back to Liverpool and hired a mason to carve a beautiful stone in pale gray granite. When it was done I returned again, and as the headstone was put firmly in place in the graveyard at Our Lady and St. Nicholas, I arranged for the bells to be rung and said my own prayers for my mother as I ran my fingers over her name—Frances Gow—carved deeply into the smooth surface. And below, in letters just as deep, Forever Cherished. Beloved Mother of Linny Gow.

I can finally wear the pendant with pride, and I wear no other jewelry but this.

When the time is right I will take David to visit his grandmother's grave. He will never know of the other grave I visited. The pink-streaked stone is barely visible, sunken into the soft grass, and yet the holly bush still stands, its spiny foliage glossy.

He listens to my stories about Liverpool with interest. He has learned to write and sends simple letters to Malti. Sometimes he draws pictures of his life in England and encloses those as well. He says he will go back to visit her someday. Malti lives with Trupti and her nieces and nephews in Delhi. They no longer have to work for others, and want for nothing.

David thrives, a healthy, strong-limbed, dark-eyed child, a child of seven who plays with his friends and complains about his daily school lessons. In this way he is an ordinary boy. But he has the love of horses in his blood. Shaker and I discovered this when I decided it was time he had his own horse. We took him to a stable, and he immediately chose a tall gleaming roan.

I thought the horse too big for him, but he was adamant. And when he was in the saddle I saw his father in him so clearly, in the way he held the short crop but was loath to use it, in his small, capable hands as they smoothed the horse's mane, as he leaned forward and instinctively whispered into the horse's ear. On that first mount, he pressed his knees into the roan's sides and was off across the field, leaving me with my mouth open in surprise and worry, and yet also with such an overpowering joy that I could not speak.

Shaker immediately took chase on a quick dappled mare, and within minutes they rode back to me, the look of pleasure on David's face unmistakable, while Shaker simply smiled with the proud, indulgent smile of a father.

He and Celina have not had the fortune to have children, and they treat David with the love and compassion they would have given freely to their own. Shaker and Celina are our family; I am like a beloved sister to them, while David is the cosseted child of us all.

And so, unlike me, who too early lost a mother, my son blossoms in the love of two women. David has his memories of the man he believes to be his father, although they are thin and rapidly fading, and soon will be reduced to the small likeness painted on a cameo. Shaker, who stands in for his father, is kind and loving. And the one who truly fathered him will remain—at least until David is no longer an impressionable child—unknown.

When he is fully grown, will I give him the missive I wrote at the end of that terrible time in Calcutta, in the days following Somers's death? Who can say? At times I take out the shakily written, ink-blotched pages and read them, seeing myself—who I was then—as if through someone else's eyes. I keep it safe, for I believe it may be important for David one day. I have come to realize that there are no certainties in this life, no promises—to others, or to oneself—that can always be kept.

There are days when the longing for the poppy is so strong I endure physical pain. I know now that it is most likely I will never lose the long-ing, but I also know that there is nothing that can ever drive me to once more be its slave. At odd times, unexpected times, perhaps when I am waking, I feel a sense of the old ebb and flow of the sweet smoke in my head. At these times I am confused momentarily, saddened, when I think over my life and see it as a disaster, a litany of errors small and huge, of lies and deception. But then I hear the sound of my son mur-muring to his pup from the other room, and I know that the long jour-ney I took has brought me to this place, with David, in the way it was meant to be. I can again bear to look at my own reflection: although my eyes are deeper, the skin around them finely lined, they are clear now. I look like a mother, an ordinary woman.

Celina has suggested that perhaps I shall soon find someone—an ordinary man—to share my life. Perhaps. I have learned that I am capable of passion, of giving and accepting love. I am twenty-eight. There is time.

For now I have my dream—the dream that has nothing to do with the poppy. This real dream, the one I can bring at will, is the memory of the copper sun, of the Kashmir valley, its carpet of flowers. Of passion and of completeness. This dream has replaced the nightmare. I am free of all that kept me prisoner for so long. And who could wish for more than this?

※※※

MY BOOK ON the medicinal plants of India, the book I began compiling when I first arrived back in England, using the case of notes I had collected over my years in India, is complete. It shall be published within a few months by Carruthers of London. Although I am known as Linny Ingram here, I put the name Linnet Gow on the book. The publisher strongly suggested that I use as the author name "A Lady"—which they prefer, or secondly, Mrs. Somers Ingram. Of course I think of myself as neither.

I wrote back that I would like it published under the name I originally indicated—Linnet Gow. They politely resisted, suggesting L. Gow.

I replied in my finest hand, stating that I insist on my choice; with all respect, I do insist.

They will come around to my bidding, of course, for I have never been one to back down. And no matter what names have been appointed, I will forever continue to think of myself as Linny Gow, the name my mother gave me, and the only name of which I am proud.

Acknowledgments

I AM GREATLY INDEBTED to my agent, Sarah Heller, for all her help with this project. I would like to thank Harriet Evans, for her instinct and her insight and her questions, and for pushing me to go further and dig deeper. She truly was instrumental in helping me make this book as close as possible to the one I envisioned. Heartfelt thanks to Catherine Cobain and Hazel Orme, and, of course, I owe much gratitude to Rachel Kahan. I must also thank Shannon Kernaghan, Donna Freeman, Irene Williams, Anita Jewell, and Kathy Lowinger, who read the manuscript in its original form and encouraged me. Last, I thank my children, Zalie, Brenna, and Kitt, for their understanding and constant support. No matter how difficult the journey, they are always willing companions.

About the Author

LINDA HOLEMAN is the author of two collections of short stories, *Flying to Yellow* and *Devil's Darning Needle,* as well as several books for young adults, including *Search for the Moon King's Daughter* and *Mercy's Birds*. She lives in Winnipeg, Manitoba.

a novel

LINDA HOLEMAN

A Reader's Guide

About the Book

Not since *The Far Pavilions* has an historical novel captured the imagination of its readers on such a showstopping scale. *The Linnet Bird* is the tale of Linny Gow: orphan, widow, mother, adventurer. Shackled by a reprehensible past, yet determined to rediscover her own dignity in the anonymity of a foreign nation, Linny braves a deadly ocean voyage—only to discover that her dark history cannot be outrun.

Gritty, provocative, and lushly imagined, Linny's heartrending story carries her from the gruesome poverty of working-class Liverpool in the thick of the Industrial Revolution to the multi-hued pageantry of India under British rule. As she quests for the elusive means to healing and freedom, Linny must lie, cheat, beg, fight—even murder—in order to survive. Yet it is a chance encounter with a dangerous stranger that unclenches Linny's pockmarked heart and fuels her ultimate transformation.

This unforgettable saga explores the back-alley depravity of child prostitution and the sociopolitical hypocrisy of colonial India with equal panache—while sensitively evoking the inner thought processes of its unforgettable heroine. The following guide is designed to help direct your group's discussion of Linda Holeman's masterpiece, *The Linnet Bird*.

Questions for Discussion

1. When Ram coerces Linny into working with the excuse, "Many a lass does help out her family when they've fallen on hard times," Linny reflects that her bloodline elevates her above this: "Of course I knew a number of the older girls . . . who worked a few hours now and then . . . when money was short at home. But I had always known I was different. I wasn't like them . . . It was in my blood, this difference" (p. 6).

Where does Linny get this notion of inherited superiority? What later event marks her first doubt about the legitimacy of her noble blood?

2. After a fruitless visit from the Ladies of Righteous Conduct, Linny reflects "I turned thirteen and knew I had grown hard. And I knew my mother would not be pleased—not because I was a whore, for that was not my fault—but because of my evil ways and my even more evil thoughts" (p. 26). What is this evil she is talking about? What attempt does she make to rectify her ways?

3. What subversive act offers Linny a sense of "small potency" while she is subject to Ram's pimping? Why doesn't she try to hoard money instead?

4. Linny's position at the library is a dream come true: a first opportunity for legitimate employment and access to unlimited books. Why is there no description of her momentous first day at work?

5. Linny is disgusted with the pretensions and prejudices of the British in India, frustrated by the limitations placed on her exploration of her surroundings, uninterested in the rampant matchmaking culture, and unable to find compatible women with whom to make friends. Why, then, does she insist that "Faced with the thought of leaving India, of returning to Liverpool, I knew then that I would do whatever I had to. Marry someone. Anyone" (p. 224)?

6. Why does Shaker refer to Linny as "his sign"? What is her reaction to this label?

7. Linny is perceptive enough to notice that opium has reduced Meg from an ambitious, flamboyant character to a shadow of her former self, "worn and listless as all the other women . . . " (p. 383). She is also aware that laudanum, Meg's favorite antidote to all her child's complaints, is potentially fatal. Why does she ignore her misgivings and indulge in opium at Meg's urging? Is this a suicidal tendency, or mere stupidity?

8. After escaping prostitution, Linny is shocked when she sees her own reflection: "I didn't know the hollow-eyed woman in the mirror" (p. 103). Ten years later, at the peak of her opium addiction, she is again unable to recognize her reflection: "I looked at myself in the mirror again . . . I had lost sight of the woman who called herself Linny Gow" (p. 399). At the end of the novel, Linny claims, "I can again bear to look at my own reflection . . . I look like a mother, an ordinary woman"

(p. 415). Discuss the use of mirrors and reflections elsewhere in the novel. Does Linny succeed in finding her true self, and, if so, where does she find this image reflected?

9. Linny makes one attempt at escaping the tedium of India. As she stands at the dock with her luggage, poised to leave, a sadhu, or holy man, speaks unintelligibly to her. Linny claims, "I understood the portent of the sadhu" (p. 232) and reverses her decision. Why does she choose to interpret the event this way?

10. Linny finds herself egging on Somers's violence: "for some inexplicable reason I sometimes found myself goading him purposely . . . I wanted to see how far I could push him before he would react . . . I think now . . . that it was a way of drawing Somers's attention—even if the attention was filled with nothing more than trepidation and fear of physical pain. I wanted to reach him in some way, in the confusing push and pull of our relationship" (p. 271). In what ways is Linny's tale a timeless look at childhood and/or marital abuse and their psychological effects on a woman? What stereotypical behaviors does she fall into? What lesson does her story provide for healing and renewal?

11. Frances Gow, Linny's "soft and dreamy" dead mother, plays a recurring role in Linny's imagination. Frances's voice soothes Linny through her first rape at the age of eleven. Her face appears, albeit drowned, as Linny struggles against chloral poisoning during her ordeal on Rodney Street. Where else does she appear? What traits does Linny assign to Frances, and what strengths does she imagine she gleans from her upbringing at her mother's hands?

12. What "strange and troubling sensation of loss" does Linny experience when she leaves her life of prostitution behind?